David Laing

## Select Remains of the Ancient Popular and Romance Poetry of Scotland

David Laing

**Select Remains of the Ancient Popular and Romance Poetry of Scotland**

ISBN/EAN: 9783337049485

Printed in Europe, USA, Canada, Australia, Japan

Cover: Foto ©Andreas Hilbeck / pixelio.de

More available books at **www.hansebooks.com**

# SELECT REMAINS

OF THE

# ANCIENT POPULAR AND ROMANCE POETRY OF SCOTLAND

COLLECTED AND EDITED

BY

## DAVID LAING, LL.D.

RE-EDITED, WITH MEMORIAL-INTRODUCTION AND ADDITIONS

BY

## JOHN SMALL, M.A.

WILLIAM BLACKWOOD AND SONS
EDINBURGH AND LONDON
MDCCCLXXXV

# MEMORIAL-INTRODUCTION

# MEMORIAL-INTRODUCTION.

T is now more than half a century since the first
edition of the 'Select Remains of the Ancient
Popular Poetry of Scotland' was issued by its
much-lamented editor, the late David Laing;
and it has been thought desirable to prefix to
this second edition a short memoir of one who did much to
illustrate the ancient history and poetry of Scotland.

David Laing was born in Edinburgh on the 20th of April
1793, and was the second son of William Laing, a well-known
bookseller in that city.   William Laing was very successful in
business, which was carried on by him, first in Chessell's Court,
Canongate, and latterly in No. 49 South Bridge Street.   He
was noted for the large store of books relating to Scotland
which he always kept in stock, and his shop was a place of
resort for the *litterati* of the day.   He published several works
of value, such as good editions of Thucydides, Herodotus, and
Xenophon, Pinkerton's 'Inquiry,' and Wyntoun's 'Chronicle
of Scotland,' edited by David Macpherson.

After being educated at the Canongate Grammar School,
David Laing attended in 1805-6 the Greek Class at the University of Edinburgh, then taught by Professor Dalzel.   There-
after he entered his father's business as an apprentice, and
soon acquired a thorough knowledge of books, for which
unusual facilities were thus afforded.

In the sketches of Edinburgh booksellers about the year
1819, which form a chapter in 'Peter's Letters to his Kins-
folk,' a well-known work by J. Gibson Lockhart, the following

account is given of Mr Laing and his son David: "As for shops of old books, classics, black-letter, foreign literature, and the like, I was never in any great town which possesses so few of them as this. It might indeed be guessed that her riches in this way would not be great, after the account I have given you of the state of scholarship among the *littérateurs* of the North. There is, however, one shop of this sort which might cut a very respectable figure, even in places where attainments of another kind are more in request; and I confess I have visited this shop more frequently, and with more pleasure, than any of its more fashionable neighbours in Edinburgh. It is situated, as it ought to be, in the immediate vicinity of the College, and consequently quite out of the way of all the fashionable promenades and lounges; but indeed, for anything I have seen, it is not much frequented, even by the young gentlemen of the University. The daily visitors of Mr Laing (for that is the name of its proprietor) seem rather to be a few scattered individuals of various classes and professions, among whom, in spite of the prevailing spirit and customs of the place, some love of classical learning is still found to linger—retired clergymen and the like, who make no great noise in this world, and, indeed, are scarcely known to exist by the most part even of the literary people of Edinburgh. The shop, notwithstanding, is a remarkably neat and comfortable one, and even a lady might lounge in it without having her eye offended or her gown soiled. It consists of two apartments, which are both completely furnished with valuable editions of old authors; and I assure you, the antique vellum bindings or oak boards of these ponderous folios are a very refreshing sight to me after visiting the gaudy and brilliant stores of such a shop as that I have just described [Messrs Manners & Miller in the High Street, near to the Parliament Square]. Mr Laing himself is a quiet, sedate-looking old gentleman, who, although he has contrived to make very rich in his business, has still the air of being somewhat dissatisfied that so much more attention should be paid by his fellow-citizens to the flimsy novelties of the day, than to the solid and substantial articles which his magazine displays. But his son is the chief enthusiast. Indeed he is by far the most genuine specimen of the true old-fashioned bibliopole that I ever saw exhibited in the person of a young man. My friend Wastle [*i.e.*, J. G. Lockhart] has a prodigious liking for him, which originated, I believe, in their once meeting casually in Rotterdam, and travelling together over most part of Holland in the Treckschuyt—and indeed this circumstance has been expressly alluded to by Wastle in one of his poems. Here Wastle commonly spends one or two hours every week he is in Edinburgh, turning over in company with his young friend all the Aldines, the Elzevirs, and Wynkin de Wordes and Caxtons, in the collection; nor does he often leave the shop without being tempted to take some little specimen of its treasures home with him. I also, although my days of bibliomania are long since over, have been occasionally induced to transgress my self-denying rule, and have picked up various curious things at a pretty cheap rate, and one book in particular, of which I shall beg your acceptance when we meet—but at present I won't tell you what it is. David Laing is still a very young man; but Wastle tells me (and so far as I have had occasion to see, he is quite correct in doing so) that he possesses a truly wonderful degree of skill and knowledge in almost all departments of bibliography. Since Lunn's death, he says, he does not think there is any of the booksellers in London superior to him in his way; and he often advises him to transfer the shop and all the treasures thither. But I suppose Mr Laing has very good reason not to be in a hurry in adopting any such advice. He publishes a catalogue almost every year, and thus carries on a very extensive trade with all parts of the island. Besides, miserable as is the general condition of old learning in Scotland, there is still, I suppose, abundant occasion for one bookseller of this kind, and, I believe, he has no rival in the whole country.  For my part, if I lived in Edinburgh, I would go to his shop every now and then, were it only to be put in mind of the happy hours we used to spend together long ago at Mr Parker's.

"This old gentleman and his son are distinguished by their classical taste in regard to other things besides books— and amongst the rest in regard to wines—a subject touching which it is fully more easy for them to excite the sympathy of the knowing ones of Edinburgh.  They give an annual dinner to Wastle, and he carried me with him the other day to one of these anniversaries.  I have seldom seen a more luxurious display.  We had claret of the most exquisite Lafitte flavour, which foamed in the glass like the cream of strawberries, and went down as cool as the nectar of Olympus.  David and Wastle entertained us with an infinite variety of stories about George Buchanan, the Admirable Crichtonius, and all the more forgotten heroes of the *Deliciæ Poetarum Scotorum.* What precise share of the pleasure might be due to the claret and what to the stories, I shall not venture to inquire; but I have rarely spent an evening more pleasantly.

"*P.S.*—They are also very curious in sherry."

As stated in the above passage, Lockhart met with young Laing when in Holland, where the latter went annually for the purpose of purchasing foreign books—his father having been one of the first Edinburgh booksellers who introduced Continental literature to any considerable extent.

In the poem referred to in the preceding extract, which was published by Lockhart in 'Blackwood's Magazine' in 1818, called "The Mad Banker of Amsterdam, or the Fate of the Brauns," there are several references to David Laing.  The first of these refers to their meeting at Mynheer Braun's house :—

> " But to return (in this new style of Frere's,
>     A phrase which oft hath been and oft must be),
>   I dined when last in Holland at Mynheer's,
>     No one was there but David Laing and me,

And a Dutch minister, one Van der Schpiers,
  Domestic tutor in the family ;
To give the vrow the praise that is her due,
The dinner much invited a set to.

In course of talk the clergyman and Braun
  Enlarged upon the charm of Dutch society,
Its comforts—none that attribute disown,
  And what some won't agree to, its variety ;
David and I sucked all the doctrines down,
  But over-doses generate satiety.
So we to pay them back in their own coin,
Begun in praise of Scotland to rejoin.

A fruitful topic, it must be confessed,
  And in good hands, I mean in Laing's and mine,
(David the most sagacious and the best,
  As all old Reekie's erudites opine,
Of Scottish bibliopoles, who knows the zest
  And name of every title-page Aldine
A famous bibliomaniac and a shrewd,
Who turns his madness to no little good.)

We touched on many topics I and David ;
  He chiefly sung the praise of a sale dinner ;
I on Young's tavern principally ravèd,
  Ore soluto—I'm a glorious spinner,
I painted to the set, in colours vivid,
  The portrait of full many a curious sinner
Who comes, with ready head and readier tongue,
To kill his evenings in thy house Bill Young."

In 1815, young Laing began to indulge his desire of publishing some of the more curious specimens of early Scottish literature; and accordingly he issued a reprint of the Catalogue of books which Drummond of Hawthornden presented to the Library of the University of Edinburgh in 1627.

In 1821 he became a partner with his father, and issued during that year reprints of Sir Thomas Craig's ' Epithalamium on the Marriage of Queen Mary and Darnley in 1565 ;' the Poems of Alexander Scott, the Scottish Anacreon, originally printed in 1568; and those of Alexander Montgomery, who wrote between 1597 and 1631. The same year he began the publication, in parts, of the 'Select Remains of the Ancient Popular Poetry of Scotland, 1420-1580,' which was completed in 1822. This work, which was elegantly printed, contained twenty-five pieces of much interest, nearly all of which were published for the first time. To these he prefixed short introductions, which evince an intimate acquaintance with early poetry. Of this work, an account of which is given in his Advertisement prefixed to it, only about 108 copies were printed; and it soon became an object of eager quest to book-collectors. Laing, however, had not then the same ease in reading early manuscripts which he afterwards attained. Numerous errors are to be found in the text of the poems; and although in the Appendix to the volume lists were given of such as he had observed, there remained many others which it has been found necessary to correct in the present edition. In his latter years, Laing proposed to reissue this work, with the addition of several new pieces; and an interleaved copy of it, in which he inserted some valuable notes, indicated the plan for the new edition, which it has been our aim to follow out.[1]

In 1818 a vacancy occurred in the librarianship of the Advocates' Library, and Laing became a candidate for the office. It was, however, filled up in 1820 by the appointment of Dr David Irving.

In 1822 Laing published a reprint of a curious Scottish poem entitled "The Pleasing History of Roswall and Lillian," and also a *facsimile* of an ancient heraldic manuscript, emblazoned by Sir David Lyndsay of the Mount, Lyon King of Arms, which is preserved in the Advocates' Library.

The Bannatyne Club, which was formed on the model of the Roxburghe Club, was originated in 1823 by Sir Walter Scott, for the purpose of reprinting rare works relating to

---

[1] Additions, for which the present Editor is responsible, are put within brackets.

Scotland. It was named after George Bannatyne, an Edinburgh citizen, who, in the time of pestilence in 1568, retired into solitude and engrossed into two large volumes a collection of the ancient poetry of Scotland, through which nearly all that is known of it has come to us. Sir Walter insisted that Laing should act as Secretary of the Club.

Lockhart, in his memoir of Scott, remarks : "At the meetings of the Bannatyne, Scott regularly presided from 1823 to 1831, and in the chair at their anniversary dinners, surrounded by some of his oldest and dearest friends—Thomas Thomson (the Vice-President), John Clerk (Lord Eldin), the Chief-Commissioner Adam, the Chief-Baron Shepherd, Lord Jeffrey, Mr Constable, and let me not forget his kind, intelligent, and industrious ally, Mr David Laing, bookseller, the Secretary of the Club. He from this time forward was the unfailing source and centre of all sorts of merriment within the limits of becoming mirth. . . . His song, composed for their first dinner (March 1823), was sung by James Ballantyne, and heartily chorused by all the aforesaid dignitaries :—

> "Assist me, ye friends of Old Books and Old Wine,
> To sing in the praises of sage Bannatyne,
> Who left such a treasure of old Scottish lore
> As enables each age to print one volume more.
> > One volume more, my friends, one volume more—
> > We'll ransack old Banny for one volume more.
>
> And first Allan Ramsay was eager to glean
> From Bannatyne's *Hortus* his bright Evergreen ;
> Two tight little volumes (intended for four)
> Still leave us the task to print one volume more.
> > One volume more, &c.
>
> His ways were not ours, for he cared not a pin
> How much he left out, how much he put in ;
> The truth of the reading he thought was a bore,
> So this accurate age calls for one volume more.
> > One volume more, &c.

Correct and sagacious, then came my Lord Hailes,
And weighed every letter in critical scales,
But left out some brief words which the prudish abhor,
And castrated Banny in one volume more.
        One volume more, my friends, one volume more—
        We'll restore Banny's manhood in one volume more.


John Pinkerton next, and I'm truly concern'd,
I can't call that worthy so candid as learn'd,
He rail'd at the plaid, and blasphemed the claymore,
And set Scots by the ears in his one volume more.
        One volume more, my friends, one volume more—
        Celt and Goth shall be pleased with one volume more.


As bitter as gall, and as sharp as a razor,
And feeding on herbs as a Nebuchadnezzar;
His diet too acid, his temper too sour,
Little Ritson came out with his two volumes more.
        But one volume more, my friends, one volume more—
        We'll dine on roast beef and print one volume more.


The stout Gothic yeditur, next on the roll,
With his beard like a brush and as black as a coal;
And honest Greysteel that was true to the core,
Lift their hearts and their hands each to one volume more.
        One volume more, &c.


Since by these single champions what wonders were done,
What may not be achieved by our Thirty-and-One?
Law, Gospel, and Commerce, we count in our corps,
And the Trade and the Press join for one volume more.
        One volume more, &c.


Ancient libels and contraband books, I assure ye,
We'll print as secure from exchequer or jury;
Then hear your Committee, and let them count o'er
The Chiels they intend in their three volumes more.
        Three volumes more, &c.


They'll produce you King Jamie the sapient and Sext,
And the Rob of Dumblane and her Bishops come next;

One tome miscellaneous they'll add to your store,
Resolving next year to print four volumes more.
Four volumes more, my friends, four volumes more—
Pay down your subscriptions for four volumes more."

This song was the first of several which were sung on these occasions, and were printed subsequently under the title of 'Bannatyne Garlands,' in black-letter, in imitation of ancient ballads. Scott's is interesting to us here, as in it are mentioned the predecessors of Laing in editing ancient Scottish poetry—viz., Allan Ramsay, Lord Hailes, John Pinkerton, Joseph Ritson, James Sibbald, and David Herd (called Greysteel by his intimate friends), in whose footsteps Laing followed with such success.

Laing discharged the duties of the office of Secretary of this famous Club with much zeal, and acted in that capacity for thirty-eight years, down to the dissolution of the Club in 1861. He refers to his long and arduous labours in connection with this Society in the following terms: "No one can imagine how much of my time was so spent,—days and nights, with frequent and sometimes distant journeys,—on matters more or less connected with the Club, and wearisome enough work besides, with doubts occasionally springing up in my mind whether a person like myself, having always a very limited income, was justified year after year in thus spending the best period of his life. Persuaded, however, that the object was laudable, and one to which I had early devoted myself, I now feel thankful at the close of such a lengthened period, to be able to say that during these thirty-eight years, neither seeking praise nor receiving reward, I never faltered from my work nor drew my hand back from the plough."

In 1823 he contributed to the Club, Holland's 'Buke of the Howlate,' which he edited from the Asloan MS. preserved at Auchinleck, Ayrshire. This allegorical poem, composed about the middle of the fifteenth century, was supposed by

Pinkerton to be a satire on King James II. of Scotland ; but
in his preface, Laing showed that this ancient work was not
written with any view to local or national politics.   To the
title-page of the volume an interesting design was contributed
by Charles Kirkpatrick Sharpe.  The same year Laing began
the publication of various pieces of Fugitive Scottish poetry of
the seventeenth century.  The first volume was finished in
1825, and was followed by a second in 1853.

In 1826 he edited the poems of George Bannatyne, whose
celebrated manuscript of ancient Scottish poetry is preserved
in the Advocates' Library.  In that year he became a Fellow
of the Society of Antiquaries of Scotland, and was for the long
period of fifty-four years one of its most active members.  For
sixteen years, at a time when its funds were in a critical state,
he acted as its Treasurer.  He also was for a time one of
the Editors of its proceedings, a Vice-President, and Foreign
Secretary.  But, while contributing to the prosperity of the
Society by his business talents, he was also a constant contrib-
utor of papers at its meetings ; and the importance of these
was acknowledged to be altogether unparalleled in its history.

Between 1825 and 1827 Laing was engaged in arrangements
for transferring the books of the University Library from the
old library to the noble hall in the present building.  The
Committee of the Senatus Academicus were so well satisfied
with Laing's labours that they drew up the following report :
" In closing the repairs of the Library, the Committee have
again to direct the attention of the Senatus to the invaluable
services of Mr D. Laing.  With a skill which very few could
have brought to the work, and with a perseverance which has
laid the University under deep obligations, he has discharged
the trust undertaken by him in May 1825.  The Committee
regret that they have no pecuniary recompense to offer which
is at all commensurate to the services of Mr Laing ; but they
unanimously and earnestly recommend that, in addition to the
hundred guineas originally stipulated for, fifty guineas should

be presented to Mr Laing by order of the Senatus, in token of their approbation."

In 1826 Laing published a little volume entitled 'Early Metrical Tales, including the History of Sir Egeir, Sir Gryme, and Sir Gray-steill.' To these poems he prefixed short introductions.

In 1827 there was published by his firm, and edited by him, a handsome volume under the title of 'The Knightly Tale of Golagrus and Gawane, and other Ancient Poems.' This was a reprint of the first book known to have been printed in Scotland (in 1508, by Walter Chepman and Andro Myllar), of which the only copy that exists is preserved in the Advocates' Library. The reprint had been announced for publication in 1814, but was delayed from various causes. After the difficulties of collation had been overcome, and the volume had been completed with the exception of the introductory remarks, a fire took place in the premises where the sheets were deposited, and the greater portion of the copies were either destroyed or rendered imperfect. Several of the sheets were, however, reprinted, and about seventy-six copies were ultimately completed and published. Nearly all of these show a few leaves bearing the marks of fire.

In conjunction with Sir Walter Scott, Laing, in 1829, edited a volume for the Bannatyne Club—'The Memorials of George Bannatyne, with an Account of his celebrated MS.' To this volume Sir Walter contributed the memoir, and Laing the account of the MS.

In 1830 Laing edited for the same Club a 'Relation of Proceedings concerning the Affairs of the Kirk of Scotland, 1637-38,' by John, Earl of Rothes. This work may be regarded as supplying authentic information relative to events which happened in the short but eventful period which it embraces. In 1831 he also edited for the Bannatyne Club a reprint of 'The Buik of the most noble and vailzeand Conqueror Alexander the Great,' originally printed in 1580; and in 1833 he edited 'A Collection of Ancient Scottish Prophecies in Alliterative Verse,' originally printed in 1603 and 1615. To this volume the preface was added by Thomas Thomson.

About the beginning of the present century, George Chalmers, the distinguished Scottish antiquary, made collections for the purpose of publishing a complete edition of the poems of William Dunbar, in his time the "Rhymer" or Poet·Laureate of Scotland. Laing having acquired these papers after the death of Chalmers, brought out in 1834 the first collected edition of Dunbar's writings. This edition was highly praised, and has long been much coveted by collectors. In 1865 he issued a supplement containing several additional poems, and some new biographical information.

In 1836 he edited for the Bannatyne Club 'A Diary of Public Transactions and other occurrences, chiefly in Scotland,' by John Nicoll, 1560-1667.' The MS. of this work is preserved in the Advocates' Library.

In 1837 he edited a long poem by John Rolland of Dalkeith, called 'The Seven Sages, 1578.' In his preface to this work, he states that nothing was known of Rolland's personal history. A charter has since been found in Laing's own collection, showing that Rolland was a notary in Dalkeith, and also a Presbyter—a conjunction not unusual in the times when he flourished.

The year 1837 was an eventful one for Laing. Macvey Napier, Professor of Conveyancing in the University, who was also Librarian to the Society of Writers to the Signet, resigned his office of Librarian. From his labours in the field of Scottish poetry, Laing was now well known to many men of eminence, and in becoming a candidate for the vacant office he received testimonials of the most gratifying character. The Hon. William Adam, Sir William Hamilton, Dr Irving, the Rev. Dr [afterwards Principal] Lee, the Rev. John Jamieson the Scottish lexicographer, Thomas Maitland, afterwards Lord Dundrennan, Robert Southey, Dr Hibbert Ware, the Rev.

Philip Bliss of Oxford, Allan Cunningham, Dr Dibdin, Sir Henry Ellis, Sir Fred. Madden, J. G. Lockhart, and Patrick Fraser Tytler, the historian of Scotland, were amongst the number of his supporters on this occasion. On the 21st of June of that year Laing was elected. He was proposed by Sir James Gibson Craig, Bart, and seconded by James Tytler Esq. of Woodhouselee.

In 1837, jointly with Mr W. B. D. D. Turnbull, Laing edited a small volume containing the poem called 'Owain Miles,' and other inedited pieces of ancient English poetry. These were derived from the Auchinleck MS. preserved in the Advocates' Library.

In 1838, Laing, in conjunction with Adam Urquhart, edited for the Bannatyne Club, 'Historical Observes of Memorable Occurrents, 1680-1686,' by Sir John Lauder of Fountainhall, one of the Senators of the College of Justice.

The Abbotsford Club, which was founded in 1834 mainly by the exertions of Mr Turnbull, now began to look to Laing for assistance. He accordingly edited, in conjunction with Mr J. Hill Burton, the 'Jacobite Correspondence of the Atholl Family during the Rebellion, 1745-1746,' which was issued to the members in 1840. This Club did not confine their printing to works connected with Scotland, but admitted all materials throwing light on the ancient history or literature of any country, anywhere described or discussed by the author of 'Waverley.'

In 1841 Laing published the 'Letters and Journals of Robert Baillie, Principal of the University of Glasgow.' These valuable papers relate to the eventful period between 1637 and 1642. This important work was reviewed by Thomas Carlyle in the 'London and Westminster Review' for 1841. Writing of Laing's editorial labours, he says: "Mr Laing, according to all appearance, has exhibited his usual industry, sagacity, correctness in this case, and done his work well. The notes are brief, illuminative, ever in the right place; and, what we will praise withal, not over plenteous, not more of them than needed. Nothing is easier than for an antiquarian editor to seize too eagerly any chance or pretext for pouring out his long-bottled antiquarian lore, and drowning his text, instead of refreshing and illustrating it—a really criminal proceeding! This we say the present editor has virtuously forborne." [1]

The Wodrow Society, instituted for the publication of works connected with the history of the Church of Scotland, began its labours in 1841. Laing, familiar with all the manuscript treasures of the various Scottish libraries, that year edited John Row of Carnock's 'History of the Kirk of Scotland from 1558 to 1639;' and for this Society, in 1846, he also issued the first volume of the Works of John Knox, which was completed in 1864 by the publication of the sixth volume. This valuable edition must be regarded as Laing's most important contribution to Scottish literature.

In 1843 Laing edited a very interesting work for the Shakespeare Society—'Notes of Ben Jonson's Conversations with Drummond the Poet of Hawthornden;' and in 1847 he edited, for the Bannatyne Club, the 'Buke of the Order of Knighthood, by Sir Gilbert Hay.'

In 1848, on the retirement of Dr Irving from the Keepership of the Advocates' Library, Laing again became a candidate for this desirable appointment. He was, however, unsuccessful, as the appointment was bestowed on Mr Samuel Halkett.

The same year he edited for the Bannatyne Club another work by Sir John Lauder of Fountainhall—viz., his 'Historical Notices of Scottish Affairs from 1661 to 1668.'

---

[1] In 1843, when Carlyle, then engaged on his 'Life of Cromwell,' came to Scotland to visit the scene of the Protector's victory at Dunbar, he states in a letter to his wife: "Before quitting Edinburgh I had gone to David Laing and refreshed all my recollections by looking at his books, one of which he even lent me out thither."—*Life by Froude*, 1831-81, vol. i. p. 325.

In 1849 he issued two volumes to the members of the Abbotsford Club,—'Sire Degarre, a Metrical Romance of the 13th Century,' and 'A Penniworth of Witte, Florice and Blauncheflour, and other pieces of ancient poetry.' These volumes were printed from the Auchinleck MS. in the Advocates' Library.

In 1851 Laing edited for the Bannatyne Club a volume of Original Letters relating to the Ecclesiastical Affairs of Scotland, chiefly written by, or addressed to, King James VI., after his accession to the English Throne, 1603-1625, in two volumes 4to.

In 1853 he published in the Shakespeare Society Series, Thomas Lodge's 'Defence of Poetry, Music and Stage Plays, An Alarum against Usurers, and the delectable History of Forbonius and Drissena, with Introduction and Notes;' and the same year he edited, in conjunction with Charles Kirkpatrick Sharpe, a new edition of Johnson's 'Scots Musical Museum.'

In 1854 Laing was elected Honorary Professor of Antiquities to the Royal Scottish Academy of Painting, Sculpture, and Architecture.

In 1855 there was issued to the members of the Bannatyne Club a series of etchings, chiefly of views in Scotland, by John Clerk of Eldin (author of the well-known work on Naval Tactics), 1773-1779, in folio. To this handsome volume Laing prefixed an account of Mr Clerk and of his numerous characteristic etchings on copper, which were long supposed to have perished. The same year the third volume of the Miscellany of the Bannatyne Club was issued, which Laing edited, and which contains several interesting papers and plates of seals. In 1855 Laing also wrote a preface to the reprint of the 'Breviarium Aberdonense,' which had been edited from the rare original by the Rev. William Blew, A.M., and was then published at London, by J. Toovey, for subscribers. Laing added a sheet "Compassio Beate Marie,' printed at

Edinburgh in 1520, from the only copy which was known to exist.

In 1856 the Archæological Institute of Great Britain and Ireland held its meeting at Edinburgh, and an exhibition of Historical Scottish Relics was held in the Galleries of the Royal Academy. Mr Laing then exhibited several highly interesting portraits — Anne of Cleves, Mary of Lorraine, Mary Stuart, and several others. Of the Relics a catalogue was published by Mr Albert Way, in 1859, to which Laing contributed an account of the Civic Insignia of Edinburgh, 1616-32.

In 1858 Laing edited the 'Letters of John Colville, 1582-1603,' for the Bannatyne Club. Colville first was minister of Kilbryde, but afterwards gave up the Church and acted as confidential correspondent of the English Court. In the prefatory memoir Laing has given a full account of his extraordinary career. Conjointly with James Macknight, Laing the same year edited for the Club 'Memoirs of the Insurrection in Scotland in 1715, by John, Master of Sinclair.' In addition to these he issued a Catalogue of the Graduates in Arts, Divinity, and Laws of the University of Edinburgh, from its foundation in 1580 to the year 1858.

In 1859 he edited for the Club the Charters of the Collegiate Church of St Giles of Edinburgh, under the title of 'Registrum Cartarum Ecclesiæ Sancti Egidii de Edinburgh, 1344-1507.' To this volume he prefixed a very interesting introduction.

In 1861 he edited for the Bannatyne Club, 'The Registers of the Church of Soutra, and those of Trinity College Church, at Edinburgh.'

In 1861 Laing at length received some recognition of his long and disinterested services to Scottish literature. At the final general meeting of the Bannatyne Club, held on 27th February 1861, a handsome silver vase, surmounted with a statuette of Sir Walter Scott, was presented to Laing by the members, who subscribed 350 guineas for a testimonial, as a mark of their high sense of the admirable manner in which the publications of the Club had been superintended by him as Honorary Secretary from its institution in 1823 to its dissolution in 1861.   The same year he was translated by the Royal Scottish Academy from their Professorship of Antiquities to their Honorary Chair of Ancient History.   During that year and the year following, he delivered to the Academy three very interesting lectures, the first being an "Inquiry into the State of the Arts of Design in Scotland at an early Period," and the second and third "On the Scottish Artists who flourished between the Union of the Crowns, A.D. 1603, and the present Century."   These lectures were highly appreciated.

In 1862, in conjunction with Professor Cosmo Innes, Laing edited a History of the University of Edinburgh that had been drawn up by Professor Dalzel from the Records of the Town Council and other sources.

In 1863 there was presented to the Spalding Club a volume containing 'Extracts from the Diary of Alexander Brodie of Brodie, 1652-1685.'   This was edited by Laing.   In that year a portrait of him, painted by William (now Sir William) Fettes Douglas, P.R.S.A., was painted and added to the Collection of Works of Art belonging to the Royal Academy.   This portrait, of cabinet size, represents Laing seated in his sanctum before a table covered with missals, charters, old books, and the vase presented to him by the Bannatyne Club.

In 1864 Laing received the honorary degree of LL.D. from the University of Edinburgh.   The degree was conferred at the same time on John Hill Burton the historian, and Joseph Robertson.   In presenting Laing to the Vice-Chancellor Sir David Brewster, Professor Innes said: "In the name of the Faculty of Law, I present to you Mr David Laing as one upon whom the Faculty and Senatus of our University think it fit to confer the honour of a degree of Doctor of Laws.   Mr Laing is one of the Foreign Secretaries of the Society of Antiquaries of Scotland, Honorary Professor of Ancient History in the Royal Scottish Academy, and a gentleman accurately learned in several departments of literature and art. Mr Laing has made a peculiar study of the early poets and poetry of Scotland, and has devoted much labour and research to our national history, especially the history of the Reformed Church in Scotland. If you desire specimens of his work, he has given an admirable edition of the poems of Dunbar—our Scottish Chaucer; and his elaborate edition of Knox, has at length placed the writings of that great Reformer on a sound foundation. Mr Laing's qualifications have been long known to men of kindred studies. At the institution of the Bannatyne Club, a society, as you know, for promoting the study of early Scottish literature—a society in which Sir Walter Scott took great delight—he selected Mr Laing for the office of Honorary Secretary; and Mr Laing held that office and discharged the duties in a most efficient manner from the birth to end of the Club, for forty years. During that long period I may say his hand was never idle. Besides the official work of Secretary, he arranged and gave to the Club a continuous series of works of history, antiquities, art, and literature—the most important of which, perhaps, is the 'Collected Correspondence of Principal Baillie.' Mr Laing has some peculiar claims upon the gratitude of our University. To him we owe the full Catalogue of our graduates from the foundation of our University. It is less generally known that the University is indebted to him for the arrangement of our Library preparatory to its being moved into the present noble room. It was a task for which he was pre-eminently qualified, and which he performed as a labour of love. I have alluded —and I can do no more than allude—to Mr Laing's knowledge of art, both native and foreign, in which, if he has equals, he has no superior among his countrymen. But one quality of Mr Laing I have not mentioned. He is a workman who knows his tools and where to find them. To many a young student he has saved the dreary and discouraging labour of informing himself where information is to be found.   His love for all letters—his willingness to assist all study—have brought it to pass that, sitting in that fine Signet Library of which he holds the keys, he is consulted by everybody in every emergency.   No wise man will undertake a literary work in Scotland without taking counsel with Mr Laing."

In 1865 Dr Laing contributed to the Abbotsford Club a volume of poems by Stephen Hawes—'The Conversion of Swerers.'

When Thomas Carlyle was elected Lord Rector of the University of Edinburgh in 1865, he selected Dr Laing as his Assessor in the University Court.   Like the Rector, his Assessor held office for the term of three years.

In 1867 Dr Laing issued to the members of the Bannatyne Club a volume of 'Royal Letters, Charters, and Tracts, relating to the Colonisation of New Scotland, and the institution of the Order of Knights Baronets of Nova Scotia, 1622-1638.'   He also presented to the members that year a volume of 'Adversaria,' or notices of some of the earlier works printed for the Club.   His edition of the Poetical Works of Robert Henryson, comprising poems and fables of the fifteenth century, appeared in the same year.

In 1868 Dr Laing published a very curious work,—'A compendious Book of Psalms and spiritual songs,' commonly known as 'The Gude and Godlie Ballates.'   In 1869 he published a series of the etchings of his old friend Charles Kirkpatrick Sharpe, with some of his poetical and prose fragments, to which he prefixed a short Memoir.

For many years Dr Laing had made collections for a complete edition of the Poetical Works of Sir David Lyndsay of the Mount, and the appearance of this work was looked forward to with much interest by his antiquarian friends.   To their great disappointment he set aside the sheets of his elaborate edition, and issued in 1871 one intended for popular use.  This edition was not well received, and many inquiries were made as to the time when the larger edition, containing much new matter, would appear.  When hard pressed one day by an old friend to say when it would be published, he only replied, "You know my name is *D(e) La( y)ing.*" The much-looked-for edition, however, did not appear in his lifetime.

While engaged so much with general literature, Dr Laing did not neglect his duties as Librarian, and in 1871 he published the first volume of the Catalogue of the printed books in the Library of the Society of Writers to H.M. Signet in Scotland.

In 1871 Dr Laing took much interest in an exhibition held at Edinburgh on the occasion of the commemoration of the Centenary of the birth of Sir Walter Scott.  In conjunction with James Drummond, R.S.A., he drew up a catalogue of the valuable pictures and relics then brought together.  In 1871-72 he published Wyntoun's 'Chronicle' in the series known as the Historians of Scotland.

In 1873, Dr Laing, who was well informed on the subject of the authorship of the beautiful "Ode to the Cuckoo," published a *brochure* in which he vindicated the claims of Logan against the statements made by the Rev. A. B. Grosart in his edition of the poems of Michael Bruce published in 1865.  In the same year he issued the Poetical Works of Alexander Craig of Rose Craig, 1604-1631, which were then for the first time collected.  This volume was issued to the members of the Hunterian Club.

·The year 1874 being the fiftieth anniversary of the admission of Dr Laing as a Fellow of the Society of Antiquaries, it was resolved that the members should show their respect for him as an antiquary, and their appreciation of his valuable services to the Society, by asking him to sit for his portrait.  The necessary sum was soon subscribed, and the execution of the work was intrusted to Robert Herdman, R.S.A., who produced a most excellent likeness.  This characteristic portrait was presented to the Society on the occasion of its anniversary meeting, held on St Andrew's Day, 1874. It is now preserved in the hall of the Society, and it is from it that the frontispiece to the present volume has been taken.

In 1875 Dr Laing brought out a volume containing the etchings of Sir David Wilkie and Andrew Geddes. The same year he also published the 'Correspondence of Sir Robert Kerr, first Earl of Ancram, and his son William, third Earl of Lothian, 1616-1667,' in two elegant volumes. This work, which was derived from papers recently discovered at New-battle Abbey, is of great historical importance, as throwing new light on the part taken by Scotland during the period of the civil wars in the seventeenth century. Copies were presented by the Marquis of Lothian to the members of the Bannatyne Club. Dr Laing also presented in that year a volume to the Hunterian Club—'The Poetical Works of Patrick Hannay,' originally printed in 1644.

In the following year, 1876, he edited 'A Theatre of Scottish Worthies,' by Alexander Garden, Advocate, Aberdeen; and in the same volume, 'The Lyf, Doings, and Death of William Elphinstone, Bishop of Aberdeen, 1619-1626.' This poetical volume was issued to the members of the Hunterian Club.

In 1878 Dr Laing prepared a set of *facsimiles* of engraved copper-plates illustrating 'Le livre de la ruyne des nobles Hommes et Femmes,' which is a translation into French prose, printed at Bruges in 1476, of Boccaccio's well-known 'Fall of Princes.' A copy of this rare edition is preserved in the library of the Marquis of Lothian at Newbattle Abbey, which has a set of plates not found in any other copy of the work known to exist.[1] In reproducing these plates, Dr Laing in his interesting preface gave an account of the earliest speci-

---

[1] Books printed in the fifteenth century which contain impressions from engraved copper-plates are so rare that they are greatly valued and sought after.

mens of engraving. A melancholy interest is attached to this volume, as it was Dr Laing's last publication; and the few copies printed were presented by him to various libraries, as a token of gratitude for the facilities they had afforded to him in his researches.

Dr Laing at this time took steps to have his immense private library arranged in a large room which he had added to his villa at Portobello. Although only the choicer portion of his books could be there accommodated, he was now enabled to show many of his treasures to his visitors. In August of that year he entertained several of his old friends, to whom he exhibited his book-rarities. It was now becoming evident that his strength was beginning to fail. A general debility soon after set in, and on the 18th of October 1878, in his eighty-sixth year, and without any severe illness, Dr Laing's long and useful life was brought to a close.

When the sad event became known, there was a general feeling that the country had sustained a great loss, and that a blank was made in Scottish literary society which it would be impossible to fill. He left a large circle of attached friends, to whom he was endeared by his genial and amiable disposition.

Dr Laing was buried in the family tomb in the New Calton Burying-ground; and the large number of attendant mourners showed the respect in which he was held.

After his death the edition of Lyndsay's 'Poems' which he had printed several years previously was published, with a glossary prepared by the writer of this memoir. The numerous *facsimiles* with which it is enriched render this one of the most beautifully illustrated of his many works. In 1879 a new edition of Sir David Lyndsay's 'Heraldic MS.,' previously mentioned, was published.

In 1880 there appeared a second edition of 'A Ballad Book,' of which Charles Kirkpatrick Sharpe printed a few copies for private friends in 1823. Sharpe was then assisting Sir Walter Scott in the preparation of his Border Minstrelsy, and this Ballad Book contained such as were not included by Scott, but still were worth preserving for their quaintness. "They were," says Sharpe, "mostly gathered from the mouths of nurses, wet and dry, singing to their babes and sucklings, dairymaids pursuing their vocation in the cow-house, and tenants' daughters while giving the lady (as every laird's wife was once called) a spinning day, whilom an anniversary tribute in Annandale. Several, too, were picked up from tailors who were wont to reside in my father's castle while misshaping clothes for the children and servants." This second edition was in process of being arranged by Dr Laing at the time of his death, and his instructions as to the additional pieces to be selected from the Sharpe and Scott MSS. were duly adhered to in the elegant volume published in 1880.

By his will, executed in 1864, Dr Laing bequeathed several valuable portraits and antiquities to the Society of Antiquaries, together with the testimonial presented to him by the Bannatyne Club. His valuable collection of manuscripts he left to the Library of the University of Edinburgh on condition of their being kept in a separate place in the Library, and of their being stamped with an appropriate stamp. He also bequeathed several pictures to the National Gallery of Edinburgh—one of these was painted in 1767 by Runciman, known as "King Lear in a Storm." To the Royal Scottish Academy he left a large collection of drawings and sketches by the old masters.

He left directions that his large private library should be sold in London by public auction. It was accordingly intrusted to Messrs Sotheby, Wilkinson, & Hodge, by whom it was sold in four portions, embracing thirty-one days' sale, in the end of 1879 and beginning of 1880. This collection being the acquisition of a long lifetime, and of one who had unequalled opportunities of securing literary treasures connected with Scotland, excited much interest, and realised the large sum of £16,137, 9s. Besides the books, a collection of his en-

gravings, etchings, and drawings, was sold in Edinburgh in
1879, and the finer portion of his prints was sold in London
in 1880.

In concluding this brief notice of Dr David Laing, we
must acknowledge its imperfection, for, in addition to the
long list of books edited by him which has been here given,
there are many others in which he had a share, or to
which he contributed valuable information. Besides, his
papers—about a hundred in number—contributed to the
Society of Antiquaries, are so replete with information, that
these alone would be sufficient to make a reputation. It
rarely falls to the lot of a biographer to record so much literary
work performed by one man as was done by Dr Laing in his
long and honourable career.

# Select Remains

## of the

# Ancient Popular Poetry
# of Scotland.

# Printed at Edinburgh.

### MDCCCXXII.

We redeth oft and findeth ywrite·
and this clerkes wele it wite·
Layes that ben in harping·
ben yfounde of ferli thing·
sum bethe of wer and sum of wo·
and sum of ioie and mirthe also·
and sum of trecherie and of gile·
of old auentours that fel while·
and sum of bourdes and ribaudy·
and mani ther beth of fairy·
of all thinges that men seth·
mest o loue forsothe thai beth·

       Lai le Freine.   Auch. MS. fol. 261.

# THE ADVERTISEMENT.

ITTLE apology, it is conceived, will be looked for, on submitting to the Publick a Collection, such as this is, of our ANCIENT POPULAR POETRY: neither is it necessary to detain the reader with any general reflections which the nature of its contents might be supposed to suggest. The remains of the Early Poetical Literature of our Country, and indeed of most Nations, are allowed to possess a value, sanctioned by Time, of which neither prejudice

nor fashion can deprive them, and this may be thought sufficient to justify any attempt that is made for their preservation. They are valuable, no less in enabling us to trace the history and progress of our language, than in assisting us to illustrate ancient manners and amusements, of which they often contain the liveliest representations.

T.HE professed object of this work was to bring together some of the rarer pieces of the ancient vernacular Poetry of Scotland. Accordingly, an endeavour has been made to collect such as either still remained unpublished, or had appeared only in a corrupted or imperfect state : and if, in the prosecution of this design, the Editor has been unsuccessful, it has, at least, arisen from no want on his part of diligence and assiduity. For it has been well observed by the excellent and ingenious HEADLEY, that "to constitute a relish for the Black-Letter (a term by which we may understand whatever relates to antiquarian knowledge), a certain degree of literary Quixotism is highly requisite : he who is unwilling to penetrate the barren heath and solitary desert ; he who cannot encounter weariness, perplexity, and disgust; he who is not actuated by an enthusiasm for his employment,—is no true knight, and unfit for such service."[1]  More especially is this the case when, in order to publish the early remains of our National Poetry with the correctness and fidelity which is requisite, recourse must be had to ancient and discordant manuscripts, where the obscurity of the language, or the labour of decyphering them, is the least perplexing or difficult part of the undertaking.

IN the APPENDIX some remarks are subjoined which have occurred since a part of the volume was printed off.  The Reader will observe that the various Pieces contained in it have, at least, in their favour, the claim of antiquity, since all of them are given from sources anterior to the close of the Sixteenth Century.  These are carefully pointed out in the short notices which it was thought necessary to prefix to the Poems for their better illustration.  At the same time, many other curious reliques might have been found worthy of being brought to light; and it will be

[1] Select Beauties of Ancient English Poetry, 8vo, p. vii.

gratifying to the Editor, if this publication prove
in any way conductive to a more extensive research after the scanty and too long neglected
Remains of this portion of our Ancient Literature.  To what extent these may have suffered
in their transmission to our times, cannot now be
ascertained.  That they have suffered greatly is,
however, beyond doubt, and was a natural conse-
quence, in their having (in the words of Bishop
PERCY) "been handed down to us with less care
than any other writings in the world."[1]

[1] Of some of the Pieces which have hitherto eluded discovery, a
short list may here be subjoined, as the best mode of exciting
attention; and the Editor should feel happy to receive information respecting any of them, or of similar compositions, either in
a printed or manuscript state, which may have escaped his researches.—This list might have been easily enlarged.

THE TALE HOW THE KING OF ESTMORELAND MAREIT THE KINGIS
    DOCHTER OF WESTMORELAND.  A modernized copy of this
    romantick tale is printed in Percy's Reliques.

THE TALE OF THE THREE FUTTIT DOG OF NORROWAY.  Mentioned
    in the Complaynt of Scotland, 1549: or, indeed, any of the
    *taylis, fabillis,* or *pleysand storeis,* enumerated in that curious
    work, which are pointed out by Dr Leyden, in his republica-
    tion of that ancient and singular composition.

THE EARL OF ERROL'S TESTAMENT, in Scotish metre, by ROBERT
    ALEXANDER, Advocate, was printed at Edinburgh some time
    after the year 1541.

CHRIST'S KIRK ON THE GREENE.  Any edition prior to that printed
    in the year 1663.

In the following stanzas of THE PALICE OF HONOUR, by Bishop
    Douglas, written in 1503, several curious tales are alluded to,
    most of which probably are no longer in existence :—

THE present work must necessarily have a very limited circulation,[1] yet, trusting that such a Col-

> I saw Raf Coilȝear with his thrawin brow,
> Craibit Johne the Reif, and auld Cowkewyis Sow
> And how the Wran came out of Ailssay,
> And Peirs Plewman that maid his workmen fow,
> Greit Gowmakmorne and Fyn Makcoul, and how
> Thay suld be Goddis in Ireland as they say;
> Thair saw I Maitland vpon auld Beird Gray,
> Robene Hude, and Gilbert with the quhite hand,
> How Hay of Nauchtoun slew in Madin land.
>
> The Nigromansie thair saw I eik anone,
> Of Benytas, Bongo, and Freir Bacone,
> With mony subtill point of juglary,
> Of Flanders peis maid mony precious stone,
> Ane greit laid sadill of a siching bone,
> Of ane nutemug thay maid a monk in hy,
> Ane paroche kirk of ane penny py.
> And Benytas of ane mussill maid ane aip,
> With mony vther subtill mow and jaip.—Edit. 1579, p. 56

THE BATTLE OF HARLAW. Anno 1411. Printed in the Evergreen, by Allan Ramsay, from (as supposed) a modernized copy. It was printed in the year 1668.

SIR EGEIR, SIR GRYME, AND SIR GRAY STEILL. An analysis of this interesting romance is given by Mr Ellis (Specimens of early English Romances, vol. iii. 308-347), from a modernized copy, in Mr Douce's possession, printed in the year 1711, pp. 84. It certainly, however, had been often printed before this edition, which bears to be "Newly corrected and amended." Indeed, in the Will of Thomas Bassandyne, a Printer in Edinburgh, dated 18th Oct. 1577, among other books of which his stock consisted, we find "Item III$^{c.}$ [300] Gray Steillis, y$^e$ pece vi$^d$, summa vii$^L$ x$^s$."—It is also supposed to have been printed at Edinburgh by Robert Smith, or by Thomas Finlason; but any copy printed in the sixteenth or seventeenth century, which might present the text in an authentick state, would be esteemed a valuable discovery.

[1] The entire impression does not exceed ONE HUNDRED AND EIGHT copies.

lection is neither unworthy of publick attention,
nor of the care that has been bestowed in forming
it, the Editor, with all due feeling of grateful
esteem, would inscribe it as a slight but sincere
tribute of respect to THE DISTINGUISHED AUTHOR,
to whom, of all others, the Literature of his Native
Country is most deeply beholden :—Whose zeal
in its cause has been shewn, no less in a friendly
and generous encouragement of those engaged in
its cultivation, than in his own successful exertions
in behalf of the unregarded and traditionary productions of former ages ;—and Who has, at the
same time, so eminently sustained and extended
the reputation of our national literary character,
by those original compositions which have shed
so much lustre over the MINSTRELSY AND ROMANCE
OF SCOTLAND, and have happily displayed the extent and fertility of his own surpassing Genius.

DAVID LAING.

EDINBURGH,
*6th November* 1822.

# THE TABLE OF CONTENTS.



[1] Not in Edition of 1822.

# SELECT REMAINS

OF THE

## ANCIENT POPULAR AND ROMANCE POETRY OF SCOTLAND

THE

# THE
# TAILL OF RAUF COILȜEAR

I.

# RAUF COILƷEAR.

THE *Tale of* Rauf Coilgear, *and that of* John the Reeve *which immediately follows, were two of the best known metrical fictions in Scotland at an early period. That they enjoyed much popularity is shown by the following lines in one of the poems of* Dunbar, *addressed to* James IV.—

> " Gentill and semple, of every clan
>   Kyne of Rauf Colȝear and Johne the Reif."

Bishop Gawain Douglas *also, in his Palice of Honour, written in the year* 1503, *among other characters of notoriety, says :*

> " I saw Raf Coilȝear with his thrawin brow,
>   Craibit Johne the Reif, and auld Cowkewyis Sow."

*The idea or plot in these pieces is not uncommon in the early literature both of England and Scotland, as it was a favourite theme of the old ballad-makers to represent the king as going about in disguise, and conversing, either by accident or design, with some of the poorest of his subjects. Of poems of this kind may be mentioned :* The King and the Miller of Mansfield; King James I. and the Tinker; King Alfred and the Shepherd; King Henry VIII. and the Cobbler; *&c.*

*The Tale of* Rauf Coilȝear, *in common with a great number of the ancient romances in our vernacular language, may possibly be traced to some Norman original. Its language,*

*the familiar structure of the stanza, and its alliterative style,
refer the composition to the later portion of the fourteenth
century. We are not, however, possessed of such evidence as
might enable us to ascribe it in particular to any one Scottish
Poet.*

*It is enumerated by the author of the Complaynt of Scot-
land, in* 1549, *among the* " taylis, fabillis, and plesand
stories " *recited by* " the scheiphirdis," *whereof* " sum vas
in prose, and sum in verse, sum var storeis, and sum
var flet taylis."

*This Tale, however, was for a length of time considered
no longer to be in existence. The short notice which occurs
in* Jos. Ames's Typographical Antiquities, 1749, 4to, *p.*
583, *is the only intimation respecting any printed edition;
but so completely had every copy eluded detection that the
repeated search and inquiry of more than half a century
failed in gratifying the curiosity excited by these different
allusions among our poetical antiquaries. In the index to
the* Asloan Manuscript, *preserved at Auchinleck,* " Item,
The Buke of Ralf Colƶear " *appears as the* lxiv. *article;
but this and some other portions of the same volume have
long since been lost.*

*The present re-impression has been made from a printed
copy discovered about the year* 1821 *in a volume of English
Tracts of extreme rarity, in the Library of the* Faculty of
Advocates. *The original, which contains sixteen leaves in
black letter, is now detached and bound separately, and a
correct facsimile of the title is prefixed to the poem. Although
seemingly printed with more accuracy than is commonly met
with in such publications, two lines in the* XI.*th, and one line
in the* LV.*th stanza appear to have been omitted. The only
liberty that has been taken, besides the change of letter, is the
substitution of* " th " *in the few instances where the Anglo-
Saxon* " þ " *had been introduced.*

*The Tale of* Rauf Coilƶear *has claims to public attention
altogether independent of its uncommon rarity; as it possesses
no inconsiderable share of poetical merit. Although, like
most poems of the same age and character, many words are
introduced merely for the sake of alliteration, the language is*

*by no means obscure. The narrative is simple and circum-
stantial; the characters are well described; and a vein of
comic humour runs through the whole. The adventures with
the Saracen towards the conclusion of the poem—very skil-
fully introduced to prevent the author from involving the
reputation either of his hero* Schir Rauf, *or of the* 'gentill
knycht,' Schir Rolland—*which terminates so happily in*
Magog's *conversion to the Christian Faith, and his marriage
with the* 'Gentill Duchess,' *may perhaps be considered as the
strongest evidence of its Norman origin.*

[*The scene of the Tale is laid in the neighbourhood of
Paris. The King, afterwards the* Emperor Charlemagne,
*is represented as having, in a storm, been separated from his
attendants, and meeting with a charcoal-burner called* Ralf,
*who gives him shelter in his house. A supper is set before
him, replete with excellent viands. The Collier requests the
King to lead his wife to the table, and when he hesitates, the
Collier gives him a blow under the ear which sends him to
the floor. After this the King does as requested, and the
entertainment begins, in which wine and venison are not
wanting. After supper* Ralf *tells many stories, and at last
asks his guest who he may be. He gives his name as* Wymond of the Wardrobe, *an attendant on the Queen. He
then tells the Collier that if he will bring a load of his charcoal to him at the palace, he will ensure him a good price
for it.*

*In the morning the King takes his leave, and soon after
meets* Sir Roland *and* Sir Oliver, *with a retinue of a thousand men, in search of him. They attend a service at the
Cathedral of St Denis, followed by Yule festivities. The
next morning the Collier sets off for the Court with a load of
charcoal. The King, remembering his engagement, requests*
Sir Róland *to proceed to the road leading to Paris, and
if he find any one, to bring him to the hall. He meets the
Collier and orders him to come with him. The Collier
demurs and offers to fight. He however consents to go to
see* Wymond of the Wardrobe. *The Knight returns,
leaving the Collier to follow. The King inquires whether
he saw any one, when he stated that he only met a poor man*

*conveying coals. By this time the Collier is at the palace gate clamouring for admittance. He gains his point through* Sir Roland's *influence. He finds himself where the King is dining in state, and at last recognises in him* Wymond of the Wardrobe ; *but he is now, however, so much grander a person than he expected, that he wishes to escape. The King smiles at his surprise, and tells the story of his reception in the forest. The courtiers think the Collier should be hanged, but the King dubs him a knight, and assigns him a retinue and a revenue. He has, however, to win his spurs. Accordingly he sets out in quest of adventures. He at last sees advancing a Saracen Knight mounted on a camel, and both prepare for combat. They rush together with terrible force, when both their chargers perish. They renew the fight on foot with short knives.* Sir Roland *runs forward and parts them, and invites the Saracen to become a Christian. He, however, defies them both, and gives* Sir Roland *a challenge from the* Khan of Tartary *to* King Charles. *He says his own name is* Magog. Sir Roland *tries to convert him with the bait of rich duchies and a worthy wife. The Saracen refuses these attractions, but if the Christian's* God *can be avouched as really so good, he will believe on him and on* Christ *his* Son. Sir Roland *thanks* God, *and all three swear on their swords to become brothers, and they proceed to Court. The King celebrates the result, the Bishop administers the sacraments, names the Saracen* Sir Walter, *and weds him to the Duchess,* Dame Jane *of Anjou.* Sir Ralf's *knighthood is approved, and he is made Marechal of France. He sends for his wife, and on the spot where he met the King founds an hospice in honour of* St Julian, *the patron of travellers.*]

# ¶ Heir beginnis the taill of Rauf coilȝear how he harbreit King charlis

# ❧ Imprentit at Sanc-

tandrois be Robert Lekpreuik. Anno. 1572.

I.

# 𝕽auf Coilȝear.

I.

IN the cheiftyme of Charlis, that chosin chiftane,
   Thair fell ane ferlyfull flan within thay fellis wyde,
Quhair Empreouris, and Erlis, and vther mony ane,
   Turnit fra Sanct Thomas befoir the ȝule tyde;
Thay past vnto Paris, thay proudest in pane,     5
   With mony Prelatis and Princis, that was of mekle
      pryde,
All thay went with the King to his worthy wane;
   Ouir the feildis sa fair thay fure be his syde;
All the worthiest went in the morning,
      Baith Dukis, and Duchepeiris,     10
      Barrounis, and Bacheleiris,
      Mony stout man steiris
        Of town with the King.

II.

¶ And as that Ryall raid ouir the rude mure,
   Him betyde ane tempest that tyme, hard I tell;   15
The wind blew out of the Eist stiflie and sture,
   The d[rift]¹ durandlie draif in mony deip dell;
Sa feirslie fra the firmament, sa fellounlie it fure,
   Thair micht na folk hald na fute on the heich fell;
In point thay war to parische, thay proudest men and
     pure,     20
   In thay wickit wedderis thair wist nane to dwell.

¹ Deip, in ed. of 1572.

Amang thay myrk montanis sa madlie thay mer,
  Be it was pryme of the day,
  Sa wonder hard fure thay
  That ilk ane tuik ane seir way,    25
   And sperpellit full fer.


### III.

Ithand wedderis of the Eist draif on sa fast,
 It all to-blaisterit and blew that thairin baid,
Be thay disseuerit sindrie, midmorne was past;
 Thair wist na Knicht of the Court quhat way the
   King raid;    30
He saw thair was na better bot God at the last,
 His steid aganis the storme staluartlie straid,
He cachit fra the Court, sic was his awin cast,
 Quhair na body was him about be fiue mylis braid.
In thay montanis, I-wis, he wox all will,   35
  In wickit wedderis and wicht,
  Amang thay montanis on hicht,
  Be that it drew to the nicht,
   The King lykit ill.


### IV.

Euill lykand was the King it nichtit him sa lait,  40
 And he na harberie had for his behufe;
Sa come thair ane cant Carll chachand the gait,
 With ane capill and twa creillis cuplit abufe;
The King carpit to the Carll withouten debait,—
 "Schir, tell me thy richt name, for the Rude lufe?" 45
He sayis, "Men callis me Rauf Coilƺear, as I weill wait,
 I leid my life in this land with mekle vnrufe,
Baith tyde and tyme in all my trauale;
  Hine ouir seuin mylis I dwell,
  And leidis coilis to sell;    50
  Sen thow speiris, I the tell
   All the suith hale."

### V.

¶ " Sa mot I thrife," said the King, " I speir for nane
　　ill ;
Thow semis ane nobill fallow, thy answer is sa fyne."
" Forsuith," said the Coilƺear, " traist quhen thow will,
　For I trow and it be nocht swa, sum part salbe thyne."
" Mary, God forbid," said the King, " that war bot lytill
　　skill,
　Baith my self and my hors is reddy for to tyne ;
I pray the, bring me to sum rest, the weddir is sa schill,
　For I defend that we fall in ony fechtine ;　　　60
I had mekill mair nait, sum friendschip to find :
　　　　And gif thow can better than I,
　　　　For the name of Sanct July,
　　　　Thow bring me to sum harbery,
　　　　　　And leif me nocht behind."　　　65


### VI.

" I wait na worthie harberie heir neir hand,
　For to serue sic ane man as me think the,
Nane bot mine awin hous, maist in this land ;
　Fer furth in the forest, amang the fellis hie,
With thy thow wald be payit of sic as thow fand ;　　70
　Forsuith thow suld be wel-cum to pas hame with me,
Or ony vther gude fallow that I heir fand
　Walkand will of his way, as me think the ;
For the wedderis are sa fell, that fallis on the feild."
　　　　The King was blyth quhair he raid,　　75
　　　　Of the grant that he had maid,
　　　　Sayand with hart glaid,
　　　　" Schir, God ƺow forƺeild."


### VII.

" Na, thank me not ouir airlie, for dreid that we threip,
　For I haue seruit the ƺit of lytill thing to ruse ;　　80
For nouther hes thow had of me fyre, drink, nor meit,
　Nor nane vther eismentis for trauellouris behuse ;

Bot, micht we bring this harberie this nicht weill to
    heip,
  That we micht with ressoun baith thus excuse ;
To-morne on the morning, quhen thow sall on leip,   85
  Pryse at the parting, how that thow dois ;
For first to lofe and syne to lak, Peter ! it is schame."
      The King said, " In gude fay,
      Schir, it is suith that ʒe say."
      Into sic talk fell thay           90
        Quhill thay war neir hame.


### VIII.

¶ To the Coilʒearis hous baith, or thay wald blin,
  The Carll had cunning weill quhair the gait lay ;
" Vndo the dure beliue !  Dame, art thow in ?
  Quhy Deuill makis thow na dule for this euill day?  95
For my gaist and I baith cheueris with the chin,
  Sa fell ane wedder feld I neuer, be my gude fay."
The gude wyfe, [was] glaid with the gle to begin,
  For durst scho neuer sit summoundis that scho hard
    him say,
The Carll was wantoun of word, and wox wonder
    wraith.           100
      All abaisit for blame,
      To the dure went our Dame,
      Scho said, " Schir, ʒe ar welcome hame,
      And ʒour gaist baith."


### IX.

¶ " Dame, I haue deir coft all this dayis hyre,     105
  In wickit wedderis and weit walkand full will ;
Dame, kyith I am cummin hame, and kendill on ane fire,
  I trow our gaist be the gait hes farne als ill ;
Ane Ryall rufe het fyre war my desyre,
  To fair the better for his saik, gif we micht win thair-
    till ;           110
Knap doun capounis of the best, but in the byre,
  Heir is bot hamelie fair, do beliue, Gill."

Twa cant knaifis of his awin haistelie he bad—
   "The ane of ȝow my capill ta,
   The vther his coursour alswa,      115
   To the stabill swyith ȝe ga."
     Than was the King glaid.


### X.

☞ The Coilȝear, gudlie in feir, tuke him be the hand,
  And put him befoir him, as ressoun had bene;
Quhen thay come to the dure, the King begouth to
    stand,      120
  To put the Coilȝear in befoir, maid him to mene;
He said, "Thow art vncourtes, that sall I warrand."
  He tyt the King be the nek, twa part in tene;
"Gif thow at bidding suld be boun or obeysand,
  And gif thow of courtasie couth, thow hes forȝet it
   ·   clene;      125
Now is anis," said the Coilȝear, "kynd aucht to creip,
   Sen ellis thow art vnknawin,
   To mak me Lord of my awin,
   Sa mot I thriue I am thrawin,
     Begin we to threip."      130


### XI.

Than benwart thay ȝeid, quhair brandis was bricht,
  To ane bricht byrnand fyre as the Carll bad;
He callit on Gyliane, his wyfe, thair supper to dicht,
  "Of the best that thair is, help that we had,
Efter ane euill day to haue ane mirrie nicht,      135
  For sa troublit with stormis was I neuer stad;
Of ilk airt of the Eist sa laithly it laid,
   Ȝit was I mekle willar than,
   Quhen I met with this man."
   Of sic taillis thay began,      140
     Quhill the supper was graid.

### XII.

¶ Sone was the supper dicht, and the fyre bet,
  And thay had weschin, I-wis, the worthiest was thair:
"Tak my wyfe be the hand, in feir, withoutin let,
  And gang begin the buird," said the Coilƶear.    145
"That war vnsemand, forsuith, and thy self vnset;"
  The King profferit him to gang, and maid ane strange
    fair.
"Now is twyse," said the Carll, "me think thow hes
    forƶet."
He leit gyrd to the King, withoutin ony mair,
And hit him vnder the eir with his richt hand.    150
      Quhill he stakkerit thair with all
      Half the breid of the hall,
      He faind neuer of ane fall,
        Quhill he the eird fand.

### XIII.

¶ He start vp stoutly agane, vneis micht he stand,  155
  For anger of that outray that he had thair tane;
He callit on Gyliane his wyfe, "Ga tak him be the
    hand,
  And gang agane to the buird, quhair ƶe suld air haue
    gane;"
"Schir, thow art vnskilfull, and that sall I warrand,
  Thow byrd to haue nurtour aneuch, and thow hes
    nane;                 160
Thow hes walkit, I wis, in mony wyld land,
  The mair vertew thow suld haue, to keip the fra
    blame;
Thou suld be courtes of kynd, and ane cunnand Courteir.
      Thocht that I simpill be,
      Do as I bid the,            165
      The hous is myne, pardie,
        And all that is heir."

### XIV.

☞ The King said to himself, " This is an euill lyfe,
 Ȝit was I neuer in my lyfe thus-gait leird ;
And I haue oft tymes bene quhair gude hes bene ryfe,
 That maist couth of courtasie in this Cristin eird. 171
Is nane sa gude as leif of, and mak na mair stryfe,
 For I am stonischit at this straik, that hes me thus
  steird."
In feir fairlie he foundis, with the gude wyfe,
 Quhair the Coilȝear bad, sa braithlie he beird.  175
Quhen he had done his bidding, as him gude thocht,
  Doun he sat the King neir,
  And maid him glaid and gude cheir,
  And said, " Ȝe ar welcum heir,
   Be him that me bocht."  180

### XV.

¶ Quhen they war seruit and set to the suppar,
 Gyll and the gentill King, Charlis of micht,
Syne on the tother syde sat the Coilȝear :
 Thus war thay marschellit, but mair, and matchit that
  nicht.
Thay brocht breid to the buird, and braun of ane bair,
 And the worthyest wyne, went vpon hicht ;  186
Thay Beirnis, as I wene, thay had aneuch thair,
 Within that burelie bigging, byrnand full bricht ;
Syne enteris thair daynteis on deis dicht dayntelie.
  Within that worthie wane,  190
  Forsuith wantit thay nane :
  With blyith cheir sayis Gyliane,
   " Schir, dois glaidlie."

### XVI.

☞ The Carll carpit to the King cumlie and cleir,
 " Schir, the forestaris, forsuith, of this forest,  195
Thay haue me all at inuy, for dreid of the deir ;
 Thay threip that I thring doun of the fattest ;

Thay say, I sall to Paris, thair to compeir
  Befoir our cumlie King, in dule to be drest;
Sic manassing thay me mak, forsuith, ilk ȝeir,     200
  And ȝit aneuch sall I haue for me and ane gest;
Thairfoir sic as thow seis, spend on, and not spair."
      Thus said gentill Charlis the Mane
      To the Coilȝear agane,
      "The King him self hes bene fane,     205
      Sum tyme of sic fair."


### XVII.

¶ Of caponnis and cunningis they had plentie,
  With wyne at thair will, and eik vennysoun;
Byrdis bakin in breid, the best that may be;
  Thus full freschlie thay fure into fusioun.     210
The Carll with ane cleir voce carpit on he,
  Said, "Gyll, lat the cop raik for my bennysoun;
And gar our gaist begin, and syne drink thow to me,
  Sen he is ane stranger, me think it ressoun."
Thay drank dreichlie about, thay wosche, and thay rais,
      The King with ane blyith cheir     216
      Thankit the Coilȝeir;
      Syne all the thre into feir
      To the fyre gais.


### XVIII.

Quhen they had maid thame eis, the Coilȝear tald   220
  Mony sindrie taillis efter suppair;
Ane bricht byrnand fyre was byrnand full bald,
  The King held gude countenance and company bair;
And euer to his asking ane answer he ȝald,
  Quhill at the last he began to frane farther mair: 225
"In faith, friend, I wald wit, tell gif ȝe wald,
  Quhair is thy maist wynning?" said the Coilȝear.
"Out of weir," said the King, "I wayndit neuer to tell;
      With my Lady the Quene,
      In office maist haue I bene,     230
      All thir ȝeiris fyftene,
      In the Court for to dwell."

### XIX.

¶ "Quhat-kin office art thow in, quhen thow art at
  hame,
  Gif thow dwellis with the Quene, proudest in pane?"
"Ane Chyld of hir Chalmer, Schir, be Sanct Jame, 235
  And thocht my self it say, maist inwart of ane;
For my dwelling to nicht I dreid me for blame."
  "Quhat sal I cal the," said the Coilʒear, "quhen
    thow art hyne gane?"
"Wymond of the Wardrop is my richt name,
  Quhair euer thow findis me befoir the, thi harberie is
    tane; 240
And thow will cum to the Court, this I vnderta,
      Thow sall haue for thy fewaill,
      For my saik, the better saill,
      And onwart to thy trauaill,
        Worth ane laid or twa." 245

### XX.

¶ He said, "I haue na knawledge quhair the Court lyis,
  And I am wonder wa to cum quhair I am vnkend;"
"And I sall say the the suith on ilk syde, I wis,
  That thow sall wit weill aneuch or I fra the wend.
Baith the King and the Quene meitis in Paris, 250
  For to hald thair ʒule togidder, for scho is efter send;
Thair may thow sell, be ressoun, als deir as thow will
    prys,
  And ʒit I sall help the, gif I ocht may amend,
For I am knawin with Officiaris in cais thow cum thair;
      Haue gude thocht on my Name, 255
      And speir gif I be at hame,
      For I suppois, be Sanct Jame,
        Thow sall the better fair."

### XXI.

¶ "Me think it ressoun, be the Rude, that I do thy red,
  In cais I cum to the Court, and knaw bot the ane, 260
Is nane sa gude as drink, and gang to our bed,
  For als far as I wait, the nicht is furth gane."

To ane preuie chalmer beliue thay him led,
  Quhair ane burely bed was wrocht in that wane,
Closit with courtingis, and cumlie cled ;      265
  Of the worthiest wyne wantit thay nane.
The Coilƺear and his wyfe baith with him thay ƺeid,
      To serue him all at thay mocht,
      Till he was in bed brocht.
      Mair the King spak nocht,      270
        Bot thankit thame thair deid.

#### XXII.

☞ Upon the morne airlie, quhen it was day,
  The King buskit him sone, with scant of squyary.
Wachis and Wardroparis all war away,
  That war wont for to walkin mony worthy.      275
Ane Pauyot preuilie brocht him his palfray,
  The King thocht lang of this lyfe, and lap on in hy ;
Then callit he on the Carll, anent quhair he lay,
  For to tak his leif, than spak he freindly ;
Than walkinnit thay baith, and hard he was thair.  280
      The Carll start vp sone,
      And prayit him to abyde none ;
      " Quhill thir wickit wedderis be done,
        I red nocht ƺe fair."

#### XXIII.

" Sa mot I thriue," said the King, " me war laith to byde,
  Is not the morne ƺule day, formest of the ƺeir ?    286
Ane man that Office suld beir betyme at this tyde,
  He will be found in his fault, that wantis foroutin weir ;
I se the Firmament fair vpon ather syde,
  I will returne to the Court quhill the wedder is cleir ;
Call furth the gude wyfe, lat pay hir or we ryde,    291
  For the worthie harberie that I haue fundin heir."
" Lat be, God forbid," the Coilƺear said,
      " And thow of Charlis cumpany,
      Cheif King of Cheualry,      295
      That for ane nichtis harbery,
        Pay suld be laid."

### XXIV.

¶ " Ʒea sen it is sa that thow will haue na pay,
  Cum the morne to the Court and do my counsall;
Deliuer the, and bring ane laid, and mak na delay,  300
   Thow may not schame with thy craft, gif thow thriue
     sall;
Gif I may help the ocht to sell, forsuith I sall assay,
  And als my self wald haue sum of the fewall."
" Peter !" he said, " I sall preif the morne, gif I may,
  To bring coillis to the Court, to se gif thay sell sall."
" Se that thow let nocht, I pray the," said the King.  306
    " In faith," said the Coilƺear,
     " Traist weill I salbe thair,
     For thow will neuer gif the mair,
      To mak ane lesing."       310

### XXV.

" Bot tell me now, lelely, quhat is thy richt name ?
  I will forƺet the morne, and ony man me greif."
" Wymond of the Wardrop, I bid not to lane,
  Tak gude tent to my name, the Court gif thow will
    preif; "       314
" That I haue said, I sall hald, and that I tell the plane;
  Quhair ony Coilƺear may enchaip I trow till encheif."
Quhen he had grantit him to cum, than was the King fane,
  And withoutin ony mair let, than he tuke his leif:
Then the Coilƺear had greit thocht on the cunnand he
    had maid,
     Went to the charcoill in hy,      320
     To mak his chauffray reddy,
     Agane the morne airly,
      He ordanit him ane laid.

### XXVI.

¶ The lyft lemit vp beliue, and licht was the day,
  The King had greit knawledge the countrie to ken:
Schir Rolland and Oliuer come rydand the way,   326
  With thame ane thousand and ma of fensabill men,

War wanderand all the nicht ouir, and mony ma than
    thay,
  On ilk airt outwart war ordanit sic ten;
Gif thay micht heir of the King, or happin quhair he
    lay,                         330
To Jesus Christ thay pray, that grace thame to len.
  Als sone as Schir Rolland saw it was the King,
      He kneillit doun in the place,
      Thankand God ane greit space;
      Thair was ane meting of grace      335
        At that gaddering.

### XXVII.

The gentill Knicht, Schir Rolland, he kneillit on his kne,
  Thankand greit God that mekill was of micht;
Schir Oliuer at his hand, and Bischoppis thre,
    Withoutin commounis that come and mony vther
      Knicht;                          340
Than to Paris thay pas, all that Cheualrie,
  Betuix none of the day and Ʒule nicht:
The gentill Bischop Turpine cummand thay se,
  With threttie Conuent of Preistis reuest at ane sicht,
Preichand of Prophecie in Processioun.      345
      Efter thame, baith fer and neir,
      Folkis following in feir,
      Thankand God with gude cheir
        Thair Lord was gane to toun.

### XXVIII.

☞ Quhen thay Princis appeirit into Paris,      350
  Ilk rew ryallie with riches thame arrayis;
Thair was digne seruice done at Sanct Dyonys,
  With mony proud Prelat, as the buik sayis.
Syne to supper they went within the Palys,
  Befoir that mirthfull man menstrallis playis;    355
Mony wicht wyfis sone, worthie and wise,
  Was sene at that semblay ane and twentie dayis;

With all-kin principall plentie for his plesance.
    Thay callit it the best Ȝule than,
    And maist worthie began,         360
    Sen euer King Charlis was man,
      Or euer was in France.

### XXIX.

¶ Than vpon the morne airlie, quhen the day dew,
  The Coilȝear had greit thocht quhat he had vnder tane;
He kest twa creillis on ane capill with coillis anew,  365
  Wandit thame with widdeis, to wend on that wane.
" Mary, it is not my counsall, bot ȝone man that ȝe knew,
  To do ȝow in his gentrise," said Gyliane.
" Thow gaif him ane outragious blaw and greit boist
    blew ;
  In faith, thow suld haue bocht it deir, and he had
    bene allane ;         370
Forthy, hald ȝow fra the Court, for ocht that may be :
    Ȝone man that thow outrayd,
    Is not sa simpill as he said,
    Thairun my lyfe dar I layd,
      That sall thow heir and se."

### XXX.

☞ " Ȝea, Dame, haue nane dreid of my lyfe to day, 376
  Lat me wirk as I will, the weird is mine awin.
I spak not out of ressoun, the suth gif I sall say,
  To Wymond of the Wardrop war the suith knawin ;
That I haue hecht I sall hald, happin as it may,    380
  Quhidder sa it gang to greif or to gawin."
He caucht twa creillis on ane capill and catchit on his
    way
  Ouir the daillis sa derf, be the day was dawin ;
The hie way to Paris, in all that he mocht,
    With ane quhip in his hand,       385
    Cantlie on catchand,
    To fulfill his cunnand,
      To the Court socht.

### XXXI.

¶ Graith thocht of the grant had the gude King,
  And callit Schir Rolland him till and gaif command-
      ment,                                              390
Ane man he traistit in, maist atour all vther thing,
  That neuer wald set him on assay withoutin his
      assent:
"Tak thy hors and thy harnes in the morning,
  For to watche weill the wayis, I wald that thow went;
Gif thow meitis ony leid lent on the ling,              395
  Gar thame boun to this burgh, I tell the mine intent;
Or gyf thow seis ony man cumming furth the way,
        Quhat sumeuer that he be,
        Bring him haistely to me,
        Befoir none that I him se                        400
        In this hall the day."

### XXXII.

¶ Schir Rolland had greit ferly and in hart kest
  Quhat that suld betakin that the King tald;
Vpon solemnit ƺule day quhen ilk man suld rest,
  That him behouit neidlingis to watche on the wald,
Quhen his God to serue he suld haue him drest,         406
  And syne, with ane blyith cheir, buskit that bald.
Out of Paris proudly he preikit full prest,
  In till his harnes all haill his hechtis for to hald;
He vmbekest the countrie, outwith the toun,            410
        He saw na thing on steir,
        Nouther fer nor neir,
        Bot the feildis in feir,
        Daillis and doun.

### XXXIII.

¶ He huit and he houerit, quhill midmorne and mair,
  Behaldand the hie hillis, and passage sa plane;   416
Sa saw he quhair the Coilƺear come with all his fair,
  With twa creillis on ane capill; thairof was he fane

He followit to him haistely, amang the holtis hair,
  For to bring him to the King, at bidding full bane. 420
Courtesly to the Knicht kneillit the Coilȝear;
  And Schir Rolland him self salust him agane,
Syne bad him leif his courtasie, and boun him to ga,
    He said, "Withoutin letting,
    Thow mon to Paris to the King, 425
    Speid the fast in ane ling,
      Sen I find na ma."

XXXIV.

¶ "In faith," said the Coilȝear, "ȝit was I neuer sa
    nyse,
  Schir Knicht, it is na courtasie commounis to scorne;
Thair is mony better than I cummis oft to Parys, 430
  That the King wait not of, nouther nicht nor morne;
For to towsill me or tit me, thocht foull be my clais,
  Or I be dantit on sic wyse, my lyfe salbe lorne."
"Do way," said Schir Rolland, "me think thow art
    not wise,
  I red thow at bidding be, be all that we haue sworne,
And call thow it na scorning, bot do as I the ken; 436
    Sen thow hes hard mine intent,
    It is the Kingis commandement,
    At this tyme thow suld haue went,
      And I had met sic ten." 440

XXXV.

¶ "I am bot ane mad man, that thow hes heir met,
  I haue na myster to matche with maisterfull men;
Fairand ouir the feildis, fewell to fet,
  And oft fylit my feit in mony foull fen;
Gangand with laidis, my gouerning to get. 445
  Thair is mony Carll in the countrie thow may nocht
    ken;
I sall hald that I haue hecht, bot I be hard set,
  To Wymond of the Wardrop, I wait full weill
    quhen."

"Sa thriue I," said Rolland, "it is mine intent,
　　That nouther to Wymond nor Will　　　　450
　　Thow sall hald nor hecht till,
　　Quhill I haue brocht the to fulfill
　　　　The Kingis commandment."


### XXXVI.

¶ The Carll beheld to the Knicht, as he stude than,
　　He bair grauit in Gold and Gowlis in grene,　　455
Glitterand full gaylie quhen glemis began,
　　Ane Tyger ticht to ane tre, ane takin of tene;
Trewlie that tenefull was trimland than,
　　Semelie schapin and schroud in that Scheild schene;
Mekle worschip of weir worthylie he wan,　　460
　　Befoir, into fechting with mony worthie sene;
His Basnet was bordourit and burneist bricht
　　　　With stanes of Beriall deir;
　　　　Dyamountis and Sapheir,
　　　　Riche Rubeis in feir,　　　　465
　　　　Reulit full richt.


### XXXVII.

His plaitis properlie picht attour with precious stanis,
　　And his Pulanis full prest of that ilk peir;
Greit Graipis of Gold his Greis for the nanis,
　　And his Cussanis cumlie schynand full cleir;　　470
Bricht braissaris of steill about his arme banis,
　　Blandit with Beriallis and Cristallis cleir;
Ticht ouir with Thopas, and trew lufe atanis,
　　The teind of his iewellis to tell war full teir;
His Sadill circulit and set, richt sa on ilk syde,　　475
　　　　His brydill bellisand and gay,
　　　　His steid stout on stray,
　　　　He was the Ryallest of array,
　　　　On Ronsy micht ryde.

### XXXVIII.

¶ Of that Ryall array that Rolland in raid,  480
 Rauf rusit in his hart of that Ryall thing :
" He is the gayest in geir that euer on ground glaid,
 Haue he grace to the gre in ilk Iornaying ;
War he ane manly man, as he is weill maid,
 He war full michtie, with magre durst abyde his
   meting."  485
He bad the Coilƶear in wraith swyth withoutin baid,
 Cast the creillis fra the capill, and gang to the King.
" In faith, it war greit schame," said the Coilƶear,
  " I vndertuk thay suld be brocht,
   This day for ocht that be mocht ;  490·
   Schir Knicht, that word is for nocht,
    That thow carpis thair."


### XXXIX.

¶ " Thow huifis on thir holtis, and haldis me heir,
 Quhill half the haill day may the hicht haue ; "
" Be Christ that was Cristinnit, and his Mother cleir,
 Thow sall catche to the Court that sall not be· to
   craue.  496
It micht be preifit preiudice, bot gif thow suld compeir,
 To se quhat granting of grace the King wald the gaif."
" For na gold on this ground wald I, but weir,
 Be fundin fals to the King, sa Christ me saue." 500
" To gar the cum and be knawin as I am command,
  I wait not quhat his willis be,
  Nor he namit na mair the,
  Nor ane vther man to me,
   Bot quhome that I fand."  505


### XL.

¶ " Thow fand me fechand nathing that followit to feid,
 I war ane fule gif I fled, and fand nane affray ;
Bot as ane lauchfull man my laidis to leid,
 That leifis with mekle lawtie and labour in fay ; 509

Be the Mother and the Maydin that maid vs remeid,
  And thow mat me ony mair, cum efter quhat sa may,
Thow and I sall dyntis deill quhill ane of vs be deid,
  For the deidis thow hes me done vpon this deir day."
Mekle merwell of that word had Schir Rolland;
        He saw na wappinis thair,        515
        That the CoilƷear bair,
        Bot ane auld Buklair,
          And ane roustie brand.


### XLI.

¶ "It is lyke," said Schir Rolland, and lichtly he leuch,
  "That sic ane stubill husband man wald stryke
    stoutly;
Thair is mony toun man to tuggill is full teuch,    521
  Thocht thair brandis be blak and vnburely;
Oft fair foullis ar fundin faynt, and als freuch;
  I defend we fecht or fall in that foly.
Lat se how we may disseuer with sobernes aneuch; 525
  And catche crabitnes away, be Christ counsall I,
Quhair winnis that Wymond thow hecht to meit to
    day?"
        "With the Quene tauld he me,
        And thair I vndertuke to be,
        Into Paris, Pardie,        530
          Withoutin delay."


### XLII.

"And I am knawin with the Quene," said Schir Rolland,
  "And with mony byrdis in hir Bowre, be buikis and
    bellis;
The King is into Paris, that sall I warrand,
  And all his aduertance that in his Court dwellis; 535
Me tharth haue nane noy of myne erand,
  For me think thow will be thair efter as thow tellis;
Bot gif I fand the, forrow now to keip my cunnand."
  "Schir Knicht," said the CoilƷear, "thow trowis me
    neuer ellis,

Bot gif sum suddand let put it out of delay,
For that I hecht of my will,
And na man threit me thair till,
That I am haldin to fulfill,
And sall do quhill I may."

XLIII.

¶ "Ȝea, sen thow will be thair, thy cunnandis to new,
I neid nane airar myne erand nor none of the day."
"Be thow traist," said the Coilȝear, "man, as I am trew,
I will not haist me ane fute faster on the way;
Bot gif thow raik out of my renk, full raith sall thow rew,
Or, be the Rude, I sall rais thy Ryall array,
Thocht thy body be braissit in that bricht hew,
Thow salbe fundin als febil of thy bone fay."
Schir Rolland said to him self, "this is bot foly,
To striue with him ocht mair,
I se weill he will be thair."
His leif at the Coilȝear,
He tuke lufesumly.

XLIV.

¶ "Be Christ," said the Coilȝear, "that war ane foull scorne,
That thow suld chaip, bot I the knew, that is sa schynand;
For thow seis my weidis ar auld and all to-worne,
Thow trowis nathing thir taillis that I am telland.
Bring na Beirnis vs by, bot as we war borne,
And thir Blonkis that vs beiris, thairto I mak ane band,
That I sall meit the heir vpon this mure to morne,
Gif I be haldin in heill, and thairto my hand,
Sen that we haue na laiser at this tyme to ta."
In ane thourtour way,
Seir gaitis pas thay,
Baith to Paris in fay,
Thus partit thay twa.

### XLV.

The gentill Knicht, Schir Rolland, come rydand full sone,
  And left the CoilƷear to cum, as he had vndertane;
And quhen he come to Paris, the hie Mes was done,
  The King with mony cumly out of the Kirk is gane;
Of his harnes in hy he hynt withoutin hone,      575
  And in ane rob him arrayit richest of ane;
In that worschipfull weid he went in at none,
  As he was wont, with the wy that weildit the wane,
On fute ferly in feir, formest of all.
        Richt weill payit was the King      580
        Of Schir Rollandis cumming,
        To speir of his tything
           Efter him gart call.

### XLVI.

The King in counsall him callit, "cum hidder Schir
    Knicht,
  Hes thow my bidding done, as I the command?" 585
"In faith," said Schir Rolland, "I raid on full richt,
  To watche wyselie the wayis; that I sall warrand.
Thair wald na douchtie this day for Iornay be dicht;
  Fairand ouir the feildis full few thair I fand;
Saif anerly ane man that semblit in my sicht,     590
  Thair was na leid on lyfe lent in this land."
"Quhat kin a fallow was that ane, Schir, I the pray?"
        "Ane man in husband weid,
        Buskit busteously on breid,
        Leidand coillis he Ʒeid,     595
           To Paris the way."

### XLVII.

"Quhy hes thow not that husband brocht, as I the bad?
  I dreid me, sa he dantit the, thow durst not with him
    deill."
"In faith," said Schir Rolland, "gif that he sa had,
  That war full hard to my hart, and I ane man in
    heill."     600

He saw the King was engreuit, and gat furth glaid,
  To se gif the Coilȝearis lawtie was leill:
" I suld haue maid him in the stour to be full hard stad,
  And I had witten that the Carll wald away steill,
Bot I trowit not the day that he wald me beget."   605
      As he went outwart bayne,
      He met ane Porter swayne,
      Cummand raith him agayne,
          Fast fra the ȝet.   609


### XLVIII.

¶ " Quhair gangis thow, Gedling, thir gaitis sa gane ? "
  " Be God," said the Grome, " ane gift heir I geif;
I deuise at the ȝet thair is ane allane,
  Bot he be lattin in beliue, him lykis not to leif;
With ane capill and twa creillis cassin on the plane,
  To cum to this Palice he preissis to preif."   615
" Gif thow hes fundin that Freik, in faith I am fane,
  Lat him in glaidly, it may not engreif;
Bot askis he eirnestly efter ony man ? "
      Than said that Gedling on ground,
      " Ȝe, forsuith in this stound,   620
      Efter ane Wymound,
          In all that he can."


### XLIX.

☞ " Pas agane Porter, and let him swyith in,
  Amang the proudest in preis, plesand in pane;
Say thow art not worthy to Wymond to win,   625
  Bid him seik him his self, gif thair be sic ane."
Agane gangis Schir Rolland, quhair gle suld begin,
  And the ȝaip ȝeman to the ȝet is gane;
Enbraissit the bandis beliue, or that he wald blin,
  Syne leit the wy at his will wend in the wane.   630
" Gang seik him now thy self," he said, vpon hicht;
      " My self hes na lasair
      Fra thir ȝettis to fair."
      " Be Christ," said the Coilȝear,
          " I·set that bot licht."   635

L.

¶ " Gif thow will not seik him, my awin self sall,  
    For I haue oft tymes swet in seruice full sair ;  
Tak keip to my capill, that na man him call,  
    Quhill I cum fra the Court," said the Coilȝear ;  
" My laid war I laith to lois, I leif the heir all,     640  
    Se that thow leis thame not, bot ȝeme them full ȝair."  
In that hardy in hy, he haikit to that hall,  
    For to wit gif Wymondis wynning was thair ;  
He arguit with the Ischar ofter than anis,  
         " Schir, can thow ocht say,     645  
         Quhair is Wymond the day ?  
         I pray the, bring him gif thow may,  
           Out of this wanis."

LI.

He trowit that the wy had witten of Wymond he wend,  
    Bot to his raifand word he gaue na reward ;     650  
Thair was na man thairin that his name kend,  
    Thay countit not the Coilȝear almaist at regaird ;  
He saw thair was na meiknes nor mesure micht mend,  
    He sped him in spedely, and nane of thame he spaird.  
Thair was na fyue of thay Freikis, that micht him furth  
         send,     655  
    He socht in sa sadly, quhill sum of thame he saird,  
He thristit in throw thame thraly with threttis ;  
         Quhen he come amang thame all,  
         Ȝit was the King in the hall,  
         And mony gude man with all,     660  
         Vngane to the meit.

LII.

¶ Thocht he had socht sic ane sicht all this seuin ȝeir,  
    Sa solempnit ane semblie had he not sene ;  
The hall was properly apperrellit and paintit but peir,  
    Dyamountis full dantely dentit betwene ;     665  
It wes semely set on ilk syde seir,  
    Gowlis glitterand full gay, glemand in grene,

Flowris with Flourdelycis formest in feir,
  With mony flamand ferly, ma than fyftene;
The rufe reulit about in reuall of Reid,        670
      Rois reulit Ryally,
      Columbyn and Lely,
      Thair was ane hailsum harbery,
        Into riche steid.

### LIII.

¶ With Dosouris to the duris dicht, quha sa wald deme,
  With all diuers dainteis dicht dantely;      676
Circulit with siluer semely to sene,
  Selcouthly in seir he was set suttelly;
Blyth byrdis abufe, and bestiall full bene,
  Fyne foullis in Fyrth, and Fischis with fry;      680
The flure carpit and cled and couerit full clene;
  Cummand fra the Cornellis closand quemely,
Bricht Bancouris about browdin ouir all,
      Greit Squechonis on hicht,
      Anamalit and weill dicht,      685
      Reulit at all richt
        Endland the hall.

### LIV.

¶ "Heir is Ryaltie," said Rauf, "aneuch for the nanis,
  With all nobilnes anournit, and that is na nay;
Had I of Wymond ane word, I wald of thir wanis,    690
  Fra thir wyis, I-wis, to went on my way;
Bot I mon ȝit heir mair quhat worthis of him anis,
  And eirnestly efter him haue myne E ay."
He thristit in throw threttie all atanis,
  Quhair mony douchtie of deid war Ioynit that day,
For he was vnburely, on bak thay him hynt;      696
      As he gat ben throw,
      He gat mony greit schow,
      Bot he was stalwart I trow,
        And laith for to stynt.      700

### LV.

¶ He thristit in throw thame, and thraly can thring,
  Fast to the formest he foundit in feir ;
Sone besyde him he gat ane sicht of the Nobill King.
  "Ƹone is Wymond, I wait, it worthis na weir ;
I ken him weill, thocht he be cled in vther clething, 705
  In clais of clene gold, kythand ƶone cleir.
  Quhen he harbreit with me, be half as he is heir,
In faith he is of mair stait, than euer he me tald.
      Allace, that I was hidder wylit,
      I dreid me sair I be begylit ! "        710
      The King preuilie smylit,
        Quhen he saw that bald.

### LVI.

¶ Thair was seruit in that saill Seigis semelie,
  Mony Senƶeorabill Syre on ilk syde seir :
With ane cairfull countenance the Coilƶear kest his E
  To the cumly Quene, courtes and cleir.      716
"Dame, of thy glitterand gyde haue I na gle,
  Be the gracious God that bocht vs sa deir,
To ken Kingis Courtasie, the Deuill come to me,
  And sa I hope I may say, or I chaip heir.      720
Micht I chaip of this chance, that changes my cheir,
      Thair suld na man be sa wyse,
      To gar me cum to Parise,
      To luke quhair the King lyis,
        In faith this seuin ƶeir ! "      725

### LVII.

¶ Quhen worthie had weschin, and fra the buirdis went,
  Thay war for-wonderit I wis of thair wyse Lord.
The King fell in carping, and tauld his Intent,
  To mony gracious Grome he maid his record :
How the busteous Beirne met him on the bent,    730
  And how the Frostis war sa fell, and sa strait ford.

Than the Coilȝear quoke as he had bene schent,
  Quhen he hard the suith say how he the King schord.
" Greit God ! gif I war now and thy self with all,
      Vpon the mure quhair we met,          735
      Baith all suddandly set
      Or ony Knicht that thow may get,
        Sa gude in thy hall."

LVIII.

¶ Thir Lordis leuch vpon loft, and lystinit to the King,
  How he was ludgeit and led, and set at sa licht :  740
Than the curagious Knichtis bad haue him to hing ;
  " For he hes seruit that," thay said, " be our sicht."
" God forbot," he said, " my thank war sic thing
  To him that succourit my lyfe in sa euill ane nicht !
Him semis ane stalwart man and stout in stryking,  745
  That Carll for his courtasie salbe maid Knicht ;
I hald the counsall full euill that Cristin man slais,
      For I had myster to haue ma,
      And not to distroy tha
      That war worthie to ga          750
        To fecht on Goddis fais."

LIX.

¶ Befoir mony worthie he dubbit him Knicht,
  Dukis and digne Lordis in that deir hall :
" Schir, se for thy self, thow semis to be wicht,
  Tak keip to this ordour, ane Knicht I the call ;   755
To mak the manly man I mak the of micht ;
  Ilk ȝeir thre hundreth pund assigne the I sall ;
And als the nixt vacant, be ressonabill richt,
  That hapnis in France, quhair sa euer it fall,
Forfaltour or fre waird, that first cummis to hand,  760
      I gif the heir heritabilly,
      Sa that I heir, quhen I haue hy,
      That thow be fundin reddy
        With Birny and brand."

LX.

¶ " It war my will, worthy, thy schone that thow wan,
  And went with thir weryouris wythest in weir ;   766

C

Heir ar curagious Knichtis, suppois thay the nocht ken,
  For thy simpill degre that thow art in heir;
I beseik God of his grace to mak the ane gude man,
  And I sall gif the to begin glitterand geir."     770
Ane Chalmer with Armour the King gart richt than
  Betaucht to ane Squyar, and maid him keipeir;
With clois Armouris of steill for that stout Knicht,
      Sextie Squyaris of fee,
      Of his retinew to be;     775
     That was ane fair cumpany,
       Schir Rauf gat that nicht.


### LXI.

¶ Upon the morne airly, Schir Rauf wald not rest,
  Bot in Ryall array he reddyit him to ryde:
"For to hald that I haue hecht, I hope it be the
      best,     780
  To ȝone busteous Beirne that boistit me to byde;
Amang the Galȝart Gromis I am bot ane Gest,
  I will the ganandest gait to that gay glyde;
Sall neuer Lord lauch on loft, quhill my lyfe may lest,
  That I for liddernes suld leif, and leuand besyde. 785
It war ane graceles gude that I war cummin to,
     Gif that the King hard on hicht
     That he had maid ane carll Knicht
     Amang thir weryouris wicht,
      And docht nocht to do."     790


### LXII.

¶ Upon ane rude Runsy he ruschit out of toun,
  In ane Ryall array he rydis full richt;
Euin to the montane he maid him full boun,
  Quhair he had trystit to meit Schir Rolland the Knicht.
Derfly ouir daillis discouerand the doun,     795
  Gif ony douchtie that day for Iornayis was dicht;
He band his blonk to ane busk on the bent broun,
  Syne baid be the bair way to hald that he had hecht.
Quhill it was neir time of the day that he had thair bene,
     He lukit ane lytill him fra,     800

He sa cummand in thra
The maist man of all tha
That euer he had sene.

### LXIII.

¶ Ane Knicht on ane Cameill come cantly at hand,
With ane curagious countenance and cruell to se ; 805
He semit baldly to abyde with Birny and with brand,
His blonk was vnburely, braid and ouir hie.
Schir Rauf reddyit him sone, and come rydand,
And in the rowme of ane renk in fewtir kest he ;
He seimit fer fellonar than first quhen he him fand, 810
He foundis throw his forcenes gif he micht him se ;
He straik the steid with the spurris, he sprent on the
    bent.
        Sa hard ane cours maid thay,
        That baith thair hors deid lay,
        Thair speiris in splenders away            815
        Abufe thair heid sprent.

### LXIV.

¶ Thus war thay for thair forcynes left on fute baith,
Thay sture hors at that straik strikin deid lay than ;
Thir riche restles renkis ruschit out full raith,
Cleikit out twa swordis and togidder ran.            820
Kest thame with gude will to do vther skaith,
Baft on thair basnetis thay Beirnis or thay blan.
Haistely hewit thay togiddir, to leif thay war laith
To tyne the worschip of weir that thay air wan ;
Na for dout of vincussing thay went nocht away :    825
        Thus ather vther can assail
        With swordis of mettaill ;
        Thay maid ane lang battaill,
        Ane hour of the day.

### LXV.

¶ Thay hard harnest men, thay hewit on in haist, 830
Thay worthit heuy with heid, and angerit with all ;
Quhill thay had maid thame sa mait, thay failƷe almaist,
Sa laith thay war on ather part to lat thair price fall ;

The riche restles men out of the renk past,
  Forwrocht with thair wapnis, and euill rent with all;
Thair was na girth on the ground, quhill ane gaif the
      gaist;                ·               836
  " Ʒarne efter ʒeilding," on ilk syde thay call.
Schir Rauf caucht to cule him, and tak mair of the licht,
      He kest vp his Veseir,
        With ane Cheualrous cheir, ·        840
      Sa saw he cummand full neir
        Ane vther kene Knicht.

LXVI.

¶ " Now be the Rude," said Schir Rauf, " I repreif the,
  Thow hes brokin conditioun, thow hes not done richt,
Thow hecht na bakheir to bring, bot anerly we;   845
  Thairto I tuik thy hand, as thow was trew Knicht."
On loud said the Saraʒine, " I heir the now lie,
  Befoir the same day I saw the neuer with sicht;
Now sall thow think it richt sone, thow hes met with me,
  Gif Mahoun or Termagant may mantene my micht."
Schir Rauf was blyth of that word and blenkit with his
      face:              851
        " Thow sayis thow art ane Saraʒine,
        Now thankit be Drichtine,
        That ane of vs sall neuer hine,
          Vndeid in this place."      855

LXVII.

¶ Than said the Saraʒine to Schir Rauf succudrously,
  " I haue na lyking to lyfe to lat the with lufe."
He gaue ane braid with his brand to the Beirne by,
  Till the blude of his browis brest out abufe.
The kene Knicht in that steid stakkerit sturely,   860
  The lenth of ane rude braid he gart him remufe;
Schir Rauf ruschit vp agane, and hit him in hy.
  Thay preis furth properly thair pithis to prufe,
Ilk ane a schort knyfe braidit out sone,
      In stour stifly thay stand,     865
      With twa knyfis in hand,
      With that come Schir Rolland
        As thay had neir done.

### LXVIII.

The gentill Knicht Schir Rolland come rydand ful richt,
  And ruschit fra his Runsy, and ran thame betwene ;
He sayis, "Thow art ane Saraȝine, I se be my sicht,
  For to confound our Cristin men that counteris sa
    kene ;
Tell me thy name tyte, thow trauelland Knicht !
  Fy on thy fechting ! fell hes thow bene,
Thow art stout and strang, and stalwart in fecht,    875
  Sa is thy fallow in faith, and that is weill sene ;
In Christ and thow will trow, thow takis nane outray."
      " Forsuith," the Saraȝine said,
      " Thy self maid me neuer sa affraid,
      That I for souerance wald haue praid,    880
      Na not sall to day."

### LXIX.

¶ " Breif me not with ȝour boist, bot mak ȝow baith
  boun,
  Batteris on baldly the best, I ȝow pray."
" Na," said Schir Rolland, "that war na resoun,
  I trow in the mekle God, that maist of michtis may.
The tane is in power to mak that presoun,    886
  For that war na wassalage sum men wald say ;
I rid that thow hartfully forsaik thy Mahoun ;
  Fy on that foull Feind, for fals is thy fay !
Becum Cristin, Schir Knicht, and on Christ call,    890
      It is my will thow conuert,
      This wickit warld is bot ane start,
      And haue him halely in hart,
        That maker is of all."

### LXX.

¶ " Schir Rolland, I rek nocht of thy Rauingis,    895
  Thow dois bot reuerance to thame that rekkis it nocht;
Thow slane hes oft, thy self, of my Counsingis,
  Soudanis and sib men, that the with schame socht.
Now faindis to haue fauour with thy fleichingis,
  Now haue I ferlie, gif I fauour the ocht :    900
We sall spuilȝe ȝow dispittously at the nixt springis ;

Mak ʒow biggingis full bair, bodword haue I brocht ;
Chace Charlis ʒour King fer out of France ;
      Fra the Chane of Tartarie,
      At him this message wald I be,                905
      To tell him as I haue tauld the,
      Withoutin plesance."

LXXI.

¶ " Tyte tell me thy name, it seruis of nocht,
   Ʒe Saraʒeins ar succuderus and self willit ay ;
Sall neuer of sa sour ane brand ane bricht fyre be brocht,
   The Feynd is sa felloun als fers as he may."        911
" Sa thriue I," said the Saraʒine, "to threip is my
      thocht,
   Quha·waitis the Cristin with cair, my cusingis ar thay ;
My name is Magog, in will and I mocht,                914
   To ding thame doun dourly that euer war in my way ;
Forthy my warysoun is full gude at hame quhair I dwel."
      " In faith," said Schir Rolland,
      " That is full euill wyn land
      . To haue quhill thow ar leuand,
      Sine at thine end hell."                920

LXXII.

¶ " Wald thow conuert the in hy, and couer the of sin,
   Thow suld haue mair profite and mekle pardoun ;
Riche Douchereis seir to be sesit in,
   During quhill day dawis, that neuer will gang doun ;
Wed ane worthie to wyfe, and weild hir with win,   925
   Ane of the riche of our Realme be that ressoun ;
The gentill Duches, Dame Iane, that claimis be hir kin
   Angeos and vther landis, with mony riche toun ;
Thus may thow, and thow will, wirk the best wise,
      I do the out of dispair,                930
      In all France in nane sa fair
      Als scho is, appeirand air
      · To twa Douchereis."

LXXIII.

¶ " I rek nocht of thy riches, Schir Rolland the Knicht,"
   Said the rude Saraʒine in Ryall array ;                935

" Thy God nor thy Grassum set I bot licht ;
  Bot gif thy God be sa gude as I heir the say,
I will forsaik Mahoun, and tak me to his micht,
  Euer mair perpetuallie as he that mair may.
Heir with hart and gude will my treuth I the plicht,
  That I sall lelely leif on thy Lord ay,                941
And I beseik him of Grace, and askis him mercy,
        And Christ his Sone full schene,
        For I haue Cristin men sene,
        That in mony angeris hes bene,                  945
           Full oft on him cry."


LXXIV.

¶ " I thank God," said Rolland, " that word lykis me,
  And Christ his sweit Sone, that the that grace send."
Thay swoir on thair swordis swyftlie all thre,
  And conseruit thame freindis to thair lyfis end,      950
Euer in all trauell to leif and to die.
  Thay Knichtis caryit to the court, as Christ had
        thame kend.
The King for thair cumming maid game and gle,
  With mony mirthfull man thair mirthis to mend.
Digne Bischoppis that day, that douchtie gart bring,
        And gaue him Sacramentis seir,                  956
        And callit him Schir Gawteir,
        And sine the Duches cleir
           He weddit with ane ring.


LXXV.

¶ Than Schir Rauf gat rewaird to keip his Knichtheid ;
  Sic tythingis come to the King within thay nyne
        nicht,                                          961
That the Marschell of France was newlingis deid ;
  Richt thair, with the counsall of mony kene Knicht,
He thocht him richt worthie to byde in his steid,
  For to weild that worschip worthie and wicht.         965
His wyfe wald he nocht forƷet, for dout of Goddis feid.
  He send efter that hende, to leif thame in richt ;
Syne foundit ane fair place quhair he met the King,

Euer mair perpetually,
In the name of Sanct July,      970
That all that wantis harbery,
     Suld haue gestning.

**Finis.**

# Imprentit at Sanc=
tandrois be Robert Lekpreuik. Anno. 1572.

# JOHN THE REEVE

# JOHN THE REEVE.

*THE Tale of* John the Reeve *was written about the close of the fourteenth century, and, as has been already mentioned in the preface to the Tale of* Rauf Coilȝear, *was very well known in Scotland at an early period. Besides being mentioned by* Dunbar *and* Gawain Douglas *in the passages already quoted (p.* 3), *it is referred to by* Sir David Lyndesay *in his Testament of the Papingo (l.* 560), *when describing the straits to which* Archbishop Beaton *was latterly reduced, not knowing where to conceal himself :—*

" Bot dissagysit lyke Ihoné the Raif he raid."

*From its being so often noticed by the Scottish Poets, it was long sought after by the lovers of our early Scottish literature.* Sir Walter Scott, *in his Minstrelsy of the Scottish Border (vol. i. p.* 20), *commenting on the passages in* Dunbar *and* Douglas, *but unaware of the actual existence of the poem, surmised that* Ralf Coilȝear *and* John the Reeve *were robbers. He further remarks, " Lord Hailes conjectures* John the Reif *to be the same with* Johnie Armstrong ; *but surely not with his usual accuracy, for the ' Palice of Honour ' was printed twenty-eight years before* Johnie's *execution."* Dr Laing, *in his edition of this work, expressed his regret at not being able to include it with the other poems. He mentions* Bishop Percy's *account of it as " being built on an adventure of the same kind with the ballad of* The King and the Miller of Mansfield, *which happened between* King Edward Longshanks *and one of his Reeves or Bailiffs. This (he adds) is a piece of great antiquity, being written before the time of* Edward IV., *and for its genuine humour, diverting incidents, and faithful picture of rustic manners, is infinitely superior to all that have since been written in imitation."* Dr Laing *on this re-marks —* "*Judging, however, from the lines which the* Bishop *elsewhere quotes,[1] the originality of conception thus assigned to this poem appears rather questionable, as there are several English ballads (such as the* King *and the* Barker, *printed by Ritson) that may vie with it in point of antiquity ; and certainly it can, by no means, be esteemed so ancient as* Ralf Coilȝear (*which, indeed, ought more explicitly to have been referred to the Fourteenth Century), with which we find a poem of a similar title specified as being popular in Scotland so early, at least, as the reign of our* James the Fourth."

-*Although the Tale was described in* Bishop Percy's *Reliques of English Poetry as being in a folio manuscript volume in his possession, it remained then still inaccessible ; and it was only about the year 1868 that the manuscript was made available for reference by being placed in the British Museum.[2] Its contents, however, have since been printed, under the editorship of* Mr J. W. Hales, *and* Mr F. J. Furnivall.

*The following is an outline of the Tale :* King Edward Longshanks, *accompanied by a Bishop and an Earl, when hawking lose their way in a storm. They meet a man on horseback, who, however, wishes to avoid them. They request him to stop, which he does with reluctance, say-ing he is afraid. They ask who he may be, when he says he is one of the King's bondmen, and that, if they will swear not to hurt him, he will give them help, and meanwhile can let them have some stale bacon and sour ale for supper. He asks in return who they are, when the Earl informs him that they live in the King's house. They reach the Reeve's dwelling, when the King asks for a fire, as the clothes of the party are wet. The Reeve, however, hesitates, and states*

---

[1] 'Reliques of English Poetry,' vol. ii. p. 84.

[2] The present text has been carefully collated with the original in the Museum.

*that as he is a bondman, were he to warm them and feed them well, it might come to some official's ear, and so do him harm. The bondman and the party at length enter his house, where they are welcomed by his wife. They are shown into a room with a fire and candles, and their horses are led to a stable. John inquires at the Earl who the long-legged fellow is, when he is informed that he is the King's head-falconer. He also tells him that the other is a poor chaplain, and that he himself is a 'sumpterman.' They all plead poverty, when John avows that although he wears russet he is rich, and that he drinks as good wine as the King. John's neighbours Hobkin and Hodgkin come in, and supper is prepared. When set at table, the King complains of the poor fare, but the bondman says he will give them no better, unless they all swear not to tell the King. To this they agree, and John orders the bad supper to be taken away, and better viands to be brought in, with plenty of good wine. The Earl declares it a royal feast. John and his neighbours get merry, and dance till they sink down. The King spends a jovial night, and in the morning he and his friends breakfast, and take their leave, promising John a reward.*

*The King returns to Windsor and tells his adventures to the Queen. She asks the King to send for the Reeve. This is done, and John makes preparations for his journey, as part of which he discusses five gallons with his neighbours, who afterwards heave him on his mare. When he reaches the castle the porter will not admit him. He observes the Earl, who tells the King that he is at the gate. The King orders the Reeve to be brought in. Finding it is the King that he sees, John reminds him of his promise not to hurt him. The King thanks him for his attentions in the forest, and then makes him a gentleman, and assigns him £100 a-year. John kneels and thanks the King, who puts a collar round his neck, and makes him a Knight. The Bishop promises to put his sons to school, and tells him that the King will marry his daughters to two squires. One of his sons is afterwards knighted, and the other, become a clergyman, gets a living. His two neighbours are made freemen, and John keeps open house till he dies.*

II.

# John the Reeue.

PART I.

I.

G OD! through thy might and thy mercy,
    All that loueth game and glee,
  Their soules to heauen bringe.
Best is mirth of all solace;
Therfore I hope itt betokens grace,      5
  Of mirth who hath likinge.

II.

As I heard tell this other yeere,
A clarke came out of Lancashire;
  A rolle he had reading,
A bourde written therein he ffound,      10
That some time ffell in England,
  In Edwards dayes our King.

III.

By East, West, North, and Southe,
All this realme well run hee cowthe,
  Castle, tower, and towne.
Of that name were Kings three;      15
But Edward with the long shankes was hee,
  A Lord of great renowne.

### IV.

As the King rode a hunting vpon a day,
Three ffawcons fflew away;　　　　　　　　　　20
　　He ffollowed wonderous ffast.
They rode vpon their horsses that tyde,
They rode forth on euery side;
　　The country they out cast;

### V.

Ffrom morning vntill eueninge late,　　　　　25
Many menn abroad they gate
　　Wandring all alone;
The night came att the last;
There was no man that wist
　　What way the King was gone,　　　　　30

### VI.

Saue a Bishopp and an Erle ffree
That was allwayes the King ffull nye,
　　And thus then gan they say:
" Itt is a ffolly, by St John,
Ffor vs thus to ryde alone　　　　　　　　　35
　　Soe many a wilsome way.

### VII.

" A King and an Erle to ryde in hast,
A Bishopp from his coste to be cast,
　　Ffor hunting sikerlye.
The whether happned wonderous ill,　　　　40
All night wee may ryde vnskill,
　　Not wotting where wee bee."

### VIII.

Then the King began to say,
" Good Sir Bishopp, I you pray
　　Some comfort if you may."　　　　　　　45

As they stoode talking all about,
They were ware of a carle stout:
  "Good deene ffellow!" can they say.


### IX.

Then the Erle was well apayd:
"You be welcome, good ffellow!" hee sayd,      50
  "Of ffellowshipp we[1] pray thee."
The carle ffull hye on horsse sate,
His leggs were short and broad,
  His stirropps were of tree;


### X.

A payre of shooes were stiffe and store,      55
On his heele a rustye spurre,
  Thus fforwards rydeth hee.
The Bishopp rode after on his palfrey;
"Abyde, good ffellow, I thee pray
  And take vs home with thee."      60


### XI.

The carle answered him that tyde,
"Ffrom me thou gett oft noe other guide,
  I sweare by sweete St John."
Then said the Erle ware and wise,
"Thou canst litle of gentrise,      65
  Say not soe ffor shame!"


### XII.

The carle answered the Erle vnto,
"With gentlenesse I haue nothing to doe,
  I tell thee by my ffay."
The weather was cold and euen roughe;      70
The King and the Erle sate and loughe,
  The Bishopp did him soe pray.

[1] MS. ee.

### XIII.

The King said, "soe mote I thee!
Hee is a carle, whosoeuer hee bee,
  I reade wee ryde him neere."
They sayd with words hend,
" Ryd saftlye, gentle ffreind
  And bring vs to some harbor."    75

### XIV.

Then to tarry the carle was lothe,
But rode forth as he was wrothe,    80
  I tell you sickerlye.
The King sayd, " by Mary bright,
I troe wee shall ryde all this night
  In wast vnskillffullye ;

### XV.

" I ffeare wee shall come to no towne,    85
Ryde to the carle and pull him downe
  Hastilye without delay."
The Bishopp said soone on hye,
" Abyde, good ffellow, and take vs with thee,
  Ffor my loue, I thee pray."    90

### XVI.

The Erle said, " by God in heauen,
Oft men meete att vnsett steuen ;
  To quite thee well wee may."
The carle sayd, " by St John
I am affrayd[1] of you eche one,    95
  I tell you by my ffay."

### XVII.

The carle sayd, " by Mary bright,
I am afrayd of you this night,

---

[1] MS. affraye.

I see you roune and reason,
I know you not, and itt were day, 100
I troe you thinke more thane you say,
  I am affrayd of treason.


### XVIII.

"The night is merke, I may not see
What kind of men that you bee.
  But and you will doe one thinge, 105
Swere to doe me not desease,
Then wold I ffaine you please,
  If I cold, with any thinge."


### XIX.

Then sayd the Erle with words ffree,
"I pray you, ffellow, come hither to mee, 110
  And to some towne vs bringe;
And after, if wee may thee kenn,
Amonge Lords and gentlemen
  Wee shall requite thy dealinge."


### XX.

"Of Lords," sayes hee, "speake no more! 115
With them I haue nothing to doe,
  Nor neuer thinke to haue;
Ffor I had rather be brought in bale,
My hood or that I wold vayle,
  On them to crouch or craue." 120


### XXI.

The King sayd curteouslye,
"What manner of man aree yee
  Att home in your dwellinge?"
"A husbandman fforsooth I am,
And the Kings bondman; 125
  Therof I haue good likinge."
D

### XXII.

"Sir, when spake you with our King?"
"In ffaith, neuer, in all my liuing;
    He knoweth not my name;
And I haue my capul and my crofft;       130
If I speake not with the King oft,
    I care not, by St Jame."

### XXIII.

"What is thy name, ffellow, by thy leaue?"
"Marry," quoth hee, "John [the][1] Reeue;
    I care not who itt heare;       135
Ffor if you come into my inne,
With beeffe and bread you shall beginn
    Soone att your supper;

### XXIV.

"Salt bacon of a yeere old,
Ale that is both sower and cold,       140
    I use neither braggatt nor beere,
I lett you witt withouten lett,
I dare eate noe other meate,
    I sell my wheate ech yeere."

### XXV.

"Why doe you, Iohn, sell your wheate?"       145
"Ffor [I][2] dare not eat that I gett.
    Therof I am ffull wrothe;
Ffor I loue a draught of good drinke as well
As any man that doth itt sell,
    And alsoe a good wheat loffe.       150

### XXVI.

"Ffor he that ffirst starueth Iohn [the] Reeue,
I pray to God hee may neuer well cheeue,

---

[1] De, in MS. throughout.         [2] MS. omits.

Neither on water nor land,
Whether itt be Sherriffe or King
That makes such statuinge,      155
   I outcept neuer a one.


### XXVII.

"Ffor and the Kings penny were layd by mine,
I durst as well as hee drinke the wine
   Till all my good were gone.
Bot sithence that wee are mett soe meete,      160
Tell mee where is your recreate,
   You seeme good laddes eche one."


### XXVIII.

The Erle answered with words ffaire,
"In the Kings house is our repayre,
   If wee bee out of the way."      165
"This night," quoth Iohn, "you shall not spill;
Such harbour I shall bring you till;
   I hett itt you to-day.


### XXIX.

"Soe that yee take itt thankeffullye
In Gods name and St Iollye,      170
   I aske noe other pay;
And if you be sturdy and stout,
I shall garr you to stand without,
   Ffor ought that you can say.


### XXX.

"For I haue two neighbors won by mee      175
Of the same ffreeledge that am I,
   Of old band-shipp are wee;
The Bishopp of Durham this towne oweth,
The Erle of Gloster—who-soe him knoweth—
   Lord of the other is hee.      180

### XXXI.

" Wist my neighbors that I were thratt,
I vow to God they wold not lett
 Ffor to come soone to mee ;
If any wrong were to mee done,
Wee three durst ffight a whole afternoone,  185
 I tell you sikerlye."

### XXXII.

The King sayd, " Iohn, tell vs not this tale ;
Wee are not ordayned ffor battell,
 Our weeds are wett and cold ;
Heere is no man that yee shall greeue.  190
But helpe vs Iohn, by your leaue,
 With bright a ffeeare and bold."

### XXXIII.

" Ifaith," sayd Iohn, " that you shall want,
Ffor ffuell heere is wonderous scant,
 As I heere haue yee told.  195
Thou getteth noe other of Iohn [the] Reeue ;
Ffor the Kings statutes, whilest I liue,
 I thinke to vse and hold.

### XXXIV.

" If thou find in my house payment ffine,
Or in my kitchin poultry slaine,  200
 Peraduenture thou wold say
That Iohn Reeue his bond hath broken ;
I wold not that such words weere spoken
 In the Kings house another day.

### XXXV.

" Ffor itt might turne me to great greeffe ;  205
Such proud ladds that beare office

Wold danger a pore man aye;
And or I wold pray thee of mercy longe,
Yett weere I better to lett thee gange
    In twentye twiine devills way."    210

### XXXVI.

Thus the[y][1] rode to the towne:
Iohn the Reeue lighted downe
    Beside a comlye hall.
Four men beliue came wight;
They hasted them ffull swyft    215
    When they heard Iohn call;
They served him honestly and able,
And [led][1] his horsse to the stable,
    And lett noe terme misfall.

### XXXVII.

Some went to warne their dame    220
That Iohn had brought guests home.
    Shee came to welcome them tyte
In a side kirtle of greene,
Her head was dight all bydeene,
    The wiffe was of noe pryde;    225

### XXXVIII.

Her kerchers were all of silke,
Her hayre as white as any milke,
    Louesome of hue and hyde;
Shee was thicke, and some deal broad,
Of comlye ffashyon was shee made,    230
    Both belly, backe, and side.

### XXXIX.

Then Iohn called his men all,
Sayes, " build me a ffire in the hall,

[1] MS. omits.

And giue their capulls meate ;
Lay before them corne and hay ;                    235
Ffor my loue rubb of the clay,
    Ffor they beene weary and wett ;


### XL.

" Lay vnder them straw to the knee,
Ffor courtye[r]s comonly wold be iollye,
    And haue but litle to spend."            240


### XLI.

Then hee said, " by St Iohn,
You are welcome euery one,
    If you take itt thankefullye !
Curtesye I learned neuer none,
But after mee, ffellowes, I read you gone,"      245
    Till a chamber they went all three ;


### XLII.

A charcole ffire was burning bright,
Candles on chandlours light,
    Eche ffreake might other see.
"Where are your sords?" quoth Iohn [the] Reeue.
The Erle said, "Sir, by your leaue,              251
    Wee weare none, pardye."


### XLIII.

Then Iohn rowned with the Erle soe ffree ;
" What long ffellow is yonder," quoth hee,
    " That is soe long of lim and lyre ? "       255
The Erle answered with words small,
" Yonder is Peeres Pay-ffor-all,
    The Queenes Cheefe ffawconer."


### XLIV.

" Ah ah ! " quoth Iohn, " ffor Gods good,
Where gott hee that gay hood,                      260

Glitering as gold itt were?
And I were as proud as hee is like,
There is no man in England ryke
   Shold garr me keepe his gleads one yeere.

### XLV.

" I pray you, sir, ffor Gods werke,        265
Who is yond in yonder serke
   That rydeth Peeres soe nye? "
The Erle answered him againe,
" Yonder is a pore chaplaine,
   Long aduanced or hee bee;        270

### XLVI.

" And I my selfe am a sumpter man,
Other craft keepe I none,
   I say you withouten misse."[1]
" You are ffresh ffellowes in your appay,
Iolly Ietters in your array,        275
   Proud ladds, and I trow penyles."

### XLVII.

The King said, " soe mote I thee,
There is not a penny amongst vs three
   To buy vs bread and fflesh."
"Ah, ha!" quoth Iohn, "there is small charge;
For courtye[r]s comonlye are att large,     281
   If they goe neuer soe ffresh.

### XLVIII.

" I goe girt in a russett gowne,
My hood is of homemade browne,
   I weare neither burnett nor greene,     285
And yett I troe I haue in store
A thousand pounds and some deale more,
   For all yee are prouder and ffine;

---

[1] miste, in MS.

### XLIX.

" Therfore I say, as mote I thee,
A bondman itt is good [to][1] bee,          290
    And come of carles kinne;
Ffor and I bee in tauerne sett,
To drinke as good wine I will not lette,
    As London Edward or his Queene."

### L.

The Erle said, "by Gods might,          295
Iohn, thou art a comly knight,
    And sturdy in euerye ffray."
"A knight!" quoth Iohn, "doe away, ffor shame!
I am the King's bondman.
    Such wast words doe away!          300

### LI.

" I know you not in your estate;
I am misnurtured, well I wott;
    I will not therto say nay.
But if any such doe me wrong,
I will ffight with him hand to hand,          305
    When I am cladd in mine array."

### LII.

The Bishopp sayd, "you seeme sturdye:
Trauelled you neuer beyond the sea?"
    Ihon sayd sharplye "nay!
I know none such strange guise,          310
But att home on my owne wise
    I dare hold the hye way;

### LIII.

" And that hath done Iohn Reeue scath,
Ffor I haue made such as you wrath

[1] MS. omits.

With choppes and chances yare." 315
"Iohn [the] Reeue," sayd our King,
"Hast thou any armouringe,
  Or any weapon to weare?"


### LIV.

"I vow, sir, to God," sayd Iohn thoe,
"But a pikefforke with graines two— 320
  My ffather vsed neuer other speare:—
A rusty sword that well will byte,
And a handffull, a thyttile syde
  That sharplye will s[h]are,


### LV.

"An acton and a habargyon a ffoote side; 325
And yett peraduenture I durst abyde
  As well as thou, Peeres, ffor all thy painted geere."
Quoth Iohn, "I reede we goe to the hall,
Wee three ffellowes; and Peeres Pay-for-all
  The proudest before shall fare." 330


### LVI.

Thither they raked anon-wright:
A charcole ffyer burning bright
  With manye a strang brand.
The hall was large and some deale wyde,
There bords were couered on euerye syde, 335
  There mirth was comanded.


### LVII.

Then the good wiffe sayd with a seemlye cheere,
"Your supper is readye there."
  "Yett watter," quoth Iohn, "letts see."
By then came Iohns neighbors two, 340
Hobkin long and Hob alsoe:
  The ffirst ffitt here ffind wee.

## PART II.

### I.

Iohn sayd, "ffor want of a marshall, I will take
    the wand:
Peeres ffauconer before shall gange;
  Begin the dish shall hee.
Goe to the bench, thou proud chaplaine,
My wiffe shall sitt thee againe;           5
  Thy meate-fellow shall shee bee."
He sett the Erle against the King;
They were ffaine att his bidding.
  Thus Iohn marshalled his meanye.

### II.

Then Iohn sperred where his daughters were:    10
"The ffairer shall sitt by the ffawconere;
  He is the best ffarrand man:
The other shall the Sompter man haue."
The Erle sayd, "soe God me saue!
  Of curtesye, Iohn, thou can."          15

### III.

"If my selfe," quoth John, "be bound,
Yett my daughters beene well ffarrand,
  I tell you sickerlye.
Peeres, and thou had wedded Iohn daughter Reeue,
There were no man that durst thee greeue    20
  Neither ffor gold nor ffee.

### IV.

"Sompter man, and thou the other had,
In good ffaith then thou were made
  For euer in this cuntrye;

Then Peeres, thou might beare the prize.          25
Yett I wold this chaplaine had a benefize,
  As mote I thariue or thee![1]


### V.

" In this towne a kirke there is ;
And I were king, it shold be his,
  He shold haue itt of mee ;          30
Yett will I helpe as well as I may."
The King, the Erle, the Bishopp, can say,
  " Iohn, and wee liue wee shall quitte thee."


### VI.

When his daughters were come to dease,
" Sitt ffarther," quoth Iohn withouten leaze,          35
  For there shalbe no more.
These strange ffellowes I doe not ken ;
Peraduenture they may be some gentlemen ;
  Therfore I and my neighbors towe,


### VII.

" Att side end bord wee will bee,          40
Out of the gentles companye :
  Thinke yee not best soe ?
For itt was neuer the law of England
To sett gentles blood with bound ;
  Therfore to supper will wee goe."          45


### VIII.

By then came in beane bread,
Salt bacon rusted and redd,
  And brewice in a blacke dish,
Leane salt beefe of a yeere old,
Ale that was both sower and cold ;          50
  This was the ffirst service :

---

[1] MS. reads three, an error for *thee*, to thrive.

### IX.

Eche one had of that ylke a messe;
The King sayd, " Soe haue I blisse,
  Such service nere[1] I see."
Quoth Iohn, " thou gettest noe other of mee        55
  Att this time but this."

### X.

" Yes, good fellow," the King gan say,
" Take this seruice here away,
  And better bread vs bringe;
And gett vs some better drinke;        60
We shall thee requite, as wee thinke,
  Without any letting."

### XI.

Quoth Iohn, " beshrew the morsell of bread
This night that shall come in your head
  But thou sweare me one thinge!        65
Swere to me by booke and bell
That thou shalt neuer Iohn Reeue bettell
  Vnto Edward our Kinge."

### XII.

Quoth the King, " to thee my truth I plight,
He shall nott witt our service,        70
  No more than he doth nowe,
Neuer while wee three liue in land."
" Thereto," quoth Iohn, " hold vp thy hand,
  And then I will thee troe."

### XIII.

" Loe," quoth the King, " my hand is heere!"        75
" Soe is mine!" quoth the Erle with a merry cheere,

[1] nerest, in MS.

" Thereto I giue God a vowe."
" Haue heere my hand ! " the Bishopp sayd,
" Marry," quoth Iohn, "thou may hold thee well apayd,
   Ffor itt is ffor thy power.              80

### XIV.

" Take this away thou hobkin long,
And lett vs sitt out of the throng
   Att a side bords end ;
These strange ffellowes thinke vncouthlye
This night att our cookerye,            85
   Such as God hath vs sent."

### XV.

By then came in the payment bread
Wine that was both white and redd
   In siluer cuppes cleare.
" A ha," quoth Iohn, " our supper begins with drinke !  90
Tasste itt, lads ! and looke how yee thinke,
   Ffor my loue, and make good cheere !

### XVI.

" Of meate and drinke you shall haue good ffare ;
And as ffor good wine, wee will not spare,
   I [giue][1] you to vnderstand.          95
Ffor euerye yeere, I tell thee thoe [2]
I will haue a tunn or towe
   Of the best that maybe ffound.

### XVII.

" Yee shall see three churles heere
Drink the wine with a merry cheere ;      100
   I pray you doe you soe ;

---

    [1] MS. goe.                   [2] Probably for true.

And when our supper is all doone,
You and mee will dance soone;
  Letts see who best can doe."


### XVIII.

The Erle sayd, " by Marry bright,          105
Wheresoeuer the King lyeth this night,
  He drinketh no better wine
Then thou selfe does att this tyde."
" In faith," quoth Iohn, " soe had leeuer I did
  Then liue ay in woe and payne.          110


### XIX.

" If I be come of Carles kinne,
Part of the good that I may winne,
  Some therof shall be mine.
He that neuer spendeth but alway spareth,
Comonlye oft the worsse he ffareth;          115
  Others will broake itt ffine."


### XX.

By then came in red wine and ale,
The bores head into the hall,
  Then sheild with sauces seere;
Capons both baked and rosted,          120
Woodcockes, venison, without bost,
  And dish meeate dight ffull deere.


### XXI.

Swannes they had piping hott,
Coneys, curleys, well I wott,
  The crane, the hearne in ffere,          125
Pigeons, partridg[e]s, with spicerye,
Elkes, fflomes, with ffroterye.
  Iohn bade them make good cheere.

### XXII.

The Erle sayd, "soe mote I thee,
Iohn, you serue vs royallye!      130
  If yee had dwelled att London,
If king Edward where here,
He might be a-payd with this supper,
  Such ffreindshipp wee haue ffound."

### XXIII.

"Nay," sayd Iohn, "by Gods grace,      135
And Edward wher in[1] this place,
  Hee shold not touch this tonne.
Hee wold be wrath with Iohn, I hope;
Thereffore I beshrew the soupe
  That shall come in his mouth!"      140

### XXIV.

Theratt the King laughed and made good cheere.
The Bishopp sayd, "wee fare well heere!"
  The Erle sayd as him thought.
They spake Lattine amongst them there:
"In faith," quoth Iohn, "and yee greeue me,   145
  Full deere itt shalbe bought.

### XXV.

"Speake English euerye-eche one,
Or else sitt still, in the devills name!
  Such talke loue I naught.
Lattine spoken amongst lewd men,      150
Therin noe reason ffind I can;
  For ffalshood itt is wrought.

### XXVI.

"Row[n]ing, I loue itt neither young nor old;
Therefore yee ought not to bee to bold,

---

[1] MS. wherin, probably for were in.

Neither att meate nor meale.         155
Hee was ffalse that rowning began;
Theerfore I say to you certaine
   I loue itt neuer a deale:

### XXVII.

"That man can [nocht] of curtesye
That lets att his meate rowning bee,    160
   I say, soe haue I se[i]le."[1]
The Erle sayd right againe,
"Att your bidding wee will be baine,
   Wee thinke you say right weele."

### XXVIII.

By this came vp ffrom the kitchin    165
Sirrupps on plates good and ffine,
   Wrought in a ffayre array.
"Sirrah," sayth Iohn, "sithe wee are mett,
And as good ffellowes together sett,
   Lett vs be blythe to-day.    170

### XXIX.

"Hodgkin long, and Hob of the Lath,
You are counted good ffellowes both,
   Now is no time to thrine;
This wine is new come out of Ffrance;
Be God! me list well to dance,    175
   Therfore take my hand in thine;

### XXX.

"For wee will ffor our guests sake
Hop and dance, and reuell make."
   The truth ffor to know,
Vp he rose, and dranke the wine:    180
"Wee must haue powder of ginger therein,"
   Iohn sayd, as I troe.

[1] MS. sele.

### XXXI.

Iohn bade them stand vp all about,
"And yee shall see the carles stout
   Dance about the bowle.          185
Hob of the Lathe and Hodgkin long,
In ffayth you dance your mesures wrong!
   Methinkes that I shold know.

### XXXII.

"Yee dance neither Gallyard nor hawe,
Trace nor true mesure, as I trowe,        190
   But hopp as yee were woode."
When they began of ffoote to ffayle,
The[y] tumbled top ouer tayle,
   And Master and Master they yode.

### XXXIII.

Forth they stepped on stones store;      195
Hob of the Lathe lay on the fflore,
   His brow brast out of blood.
"Ah, ha!" quoth Iohn, "thou makes good game!
Had thou not ffalled, wee had not laught;
   Thou gladds vs all, by the rood."      200

### XXXIV.

Iohn hent vp Hobb by the hand,
Sayes, "methinkes wee dance our measures wronge,
   By him that sitteth in throne."
Then they began to kicke and wince,
Iohn hitt the king ouer the shinnes     205
   With a payre of new clowted shoone.

### XXXV.

Sith King Edward was mad a knight,
Had he neuer soe merry a night
   As he had with Iohn [the] Reeue.

To bed they busked them anon,                    210
Their liueryes were serued them vp soone
  With a merry cheere;


### XXXVI.

And thus they sleeped till morning att pri[m]e[1]
In ffull good sheetes of line.
  A masse he garred them to haue,               215
And after they dight them to dine
With boyled capons good and ffine.
  The Duke sayd, "soe God me saue,
If euer wee come to our abone,
We shall thee quitt our warrison;              220
  Thou shalt not need itt to craue."


------------


## PART III.


### I.

The king tooke leaue att man and mayde;
Iohn sett him in the rode way;
  To Windsor can hee ryde.
Then all the court was ffull faine
That the king was comen againe,                 5
  And thanked Christ that tyde.


### II.

The Ierfawcons were taken againe
In the fforrest of Windsor without laine,
  The lords did soe provyde,

[1] prine, in MS.

They thanked God and St Iollye.            10
To tell the Queene of their harbor[ye][1]
  The lords had ffull great pryde.


### III.

The Queene sayd, " Sir, by your leaue,
I pray you send ffor that noble Reeue,
  That I may see him with sight."            15
The messenger was made to wend,
And bidd Iohn Reeue goe to the King
  Hastilye with all his might.


### IV.

Iohn waxed vnfaine in bone and blood,
Saith, " dame, to me this is noe good,            20
  My truth to you I plight."
" You must come in your best array."
" What too," sayd Iohn, " Sir, I thee pray ? "
  " Thou must be made a Knight."


### V.

" A Knight," sayd Iohn, " by Marry myld,            25
I know right well I am beguiled
  With the guests I harbord late.
To debate they will me bring ;
Yett cast I mee ffor nothinge
  Noe sorrow ffor to take ;            30


### VI.

" Allice, ffeitch mee downe my side acton,
My round pallett to my crowne,
  Is made of Millayne plate,
A pitch-fforke and a sword."
Shee sayd shee was affrayd            35
  This deede wold make debate.

---

[1] Harbor, in MS.

### VII.

Allice ffeitched downe his acton syde;
Hee took itt ffor no litle pryde,
  Yett must hee itt weare.
The scaberd was rent withouten doubt,     40
A large handfull the bleade hanged out:
  Iohn the Reeue sayd there,

### VIII.

"Gett lether and a nayle," Iohn can say,
"Lett me sow itt a chape to-day,
  Lest men scorne my geere.     45
Now," sayd Iohn, "will I see
[W]hether itt will out lightly
  Or I meane itt to weare."

### IX.

Iohn pulled ffast at the blade:
(I wold hee had kist my arse that itt made!)   50
  He cold not gett itt out.
Allice held, and Iohn draughe,
Either att other ffast loughe,
  I doe yee out of doubt.

### X.

Iohn pulled att the scaberd soe hard     55
Againe a post he ran backward
  And gaue his head a rowte.
His wiffe did laughe when he did ffall,
And soe did his meanye all
  That were there neere about.     60

### XI.

Iohn sent after his neighbors both
Hodgkine long and Hobb of the Lath.

They were beene att his biddinge.
3 pottles of wine in a dishe
They supped itt all off, as I wis, 65
    All there att their partinge.

#### XII.

Iohn sayd, " And I had my buckler,
Theres nothing that shold me dare,
    I tell you all in ffere.
Ffeitch me downe," quoth he, " my gloues ; 70
They came but on my hands but once
    This twenty-two yeere.

#### XIII.

" Ffeitch mee my capull," sayd hee there.
His saddle was of a new manner,
    His stirropps were of a tree. 75
" Dame," he sayd, " Ffeitch me wine ;
I will drinke to thee once againe,
    I troe I shall neuer thee see.

#### XIV.

" Hodgkin long, and Hob of the Lathe,
Tarry and drinke with me bothe, 80
    Ffor my cares are ffast commannde."
They dranke five gallons verament :
" Ffarwell ffellowes all present,
    Ffor I am readye to gange ! "

#### XV.

Iohn was soe combred in his geere 85
Hee cold not gett vpon his mare
    Till Hodgkinn heaue vp behind.

#### XVI.

" Now ffarwell, Sir, by the roode ! "
To neither Knight nor Barron good

His hatt he wold not vayle            90
Till he came to the Kings gate :
The Porter wold not lett him in theratt,
 Nor come within the walle,


### XVII.

Till a Knight came walking out.
They sayd, " yonder standeth a carle stout      95
 In a rusticall arraye."
On him they all wondred wright,
And said he was an vnseemelye wight,
 And thus to him they gan say :


### XVIII.

" Hayle, ffellow ! where wast thou borne ?    100
Thee besseemeth ffull well to weare a horne !
 Where had thou that ffaire geere ?
I troe a man might seeke ffull long,
One like to thee ar that hee ffound,
 Tho he sought all this yeere."          105


### XIX.

Iohn bade them kisse the devills arse :
" Ffor you my geare is much the worsse !
 You will itt not amend,
By my ffaith, that can I lead !
Vpon the head I shall you shread .          110
 But if you hence wende !


### XX.

" The devill him speede vpon his crowne
That causeth me to come to this towne,
 Whether he weare Iacke or Iill !
What shold such men as I doe heere          115
Att the kings Manner ?
 I might haue beene att home still."

### XXI.

As Iohn stoode fflyting ffast,
He saw one of his guests come at the last;
  To him he spake ffull bold,     120
To him he ffast ffull rode,
He vayled neither hatt nor hood;
  Sayth, "thou hast me betold!

### XXII.

"Full well I wott by this light
That thou has disdainde mee right;     125
  Ffor wrat[h] I waxe neere wood!"
The Erle sayd, "by Marry bright,
Iohn, thou made vs a merry night;
  Thou shalt haue nothing but good."

### XXIII.

The Erle tooke leaue att Iohn Reue,     130
Sayd, "thou shalt come in without greefe;
  I pray thee tarry a while."
The Erle into the hall went,
And told the King verament
  That Iohn Reeue was att the gate;     135
"To no man list hee lout.
A rusty sword gird him about,
  And a long ffawchyon, I wott."

### XXIV.

The King said, "goe wee to meate,
And bringe him when wee are sett;     140
  Our dame shall haue a play.
He hath 10 arrowes in a thonge,
Some are short and some are long,
  The sooth as I shold say;

### XXV.

"A rusty sallett vpon his crowne,     145
His hood were made home browne;

There may nothing him dare;
A thytill hee hath ffast in his hand
That hangeth in a peake band,
　　And sharplye itt will share.　　　　　　　　150

### XXVI.

" He hath a pouch hanging ffull wyde,
A rusty Buckeler on the other syde,
　　His mittons are of blacke clothe.
Who-soe to him sayth ought but good,
[I swear it to you by the rood,][1]　　　　　155
　　Ffull soone hee wilbe wrothe."

### XXVII.

Then Iohn sayd, " Porter, lett mee in !
Some of my goods thou shalt win;
　　I loue not ffor to pray."
The Porter sayd, " stand abacke !　　　　　160
And thou come neere I shall thee rappe,
　　Thou carle, by my ffay ! "

### XXVIII.

Iohn tooke his fforke in his hand,
He bare his fforke on an end,
　　He thought to make a ffray;　　　　　　165
His capull was wight, and corne ffedd;
Vpon the Porter hee him spedd,
　　And him had wellnye slaine.

### XXIX.

He hitt the Porter vpon the crowne,
With that stroke hee ffell downe,　　　　　170
　　Fforsooth as I you tell;
And then hee rode into the hall,
And all the doggs both great and small
　　On Iohn ffast can the[y] yell.

---

[1] Line wanting in MS., supplied from Bp. Percy's Folio MS. ed.
Hales and Furnivall.

### XXX.

Iohn layd about as hee were wood,    175
And 4 hee killed as hee stood;
  The rest will now be ware.
Then came fforth a squier hend,
And sayd, "Iohn I am thy ffreind,
  I pray you light downe heere."    180

### XXXI.

Another sayd, "giue me thy fforke,"
And Iohn sayd, "nay by St William of Yorke,
  Ffirst I will cracke thy crowne!"
Another sayd, "lay downe thy sword;
Sett vp thy horsse; be not affeard;    185
  Thy bow, good Iohn, lay downe;

### XXXII.

"I shall hold your stirroppe;
Doe of your pallett and your hoode
  Ere the[y] ffall, as I troe.
Yee see not who sitteth att the meate;    190
Yee are a wonderous silly ffreake,
  And alsoe passing sloe!"

### XXXIII.

"What devill," sayd Iohn, "is that ffor thee?
Itt is my owne, soe mote I thee!
  Therfore I will itt weare."    195

### XXXIV.

The Queen beheld him in hast;
"My lord," shee sayd, "ffor Gods ffast,
  Who is yonder that doth ryde?
Such a ffellow saw I neuer yore!"
Shee saith, "hee hath the quaintest geere,    200
  He is but simple of pryde."

### XXXV.

Right soe came Iohn as hee were wood;
He vayled neither hatt nor hood,
　　He was a ffaley ffreake;
He tooke his fforke as hee wold iust;　　205
Vp to the dease ffast he itt thrust.
　　The Queene ffor ffeare did speake,

### XXXVI.

And sayd, "lords, beware, ffor Gods grace!
Ffor hee will frowte some in the fface
　　If yee take not good heede!"　　210
The[y] laughed without doubt,
And soe did all that were about,
　　To see Iohn on his steede.

### XXXVII.

Then sayd Iohn to our Queene,
"Thou mayest be proud, dame, as I weene,　215
　　To haue such a ffawconer!
Ffor he is a well ffarrand man,
And much good manner hee can,
　　I tell you sooth in ffere.

### XXXVIII.

[　.　　.　　.　　.　　.　　.　　.　]¹
But, lord," hee sayd, "my good, its thine;　220
My body alsoe, ffor to pine,
　　Ffor thou art king with crowne.
But, lord, thy word is honorable,
Both stedffast, sure, and stable,
　　And alsoe great of renowne!　　225

### XXXIX.

"Therefore haue mind what thou me hight
When thou with me [harbord]² a night,

¹ There is no break in the MS. here, but something is wanting to complete the sense.　² MS. omits.

A warryson that I shold haue."
Iohn spoke to him with sturdye mood,
Hee vayled neither hatt nor hood,          230
  But stood with him checkmate.


### XL.

The King sayd, " fellow mine,
Ffor thy capons hott, and good red wine,
  Much thankes I doe giue thee."
The Queene sayd, " by Mary bright,          235
Award him as his right;
  Well aduanced lett him bee ! "


### XLI.

The King sayd vntill him then,
" Iohn, I make thee a gentleman;
  Thy manner place I thee giue,          240
And a 100$^{li}$ to thee and thine,
And euery yeere a tunn of red wine
  Soe long as thou dost liue."


### XLII.

But then Iohn began to kneele:
" I thanke you, my Lord, as I haue soule,          245
  Therof I am well payd."
The King tooke a coller bright,
And sayd, " Iohn, heere I make thee a knight
  With worshippe:" when hee sayd,


### XLIII.

Then was Iohn euill apayed,          250
And amongst them all thus hee sayd,
  " Ffull oft I haue heard tell
That after a coller comes a rope;
I shall be hanged by the throate;
  Methinkes itt doth not well."          255

### XLIV.

" Sith thou hast taken this estate,
That euery man may itt wott,
   Thou must begin the bord."
Then Iohn therof was nothing ffaine—
I tell you truth with-outen laine,—     260
   He spake neuer a word.

### XLV.

But att the bords end he sate him downe;
Ffor hee had leeuer beene att home
   Then att all their ffrankish ffare;"
Ffor there was wine, well I wott;     265
Royall meates of the best sortes
   Were sett before him there.

### XLVI.

A gallon of wine was put in a dishe;
Iohn supped itt of, both more and lesse,
   " Ffeitch," quoth the King, "such mare."   270
" By my Lady," quoth Iohn, " This is good wine!
Let us make merry, ffor now itt is time;
   Christs curse on him that doth itt spare!"

### XLVII.

With that came in the Porter hend
And kneeled downe before the King,    275
   Was all berunnen with blood.
Then the King in hart was woe,
Sayes, " Porter, who hath dight thee soe?
   Tell on; I wax neere wood."

### XLVIII.

"Now infaith," sayd Iohn, "that same was I,   280
For to teach him some curtesye,

Ffor thou hast taught him noe good.
For when thou came to my pore place,
With mee thou found soe great a grace,
  Noe man did bidd thee stand without;      285


### XLIX.

" Ffor if any man had against thee spoken,
His head ffull soone I shold haue broken,"
  Iohn sayd, " with-outen doubt.
Therefore I warne thy porters ffree,
When any man [comes][1] out of my countrye,    290
  Another [time][1] lett them not be soe stout.


### L.

" If both thy porters goe walling wood,
Begod I shall reaue their hood,
  Or goe on ffoote boote.
But thou, Lord, hast after me sent,    295
And I am come att thy commandement
  Hastilye withouten doubt."


### LI.

The King sayd, " by St Iame!
Iohn, my porters were to blame;
  Yee did nothing but right."    300
He tooke the case into his hand;
Then to kisse hee made them gange;
  Then laughed both King and Knight.
" I pray you," quoth the King, " good ffellowes bee."
" Yes," quoth Iohn, " soe mote I thee,    305
  We were not wrathe ore night."


### LII.

Then the [2] Bishopp sayd to him thoe,
" Iohn, send hither thy sonnes 2 ;

---

[1] MS. omits.          [2] They, in MS.

To the schoole I shall them ffind,
And soe God may for them werke,                310
That either of them haue a kirke,
  If ffortune be their ffreind.


### LIII.

"Also send hither thye daughters both;
2 marryages the King will garr them to haue,
  And wedd them with a ringe.                  315
Wend[1] fforth, Iohn, on thy way,
Looke thou be kind and curteous aye,
  Of meate and drinke be neuer nithing."


### LIV.

Then Iohn tooke leaue of King and Queene,
And after att all the court by-deene,          320
  And went fforth on his way.
He sent his daughters to the King,
And they were wedded with a ringe
  Vnto 2 squiers gay.


### LV.

His sonnes both hardye and wight,              325
The one of them was made a Knight,
  And fresh in euery ffray;
The other a parson of a kirke,
Gods seruice ffor to worke,
  To serue God[2] night and day.               330


### LVI.

Thus Iohn Reeue and his wiffe
With mirth and Iol[i]ty ledden their liffe;
  To God they made laudinge.
Hodgikin long and Hobb of the Lathe,
They were made ffreemen bothe                  335
  Through the grace of the hend King.[3]

[1] Went, in MS.     [2] To God serue, in MS.     [3] Kinghend, in MS.

### LVII.

Then thought [Iohn][1] on the Bishopps word,
And euer after kept open bord
  Ffor guests that God him send;
Till death ffeitcht him away       340
To the blisse that lasteth aye:
  And thus Iohn Reeue made an end.

### LVIII.

Thus endeth the tale of Reeue soe wight.
God that is soe ffull of might,
  To heauen their soules bring      345
That haue heard this litle story,
That liued sometimes in the south-west countrye
  In long Edwards dayes our King.

[1] MS. omits.

# THE AWNTYRS OF ARTHURE AT THE TERNE WATHELYN

F

# III.

# THE AWNTYRS OF ARTHURE AT THE TERNE WATHELYN.

*THE History of the Romance - Poetry of our country, owing to the peculiar circumstances attending its transmission to modern times, is unfortunately involved in great obscurity. Although the more ancient of these remains occasionally bear internal evidence of having proceeded from the celebrated* Makars *of the* Northe Countreye, *we remain in ignorance respecting the individuals who contributed so much to the amusement of our ancestors in these remote times, and even possess little or no positive evidence that might help us to distinguish the productions of Scottish writers from those of the English Minstrels. This may indeed be esteemed a matter of extreme unimportance, since the most valuable specimens of romantick fiction that are extant, have, in one shape or other, been made publick. The '*Sir Tristrem,' *by our venerable poet,* Thomas of Ersyldoune, *who flourished about the middle part of the* 13th Century, *has received every possible advantage in the illustrations of its distinguished Editor :— the* Geste of King Horn, *perhaps the next in point of antiquity, has been faithfully printed by* Ritson: *and the* Lyf *of* Alexander (*erroneously assigned to an English poet in the age of* Edward II.) *is given with no less accuracy by* Weber, *in his excellent Collection of Metrical Romances.*

*The Romance which follows bears such a close resem-blance in subject, style, and manner to* the Knightly tale of Golagros and Gawane, *that both have generally been at-tributed to one and the same author. The antiquity of these tales unquestionably is considerable; and but for our know-ledge of other similar alliterative poems, of which the dates are ascertained, and go far to rival these in point of obscurity, we might be justified in carrying them back to a very remote period. The only conjecture that can be offered respecting their author, is founded on the slight allusion in* Dunbar's '*Lament for the Death of the Makers,' where he says,*

> " Clerk of Tranent eik he has tane
> That made the anteris of Sir Gawane."

*As different poems of the Adventures of Sir Gawane are known, we are prevented from ascribing one or other of them to* Clerk *with any degree of certainty; besides, we have the authority of* Wyntoun *for assigning them to* Hucheon, *another of our early Poets (by whom the reader will find a specimen, in the same alliterative style, in the present volume), who says,*

> " He made the gret Gest of Arthure,
> And the Awntyre of Gawane."—

*The Author of these Romances, whoever he may have been, has certainly added something new to the Poetry of his Country.  In them there is both originality of incident and manner:—for, although they doubtless were founded on popular tradition, the Author surely would not have chosen such an intricate and cumbrous mode of versification, had they been mere translations, or had he profited by the ex-ample of the numerous productions of English Romance-Poetry, during its best period, namely, from the middle of the fourteenth to the early part of the fifteenth Century.*
*[Of this Romance three manuscripts are known to exist. Of these the first is one written by* Robert Thornton *of East Newton, Yorkshire, between* A.D. 1430 *and* 1440, *and preserved in the* Cathedral Library, Lincoln, *which*

*has also furnished the text of* Thomas of Ersyldoune *in the present volume.   A short account of this valuable MS. is given in the Appendix.   The second MS., consisting of eleven leaves in folio, written in a fair and legible hand, is pre-served in the* Bodleian Library, Oxford.   *It previously belonged to* Baynes, Ritson, and Douce.   *It was printed very incorrectly in* 1792 *by* Pinkerton, *under the title of* SIR GAWAN AND SIR GALARON OF GALLOWAY, *in the third volume of his* "Scotish Poems Reprinted from Scarce editions."   *This MS. has supplied the omissions of the* Lincoln *copy, and the words or lines in the text within brackets are those which it has furnished, unless otherwise stated.   According to* Sir Frederick Madden, *these two Manuscripts, being written in England, do not present a genuine Scottish text; still, they sufficiently prove the Ro-mance to have been of Northern origin.   The third MS. is known as the* Ireland Manuscript, *and is preserved at* Hale, Lincolnshire, *the seat of* J. I. Blackburn, Esq.   *It is written in the dialect peculiar to the north-western parts of that county.   It was edited in* 1842 *for the* Camden Society *by* John Robson, *Esq.*

*The scene of the* Awntyrs *is laid at* Tern Wathelayne *or* Tearn Wadling, *a small lake, about* 100 *acres in extent, near* Hesketh *in* Cumberland, *celebrated in several old ballads and romances.   The following is an outline of the tale :—*King Arthur *and his* Queen, Gaynour *or* Gui-never, *having established their court at Carlisle, go to hunt in the adjoining forest of Inglewood, sometimes also called the English wood, which reached as far as Penrith.   They are attended by their favourite knight,* Sir Gawan, *and many others.*   Gaynour *and* Sir Gawan, *when at a dis-tance from the party, are overtaken with darkness.   To their surprise the ghost of the Queen's mother appears.   They in-quire the cause of its frightful appearance and miserable con-dition.   The ghost then describes the torments to which it has been subjected, which, however, it states, can be miti-gated by masses.   These the* Queen *and* Sir Gawan *promise to have performed for its relief.   After admonishing them to avoid a similar destiny, the ghost vanishes.   This part of the* *tale is founded on a religious legend popular amongst the Latin writers of the middle ages. After the disappearance of the ghost the day clears, and the* Queen *and* Sir Gawan *join the Court. When at supper a knight-errant named* Sir Galaron *is introduced, who claims from the* King *lands which the latter had conquered.* Sir Galaron *challenges the knights present to single combat in defence of his claim. The* King *entertains him, and orders him to be taken to a pavilion for the night. It is arranged that he shall fight* Sir Gawan *next day. The lists are prepared, and the combat begins. Both knights are wounded.* Sir Galaron *at length yields, and* Arthur *commands peace.* Sir Gawan *gets from the* King *lands in Wales, and* Sir Galaron, *at the* Queen's *intercession, is reinstated in his lands in Galloway. He is also made a Knight of the Round Table. Finally, the* Queen *orders millions of masses to be performed for the repose of her mother's ghost.*]

III.

# Here bygynnes
# The awntyrs off Arthure at the
# Terne Wathelyn.

I.

IN Kyng Arthure tym ane awntir by-tyde,
  By the Terne Wathelyn, als the buke tellis;
Als he to Carelele was commen, that conqueroure kyde,
  With dukes, and with ducheperes, that with that
    dere duellys,
For to hunte at the herdys, that lange hase bene hyde; 5
  And one a day thay tham dighte to the depe dellis,
To felle of the femmales in the foreste, wele frythede,
  Faire in the fernysone tyme, by frythis, and fellis:
    Thus to the wode are thay wente, the wlonkeste in
      wedys,
        Bothe the Kynge, and the Qwene,          10
        And all the doghety by-dene;
        Schir Gawane gayeste one grene,
        Dame Gayenoure he ledis.

*The following variations are taken from the Douce MS. :—*

I.—1. 'In the tyme of Arthur an aunter by tydde.'  2. 'Turnewathelan,'
or Tearn Wadling, in Cumberland.  3. 'and conquerour kydde.'  4. 'the
dere.'  7. 'in forest and frydde.'  8. 'Fayre by the Firmysthamis, in
frithes.'

## II.

And thus Schir Gawane the gay, dame Gayenour he
　　ledis,
　In a gletterande gyde, that glemet full gaye;　　　15
With rich rebanes reuerssede, who that righte redys,
　Raylede with rubes one royalle arraye:
Hir hude was of hawe hewe that hir hede hydys,
　Wroghte with peloure, and palle, and perrye to paye;
Schruedede in a schorte cloke, that the rayne schrydes,
　Sett ouer with safyrs, full sothely to saye;　　　21
　　And thus wondirfully was all the wyghtis wedys,
　　　Hir sadill semyde of that ilke,
　　　Semlely sewede with sylke;
　　　One a muyle als the milke,　　　25
　　　Gayely scho glydis.


## III.

Thus alle in gleterande golde gayely scho glydis
　The gates, with Schir Gawane, by a grene welle;
Nane bot hym selfe one a blonke, by that birde bydis,
　That borne was in Burgoyne, by buke, and by belle. 30
He ledde that lady so lange by those landes sydys,
　Sythen vndir a lorere scho lyghte lawe by a felle.
Schir Arthure, with his Erles, full ernestly rydis,
　To teche thame to thaire tristis, trewely to telle:
　　To thaire tristis he tham taughte, who that righte
　　　trowes,　　　35
　　　Ilke a lorde, with owttyn lett,
　　　At his triste was he sett,
　　　With bowe and with barcelett,
　　　Vndir those bewes.


II.—3. 'With riche ribaynes reuersset.'　4. 'rubes of rial.'　5. 'of herde
hawe.'　7. 'Schurde in a schort cloke that the rayne shedes.'　8. 'with
saffres and seladynes, set by the sides.'

III.—3. 'And that barne on his blonke with the quene bidis.'　5. 'by
the lawe sides.'　8. 'the trouth for to telle.'　9. 'who the trouth trowes.'
11. 'To an oke he hem sett.'

IV.

Vndir those bewes thay bade, those beryns so balde,   40
    To bekire at those barrayne, in bankis so bare ;
Thay keste of thaire copills, in clyffes so calde ;
    Thay recomforthed thaire kenettis, to kele tham of
        care ;
Thare  myght  hirdmen,  hendely  forsothe,  herdis  by-
        halde,
    Herkyn huntyngis with hornnes, in holtis so hare, 45
Thay fellede downe the femmalls, full thikke folde,
        With fresche hundis, and felle, felonosly thay fare ;
            .Thay questede and quellys,
            By frythis and fellis,
            That the dere dwellys,                          50
            And darkys and darys.


V.

Alle darkis the dere, and to down schowys,
    And, for the dowte of the dede drowpys the daa,
And by the stremys, so strange, that swyftly swoghes,
    Thay wery the wilde swyne, and wyrkkis tham waa ;
Thay hunte, and halowes, in holttis and hillys,        56
    And till thair riste, raches relyes on thaire raye ;
Thay gafe no gamen, no grythe, that one grownde
        growes,
    Grete hundis [in the greues] full gladly gan gaa.
        Thus thies gomes, thay ga in greuys so grene,   60
            And boldly blawes rechayse,
            And folowes faste one the trase,
            With many sergaunte of mace,
            Swylk solauce to sene.

IV.—5. 'There might hatheles in high, herdes be holde.'  6. 'huntyng
in haste.'  8. 'thei folowen her fare.'  9. A line seems to be wanting in
this stanza in both MSS.  9. 'With gret questis and quellis.'  10. 'Both
in frithis and fellis.'  11. 'All the dere in the delles.'  12. 'Thei durken
and dare.'

V.—1. 'Thei durken the dere in the dyme skuwes.'  2. 'that for drede
of the deth.'  3. This line omitted in MS. D.  5. 'in hurstis and huwes.'
6. 'And bluwe rechas, ryally thei ran to ro.'  10. 'The King blowe.'

### VI.

Thus with  solauce thay  semelede, the  prowdeste  in
  palle,           65
 And sew to the soueraygne, in cleues so clene ;
Nane bot Schir Gawane, the gayeste of alle,
 By-leuys with dame Gaynoure in those greues grene :
Vndir a lorrere scho laye, that lady so smalle,
 Off boxe, and of barborane, byggyde full bene ; 70
Ffaste by-fore vndrone, this ferly gun falle,
 And this meikill mervelle, that I of mene.
  . Now will I of this mervelle meen, ȝif I mote,
   The daye woxe als dirke,
    Als it were mydnyghte mirke,  75
   Ther of Schir Gawane was irke ;
    And lyghte one his fote.

### VII.

Thus one fote are thay lyghte, those frekis vn-fayne,
 And fledde faste [fro] the foreste to the fawe fellis ;
Thay rane fast to the roches, for reddoure of the rayne,
 For the slete, and the snawe, that snayppede tham
  so snelle :         81
Thare come a lowe one the loughe, in lede es noghte to
  layne,
 In the lyknes of Lucyfere, layetheste in helle,
And glyddis to dame Gaynoure, the gatis full gayne,
 Ȝollande ȝamyrly, with many lowde ȝelle ;  85
  It ȝellede, it ȝamede with vengeance full wete ;
   And saide, oft syghande full sare,
    " I ame the body that the bare,
   Allas ! now kyndyls my kare,
    I gloppyn and I grete ! "  90

VI.—1. 'they sembled.' 2. 'within schaghes schene.' 3. 'Al bot.'
6. 'and of barber.' 9. 'meve if I mote.' 12. 'Thereof the King.'

VII.—1. 'Thus to fote ar thei faren.' 2. 'And fleen fro the fforest to the
fewe fellis.' Lines 3 and 6 are omitted in MS. D. 4. 'For the sueterand
snawe suartly hem snelles.' 5. 'a lede of the lawe, in land is.' 7. 'And
glides to Schir Gawayne the gates to gayne.' 8. 'Ȝanland and Ȝomerand.
9. 'Hit Ȝaules, hit Ȝamers with waymeyngis wete.' 11. 'I ban the body
me bare.'

VIII.

Thane gloppenyde, and grett, dame Gaynoure the gay,
  And askede Schir Gawayne, whatt was his beste
      rede ?—
" It es the clippes of the Mone, I herde a clerke saye;"
  And thus he comforthede the Qwene, with his
      knyghtehede.
" Schir Cadore, Schir Caduke, Schir Costarde, Schir
    Kaye,                            95
  Thir knyghtes are vn-curtayse, by crose, and by crede,
That thus me hase lefte in this erthe at my dede daye,
  With the gryselyeste gaste, that euer herde I grete!"—
    " At this gaste," quod Schir Gaweayne, " greue
      ȝowe no more,
      I salle speke with ȝone spyrete,       100
      In ȝone wayes so wete,
      If I maye the bales bete,
        Of ȝone body bare."

IX.

Bare was hir body, and blake to the bane,
  Alle by-claggede in claye, vn-comlyly clede :    105
It weryit, it wayemettede, lyke a womann,
  That nowther one hede, ne one hare, hillynge it hade ;
It stottyde, it stounnede, it stode als a stane,
  It marrede, it monede, it moyssed for made.
Vn to that grysely gaste Schir Gaweane es gane,   110
  He raykede to it one a rase, for he was neuer rade :
    For rade was he neuer, nowe who that ryghte
      redis,
      One the chefe of the cholle,
      A tade pykit one hir polle,
      Hir eghne ware holkede full holle,    115
      Glowand als gledis.

VIII.—3. 'the clippes of the Son.'  5. 'Schir Cador, Schir Clegis,
Schir Costardyne, Schir Cay.'  9. 'Of the goost, quod the grome.'

IX.—4. 'But on hide, ne on huwe, no helling.'  5. 'Hit stemered, hit
stounade.'  8. 'neuer drade.'  9. 'drade was he.'  10. 'chef of the clolle.'

### X.

Alle glowede als gledis, the gaste whare scho glydis,
  Vmbyclede in a clowde, with clethynge vn-clere ;
Cerkelytt with serpentes that satt by hir sydes,
  To tell the dedis ther one, my tongue wer to tere. 120
The beryn brawndeche owte his brande, and the body
      bydis,
  Therefore that cheualrous knyghte thoghte it no chere;
The hundes are to hillys, and thaire hedes hydes,
  Ffor that grysely gaste made so gryme bere :
    The grete grewhundes were agayste, for that grym
      bere, 125
      The birdes on the bewes,
      That one that gaste g[lo]wes,
      Thay clyme in the clewes,
        That hedows when thay here.

### XI.

Who that myghte that hedows see, hendeste in haulle,
  How hir cholle chatirede, hir chaftis, and hir chyne ;
Thane coniurede hir that knyghte, and one Criste gun
    he calle, 132
  "Alls thou was crucyfyede one croyse, to saue ws fra syn,
Thou spirette saye me the sothe, whedir that thou sall,
  And whi that thow walkes thies wayes, thies woddis,
    with inn ? " 135
—" I was of ffegure, and of flesche, the fayereste of alle,
  Cristenede, and krysomede, with kynges in my kyn :
    I hafe kynges in my kyn, knawen kyde full kene,
      God hase sent me this grace,
      To drye my paynes in this place, 140
      And nowe am I commen one a pase,
        To speak with ȝoure Qwene.

X.—2. 'Vmbeclipped with a cloude.' 3. 'Skeled with serpentes all
aboute the sides.' 6. 'charged no chere.' 7. 'The houndes hiȝen to the
wode.' 11. 'the gooste glowes;' L. MS. reads 'gewes.' 12. 'Thei skryke
in the skowes.' 13. 'That hatheles may here.'

XI.—1. 'Hathelesse might here so fer into halle.' 2. 'How chatered
the cholle, the challus, on the chyne.' 7. 'figure and face.' 8. 'and
knowen.' 12. 'I am comen in this cace.'

XII.

" Qwene was I whilome, wele bryghtere of browes,
  Than Beryke, or Brangwayne, the byrdis so balde;
Of any gamnes, or gudis, that one the grownde growes,
  Wele grettere than Gaynoure, of garsomes, and of
      golde,                  146
Of pales, of powndis, of parkes, of plewes,
  Of townnes, of towris, of tresoures vn-tolde;
Of contres, of castells, of cragges, of clewes;
  And now am I cachede owte of kythe, in carys so
      colde:                 150
    In care am I cachede, and cowchede in claye;
        Loo! curtayse knyghte,
        How that dede hase me dyghte,
        Nowe gyffe me anes a syghte,
          Of Gayenour the gaye."      155

XIII.

Nowe to Gayenour the gaye, Schir Gaweayne es gane,
  And to that body hase he broghte that birde then so
      bryghte:
" Welecome, Waynoure!" scho says, "thu worthye in
      wane!
Loo! howe that dulefull dede, hase thi dame dyghte,
I was reddare in rode than rose in the rayne;    160
  My lyre als the lely, lufely to syghte,
And nowe I am a gresely gaste, and grymly granes,
  With Lucefere in a lake lawe ame I lyghte;
    Thus am I lyke to Lucefere, takis witnes by mee,
        Ffor all ȝoure fresche fauoure,      165
        Now moyse one this mirroure,
        Ffor bothe Kynge and Emperoure,
        Thus sall ȝe bee.

XII.—2. 'Than berell.'  11. 'How delfulle deth has me dight.'  12.
'Lete me onys haue a sight.'

XIII.—3. 'Waynoure' here, and in some of the subsequent stanzas in
both MSS., is written instead of 'Gaynoure.' It was thought unnecessary
to correct this, although at first it might appear to be the name of the
apparition of Gaynoure's mother, but whose name is not mentioned. In the
same manner Wawayn occurs elsewhere instead of Gawayn.  6. 'lonched
on hight.'

### XIV.

"And thus dede will ȝow dyghte, [take thare of no
  dowte,]
  And there one hertly takis hede, whils that thu es
  here,                                                       170
When thou es richely arrayede, and rydes in a rowte,
  Hafe than pete, and mynd one the pore, for thu
  arte of powere,
Beryns, and byrdis, are besye the abowte,
  When thi body is bawmede, and broghte appone
  bere,
Than will thay leue the lyghtely, that nowe will the
  lowte,                                                      175
  And thane helpes the no thynge, bot halye prayere:
    The prayere of the pore, chasses the from helle,
      Of thase that ȝellis at thi ȝate,
      When thu sittis in thi sette,
      With all mirthes at thi mete,                           180
      Some dayntes thou dele.

### XV.

"With daynteths one desse, thi dyetes are dyghte;
  And thus in dawngere, and dole I downe, and I
  duelle,
Nasty, and nedfull, and nakede one nyghte,
  There ffolowes me a ferde of ffendis ffull ffell:     185
Thay harle me vnhendely, and hewys me one hyghte;
  In brasse, and in bromstane, I birne als a belle:
Was neuer wroghte in this werlde, a wafullere wyghte,
  It were tore till any tonge my tourmenttis to telle!
    Bot now will I of my tourment talke, or I gaa; 190
      Thynke hertly on this,
      Now fande to mende of this mys;
      Ffor thou erte warnede I wysse,
        Be warre now, be my waa!"

XIV.—1. 'takis witness by me,' MS. L.   7. 'Than lite wyn the light.'
9. 'may purchas the pes.'   13. 'and dayntes on des.'
  XV.—2. 'in dongon I dwelle.'   4. 'fendes of helle.'

### XVI.

"Now wo es me! for thi waa," sayd Waynour, "I
    wysse,        195
Bot a worde wolde I wete, and thi will ware;
Gyff matyns, or messes, myghte oghte menden thi
    mysse,
  Or any mobylls on molde, my myrthis ware the mare;
Or bedis of bechopes, myghte brynge the to blysse;
  Or couentis in cloysters, myghte kele the of care; 200
Ffor if thou be my modir, grete mervelle it es,
  That thi burlyche body es blakenede so bare!"—
    "I bare the of my body; whate bote es to lye?
      Be that to takenynge thou trowe,
      I brake a solempne a-vowe,    205
      That none wyste bot I, and thowe,
        And therfore dole I drye."

### XVII.

"Telle me now sothely, what may safe thi sytis,
  And I sall garre seke sayntes, for thi sake;
Bot of thase balefull bestis, that one thi body bytys,
  Alle blendis my blode, thi blee es soo blake."—  211
"This es it to luffe paramoures, and lustys, and litys,
  That gerse me lyghte, and lenge so lawe in this
    lake;
Ffor alle the welthe of this werlde, thus awaye wytis;
  This werlde es wandrethe, that wirkes me wrake: 215
    Ffor wrake it me wirkes, now Waynoure, I wysse!
      Were thritty trentalls done,
      By-twyxen vndrone and none,
      My saule were saluede full sone,
        And broghte in to blysse."    220

XVI.—8. 'is brought to be so bare.'   9. 'what bote is hit I layn.'
12. 'And no man wist ht but thowe.'   13. 'that sothely I sayn.'

XVII.—1. 'what may the sauen y-wis.'   2. 'And I sall make sere men
to singe for thi sake.'   4. 'Al bledis my ble, thi bones.'   8. 'With the
wilde wormis that worche me wrake.'   12. 'socoured with son.

### XVIII.

" To blysse brynge the that barne, [that boghte the on
  rode,]
 That was crucyfiede one croyse, and crownnede with
  thorne ;
Crystynnede, and krysommede, with candills and coude,
 Ffullede in funstane, full frely by-forne ;
Mary, that es myghty, and myldest of mode,     225
 That bare that blysschede, in Bedleme was borne,
Gyffe me grace for to grete thy saule with some gude ;
 And mene the with messes, and matynes one
  morne."—
  " To mene me with messes, grete menske nowe it
   were,
   Ffor hym, that ryste on the rode,     230
   Gyffe nowe faste of thy gude,
   To folke that fayles the fude,
    Whylls that thou erte here."


### XIX.

" Now here hertly one hande, I hete the to halde,
 With a melyone of messes to make thy menynge. 235
Bot one worde," saide dame Waynoure, " now wiete
  that I walde,
 Whate greues Gode moste of any kyns thynge ? "—
" Pride, with apparementis, als prophetis haue talde,
 By-fore the pople, appertly in thaire prechynge ;
The [bowe] is full bittire, thare of be thou balde,   240
 It makis beryns full balde, to breke his byddynge ;
  Who so his byddyng brekis, bare he es of blysse ;
   Bot thay be salued of that sare,
   Certis, or thay hethyn fare,
   Thay mon wiete of calde care,     245
    Waynoure, I wys."


XVIII.—1. 'that dere has the boghte,' MS. L. 4. 'Ffolowed in fonte-
stone.' 9. 'grete myster.'

XIX.—4. 'What wrathed God most.' 5. 'with appurtennance.' 8.
'burnes so bly.'

XX.

"Telle me," sayde Waynoure, "a worde ʒif thou woste,
    Whate dedis myghte me beste in to blys brynge? "—
"Mekenesse and mercy," scho saide, "tho are the
        moste,
    Hafe petie on the pore, thane plesys thou owre Kynge;
Sythen after that, do almous dedis of alle other thynge,
    Thies aren the gud gyftis of the Holy Goste,      252
That enspyres alle sperites, withowttyn spillynge;
    Ffor to come to that blysse, that euer more sall laste,
        Of thies speritualc thinges, spyre me na mare,  255
            Whills thou arte Qwene in thi quarte,
            Halde thies wordis in thyn herte,
            Ffor thou sall lyffe bot a starte;
                Hethyn sall thu ffare."

XXI.

" How sall we fare," saide the freke, "that fowndis to
        fyghte,                                        260
    That ofte foundis the folkes, in fele kyngis landis;
That riche rewmes ouer rynnes, agaynes the ryghte,
    And wynnes wirchippis, and welthis, by wyghtenes
        of handis ? "—
—"ʒowre Kynge es to couetous, I tell thee, schir knyghte;
    May no man stere hym of strenghe, whills the whele
        standis,                                       265
When he es in his mageste hegheste, and maste es of
        myghte,
    He sall lighte full lawe, appone the see sandis :
        Thus ʒoure cheualrous Kynge chefe schalle a
            chawnce,
            Ffalse fortune in fyghte,
            That wondirfull whele-wryghte,             270
            Mase lordis lawe for to lyghte;
                Takes witnes by Fraunce.

XX. This stanza in the Lincoln MS. is misplaced, as it is there introduced as the XVIII.   9. 'spute thou na mare.'

XXI.—2. 'And thus defoulen the folke.'   4. 'wynnen worshipp in werre
thorgh.'   6. 'May no man stry him with strength, while his whele stondes.'
9. 'chiualrous knight.'   10. 'Ffalsely fordone in fight.'   11. 'With a won-
derfull wight.'

### XXII.

" Ffraunce hafe ȝe frely with ȝour fyghte wonnen ;
  The Ffrolo and the Ffarnaghe es frely by-leuede ;
Bretayne, and Burgoyne, es bothe to ȝow bownen,
  And alle the Dugepers of Ffraunce with the dyn
      dreuede :	276
Gyane may gretyn that the werre was by-gounnen ;
  Es noghte a lorde in that lande, appon lyfe leuede ;
ȝete sall the riche Romaynes with ȝow ben ouer
    ronnen,
  And alle the Rownde Tabill thaire rentis be reuede.
    Thay sall ȝitt be Tybire tymbire ȝow tene ;	281
      Gete the, Schir Gawayne
      Turne thou to Tuskayne,
      Ffor [lese] thu sall Bretayne,
        With a knyghte kene.	285

### XXIII.

" A knyghte sall kenly closen the crowne,
  And at Carelyone be crownede for kynge :
That sege sall be sesede at a sesone,
  That mekill bale, and barete till Ynglande sall
      brynge ;
Ther sall in Tuskane be tallde of that tresone,	290
  And torne home aȝayne for that tydynge ;
And ther sall the Rownde Tabille losse the renowne,
  Be-syde Ramessaye, full ryghte at a rydynge,
    And at Dorsett sall dy the doghetyeste of alle.
      Gette the, Schir Gawayne,	295
      The baldeste of Bretayne ;
      Ffor in a slake thu sall be slayne,
        Swylke ferly sall falle !

XXII.—2. ' Freol and his folke fey ar they leued.'  3. ' to ȝow bowen.'
9. ' Thus shall a Tyber vntrue tymber with tene.'

XXIII.—1. 'This knight shal be clanly enclosed with a crowne.'  2. ' at
Carlele shal that comly.'  3. ' A sege shal be seche with a cession.'  4. ' to
Bretayn.'  8. ' Beside Ramsey full rade.'

G

### XXIV.

" Siche ferly sall falle, with owtten any fabille,
  Appone Cornewayle coste, with a knyghte kene :  300
Arthure the auenante, that honeste es and abill,
  Sall be wondid, I wysse, full wathely, I wene :
[And al the rial rowte of the Rounde Tabille,
  Thei shullen dye on a day, the doughty by-dene ;]
Supprysede with a sugette, that beris of sabille        305
  A sawtire engrelede of siluer full schene.
      He beris [it] of sabille, sothely to saye ;
          In kyng Arthures haulle
          The childe playes hym at the balle
          That sall owttraye ʒow alle,                  310
              Full derfely a daye.


### XXV.

" Hafe gud daye, dame Gaynoure, and Gawane the gude ;
  I hafe no langare tyme, mo tales to telle,
Ffor me buse wende one my waye, thorowte this
      wode,
  Vn-to my wonnynge wane, in waa for to welle :   315
Ffor him that rewfully rase, and rente was one rude,
  Thynke one the dawngere, and the dole, that I in
      duelle ;
And fede folke, for my sake, that fawtes the fude,
  And mene me with messes, and matyns in melle :
      [Masses arn medecynes to vs that bale bides ;]
          Vs thynke a messe als swete,                  321
          Als any spyce that euer thu ete."
          And thus with a grysely grete,
          The gaste awaye glydis.

### XXVI.

[With a grisly grete, the gooste awey glydis;                325
  And goes, with gronyng sore, thorgh the greues
    grene :]
The wynde, and the wedyrs, than welken in hydis;
  Than vnclosede the clowddis, the sone schane
    schene.
The kynge his bogill hase blowen, and on the bent bydis,
  His fayre folke in firthes, flokkes in fere;                330
All that royalle rowte, to the Qwene rydys,
  And melis to hir mildely, one thaire manere;
    The wyes on swilke wondirs a-wondirde thaire were;
      The prynces prowdeste in palle,
      Dame Gaynoure, and alle,                335
      Wente to Randolfe sett haulle,
        To thaire sopere.

### XXVII.

The Kynge was sett to the supere, and serued in sale,
  Vndir a seloure of sylke, full daynetyuousely dighte;
With alle the wirchipe to welde, and wyne for to wale,
  Birdis in brede, of brynt golde bryghte.                341
Ther come two setolers in, with a symbale,
  A lady, lufesome of late, ledande a knyghte;
Scho rydes vp to the heghe desse, by-fore the royalle,
  And askede Schir Arthure, full hendely one highte,
    Scho saide to that souerayne, wlonkeste in wedis,
      " Mane moste of myghte,                347
      Here es comyn ane armede knyghte;
      Now do hym resone and ryghte,
        Ffor thi manhede."                350

XXVI.—1 and 2. These lines are wanting in MS. L.   3. 'the welkyn
vnhides.'   6. 'in the frith thei flokken by-dene.'   8. 'She sayis hem the
selcouthes that thei hadde thair seene.'   9. 'The wise of the weder.'   12.
'Went to Rondoles halle.'

XXVII.—1. 'serued in halle.'   3. 'worshipp and wele, mewith the
walle.'   4. 'Briddes branden, and brad, in bankers bright.'   7. 'Ho raykes
vp, in a res.'   8. 'And halsed.'   9. 'Ho said.'   10. 'Mon makles.'   11.
'an errant knight.'

### XXVIII.

The mane in his mantyll syttis at his mete,
  In paulle purede with pane, full precyously dyghte,
Trofelyte, and trauerste with trewloues in trete;
  The tasee was of topas that ther to was tyghte:
He glyfte vpe with hys eghne, that gray ware, and
    grete,
  With his burely berde, one that birde bryghte.      356
He was the souerayneste sir, sittande in sette,
  That euer any segge saughe, or sene was with syghte.
    Thus the kyng, crowned in kythe, carpis hir till;
      "Welecome, worthyly wyghte!                     360
      Thou sall hafe resone and ryghte;
      Whythen es this comly knyghte,
        If it be thi will?"

### XXIX.

Scho was the worthilieste wyghte, that any wy myghte
    welde;
  Hir gyde was gloryous, and gaye, alle of gyrse grene;
Hir belle was of plonkette, with birdis full baulde,  366
  Botonede with besantes, and bokellede full bene;
Hir faxe in fyn perrye frette was in fowlde,
  Conterfelette in a kelle colourede full clene,
With a crowne of crystalle, and of clere golde:      370
  Hir courchefes were coryouse, with many prowd
    pyn,
    [Her perre was praysed, with prise men of might;]
      The bryghte byrdis, and balde,
      Had note ynoghe to by-halde
      One that freely to fawlde,                       375
        And one that hende knyghte.

XXVIII.—2. 'pured to pay, prodly pight.'  3. This line is omitted in
MS. D.  6. 'With his beueren berde.'  9. 'talkis hir tille.'

XXIX.—1. 'that eny wede wolde.'  3. 'Here belle was of blunket.'
4. 'Branded with brende golde.'  7. 'With a crowne craftly al of clene
golde.'  9. Omitted in MS. L.

XXX.

That knyghte in his coloures was armede full clene,
  With his comly creste, full clene to by-holde;
His brenyes, and his bacenett, burneschet full bene,
  With a bourdoure abowte, alle of brynte golde;   380
His mayles was mylk-whytte, enclosede so clene;
    His horse trappede with the same, als it was me
      taulde.
The schelde one his schuldir, of syluere full schene,
  With bare-heuedis of blake, burely, and baulde;
    His horse withe sendale was teldede, and trappede
      to the hele;   385
        And his cheuarone by-forne,
        Stode als ane vnycorne,
        Als so scharpe as any thorne,
        And mayles of stele.

XXXI.

In stele wes he stuffede, that steryn was one stede,  390
  Alle of sternys of golde, that stekillede was one
    straye;
He, and his gambesouns, glomede als gledys,
  With graynes of rubyes, that graythede were gaye,
And his schene schynbawdes, scharpe for to schrede;
  [His polemus with pelicocus were poudred to pay.]
Thus with a lance appon lofte, that lady gun he lede;
  A swayne, one a fresone, folowde him, in faye.   397
    [The ffreson was afered, for drede of that fare;]
      He was seldom wounte
      To see the tabille at his frounte,   400
      Swilke gammenes was he wonte
      [Saȝ he neuer are.]

XXX.—5. 'were mylke white . . . many hit seen.' 6. 'trapped of that ilke as true men me tolde.' 8. 'of brake browed ful bolde.' 9. 'in fyne sandel was trapped.' 11. 'Stode as an.' 13. 'An anlas of stele.'

XXXI.—2. 'his pencell displaied.' 3. 'His gloues, his gamesouns, glowed as a glede.' 5. 'schynbandes.' 6. This line is wanting in MS. L., and also the 9th in this stanza. 8. 'A freke, on a freson.' 10. 'For he was selden wonte to see.' 11. 'the tablet floure.' 12. 'Siche gamen ne gle.' 13. 'Full seldome to see,' MS. L.

### XXXII.

Arthure askede in hye, one herande tham alle,
  "Whate woldest thu, Wy, ʒif it were thi wille?
Tell me whate thu sekis, and whedir that thu schalle,
  And why thu stonyes on thi stede, and stondis so
    stille?"                                                    406
He lyfte vpe his visare fro the ventalle,
  And with a knyghtly contenance he carpis hym till:
"Be thu kaysere, or kynge, here I the be-calle,
  To fynde me a freke, to fyghte one my fill:        410
    Ffor fyghtynge to frayste, I fowndede fra hame."
      The kynge carpede on heghte,
      "Lyghte, and lende alle nyghte,
      If thou be curtayse knyghte,
        And tell me thi name."                          415


### XXXIII.

"My name es Schir Galleroun, with owttyn any gyle,
  The gretteste of Galowaye, of greues and of gyllis;
Of Konynge, of Carryke, of Connygame, of Kylle,
  Of Lomonde, of Lenay, of Lowthyane hillis.
Thou hase wonnen thaym one werre, with owttrageouse
    will;                                                      420
  And gyffen tham Schir Gawayne, and that myn herte
    grilles.
[But he shal wring his honde, and warry the wyle,]
  Or he welden my landes, at myn vn-thankes:
    By alle the welthe of this werlde, he sall tham
      neuer welde,
      Whills I my hede may bere;                       425
      Bot he wyn tham one werre,
      Bothe with schelde, and with spere,
        Appone a fair felde!

XXXII.—4. 'sturne on thi stede.' 5. 'He wayned up his viser.' 10. 'Then
said the King vppon hight.'

XXXIII.—3. 'Of Connok, of Conyngham, and also Kyle.' 4. 'Of
Lomand, of Losex.' 5. 'with a wrange wille.' 7. This line is wanting in
MS. L. 8. 'Er he weld hem, y-wis agayn myn vmwylles.'

### XXXIV.

" I will fighte on a felde, and ther-to make I my faythe,
  With any freke one the foulde, that frely es borne :
To losse swylke a lordschipe, me thynke it full laythe ;
  And ilke a leueande lede wolde laughe me to
    skorne."—                                432
" We aren here in the wode, walkand one our wathe,
  We hunte at the herdis, with hundes, and with
    horne ;
We aren one owre gamen, we ne hafe no gude graythe,
  Bot ȝitt thu sall be machede by middaye to morne.
    And forthi I rede the, thu rathe mane, thu riste
      the alle the nyghte."               437
        Than Gawayne, gayest of alle,
        Ledis hym owte of the haulle,
        Vn-till a paveleone of paulle,       440
          That prowdely was pyghte.

### XXXV.

Pighte was it prowdely, with purpure and paulle,
  With dossours, and qweschyns, and bankowres full
    bryghte ;
Withinn was a chapelle, a chambir, and ane haulle ;
  A chymneye with charecole, to chawffen that knyghte,
His stede was sone stabillede, and lede to the stalle,
  And haye hendly heuyde in hekkes one hyghte.   447
Sythen he braydes vp a burde, and clathes gun calle ;
  Sanapes, and salers, full semly to syghte,
    Preketes, and broketes, and standertis by-twene :
      Than thay seruede that knyghte,      451
      And his worthy wyghte,
      With full riche daynteths dyghte,
      In siluere full schene.

XXXIV.—4. 'And siche [iche ?] lede opon lyve.' 5. 'went to walke.'
7. 'gome graithe.' 10. 'grathest of alle.'

XXXV.—2. 'Birdes branden above, in brend gold bright.' 3. 'Inwith
was a.' 6. 'Hay bertly he had in haches on hicht.' 7. 'thei braide.'
9. 'Torches.' 10. 'Thus thei.'

### XXXVI.

In siluer sa semly thay serue tham of the beste,    455
  With vernage, in verrys and cowppys sa clene :
And  thus  thase  gleterande  gommes, gladdis  thaire
      gestis,
  With riche daynteths, endorrede, in dysches by-dene.
When the ryalle renke was gone to his ryste,
  The Kynge in to concelle hase callede his knyghtis
      so kene ;    460
Sayse "lukes nowe, ȝe lordyngs, oure lofe be noghte lost,
  Who sall enconter with ȝone knyghte, now lukes vs
      by-twene."
    Thane  said  Schir  Gawayne,  "he  sall  vs  noghte
        greue,
      Here my trouthe I ȝow plyghte,
      I sall feghte with ȝone knyghte,    465
      In the defence of my ryghte,
        My lord, with ȝowre lefe."


### XXXVII.

"I leue wele," quod the kynge, "thi latis are [liȝt,
  But I nolde, for no lordeshippe, se thi life lorne.]
"Late gaa," quod Schir Gawayne, "Gode stond with
      the riȝt,    470
  If he skape skatheles, [hit were a foule skorne]."
In the dawynge of the [day, the doughti were dight ;]
  Thaye herde matyns [and masse, erly on morne.]
By that, one [Pluton land a palais was piȝt,]
  Whare neuer [freke opon folde had fouȝten biforne.]
    [Thei setten listes by-lyue on the loȝ lande :    476
      Twa sop[pes de mayn]
      Thei b[roght to Schir Gawayn,]
      For [to confort his brayn,
        The King gared commaunde.]    480

XXXVI.—3. 'And thus Schir Gawayn the good.'  8. 'kestis ȝou bi-
twene.'  9. 'Then said Gawayn the goode.'  10. 'Here my honde I you
highte.'

XXXVII.—The greater part of this, and the two first lines of the next
stanza are torn away in MS. L.

### XXXVIII.

The [King commaunded Krudely, the Erles son of
    Kent,]
[Curtaysly in this case, take kepe to the Knight.]
With riche daynteths, that day, he dynede in his tente,
    With birdes baken in brede, of brynte golde bryghte;
And sythen vnto dame Waynour full wyesely he wente;
    And lefte with hir in warde his worthily wyghte : 486
And than thies hathells full hendely thaire horsses hase
      hent,
    At the lycence of the lorde, that lordely gun lyghte,
      Alle bot thir [two] beryns, bouldeste of blode.
        The kynges chayere was sette, 490
        A-bowne on a chasselett ;
        And many a gaylyarde grett
          Ffor Gawayne the gude.

### XXXIX.

Gawayne and Galleron dyghtis thaire stedis,
    Alle of gleterande golde, full gaye was thaire gere ;
Twa lordes be-lyfe to thaire lystes thaym ledis, 496
    With many sergeauntes of mace ; it was the manere ;
The beryns broches thaire blonkes to thair sydes bledis.
    Aythire freke appon felde hase fichede thaire spere,
Schaftis of schene wode thay scheuerede in schides ;
    So jolyly those gentill men justede one were ! 501
      Schaftis thay scheuer in schydes full schene :
        Sythen, with brandes full bryghte,
        Riche mayles thay righte ;
        Thus enconterde the knyghte 505
          With Gawayne, one grene.

XXXVIII.—3. 'or day.' 4. 'After buskis him in a brene, that burneshed
was bright.' 6. 'He in here.' 7. 'After aither in high hour horses thei
hent.' 8. 'And at the listes on the lande.' 9. 'Bothe thes two burnes.'
11. 'Quene on a chacelet.'

XXXIX.—1. 'gurden her stedes.' 6. 'has fastned his spere.' 7. 'thei
shindre.' 9. 'Sbaftes thei shindre in sheldes so shene.'

### XL.

Gawane was graythely graythede on grene,
  With griffons of golde, engrelede full gaye,
Trayfolede with trayfoles, and trewluffes by-twene,
  One a stirtande stede he strykes one straye.      510
[That other in] his turnynge he talkis with tene;
  "[Whi drawes thou the] one dreghe, and makis
    swilke delay?"
[He swapped him then at the swyre] with a swerde
  ˙ kene:
  [That greued Schir Gawayn, to] his dede day.
    [The dyntes of that doughty, were do]wttous by-
        dene.      515
      [Fyfte mayles, and mo,
      The swerde swapt in two,
      The canel-bone also,
        And clef his] schelde schene.


### XLI.

[He clef thorgh the cantell that couered the Knight,
  Thorgh the shinand shelde, a shaftmon and mare;
And then the lady loude lowe vppon hight,      522
  And Gawayn greches therwith, and gremed ful sare:
" I shal rewarde the thi route, if I con rede right."
  He folowed in on the ffreke, with a fressh fare,      525
Thorgh blason, and brene, that burneshed wer bri3t,
  With a burlich bronde, thorgh him he bare.
    The bronde was blody, that burneshed was bri3t;
      Then gloppened that gay:
      Hit was no ferly, in fay,      530
      The sturne strikis on stray,
        In stiropes stri3t.


XL.—1. 'gaily grathed in grene.'  3. 'Trifeled with traues.'  4. 'On a
stargand stede.'  5—13. These lines, partly destroyed in MS. L., are filled
up from MS. D.

XLI.—A leaf in the Lincoln Manuscript appears unfortunately to be lost.
This and the next five stanzas, and part of the XLVII., which it seems
to have contained, are therefore printed from the other copy.

### XLII.

Streyte in his steroppes, stoutely he strikes,
  And waynes at Schir Wawayn, als he were wode;
Then his leman on lowde skirles, and skrikes,      535
  When that burly burne blenket on blode:
Lordes and ladies of that laike likes;
  And thonked God fele sithe for Gawayn the gode.
With a swap of a swerde, that swathel him swykes,
  He stroke of the stede hede, streite there he stode;
    The faire fole fondred, and fel to the grounde.  541
      Gawayn gloppened in hert,
      Of he were hasty and smert,
      Oute of steropis he stert,
        Fro Grissell the goode.      545


### XLIII.

" Grissell," quod Gawayn, " gon is, God wote!
  He was the burlokest blonke, that euer bote brede!
By him, that in Bedeleem was borne, euer to ben our
    · bote,
  I shall venge the to day, if I con right rede!
Go fecche me my freson, fairest on fote,      550
  He may stonde the in stoure, in as mekle stede;
No more for the faire fole, then for a rissh rote,
  But for doel of the dombe best, that thus shuld be dede.
    I mone for no montur, for I may gete mare;"
      Als he stode by his stede,      555
      That was so goode at neede:
      Ner Gawayn wax wede,
        So siked he sare.


### XLIV.

Thus wepus for wo, Wawayn the wight;
  And wenys him to quyte, that wonded is sare.      560
That other droȝ him on dreȝt, for drede of the kniȝt,
  And boldely broched his blonk on the bent bare.

XLII.—4. ' burne ' here, and elsewhere in MS. D., for ' barne ' or
' beryn.'

Thus may thei dryve forthe the day, to the derk night :
  The son was passed, by that, mydday, and mare.
Within the listes the lede lordly don light,          565
  Touard the burne, with his bronde, he busked him
      thare :
    To bataile they bowe with brondes so bright,
        Shene sheldes wer shred ;
        Bright brenes by-bled ;
        Many douȝti were a-dred :                     570
        So fersely thei fight.


### XLV.

Thus thei feght on fote, on that fair felde,
  As fressh as a lyon, that fautes the fille ;
Wilele thes wight men, thair wepenes they welde, . . .
He bronched him yn with his bronde, vnder the brode
      shelde,                                          575
  Thorgh the waast of the body, and wonded him ille :
The swerde stent for no stuf, hit was so wel steled ;
  That other startis on bak, and stondis ston stille :
    Though he were stonayed that stonde, he strikis
        ful sare ;
        He gurdes to Schir Gawayn,                     580
        Thorgh ventaile, and pesayn ;
        He wanted noȝt to be slayn
        The brede of an hare.


### XLVI.

Hardely then thes hatheles on helmes they hewe,
  Thei beten downe beriles, and bourdures bright ; 585
Shildes on shildres, that shene were to shewe,
  Fretted were in fyne golde, thei failen in fight ;
Stones of iral they strenkel, and strewe ;
  Stithe stapeles of stele they strike don stight ;
Burnes bannen the tyme the bargan was brewe,        590
  The doughti with dyntes, so delfully were dight.
    Then gretes Gaynour, with bothe her gray ene ;

XLV.—The fourth line in this stanza is wanting in MS. D.

For tho douȝti that fight,
Were manly mached of might,
With oute reson, or right,                              595
    As al men sene.

### XLVII.

Thus gretis Gaynour, with bothe her gray yene,
  For gref of Schir Gawayn, grisly was wounded :
The Knight of corage was cruel and kene ;
  And with a stele bronde, that sturne oft stonded ; 600
Al the cost of [the] Knyght, he carf downe clene,
  Thorgh the riche mailes, that ronke were, and
    rounde ;]
Swilke a touche at that tyme, he taughte hym in tene ;
  He girdede Schir Galleron growellynge one grownde.
    Galleron full greuousely granes on the grene ;   605
      And als wondede als he was,
      Swyftly vpe he rase,
      And folowde in faste on his faas,
        With a swerde schene.

### XLVIII.

Clenly that crewelle couerde hym on highte,            610
  And with a caste of the care, in kautelle he strykis ;
Ffull ȝerne he wayttis Schir Wawayne the wighte,
  Bot hym lympede the werse ; and that me wele lykis ;
He etyllde with a slynge hafe slayne hym with slighte,
  The swerde sleppis on slante, and one the mayle
    slydys,                                           615
And Schir Gawayne by the colere clekis the knyghte,
  Than his leman so lowde skremes and skrykis.
    Scho grete one dame Gaynour, with granes so grylle,
      And saide, "lady ! makles of myghte,
      Hafe now mercy one ȝone knychte,          620
      That es so dulefully dyghte,
        Giffe it be thi will."

XLVII.—7. 'With a teneful touche.'  11. 'Sone buredely he ras.'

XLVIII.—1. 'Kenely.'  3. 'And waynes at Schir Wawayn.'  5. 'He
atteled with a slenk.'  6. 'The swerde swapped on his swange.'  7. 'keppes
the knight.'  8. 'skrilles and skrikis.'

### XLIX.

Than wilfully dame Waynour vnto the kynge went,
 Scho caught of hir coronalle ; and knelyd hym till :
"Als thu erte Roye ryalle, and recheste of rent,  625
 And I thyn wyfe, weddid at myn awen will,
ȝone beryns in ȝone batelle, that bledis one ȝone bent,
 Thay are wery, I wysse ; and wondide full ille,
Thurgh [thaire] schene  schildis  thaire  schuldirs  are
   schent ;
 [The granes of Schir Gawayne dos my hert grille.]
  The granes of Schir Gawayne greuys me full sare :
   Wolde thu, lufly lorde   632
    Gare the knyghtis accorde,
    It ware grete comforde,
     Till alle that here ware."   635


### L.

Bot than hym spake Galleron to Gawayne the gude :
 "I wende no wy in this werlde, were haluendelle so
  wyghte.
Here I make the relese, in my rentis, by the rode !
 And by-fore thiese ryalle, resynge the my ryghte ;
And sythen I make the manreden with a mylde mode,
 Als to mane in this medil erthe makles of myghte."
He talkes to-warde the knyghte, one heghte there he
  stode,   642
 He bedde that burely his brande, that burneschede
  was bryghte :
  "Of renttis and reches I make the relese."
   Downe knelis that knyghte,   645
   And carpis thies wordes one highte ;
   The kyng stude vp-ryghte,
   And commandis the pese.


XLIX.—1. 'Wisly dame Waynour.' 4. 'at thi awen wille.' 8. This
line is omitted in MS. L. 10. 'Woldest thou leve lorde.'

 L.—4. 'relese the my right.' 12. 'The kyng stode vp right.'

LI.

The kynge commandis the pese, and cryes one highte;
 And Gawayne was gudly, and lefte for his sake.  650
And than to the lystis the lordis leppis full lyghte,
 Schir Owayne, Fytz-Vryene, and Arrake full rathe:
Marrake, and Menegalle, that maste were of myghte,
 Bathe thase trauelde knyghtis trewly thay taghte:
Vnnethes myghte those knyghtes stande vp ryghte,  655
 Thay were for-bett, and for-blede, thaire wedis wexe
   blake;
  [Her blees were brosed, for beting of brondes;]
   With owtten more lettynge,
   Was dighte there thiere semblynge,
   By-fore that comly kynge,   660
    And helde vpe thair handes.


LII.

"I gyffe to the, Schir Gawayne," quode the kynge,
  "tresoure, and golde,
Glamorgans landis, with greuys so grene,
The wirchipe of Wales, to welde and to wolde;
 With Gryffons castelle, kirnelde so clene;  665
And the Husters Haulle, to hafe, and to holde;
 Wayfurthe, and Wakfelde, wallede I wene;
Twa baronryse in Burgoyne, with burghes so balde,
 That are moted abowte, and byggede full bene:
  I sall endowe the als a duke, and dub the with
   myn hand,   670
   With-thi thu saughtill with ʒone gentill
    knyghte,
   That es so hardy and wyghte,
   And relese hym thi ryghte,
   And graunte hym his lande."

LI.—4. 'Schir Ewayn, Schir Erian, and Arrak, Schir Lake.' 5. 'Schir
Dowrelat and Moylard that most wer of might.' 8. 'What for buffetes and
blode, her blees wex blake.' 9. This line is omitted in MS. L. 11. 'Dight
was here saughtlying.'

LII.—1. 'with gerson and golde.' 2. 'All the Glamorgan lande.'
5. 'Eke Ulstur halle.' 6. 'Wayford and Waterforde in Wales I wene.'
7. 'Two baronrees in Bretane.' 8. 'That arn batailed about.'

### LIII.

" Now, and here I gyffe hym," quod  Gawayne, " with-
    owttyn ony gyle,                                                          675
  Alle the landes, and the lythes, fra Lowyke to Layre;
Commoke, and Carrike, Connynghame, and Kylle,
  Als the cheualrous knyghte hase chalandchede als
    ayere;
The Lebynge, the Lowpynge, the Leveastre Ile,
  Bathe frythes, and forestes, frely and faire:        680
[Vnder ȝour lordeship to lenge the while,
  And to the Rounde Table to make repaire;
    I shall reseff him in felde, in forestis so faire :]"
      Than the Kynge, and the Quene,
      And alle the doghety by-dene,                              685
      Thorow the greuys so grene,
      To Carlele thay kayre.


### LIV.

The Kyng to Carelele es comen, with knyghttis so kene,
  To halde his Rownde Tabill, one ryalle array;
Those knyghtes, that were wondede full wathely, als I
    wene,                                                                         690
  Surgeons [sone] sanede thaym, sothely to saye;
Bothe comforthede thaym than, the Kynge and the
    Qwene;
  Thay ware dubbyde Dukes bothe one a daye.
And ther Schir Galleron weddid his wyfe, that semly
    and schene,
  With gyftis and gersomes of Schir Gawayne the
    gaye.                                                                           695
  And thus those hathells with haldis that hende:

LIII.—1. ' Here I gif Schir Galeron, quod G.'  2. 'fra Lauer.'  3. ' Connok and Carlele.'  5. ' The Lother, the Lemok, the Loynak, the Lile.'
6. ' forestes and fosses so faire.'  7—9. These lines are not in MS. L.

LIV.—2. ' And al the rounde table.'  3. ' The wees that were.'
5. ' Bothe confortes the knyghtis.'  7. ' There he wedded his wife,
slonkest I wene.'  8. ' Schir Galeron the gaye.'  9. ' Thus that hathel
in high.'

And when he was saned, and sownde,
Thay made hym sworne to Schir Gawane in
    that stownde,
And sythen, a knyghte of the Tabille Rownde,
    Vntill his lyues end.                    700


LV.

Dame Gaynour garte besyly wryte in to the weste,
    To alle manere of relygeous, to rede and to synge;
Pristes with processyons, [to pray were prest,
    With a mylion of] messis, to make hir menynge;
Dukes, Erles, Barouns, and bechoppes of the beste,
    Thurghe alle Ynglande scho garte make menynge.
And thus this ferlyes by-felle in a fforeste,          707
    Vndir an holte so bare, at an hunttynge;
        Swylke hunttynge in holtis, sulde noghte ben
            hyde :—
                Thus to the fforestes thay fure,          710
                Steryn knyghtes and sture :
                And in the tym of Arthure
                This awntyr by-tyd.


This ferly by-felle, full sothely to sayne,
In Yggillwode fforeste, at the Ternwathelayne.


explicit.

11. 'Thei made Schir Galeron that stonde.'  12. 'A knight of the
Table Ronde.'

LV.—1. 'Waynour gared wisely.'  3, 4. The words within brackets
are wanting in MS. L.  5. 'Buke lered men; bisshops the best.'  6.
'Thorgh al Bretayne besely the burde gared rynge.'  7. 'This ferly
bifelle in Englond forest.'  8. 'a holte so bore.'  10. 'thay fore.'
11. 'and store.'

H

# ORFEO AND HEURODIS

IV.

# ORFEO AND HEURODIS.

———

" Herken, lordyngys, that ben trewe,<br>
And Y wol ʒou telle of Sir Orphewe."

*THE fairy tale of* Orfeo *and* Heurodis *is possessed of a very distinct, though not less interesting character, from the numerous remains of early Romantic fiction. In the concluding lines it professes to be a lay of* Bretaigne, *but whether a translation or not, there can be no doubt that it was formed on the classical story of* Orpheus *and* Eurydice. *This tale was extensively known at an early period, owing to the circulation of the* Latin *poets and the works of other ancient authors in which it has been so beautifully narrated. In proof of this,* Mr Turner, *in his valuable and instructive history, has shown that, during the* 11th *century,* King Alfred, *when translating the* Metrum *to the* Consolations *of* Philosophy, *in his* Anglo-Saxon *version of* Boethius, *where the incident is described in a general manner by that popular writer, has told " the story so completely in his own way, and with so many of his own little touches and additions, as to make his account an original tale."* [1] *In the present instance, the narrative (as observed by a distinguished writer of our times, who, in a felicitous manner, has employed it to illustrate a highly interesting Essay on the*

---

[1] History of the Anglo-Saxons, vol. ii. p. 157, edit. 1820.

Fairies of Popular Superstition [1]) *has been transformed into a beautiful romantic tale of Faery, in which the Gothick Mythology and the usages of Chivalry are with singular skill engrafted on the fables of Greece.*

*Among the* pleysand storeis *enumerated in* The Complaynt of Scotland, 1549, *as being popular, is* Opheus, kyng of Portingal; *but no romance of this particular title is known.* It is therefore more than probable that it might have been some corruption of the present story; as we know how little stress should be laid on the geographical correctness or consistency of the Minstrel-writers. Thus in the following tale, we have* Orfeo *represented as King of Winchester, the ancient name of which, " the Romancer, with unparalleled ingenuity, discovers to have been Traciens or Thrace:"* [2] *and, in the burlesque interlude of the laying of a gaist, printed in this collection, " the Gaist" is married to " the Spenzie flie "—*

> " And crownd him kyng of Kandelie :
> And thay gat thame betwene
> *Orpheus* Kyng, and *Elpha* quene."

*The story of* Orpheus *and* Eurydice, *in the latter part of the fifteenth century, was moralised by* Robert Henryson, *the* Scotish *poet.* It was first printed at* Edinburgh, *in the year* 1508, *with the title—*Heir begynnis the traitie of Orpheus kyng, and how he ʒeid to hewyn and to hel to seik his quene. *After detailing, with minute fidelity to his classical authorities, the genealogy and history of the* King of Thrace, Henryson *introduces, in a different kind of measure, the* " mone lamentable " *of* Orpheus, *beginning*

> " O dulfull harpe ! with mony dolly string,
> Turne all thi mirth and musik in murnyng,
> And ceiss of all thi subtell sangis sweit—"

*After this pathetic lamentation, the poet having related his visit to the celestial spheres, conducts him to the infernal regions in search of* Eurydice. *From this part of* Henry-

---

[1] Minstrelsy of the Scottish Border, vol. ii. p. 174, edit. 1803.
[2] *Ibid.*, vol. ii. p. 203.

son's *performance a few stanzas, by way of specimen, may
be given.*

> " He passit furth the space of xx. dayis,
> Fer and full ferther than I can tell,
> And ay he fand stretis and redy wayis,
> Tyll at the last, vnto the yett of hell
> He com; and thare he fand a portar fell
> With thre hedis, was callit Cerberus;
> A hund of hell, a monster meruailus ! "

*He charms Cerberus, and then the " three sisters," Alecto,
Megera, and Thesiphone, whose employment was turning
round the wheel on which Ixion was spread.   " Syne," the
poet says—*

> " Syne come he till a wonder grisely flud,
> Droubly and depe, that rathly doun can ryn,
> Quhare Tantalus nakit full thristy stude,
> And yit the water yede abone his chyn;
> Thouch he gapit thare wald na drop cum in,
> Quhen he dulkit the water wald descend;
> Thus gat he noucht his thrist to slake no mend.
>
> Before his face ane apill hang also
> Fast at his mouth apon a tolter threde,
> Quhen he gapit it rokkit to and fro
> And fled, as it refusit hym to fede :
> Than Orpheus had reuth of his grete nede
> Tuke out his harp, and fast on it can clink,
> The water stude, and Tantalus gat drink."

*The next object which presents itself in his progress, is
Theseus preyed on by a " grisely gripe " or vulture, which
also excites the compassion of* Orpheus.   *On entering " hy-
douse hellis house," he exclaims—*

> " O dolly place and groundles depe dungeoun !
> Furnes of fyre, with stynk intollerable,
> Pit of dispair, wythout remissioun,
> · Thy mete venym, thy drynk is poysonable,
> Thy grete panis to compt vnnowmerabil ;
> Quhat creature cummys to duel in the
> Is ay deyand, and newir more may dee ! "

*We must pass over the different personages whom he here
beholds, in order to make room for the description of his
meeting with* Eurydice.

" Syn nethir mare he went quhare Pluto was
And Proserpine, and thiderward he drewe,
Ay playand on his harpe as he coud pas,
Till at the last Eurydices he knewe;
Lene and dedelike pitouse and pale of hewe,
Rycht warsch and wan, and walowit as a wede,
Hir lily lyre was lyke vnto the lede.

Quod he, ' My lady lele, and my delyte,
Full wa is me, to se yow changit thus !
Quhare is thy rude as rose with chekis quhite ?
Thy cristall eyne with blenkis amorouse ?
Thi lippis rede, to kis deliciouse ? '—
Qnod scho, ' As now I dar noucht tell, perfay,
Bot ye sall wit the cause ane other day.' "

*The present tale has been justly admired no less for the
harmony of its versification, than for the beautiful description
which it contains of Fairy-land.  [The following is its outline : Heurodis, queen of Winchester, unwarily falling
asleep one day under an ymp tree in the orchard of the palace,
dreams that two knights appear to her, who request her to go
with them and speak with their king.  On her refusal, the
king of Faery comes in person with a thousand knights, and
carries her off.  He shows her his palace, and then brings
her home.  After this, he orders her, under a dreadful penalty,
to meet him next morning under the ymp tree.  Orfeo
and a thousand knights surround the tree to protect her,
but she is suddenly snatched away from their sight.  Orfeo,
in despair, abandons his throne and retires to the wilderness,
where he solaces himself with his harp.  The wild beasts of
the forest, and even the birds, are charmed with his melody.
Sometimes he sees the king of Faery hunting with his attendants.  One day he observes sixty ladies on horseback hawking by the river.  Amongst them he recognises his lost queen,
and he then determines to follow the party and rescue her
if possible.  The cavalcade disappear in a cleft of a rock,
into which he follows them.  After proceeding for several
miles, he at last finds himself in a beautiful country, in
which is a castle with walls clear as crystal.  Orfeo makes
his way into the palace, and so charms the king with his
melody that he gives him back his wife.  They return to*

*Winchester, where they are received with great rejoicings,
and afterwards reign in peace and happiness.*]

*The reader will perceive that in this story the catastrophe
is different; but, if less pathetic, it certainly is more agree-
able than that of the classical fiction.*

[*Of this beautiful fairy-romance poem three Manuscripts
exist. The present copy is taken from the oldest version,
which exists in the* AUCHINLECK MANUSCRIPT, *preserved
in the* Advocates' Library.[1] *The period of its composition was probably the beginning of the* FOURTEENTH CEN-
TURY, *as the volume which contains it was apparently
written during the minority of* Edward III. *Another copy
is to be found in a Manuscript in the* Harleian Collection,[2]
*from which it was published by* Ritson.[3] *As the first
twenty-four lines are wanting in the* Auchinleck MS.,—*a
leaf immediately before the line,*

" Orfeo was a king,"

*having been torn out for the sake of the illumination,—these
are here supplied from the* Harleian MS. *It is somewhat
remarkable that the first twenty-two of these correspond almost exactly with the opening lines in the English version
of the* Lai le Freine de Marie de France, *as given in*
Weber's Metrical Romances, *vol.* I. *p.* 357. *The third
copy of this tale exists in MS.* Ashmole, No. 61, *an account
of which is given in the Appendix. This copy agrees rather
closely with the* Auchinleck MS., *but it is supposed not to be
more ancient than the time of* Henry VI.[4]]

---

[1] Fol. 300ᵃ-303ᵃ.                    [2] MS. Harl., No. 3810.
[3] Ancient English Metrical Romances, vol. ii. pp. 248-269, 1802.
[4] [As showing how generally this tale was known in Scotland, Professor
Child inserts in his Collection of Ballads, Part i. p. 215, a fragment of it
in the dialect of Shetland as recited by Andrew Coutts, an old man in the
island of Unst.]

# Orfeo and Heurodis.

[WE redyn ofte and fynde ywryte,
    As Clerkes don us to wyte,
The layes that ben of harpyng
Ben yfounde of frely thing.
Sum ben of wele and sum of wo,        5
And sum of joy and merthe also,
Sum of trechery and sum of gyle,
And sum of happes, that fallen by whyle,
Sum of bourdys and sum of rybaudry,
And sum ther ben of the feyre.        10
Off alle thing that men may se
Mooste o lowe forsothe they be.
In Brytain this layes arne ywryte,
Furst yfounde and forthe ygete,
Of aventures that fillen by dayes,        15
Wherof Brytouns made her layes,
When they myght owher heryn
Of aventures that ther weryn,
They toke her harpys with game
Maden layes and zaf it name.        20
Of aventures that han befalle,
Y can sum telle, bot nought all.
Herken, lordyngs that ben trewe,
And Y wol zou telle of Sir Orphewe.]
Orfeo was a king,        25
In Inglond an heighe lording,
A stalworth man and hardi bo,
Large and curteys, he was also ;

His fader was comen of king Pluto,
And his moder of [quene] Juno,     30
That sum time were as godes y-hold,
For auentours that thai dede and told.
[Orpheo most of ony thing
Lovede the gle of harpyng;
Syker was euery gode harpoure     35
Of hym to haue moche honour.
Hymself loved for to harpe
And layde theron his wittes scharpe.
He lernyd so, ther nothing was
A better harper in no plas.     40
In the world was neuer man born
That euer Orpheo sat biforn,
And he mygt of his harpyng her,
He schulde thinke that he wer
In one of the joys of paradys,     45
Suche joy and melody in his harping is.]
This king soiurnd in Traciens,
That was a cite of noble defens,
For Winchester was cleped tho
Traciens, withouten no:     50
The king hadde a quen of priis,
That was y-cleped dame Herodis,
The fairest leuedi for the nones
That might gon on bodi and bones,
Ful of loue and of godenisse,     55
Ac no man may telle hir fairnisse.
    ¶ Bifel so in the comessing of May,
When miri and hot is the day,
And oway beth winter schours,
And eueri feld is ful of flours,     60
And blosme breme on eueri bough,
Ouer al wexeth miri anough,
This ich quen dame Heurodis,
Tok to maidens of priis,
And went in an vndren tide     65
To play bi an orchard side,

L. 30. 'king,' MS.         L. 64. 'to,' MS. p. 'two.'

To se the floures sprede and spring,
And to here the foules sing:
Thai sett hem doun al thre,
Vnder a fair ympe tre,                                    70
And wel sone this fair quene,
Fel on slepe opon the grene:
The maidens durst hir nought awake,
Bot lete hir ligge and rest take,
So sche slepe til after none,                            75
That vnder tide was al y-done;
Ac so sone as sche gan awake,
Sche crid and lothli bere gan make;
Sche froted hir honden and hir fet,
And crached hir visage, [till] it bled wete,    80
Hir riche robe hye al torett,
And was reneyd out of hir witt:
The tvo maidens hir biside,
No durst with hir no leng abide,
Bot ourn to the palays ful right,                        85
And told bothe squier and knight,
That her quen awede wold,
And bad hem go and hir at hold.
Knightes vrn, and leuedis also,
Damisels sexti and mo,                                   90
In the orchard to the quen hye come,
And her vp in her armes nome,
And brought hir to bed atte last,
And held hir there fine fast;
Ac euer sche held in o cri,                              95
And wold vp and owy.
When Orfeo herd that tiding,
Neuer him nas wers for no thing;
He come with knightes tene,
To chaumber right bifor the quene,                      100
And biheld, and seyd with grete pite:
" O lef liif, what is te?
That euer ȝete hast ben so stille,
And now gredest wonder schille!
Thi bodi, that was so white ycore,                       105
With thine nailes is al to-tore!

Allas! thi rode, that was so red,
Is as wan as thou were ded!
And also thine fingres smale,
Beth al blodi and al pale!　　　　　　　110
Allas! thi louesum eyghen to
Loketh so man doth on his fo;
A dame, Ich biseche merci!
Lete ben al this reweful cri,
And tel me, what the is, and hou,　　　115
And what thing may the help now!"
Tho lay sche stille atte last,
And gan to wepe swithe fast,
And seyd thus the king to,
"Allas! mi lord, sir Orfeo!　　　　　　120
Seththen we first togider were,
Ones wroth neuer we nere,
Bot euer Ich haue y-loued the,
As mi liif, and so thou me,
Ac now we mot delen ato,　　　　　　125
Do thi best, for Y mot go."
"Allas!" quath he, "forlorn Ich am!
Whider wiltow go and to wham?
Whider thou gost, Ichil with the,
And whider Y go, thou schalt with me."　130
"Nay, nay, sir, that nought nis,
Ichil the telle al hou it is:
As Ich lay this vnder tide,
And slepe vnder our orchard side,
Ther come to me to fair knightes　　135
Wele y-armed al to rightes,
And bad me comen an heighing,
And speke with her lord the king.
And Ich answerd at wordes bold,
Y durst nought, no Y nold:　　　　　140
Thai priked oghain as thai might driue,
Tho com her king, al so bliue,
With an hundred knightes and mo,
And damissels an hundred also;
Al on snowe-white stedes,　　　　　145
As white as milke were her wedes.

Y no seighe neuer ȝete bifore  
So fair creatours ycore;  
The king hadde a croun on hed,  
It nas of siluer, no of gold red,      150  
Ac it was of a precious ston;  
As bright as the sonne it schon:  
And as son as he to me cam,  
Wold Ich, nold Ich, he me nam,  
And made me with him ride,      155  
Opon a palfray bi his side,  
And brought me to his palays,  
Wele atird in ich ways;  
And schewed me castels and tours,  
Riuers, forestes, frith with flours;      160  
And his riche stedes ichon,  
And seththen me brought oȝain hom,  
In to our owhen orchard,  
And said to me thus afterward:  
'Loke, dame! to morwe thatow be      165  
Right here vnder this ympe tre;  
And than thou schalt with ous go,  
And liue with ous euer mo,  
And ȝif thou makest ous y-let,  
Where thou be, thou worst y-fet,      170  
And to-tore thine limes al,  
That nothing help the no schal,  
And thei thou best so to-torn,  
Ȝete thou worst with ous y-born.'"  
   ¶ When king Orfeo herd this cas,      175  
"Owe!" quath he, "allas! allas!  
Leuer me were to lete mi liif,  
Than thus to lese the quen mi wiif!"  
He asked conseyl at ich man,  
Ac no man him help no can.      180  
Amorwe the vnder tide is come,  
And Orfeo hath his armes y-nome,  
And wele ten hundred knightes with him,  
Ich y-armed stout and grim;  
And with the quen wenten he,      185  
Right vnto that ympe tre:

Thai made scheltrom in ich aside,
And sayd thai wold there abide,
And dye ther euerichon,
Er the quen schuld from hem gon.                     190
Ac ȝete amiddes hem ful right,
The quen was oway y-tvight,
With fairi forth y-nome,
Men wist neuer wher sche was bicome.
Tho was ther criing, wepe and wo!                    195
The king in to his chaumber is go,
And oft swoned opon the ston,
And made swiche diol and swiche mon,
That neighe his liif was y-spent;
Ther was no amendement.                              200
He cleped togider his barouns,
Erls, lordes of renouns;
And when thai al y-comen were,
" Lordinges," he said, "bifor ȝou here
Ich ordainy min heighe steward                       205
To wite mi kingdom afterward,
In mi stede ben he schal,
To kepe mi londes ouer al,
For now Ichaue mi quen y-lore,
The fairest leuedi that euer was bore.               210
Neuer eft Y nil no woman se,
Into wildernes Ichil te,
And liue ther euer more
With wilde bestes in holtes hore.
And when ȝe vnderstond that Y be spent,              215
Make ȝou than a parlement,
And chese ȝou a newe king:
Now doth ȝour best with al mi thing."
    ¶ Tho was ther wepeing in the halle
And grete cri among hem alle;                        220
Vnnethe might old or ȝong
For wepeing speke a word with tong.
Thai kneled adoun al yfere,
And praid him, ȝif his wille were,
That he no schuld nought fram hem go.                225
" Do way!" quath he, "it schal be so."

Al his kingdom he forsoke,
Bot a sclauin on him he toke;
He ne hadde kirtel, no hode,
Schert, non other gode.                          230
Bot his harp he tok algate,
And dede him barfot out atte ʒate:
No man most with him go.
Oway! what ther was wepe and wo,
When he, that hadde ben king with croun,         235
Went so pouerlich out of toun!
Thurch wode, and ouer heth,
Into the wildernes he geth,
Nothing he fint that him is ays,
Bot euer he liueth in gret malais.               240
He, that hadde y-werd the fowe and griis,
And on bed the purper biis,
Now on hard hethe he lith,
With leues and gresse he him writh:
He, that hadde castels, and tours,               245
Riuer, forest, frith with flours;
Now, thei it commenci to snewe and frese,
This king mot make his bed in mese.
He that had y-had knightes of priis
Bifor him kneland, and leuedis,                  250
Now seth he no thing that him liketh,
Bot wilde wormes bi him striketh.
He, that had y-had plente
Of mete and drink, of ich deynte,
Now may he al day digge and wrote,               255
Er he finde his fille of rote.
In somer he liueth bi wild frut,
And berren, bot gode lite;
In winter may he no thing finde,
Bot rote, grases, and the rinde.                 260
Al his bodi was oway duine,
For missays, and al to-chine.
Lord! who may telle the sore,
This king sufferd ten ʒere and more!
His here of his berd, blac and rowe,             265
To his girdel-stede was growe;

His harp, whereon was al his gle,
He hidde in an holwe tre;
And, when the weder was clere and bright,
He toke his harp to him wel right,                    270
And harped at his owhen wille;
Into alle the wode the soun gan schille,
That alle the wilde bestes that ther beth,
For ioie abouten him thai teth;
And alle the foules that ther were              275
Come and sete on ich a brere;
To here his harping a-fine,
So miche melody was therin.
And when he his harping lete wold,
No best bi him abide nold.                        280
    ¶ He might se'him bisides
Oft in hot vnder tides
The king o Fairi with his rout,
Com to hunt him al about,
With dun cri and bloweing,                       285
And houndes also with him berking.
Ac no best thai no nome,
No neuer he nist whider-thai bicome.
And other while he might him se
As a gret ost bi him te,                             290
Wele atourned ten hundred knightes,
Ich y-armed to his rightes;
Of contenaunce stout and fers,
With mani desplaid baners;
And ich his swerd y-drawe hold,              295
Ac neuer he nist whider thai wold.
And other while he seighe other thing;
Knightes and leuedis com daunceing
In queynt atire gisely,
Queynt pas, and softly:                             300
Tabours and trimpes ӡede hem bi,
And al maner menstraci.
    ¶ And on a day he seighe him biside
Sexti leuedis on hors ride,
Gentil and iolif, as brid on ris,                   305
Nought o man amonges hem ther nis;

And ich a faucoun on hond bere,
And riden on haukin bi o riuere,
Of game thai founde wel gode haunt,
Maulardes, hayroun and cormeraunt;                310
The foules of the water ariseth,
The faucouns hem wele deuiseth,
Ich faucoun his pray slough.
That seighe Orfeo, and lough.
"Parfay," quath he, "ther is fair game!            315
Thider Ichil bi Godes name,
Ich was y-won swiche werk to se."
He aros, and thider gan te.
To a leuedi he was ycome,
Biheld, and hath wele vndernome,                  320
And seth, bi al thing, that it is
His owhen quen dam Heurodis.
Ȝern he biheld hir, and sche him eke,
Ac noither to other a word no speke:
For messais, that sche on him seighe,             325
That had ben so riche and so heighe,
The teres fel out of her eighe;
The other leuedis this y-seighe,
And maked hir oway to ride,
Sche most with him no lenger abide.               330
"Allas!" quath he, "now me is wo!
Whi nil deth now me slo!
Allas! wreche, that Y no might
Dye now, after this sight!
Allas! to long last mi liif,                      335
When Y no dar nought with mi wiif,
No hye to me, o word speke.
Allas! whi nil min hert breke!
Parfay," quath he, "tide wat bitide,
Whider so this leuedis ride,                      340
The selue way Ichil streche,
Of liif, no deth, me no reche."
His sclauain he dede on, al so spac,
And henge his harp opon his bac,
And had wel gode wil to gon,                      345
He no spard noither stub no ston.
                    I

In at a roche the leuedis rideth,
And he after, and nought abideth;
When he was in the roche y-go,
Wele thre mile, other mo,                          350
He com in to a fair cuntray,
As bright so sonne on somers day,
Smothe, and plain, and al grene,
Hille, no dale, was ther non ysene.
Amidde the lond a castel he sighe,                 355
Riche, and real, and wonder heighe;
Al the vtmast wal
Was clere and schine as cristal.
An hundred tours ther were about,
Degiselich and bataild stout;                      360
The butras com out of the diche,
Of rede gold y-arched riche;
The bonsour was auowed al
Of ich maner diuers animal.
Within ther wer wide wones                         365
Al of precious stones.
The werst piler on to biholde,
Was al of burnist gold.
Al that lond was euer light,
For when it schuld be therk and night,             370
The riche stones light gonne,
As bright as doth at none the sonne.'
No man may telle, no thenche in thought,
The riche werk that ther was wrought,
Bi al thing, him think that it is                  375
The proude court of paradis.
In this castel the leuedis alight,
He wold in after, ʒif he might.
    ¶ Orfeo knokketh atte gate,
The porter was redi therate,                       380
And asked, what he wold haue y-do?
" Parfay," quath he, "Icham a minstrel, lo!
To solas thi lord with my gle,
ʒif his swete wille be."
The porter vndede the ʒate anon                    385
And lete him into the castel gon.

¶ Than he gan bihold about al,
And seighe ful liggeand within the wal
Of folk, that were thider y-brought,
And thought dede and nere nought:                    390
Sum stode withouten hade,
And sum non armes nade,
And sum thurch the bodi hadde wounde,
And sum lay wode y-bounde,
And sum armed on hors sete,                          395
And sum astrangled as thai ete,
And sum were in water adreynt,
And sum with fire al forschreynt ;
Wiues ther lay on child bedde,
Sum ded, and sum awedde ;                            400
And wonder fele ther lay bisides,
Right as thai slepe her vndertides ;
Eche was thus in this warld y-nome,
With fairi thider y-come.
Ther he seighe his owhen wiif,                       405
Dame Heurodis his liif liif
Slepe vnder an ympe tre ;
Bi her clothes he knewe that it was [s]he.
¶ And when he hadde bihold this meruails alle,
He went in to the kinges halle.                      410
Than seighe he ther a semly sight,
A tabernacle blisseful and bright,
Therin her maister king sete,
And her quen fair and swete.
Her crounes, her clothes schine so bright,           415
That vnnethe bihold he hem might.
When he hadde biholden al that thing,
He kneled adoun bifor the king :
"O Lord," he seyd, " ʒif it thi wille were,
Mi menstraci thou schust y-here."                    420
The king answerd, "What man artow,
That art hider ycomen now ?
Ich, no non that is with me,
No sent neuer after the,

Ll. 408 and 446. 'he' p. 'she,' MS.

Seththen that ich here regni gan,     425
Y no fond [neuer] so folehardi man,
That hider to ous durst wende,
Bot that Ichim wold of-sende."
"Lord," quath he, "trowe ful wel,
Y nam bot a pouer menstrel,     430
And, sir, it is the maner of ous
To seche mani a lordes hous;
Thei we nought welcom no be,
Ʒete we mot proferi forth our gle."
    ¶ Bifor the king he sat adoun     435
And tok his harp so miri of soun,
And tempreth his harp, as he wele can,
And blisseful notes he ther gan,
That al that in the palays were,
Com to him for to here,     440
And liggeth adoun to his fete,
Hem thenketh his melody so swete.
The king herkneth, and sitt full stille,
To here his gle he hath gode wille;
Gode bourde he hadde of his gle,     445
The riche quen al so hadde [s]he;
When he hadde stint his harping,
Than seyd to him the king:
"Menstrel, me liketh wele thi gle,
Now aske of me what it be,     450
Largelich Ichil the pay,
Now speke and tow might asay."
"Sir," he seyd, "Ich biseche the,
Thatow woldest ʒiue me
That ich leuedi bright on ble,     455
That slepeth vnder the ympe tre."
"Nay," quath the king, "that nought nere!
A sori couple of ʒou it were,
For thou art lene, rowe and blac,
And sche is louesum withouten lac.     460
A lothlich thing it were forthi,
To sen hir in thi compayni."
    ¶ "O sir," he seyd, "gentil king,
Ʒete were it a wele fouler thing,

To here a lesing of thi mouthe,                     465
So, sir, as ӡe seyd nouthe,
What Ich wold aski, haue Y schold,
And nedes thou most thi word hold."
The king seyd, " Seththen it is so,
Take hir bi the hond, and go.                       470
Of hir Ichil thatow be blithe."
He knelyd adoun, and thonked him swithe,
His wiif he tok bi the hond
And dede him swithe out of that lond,
And went him out of that thede,                     475
Right as he come the way he ӡede.
So long he hath the way ynome,
To Winchester he is ycome,
That was his owhen cite ;
Ac no man knewe that it was he.                     480
No forther than the tounes ende,
For knoweleche ne durst wende.
Bot with a begger y-bilt ful narwe,
Ther he tok his herbarwe
To him and to his owhen wiif,                       485
As a minstrel of pouer liif,
And asked tidinges of that lond,
And who the kingdom held in hond.
The pouer begger in his cote
Told him euerich a grot ;                           490
Hou her quen was stole owy,
Ten ӡer gon, with fairy,
And hou her king in exile ӡede,
Bot no man niste in wiche thede,
And hou the steward the lond gan hold,              495
And other mani thinges him told.
   ¶ A morwe oӡain none tide
He maked his wiif ther abide,
The beggers clothes he borwed anon,
And heng his harp his rigge opon,                   500
And went him in to that cite,
That men might him bihold and se.
Erls, and barouns bold,
Buriays, and leuedis, him gan bihold.

"Lo!" thai seyd, "swiche a man!                   505
Hou long the here hongeth him opan!
Lo! hou his berd hongeth to his kne!
He is yclongen al so a tre!"
And as he ȝede in the strete,
With his steward he gan mete,                    510
And loude he sett on him a crie,
"Sir steward," he seyd, "merci!
Icham an harpour of hethenisse,
Help me now in this distresse!"
The steward seyd, "Com with me, come,            515
Of that Ichaue thou schalt haue some.
Euerich gode harpour is welcom me to
For mi lordes loue, sir Orfeo."
      ¶ In the castel the steward sat atte mete,
And mani lording was bi him sete.                520
Ther were trompour and tabourers,
Harpours fele and crouders,
Miche melody thei maked alle,
And Orfeo sat stille in the halle
And herkneth.   When thai ben al stille,         525
He toke his harp and tempred schille,
The blissfulest notes he harped there,
That euer ani man y-herd with ere:
Ich man liked wele his gle;
The steward biheld and gan y-se,                 530
And knewe the harp als bliue;
"Menstrel," he seyd, "so mot thou thriue,
Where hadestow this harp, and hou?
Y pray that thou me telle now."
      ¶ "Lord," quath he, "in vncouthe thede,     535
Thurch a wildernes as Y ȝede,
Ther Y founde in a dale
With lyouns a man to-torn smale,
And wolues him frete with teth so scharp;
Bi him Y fond this ich harp;                     540
Wele ten ȝere it is ygo."
"O!" quath the steward, "now me is wo!
That was mi lord, sir Orfeo!
Allas! wreche, what schal Y do,

That haue swiche a lord y-lore! 545
Away, that Ich was y-bore!
That him was so hard grace y-ȝarked,
And so vile deth y-marked!"
Adoun he fel aswon to grounde,
His barouns him tok vp in that stounde, 550
And telleth him hou it geth,
It nis no bot of manes deth.
  ¶ King Orfeo knewe wele bithan,
His steward was a trewe man,
And loued him, as he aught to do, 555
And stont vp, and seyt thus: " Lo,
Steward, herkne now this thing,
Ȝif Ich were Orfeo the king,
And hadde y-suffred ful ȝore,
In wildernisse miche sore; 560
And hadde y-won mi quen owy
Out of the lond of Fairy,
And hadde ybrought the leuedi hende
Right here to the tounes ende,
And with a begger her in y-nome, 565
And were miself hider y-come,
Pouerlich to the thus stille,
For to asay thi gode wille;
And Ich founde the thus trewe,
Thou no schust it neuer rewe: 570
Sikerlich for loue, or ay
Thou schust be king after mi day,
And ȝif thou of mi deth hadest ben blithe,
Thou schust ben voided al so swithe."
  ¶ Tho al tho that therin sete, 575
That it was king Orfeo vnderȝete,
And the steward him wele knewe,
Ouer and ouer the bord he threwe,
And fel adoun to his fet;
So dede euerich lord that ther sete, 580
And al thai seyd at o criing:
" Ȝe beth our lord, sir, and our king!"
Glad thai were of his liue,
To chaumber thai ladde him als bliue,

And bathed him and schaued his berd,  585
And tired him as a king apert.
And seththen with gret processioun,
Thai brought the quen in to that toun
With al maner menstraci.
Lord, ther was grete melody!  590
For ioie thai wepe with her eighe,
That hem so sounde y-comen seighe.
Now king Orfeo newe coround is,
And his quen dame Heurodis;
And liued long afterward,  595
And seththen was king the steward.
Harpours in Bretaine after than
Herd hou this meruaile bigan,
And made herof a lay of gode likeing,
And nempned it after the king:  600
That lay Orfeo is y-hote,
Gode is the lay, swete is the note.
Thus com sir Orfeo out of his care;
God graunt ous alle wele to fare!  Amen.


**EXPLICIT.**

# THOMAS OF ERSYLDOUNE
## AND THE QUENE OF ELF-LAND

V.

# THOMAS OF ERSYLDOUNE
# AND THE QUENE OF ELF-LAND.

---

*THERE are, perhaps, few poems now extant that may so
well as the following beautiful and interesting tale of* Fairy
Land, *exemplify the practice of those whose employment it
was to chaunt or rehearse the effusions of the Minstrels.
This legend of* Thomas of Ersyldoune, *in its present state,
evidently owes much to that facility and readiness of composition, which at times might enable them to enlarge and
amplify the productions of others, in order to suit existing
circumstances, and serve for the amusement of their auditors.
The exordium is professedly the work of an English reciter,
anxious to draw the attention of the assembled company to
the ' mervelles' and predictions of which he was about to tell.
Nor is it less evident, but that the prophetick parts, however
obscure their object may now be, or uncertain from what
materials they were constructed, were either added at a subsequent period, or so altered as to be instrumental to some
political purpose. Of the poems or prophecies attributed to*
Thomas the Rhymer, *we unfortunately have none but
what are preserved in English manuscripts, in which they
have lost much of their individuality ; the orthography being
uniformly accommodated to that of the transcriber.*

*This poem is preserved in five ancient manuscripts ; each
of them in a state more or less mutilated, and varying in no*

*inconsiderable degree from the other. A portion of it was
first printed in the* Border Minstrelsy, *from the fragment
in the* British Museum, *among the* Cotton MSS.[1]
*One which* Mr Jamieson *adopted in his Collection of*
Popular Ballads and Songs, *was carefully decyphered
from a volume of no ordinary curiosity, in the* University
Library, Cambridge,[2] *written in a very illegible hand,
about the middle of the* 15th *century. This MS. is valuable as containing several stanzas which are wanting in the
others. The third and fourth are preserved in the* British
Museum, *and are the* Lansdowne MS., No. 792, *and the*
Sloane MS., No. 2578. *The present text is taken from the*
Thornton MS., *preserved in the* Cathedral Library of
Lincoln, *before referred to (p. 83). As there are several
places where gaps occur, these are filled up by lines taken
from the* Cambridge *and* Lansdowne MSS. *The words
or lines thus supplied are distinguished by being printed
within brackets.*

*After the copious illustrations of this poem by its former
Editors, in works which either are, or ought to be, in the
hands of every possessor of this collection, little farther can
be required. The reader will perceive the great beauty of
the descriptive parts, and the fine vein of imagination that
runs through nearly the whole of the First Fytt. It is indeed
impossible to read this and suppose that the poem could have
been written by any other than* Thomas *himself, however
much it may have suffered by subsequent interpolation. "In
the introduction to the prophecies," as* Mr Jamieson *has
well observed, "there is so much more fancy and elegance
than in the prophecies themselves, that they can hardly be
supposed to be the composition of the same person. Indeed,
the internal evidence to the contrary almost amounts to a proof
that they are not, and that the romance itself was of Scotish
origin, although no indubitably Scotish copy is known to be
in existence." "It is remarkable," Mr J. continues, "that*

---

[1] Cotton MSS. Vitellius. E. x., written on paper, consisting of 242 leaves,
much injured by fire.

[2] Bishop More's MSS. Ff. v. 48, written on paper of 140 leaves, dating
about the middle of the 15th century.

*in all the three copies, the poet begins the story in the* first
person, *and seems disposed to tell the incidents as if they
had really happened to himself:*"

> St. 1. " As *I me* went this Andyrs day,
>     Fast on *my* way making *my* mone," &c.

> St. 3. " Alle in a longyng as *I* lay,
>     Vnderneth a semely tre,
>     Saw *I* wher a lady gay,
>     Came ridand ouer a lonely le," &c.

" *And although he afterwards, awkwardly and unnaturally
enough, speaks of* Thomas *as a third person, yet even then
he seems to insinuate that the story, which he is garbling,
was told by another before him :*

> St. 14. " And certenly, *as the story sayes,*
>     He hir mette at Eldyn tre."

*If he assumes the mask with a bad grace here, he shows
still less address when he drops it again at stanza 52 of the
First Fitt :*

> " Ther was revell, game, and play,
>     More than I yow say, pardye,
> Till hit fell upon a day,
>     *My* lufty lady seid to *me :*

> Busk *the, Thomas,* for *thu* most gon ;
>     For here no longer mayst *thu* be,
> Hye *the* fast, with mode and mone ;
>     I shall *the* bryng to Eldyn tre."

*Would it not be pardonable, from such instances as these, to
suppose it at least probable that* Thomas Rymour *was really
the original author of this romance ; and that, in order to
give a sanction to his predictions, which seem all to have been
calculated, in one way or other, for the service of his country,
he pretended to an intercourse with the Queen of Elfland, as
Numa Pompilius did with the nymph Egeria ?  Such an
intercourse, in the days of True* Thomas, *was accounted
neither unnatural nor uncommon.*" [1]

*[The Huntly bank on which* Thomas *is said to have met*

---

[1] Popular Ballads, vol. ii. p. 5, with which the numbers of the stanzas
quoted above correspond.

*the* Queen of Faery *is situated on the slope of the eastmost of the three Eildon Hills, a little more than a mile from Melrose. Not far distant was the Eildon Tree, the site of which is indicated by a large stone, called the Eildon Tree Stone.* Sir Walter Scott *gave to a picturesque ravine at the base of the western Eildon Hill the name of the Rhymer's Glen, which, however, is about two miles distant from the Eildon Tree. This glen was purchased by* Sir Walter, *and by calling it after the Rhymer, he added some of the romance of the following tale to his estate of Abbotsford.* Sir Walter *by his publication of the ancient metrical version of* Sir Tristrem, *which he attributed to* Thomas of Ersyldoune, *gave a degree of interest to the character of* Thomas, *which as being one of the earliest of our poets he might not otherwise have enjoyed.*[1]]

*With respect to the prophetick character of* Thomas *we have sufficient evidence in the testimony of such early writers as* Barbour *and* Wyntown. *The latter, in describing the battle of Kylblene, in the year* 1335, *says:*

> " Off this fycht qwhilum spak Thomas
> Off Ersyldowne, that sayd in derne
> Thare suld mete stalwartly stark and sterne :
> He sayd it in his prophecy ;
> Bot, how he wyst it, wes ferly." [2]

*—but whether or not this be one of the predictions contained in the following poem is uncertain.—The prophetick parts of which might afford ample scope for illustration, were this the object of the Editor; though, indeed, it would be no easy matter to reconcile them with any degree of satisfaction to the various national events that seem to have been foretold.*

---

[1] [The claim of Ersyldoune to the authorship of Sir Tristrem is now considered doubtful, as that romance is known to exist in several European languages before the time when he flourished.]

[2] Wyntoun, B. viii. c. 31.

## V.

# 𝕮omas off 𝕰rsselvoune.

LYSTYNS, lordyngs, bothe grete and smale,
    And takis gude tente what I will saye:
I sall ȝow telle als trewe a tale,
    Als euer was herde by nyghte or daye:
And the maste meruelle fforowttyn naye,         5
    That euer was herde by-fore or syene,
And therfore pristly I ȝow praye,
    That ȝe will of ȝoure talkyng blyne.
It es an harde thyng for to [lere]
    Of doghety dedis that hase bene done;     10
Of felle feghtyngs and batells sere;
    And how that thir knyghtis hase wonne thair schone.
Bot Jhesu Crist, that syttis in trone,
    Safe Ynglysche men bothe ferre and nere;
And I sall telle ȝow tyte and sone,         15
    Of battells donne sythen many a ȝere;
And of batells that done sall bee;
    In whate place, and howe and where;
And wha sall hafe the heghere gree;
    And whethir partye sall hafe the werre;     20
Wha sall takk the flyghte and flee;
    And wha sall dye, and byleue, thare:
Bot Jhesu Crist, that dyed on tre,
    Saue Inglysche mene whareso thay fare.

## '𝕿𝖍𝖊 𝕱𝖞𝖗𝖘𝖙 𝕱𝖞𝖙�™.'

A LS I me wente this endres daye,
    Ffull faste in mynd makand my mone,
In a mery mornynge of Maye,
    By Huntle bankkes my selfe allone.

I herde the jaye, and the throstylle cokke,     5
    The mawys menyde of hir songe,
The wodewale beryde als a belle,
    That alle the wode abowte me ronge.

Allone in longynge, thus als I laye,
    Vndre-nethe a semely tre,     10
[Saw I] whare a lady gaye,
    [Came ridand] ouer a longe lee.

If I suld sytt to domesdaye,
    With my tonge, to wrobbe and wrye,
Certanely that lady gaye,     15
    Neuer bese scho askryede for mee.

Hir palfraye was a dappill graye;
    Swylke one ne saghe I neuer none:
Als dose the sonne, on someres daye,
    That faire lady hir selfe scho schone.     20

Hir selle it was of roelle bone;
    Ffull semely was that syghte to see!
Stefly sett with precyous stone,
    And compaste all with crapotee.

Stones of oryente grete plente;     25
    Hir hare abowte hir hede it hange;
Scho rade ouer that lange lee,
    A whylle scho blewe, a-nother scho sange.

L. 5. Instead of the 'throstylle cokke,' the Cambr. MS. simply reads 'the
throstelle,' which thus serves as the proper rhyme to 'belle.'

Hir garthes of nobyll sylke thay were ;
　　The bukylls were of berelle stone ;　　　　30
Hir steraps were of crystalle clere,
　　And all with perelle ouer-by-gone.

Hir payetrelle was of irale fyne ;
　　Hir cropoure was of orphare ;
And als clere golde hir brydill it schone ;　　35
　　One aythir syde hange bellys three.

[Scho led thre grehoundis in a leeshe ;]
　　And seuen raches by hir thay rone ;—
Scho bare an horne abowte hir halse ;
　　And vndir hir belte full many a flone.　　40

Thomas laye and sawe that syghte,
　　Vndir-nethe ane semly tree ;
He sayd, " ʒone es Marye most of myghte,
　　That bare that childe that dyede for mee.

Bot if I speke with ʒone lady bryghte,　　　45
　　I hope myn herte will bryste in three ;
Now sall I go with all my myghte,
　　Hir for to mete at Eldoune tree."

Thomas rathely vpe he rase,
　　And he rane ouer that mountayne hye ;　　50
Gyff it be als the storye sayes,
　　He hir mette at Eldone tree.

He knelyde down appon his knee,
　　Vndir-nethe that grenwode spraye :—
And sayd, " lufly ladye ! rewe one mee ;　　55
　　Qwene of heuen, als thou wele maye."

Than spake that lady milde of thoghte :—
　　" Thomas, late swylke wordes bee ;
Qwene of heuenne, ne am I noghte,
　　Ffor I tuke neuer so heghe degre.　　　60

---

L. 37. is omitted in the MS.　In the Cambr. MS. this stanza is unneces-
sarily enlarged into eight lines.

Bote I ame of ane other countree,
  If I be payrelde moste of prysse;
I ryde aftyre this wylde fee,
  My raches rynnys at my devyse."

" If thou be parelde moste of prysse,      65
  And here rydis thus in thy folye,
Of lufe, lady, als thou erte wysse,
  Thou gyffe me leue to lye the bye."

Scho sayde, "thou man, that ware folye;
  I praye the, Thomas, thou lat me bee;     70
Ffor I saye the full sekirlye,
  That synne will for-doo all my beaute."

" Now, lufly ladye, rewe on mee,
  And I will euer more with the duelle;
Here my trouthe I [plyghte to thee.]     75
  Wethir thou will in heuen or helle."

" Mane of molde, thou will me marre,
  Bot ȝitt thou sall hafe all thy will;
And trowe it wele, thou chewys the werre,
  Ffor alle my beaute will thou spylle."     80

Down thane lyghte that lady bryghte,
  Vndir-nethe that grenewode spraye;
And, als the storye tellis full ryghte,
  Seuene sythis by hir he laye.

Scho sayd, "mane, the lykes thy playe:     85
  What byrde in boure may delle with the?
Thou merrys me all this longe daye,
  I pray the, Thomas, late me bee."

Thomas stode wpe in that stede,
  And he by-helde that lady gaye;     90
Hir hare it hange all ouer hir hede,
  Hir eghne semede owte, that are were graye.

L. 75. ' will the plyghte.' MS. Linc.

K

And all the riche clothynge was a-waye,
   That he byfore sawe in that stede;
Hir a schanke blake, hir other graye,                    95
   And all hir body lyke the lede.

Thomas laye, and sawe that syghte,
   Vndir-nethe that grenewod tree.

Than sayd Thomas, "allas! allas!
   In faythe this es a dullfull syghte,                    100
How arte thou fadyde thus in the face,
   That schane by-fore als the sonne so bryghte!"

[On euery syde he lokyde abowete,
   He sau he myght no whare fle;
Sche woxe so grym and so stoute,                    105
   The dewyll he wende she had be.

In the name of the Trynite,
   He coniuryde here anon right,
That she sholde not come hym nere,
   But wende away of his syght.                    110

She said, "Thomas, this is no nede,
   For fende of hell am I none;
For the now am I grete desese,
   And suffre paynis many one.

This xij mones thou shalt with me gang,                    115
   And se the maner of my lyffe;
For thy trowche thou hast me tane,
   Ayene that may ye make no stryfe."][1]

Scho sayd, "Thomas, take leue at sonne and mone,
   And als at lefe that grewes on tree;                    120
This twelmoneth sall thou with me gone,
   And medill-erthe sall thou none see."

        [1] Ll. 103-118 from Lansdowne MS.

He knelyd downe appone his knee,
  Vndir-nethe that grenewod spraye;
And sayd, "lufly lady! rewe on mee,      125
  Mylde qwene of heuen, als thou beste maye.

Allas!" he sayd, "and wa es mee!
  I trowe my dedis wyll wirke me care;
My saulle, Jhesu, by-teche I the,
  Whedir-some euer my banes sall fare."     130

Scho ledde hym in at Eldone hill,
  Vndir-nethe a derne lee;
Whare it was dirk as mydnyght myrke,
  And euer water till his knee.

The montenans of dayes three,     135
  He herd bot swoghynge of the flode,
At the laste, he sayde, "full wa es mee!
  Almaste I dye, for fawte of fode."

Scho lede hym in-till a faire herbere,
  Whare frwte was growand gret plentee;    140
Pere and appill, bothe rype thay were,
  The date, and als the damasee;

The fygge, and als so the wyneberye;
  The nyghtgales byggande on thair neste;
The papeioyes faste abowte gan flye;    145
  And throstylls sange wolde hafe no reste.

He pressede to pulle frowyte with his hande;
  Als mane for fude that was nere faynt.
Scho sayd, "Thomas! thou late thame stande,
  Or ells the fende the will atteynt.    150

L. 123. These lines seem to be an improper repetition of a former stanza.
In the Cambr. MS. Thomas kneels down, and makes his mone to 'Mary
mylde,' and says,—'but thou rew on mee
          Alle my games fro me ar gone.'—
L. 131 should perhaps read, as in Cambr. MS., 'to the Eldoun birke.'

If thou it plokk, sothely to saye,
  Thi saule gose to the fyre of helle ;
It comes neuer owte or domesdaye,
  Bot ther in payne ay for to duelle.

Thomas, sothely, I the hyghte,            155
  Come lygge thyn hede downe on my knee,
And [thou] sall se the fayreste syghte,
  That euer sawe mane of thi contree."

He did in hye als scho hym badde ;
  Appone hir knee his hede he layde,       160
Ffor hir to paye he was full glade,
  And thane that lady to hym sayde—

" Seese thou nowe ȝone faire waye,
  That lyggis ouer ȝone heghe mountayne ?—
Ȝone es the waye to heuen for aye,       165
  When synfull sawles are passed ther payne.

Seese thou nowe, ȝone other waye,
  That lygges lawe by-nethe ȝone rysse?
Ȝone es the waye, the sothe to saye,
  Vnto the joye of paradyse.             170

Seese thou ȝitt ȝone thirde waye,
  That ligges vndir ȝone grene playne?
Ȝone es the waye, with tene and traye,
  Whare synfull saulis suffirris thaire payne.

Bot seese thou nowe ȝone ferthe waye,    175
  That lygges ouer ȝone depe delle ?
Ȝone es the way, so waylawaye,
  Vnto the byrnande fyre of hell.

Seese thou ȝitt ȝone faire castelle,
  That standes vpone ȝone heghe hill ?     180
Of towne and towre, it beris the belle ;
  In erthe es none lyk it vn-till.

Ffor sothe, Thomas, ȝone es myn awenne,
  And the kynges of this countree;
Bot me ware leuer be hanged and drawene,   185
  Or that he wyste thou laye me by.

When thou commes to ȝone castelle gaye,
  I pray the curtase mane to bee;
And whate so any mane to the saye,
  Luke thou answere none bott mee.   190

My lorde es seruede at ylk a mese,
  With thritty knyghttis faire and free;
I sall saye, syttande at the desse,
  I tuke thi speche by-ȝonde the see."

Thomas still als stane he stude,   195
  And he by-helde that lady gaye;
Scho come agayne als faire, and gude,
  And also ryche one hir palfraye.

[Thomas said, " Lady, wele is me,
  That euer I baide this day;   200
Nowe ye bene so fayre and whyte
  Byfore ye war so blake and gray!

I pray you that ye wyll me say,
  Lady, yf thy wyll be,
Why ye war so blake and gray?   205
  Ye said it was because of me."

" Forsothe, and I had not been so,
  Sertayne sothe I shall the tell;
Me had been as good to goo
  To the brynnyng fyre of hell;   210

My lord is so fers and fell,
  That is king of this contre,
And fulle sone he wolde haue the smell
  Of the defaute I did with the."][1]

[1] Ll. 199-214 from Lansdowne MS.

Hir grewehundis fillide with dere blode;        215
  Hir rachis couplede by my faye;
Scho blewe hir horne with mayne and mode,
  Vn-to the castelle scho tuk the waye;

Into the haulle sothely scho went;
  Thomas foloued at hir hande;        220
Than ladyes come, bothe faire and gent,
  With curtassye to hir knelande.

Harpe and fethill bothe thay fande,
  Getterne and als so the sawtrye;
Lutte, and rybybe, bothe gangande,        225
  And all manere of mynstralsye.

The most meruelle that Thomas thoghte,
  When that he stode appone the flore;
Ffor feftty hertes in were broghte,
  That were bothe grete and store.        230

Raches laye lapande in the blode,
  Cokes come with dryssynge knyfe;
They brittened tham als thay were wode;
  Reuelle amanges thame was full ryfe.

Knyghtis dawnesede by three and three,        235
  Thare was revelle, gamen, and playe,
Lufly ladyes faire and free,
  That satte and sange one riche araye.

Thomas duellide in that solace,
  More thane I ȝowe saye parde;        240
Till one a daye, so hafe I grace,
  My lufly lady sayde to mee.

" Do busk the, Thomas, the buse agayne,
  Ffor thou may here no lengare be;
Hye the faste, with myghte and mayne;        245
  I sall the brynge till Eldone tree."

Thomas sayde thane with heuy chere,
　" Lufly lady, nowe late me bee;
Ffor certis, lady, I hafe bene here
　Noghte bot the space of dayes three."　　　250

" Ffor sothe, Thomas, als I the telle,
　Thou hase bene here thre ʒere and more;
Bot langere here, thou may noghte duelle,
　The skylle I sall the telle whare-fore.

To morne, of helle the foulle fende,　　　255
　Amange this folke will feche his fee;
And thou arte mekill mane and hende,
　I trowe full wele he wolde chese the.

Ffor all the gold that euer may bee,
　Ffro hethyne vnto the worldis ende,　　　260
Thou bese neuer betrayede for mee;
　There-fore with me I rede thou wende."

Scho broghte hym agayne to Eldone tree,
　Vndir-nethe that grenewode spraye,
In Huntlee bannkes es mery to bee,　　　265
　Whare fowles synges bothe nyght and daye.

" Fferre owtt in ʒone mountane graye,
　Thomas, my fawkone, byggis a neste;—
A fawcoun is an Erlis[1] praye;
　Fforthi in na place may he reste.　　　270

Ffare wele, Thomas; I wend my waye;
　Ffor me byhouys ouer thir benttis brown."
—Loo here a fytt: more es to saye,
　All of THOMAS OF ERSELLDOWNE.—

　　　[1] herons, Lansdowne MS.; yrons, Cambr. MS.

### ' The Second Fytt.'

" FARE wele, Thomas;  I wend my waye ;
　　I may no lengare stande with the."—
" Gif me a tokynynge, lady gaye,
　　That I may saye I spake with the."

" To harpe or carpe, whare-so thou gose,　　5
　　Thomas, thou sall hafe the chose sothely."
And he said, "harpynge kepe I none ;
　　Ffor tonge es chefe of mynstralsye."

" If thou will spelle, or tales telle,
　　Thomas, thou sall neuer lesynge lye :　　10
Whare euer thou fare, by frythe or felle,
　　I pray the speke none euyll of me.

Ffare wele, Thomas, with-owttyn gyle ;
　　I may no lengare duelle with the."—
" Lufly lady, habyd a while,　　15
　　And telle thou me of some ferly."

" Thomas, herkyn what I the saye,
　　When a tree rote es dede,
The leues fadis thane, and wytis a-waye ;
　　And froyte it beris nane thane, whyte ne rede.

Of the Baylliolfe blod so sall it falle ;　　21
　　It sall be lyke a rotyne tre ;
The Comyns, and the Barlays alle,
　　The Russells, and the Ffresells free.

All sall thay fade, and wyte awaye ;　　25
　　Na ferly if that froyte than dye !
And mekill bale sall after spraye,
　　Whare joy and blysse was wonte [to bee.]

Ffare wele, Thomas, I wende [my way ;]
  I may no longer stand [with thee.]"      30
" Now lufly lady, gude [and gay,]
  Telle me ȝitt of some ferly."

" Whatkyns ferlys, Thomas gode,
  Sold I thee telle, and thi wills bee ? "
" Telle me, of this gentill blode,      35
  Wha sall thrife, and wha sall thee ;

Wha sall be kynge, wha sall be none,
  And wha sall welde this Northe countre ;
Wha sall flee, and wha sall be tane,
  And whare thir batells donne sall bee ? "      40

" Thomas, of a batelle I sall the telle,
  That sall be done righte sone at wille :
Beryns sall mete bothe fers and felle,
  And freschely fighte at Eldone hille.

The Bretons blode sall vndir fete,      45
  The Bruyse blode sall wyne the spraye ;
Sex thowsande Ynglysche, wele thou wete,
  Sall there be slayne that ilk day.

Ffare wele, Thomas ; I wende my waye ;
  To stande with the, me thynk full irke.      50
Of a batell I will the saye,
  That sall be done at Fawkirke.

Baners sall stande, bothe [large and lange,]
  Trowe this wele, with mode and mayne ;
The Bruysse blode sall vndir gane,      55
  Seuene thowsande Scottis ther sall be slayne.

L. 44. 'Ledyn hill,' MS. Cambr.; 'Helyndowne hill,' MS. Lansdowne.
L 53. 'lang and lange,' in Linc. MS. ; 'large and lange,' Cott. MS.

Ffare wele, Thomas; I pray the sesse;
  No lengare here thou tarye mee;
My grewehundis, thay brek thaire lesse,
  And my raches thaire copills in three;        60

Loo! whare the dere by twa and twa,
  Haldis ouer ȝone montane heghe.".—
Thomas said, "God schilde, thou gaa,
  Bot telle me ȝitt of some ferly."

[Holde thi greyhoundis in thi honde;        65
  And coupill thi raches to a [tre;]
And lat the dere reyke ouer the londe;—
  Ther is a herd in Holtely.]

[Off] a batelle I sall the saye,
  [That sall] gare ladyse morne in mode:        70
[At Bannokburne] bothe water and claye,
  Sall be mengyde with mannes blode.

Stedis sall stombill with tresoune,
  Bothe baye and broun, grysselle and graye;
Gentill knyghtis sall stombill downe,        75
  Thorowe the takynge of a wykkide waye.

The Bretons blode sall vndir falle;
  The Bruysse blode sall wynn the spraye;
Sex thowsand Ynglysche, grete and smale,
  Sall there be slane that ilk a daye.        80

Than sall Scottland kyngles stande;
  Trow it wele, that I the saye;
A tercelet of the same lande,
  To Bretane sall take the redy waye,

And take tercellettis grete and graye,        85
  With hym owte of his awen contree;
Thay sall wende on an ryche arraye,
  And come agayne by land and see.

---

Ll. 65-68 do not occur in the Linc. MS.—they are supplied from the
Cambr. copy; l. 71 from Sloane MS.

He sall stroye the north contree,
　　Mare and lesse hym by-forne;　　　　90
Ladyse sall saye, allas! and walowaye!
　　That euer that royalle blode was borne.

He sall ryse vpe at Kynkehorne,
　　And tye the [schippis] vn-to the sande;
At Dipplynge more, appon the morne,　　95
　　Lordis will thynke full lange to stande.

Bytwix Depplynge and the dales,
　　The watir that rynnes on rede claye:
Thare sall be slayne, for sothe, Thomas,
　　Eleuen thowsande Scottis, that nyght and daye.

Thay sall take a townn of grete renowne,　　101
　　That standis nere the water of Taye,
The ffadir, and the sone, sall be dongene downe,
　　And with strakis strange be slayne awaye.

Whene thay hafe wone that wallede towne,　　105
　　And ylke man hase cheuede thayre chaunce,
Than sall thir Bretons make tham bowne,
　　And fare forthe to the werre of Fraunce.

Than sall Scotland kyng-lesse stande,
　　And be lefte, Thomas, als I the saye;　　　110
Than sall a kyng be chosene, so ȝynge,
　　That kane no lawes lede, parfaye.

Dauid, with care he sall begynne,
　　And with care he sall wende awaye;
Lordis and ladyse, more and myne,　　　　115
　　Sall come appone a riche araye,

L. 94. 'chippis,' Linc. MS.
Ll. 113-116. According to the Cambr. MS. they read—
　　' Robert, with care he shall reng,
　　　And also he shalle wynd awaye;
　　Lordys and ladys, bothe old and yeng,
　　　Shall draw to hym with owtyn naye.'

And croune hym at the town of S[cone]
    Appon an certane solempne daye :
Beryns balde, bothe alde and ȝonge,
    Sall till hym drawe with-owttyn naye.      120

Euyn he sall to Ynglande ryde,
    Este and weste als lygges the waye.
[And take a·towne with greate pride
    And let the menn be slaine awaye.]

Betwixe a parke and an abbaye,      125
    A palesse and a paresche kyrke,
Thare sall ȝour kynge faill of his praye,
    And of his lyfe be wondir irke.

He sall be tane so wondir sare,
    So that awaye he sall noghte flee ;      130
Heys nebbe sall rynne, or he thethyn fare,
    The rede blode tryklelande vnto his knee.

He sall than be, with a false [fode]
    Betrayede of his awen [lond],
And whether it torne [to ewyll or good],      135
    He sall byde [in a rauenes honde].

That ra[uyne shall the goshawke woyne,
    Thowghte his fedres be neuer so blake,
And lede hym to London towne,
    There shall the goshawke fynd his make.     140

The rauen shall his fedres shake,
    And take tarsletis grete and gay,
The king shall hym maister make]
    In the North to do outtraye.

L. 117. Skyme, Linc. MS.
Ll. 123, 124 from Sloane MS.
L. 131. 'his neb shall rise,' MS. Cambr.
Ll. 133-136 and 137-143 completed from Lansdowne MS.

And when he es mane moste of mayne,    145
  And hopis beste thane for to spede,
On a ley lande, sall he be slayne
  Besyde a waye, forowttyne drede ;

Sythen sall selle Scotland, par ma faye,
  Ffulle, and fere, full many ane,    150
Ffor to make a certane paye,
  Bot ende of it sall neuer come nane.

And thane sall Scotland kyngles stande,
  Trowe this wele, that I telle the ;
Thre tercelettis of the same lande,    155
  Sall stryfe to bygg and browke the tree.

He sall bygg, and browke the tree,
  That hase no flyghte to fley awaye ;
Thay sall with pryde to Ynglande ryde,
  Este and weste, als lygges the waye.    160

[A cheftan then sall ryse with pride,
  Of all Scotland sall bere the floure :
He sall into Yngland ryde
  And make men hafe full scharpe schoure.]

Haly kyrke bese sett besyde,    165
  Relygyous byrnede on a fyre ;
Sythene sall thay to a castelle gl[yde,]
  And schewe tham thare with [mykell ire].

[Betwene a wycked way and a water,
  A parke and a stony way then,    170
Ther shal a cheften mete in fere ;
  A ful doughty ther shalbe slayn.

Ll. 161-164 from Lansdowne MS.
L. 169. The following stanza in the Cotton MS. is here added, as it
varies from that given above :—
      ' Bytwys a wethy and a water,
        A wel and a haly stane,
        Ther sal two chyſtans met in fer ;
          The Doglas ther sall be slane.'

The toder cheftan shalbe tane,
  A pesans of blode hym shal slee,
And lede hym away in won,          175
  And cloyse hym in a castell hee.

Ffare wel, Thomas; I wende my way;
  Ffor I must ouer ȝone bentis brown.
Here ar twoo fyttis; on is to say
  Off Thomas of Erseldown.][1]     180

[1] The conclusion of the Second Fytt (ll. 169-180), which is wanting in Lincoln MS., is here added from the Cambridge Manuscript.

## '𝔗𝔥𝔢 𝔗𝔥𝔦𝔯𝔡 𝔉𝔶𝔱𝔱.'

NOWE, lufly lady, gente and hende,
  Tell me, ȝif it thi willis bee,
Of thyes batells, how thay schall ende,
  And whate schall worthe of this northe countre?

"This worlde, Thomas, sothely to telle,     5
  Es noghte bot wandrethe and woghe!
Of a batelle, I will the telle,
  That schall be done at Spynkarde cloughe.

The Bretons blode schalle vndir falle;
  The Bruyse blode schalle wyn the spraye;     10
Sex thowsande Ynglysche, grete and smalle,
  Salle thare be slayne that nyghte and day.

The rerewarde sall noghte weite, parfaye,
  Of that ilke dulfulle dede;
Thay sall make a grete journaye,     15
  Dayes tene, with owttyn drede.

And of a batelle I will the telle,
  That sall be done now sone at will;
Beryns sall mete, bothe ferse and felle,
  And freschely fyghte at Pentland hyll.     20

Bytwyx Sembery and Pentlande,
  The haulle that standis appone the rede claye,
There schall be slayne eleuene thowsande
  [Off Sco]ttis men, that nyghte and daye.

[They sall take a] towne of grete renown,     25
  [That standis on the] water of Taye,
[Knyghtes shall wyne the waryson,
  By dyntes of swerde for ones and aye.

L. 21. Instead of 'Sembery,' the Cambr. MS. reads 'Edynborow.'

And whan they haue toke that walled towne,
  And eche man hathe take his chaunce,       30
The Britons blode shall make hym boune,
  And fare agan to werres of Fraunce.

Then shall they be in Fraunce full longe;
  Thomas, thre yere and mare;
And dyng downe castellis and towres stronge,     35
  And then shall euery man home fare.

They shall mete bothe fers and stronge,
  Bytwyx Ceton and the see;
The Englyshe shall ly in craggis amongè,]¹
  The tother oste at Barboke.      40

Fforryours furthe sall flee,
  On a Sonondaye, byfore the messe;
Seuen thowsandes sothely sall be slayne,
  One aythir partye, more and lesse.

Ffor ther sall be no baneres presse,     45
  Bot ferre in sondir sall they bee;
Carefull sall be the after mese,
  Bytwixe Cetone and the See.

Schippis sall stande appone the sande,
  Wayffande with the sees fame;     50
Thre ȝere and mare than sall thay stande,
  Or any beryne come feche thame hame.

Stedis awaye maysterles sall flynge,
  Ouer the mountans too and fraa;
Thaire sadills one thaire bakkis sall hynge,     55
  Vnto the garthis be rotyne in twaa.

Ȝitt sall thay hewe one all the daye,
  Vnto the sone be sett nere weste;
Bot thare es no wighte that ȝitt wiete maye,
  Whether of thaym sall hafe the beste.     60

¹ Ll. 27-39 from Lansdowne MS.
L. 40. Barvik fre, Sloane MS.

Thay sall plante down thaire [baners] thare,
  Worthi men all nyghte sall dye;
Bot one the morne, ther sall be care,
  Ffor nowther syde sall hafe the gree.

Than sall thay tak a trewe and swere,      65
  Ffor thre ȝere, and more, I vndirstande;
That nane of tham sall other dere,
  [Nowther] by see, ne ȝitt by lande.

[Betwene twoo seynte Marye dayes,
  When the tyme waxis nere longe,      70
Then shalle thei mete and banerse rese,
  In Gleydes-more that is so long.

Gladysmore, that gladis us all;
  This is beginning of oure gle;
Gret sorow then shall fall,      75
  Wher rest and pees were wont to be.

Crowned kyngus ther shalbe slayn,
  With dyntis sore, and wonder [to] se,
Out of a more a rauen shal cum,
  And of hym a schrew shall flye,      80

And seke the more with-owten rest,
  Aftur a crosse is made of stan,
Hye and lowe, both est and west;]
  Bot wiete wele, Thomas he sall fynd nane.

He sall lyghte whare the crose solde bee,      85
  And holde his nebbe vp to the skye;
And drynke of gentill blode and free,
  Thane ladys, waylowaye! sall crye.

Ther sall a lorde come to that werre,
  That sall be of full grete renowne;      90
And in his banere sall he bere,
  Triste it wele, a rede lyone.

Ll. 69-83 from Cambr. MS.

Thar sall another come to that werre,
   That sall fyghte full fayre in [molde ;]
And in his banere sall he bere          95
   A schippe with an ankyre of golde.

Ȝit sall another come to that werre
   That es noghte knawen by northe [ne southe,]
And in his banere sall he bere
   A wolfe with a nakede childe in his [mouthe].  100

Ȝitt sall the ferthe lorde come to that [werre]
   That sall grete maystries after make
And in his [banere sal he bere]
   The bere [bounden to a stake.]

[Although the first letters remain of the next eighteen lines, which are torn away, they are not serviceable in enabling us to perfect them from the other MSS.—But a still more considerable deficiency occurs in this part of the poem, as two whole columns, containing thirty-five lines in each, have at the same time been destroyed, thus leaving a hiatus altogether of about twenty-two stanzas. The conclusion of the poem, written on the reverse corner of the same leaf, has fortunately been preserved. The seventeen following stanzas are given from the Cambridge MS., since there is no reason to doubt that they formed a part of those of which we have now had occasion to mention the loss.]

[Then shal they fight with helme and schilde,   105
   Vnto the sun be set nere west;
Ther is no wyght in that fylde
   That wottis qwylke side shall haue the best.

A bastarde shall cum fro a forest,
   Not in Ynglond borne shall he be,—     110
And he shalle wyn the gre for the best,
   Alle men leder of Bretan shal he be.

And with pride to Englond ride,
   Est and west in [hys tyme];
And holde a parlement [of moche pryde],   115
   Wher neuer non byfore was seyne.

Alle false lawes he [shalle laye doune,]
   That are begune in that cuntre;
Truly to wyrke he shalbe boune,
   And alle leder of Bretans shal he be.     120

The bastarde shal get hym power strong,
   And alle his foes he shall doune dyng;
Of alle the v kingys landis,
   Ther shal non bodword home bryng.

The bastard shalle dye in the Holy Land;   125
   Trow this wel as I the say :
Take his [sowle] to his hande,
   Jhesu Christe that mycull may.

Thomas [truly] I the say,
   This is [trewth] ylke a worde ;—     130
Of that laste battel I the say,
   It shalbe don at Sandeforde.

Nere Sandyforth ther is a wroo,
   And nere that wro is a well;
A ston there is the wel euen fro,     135
   And nere the wel truly to tell,

On that grounde ther groeth okys thre,
   And is called Sandyford ;
Ther the last battel done shalbe ;
   Thomas, trow thou ilke a worde ; "    140

Then she seid with heuy chere ;
   The terys ran out of hir een gray.—
" Lady, or thou wepe so sore,
   Take thi houndis, and wend thi way."

" I wepe not for my way-walkyng,    145
   Thomas, truly I the say ;
But fer ladys shal wed laddys ȝong,
   When ther lordis are ded away.

L. 134. ' wroo,' in MS. Cotton it is ' bro.'

He shall haue a stede in stabul fed,
   A hauke to beyre vpon his hond ;        150
A bright lady to his bed,
   That before had non londe.

Ffare wel, Thomas ; I wende my way ;
   Alle this day thou wil me marre."—
" Lufly lady, tel thou me        155
   Of Blake Agnes of Donbar.

And why she haue gyven me the warre,
   And put me in her prison depe ;
Ffor I walde dwel with her [euer mar,]
   And kepe hir ploos and hir shepe."       160

" Off Blake Agnes cum neuer gode ;
   Wher for, Thomas, she may not the ;
Ffor al hir welth and hir wordly gode,
   In London cloysed shal she be.

Ther preuysse neuer gode of hir blode,       165
   In a dyke then shall she dye ;
Houndis of hir shall have ther fode,
   Magrat of all hir kyng of le."

Then Thomas a sory man was he,
   The terys ran out of his een gray :—       170
" Lufly lady, ʒet tell thou me,
   If we shall parte for ever and ay ? "—

" Nay ; when thou sittes at Erseldown,]
   To Huntlee bankkis thou take the waye,
Ther sall I sekirly be bowne,       175
   And mete the, Thomas, whene I maye.

[I sall] the kenne whare euer thou gaa,
   [To ber] the pryce of curtaysye ;
[For tu]nge es wele, and tunge es waa,
   [And] tunge es chefe of mynstrallsye."      180

[Scho ble]we hir horne on hir palfraye,
  [And lefte] Thomas vndir-nethe a tre ;
[To Helmesd]ale scho tuke the waye,
  [And thus de]partede scho and hee.

[Of swilke] an hirdman wolde I here     185
  [That couth] me telle of swilke ferly ;
[Ihesu] corounde with a crown of brere,
  [Bry]nge vs to his heuene so hye.
               Amen.  Amen.


EXPLICIT THOMAS OF ERSELEDOWNNE.

THE

# PYSTYL OF SWETE SUSAN

# VI.

# THE PYSTYL OF SWETE SUSAN.

HUCHEON of the Awle Ryale, *as we learn from* Wyntoun's *Metrical Chronicle, was the author of this very ancient and curious relique of Scotish Poetry. His great work was the 'Gest Historiale,' in which, according to the same authority,* Hucheon

> ——"has tretyd curyously
> In Gest of Broyttys auld story;"

*and the Prior of Lochleven, defends him, and 'the Auctore,' from whom his work was perhaps translated, against the exceptions that in his time had been made to some of the statements which it contained.* Wyntoun, *to whom we owe all the information we possess respecting* Hucheon *and his writings, says,*

> ——Men of gud discretyowne
> Suld excuse and love Huchowne
> That cunnand wes in literature.
> He made the gret Gest of Arthure,
> And the Awntyre off Gawane,
> The Pystyl als off Swete Swsan;
> He wes curyws in hys style,
> Fayre off facund, and subtille,
> And ay to plesans and delyte,
> Made in metyre mete his dyte,
> Lytil or nowcht nevyrtheles
> Waverand fra the suthfastnes.
>   —B. v. xii. 4321-4332.

*From* Hucheon's *being thus called of ' the Awle Ryale,' or Royal hall, or palace, Macpherson, the learned editor of Wyntoun's Chronicle, supposes he may have been the King's Poet. It seems, however, agreed among our poetical antiquaries that this* Hucheon *was one and the same person with* Sir Hugh of Eglynton, *a Scotish Poet, of the fourteenth century, who is mentioned by* Dunbar *in his ' Lament for the Death of the Makars.' " He flourished," (says* Mr George Chalmers, *in a letter to the Editor,) " under David II. and died under Robert II. I think there cannot be any doubt whether* Sir Hugh de Eglynton *were not* Hucheon of the Awle Ryale. *He is supposed to have died about the year* 1381. *As he was a busy Knight, in his day, so are there many notices about him."*

*[Besides having been connected with the Scottish Court in the reigns of the monarchs above mentioned,* Sir Hugh *was Justiciary of Lothian in* 1361, *and in* 1367 *was one of the commissioners for negociating a treaty with England. His wife was* Egidia, *the half-sister of* Robert II.; *and his daughter, who inherited his extensive estates, married* John Montgomery of Eglisham, *ancestor of the noble family of* Eglintoun.]

*No other production, by our author, besides the following, is known to be extant, unless, on the authority of* Wyntoun, *we should attribute to him one or other of the curious metrical romances of the adventures of Arthur and Gawane.*

*In the present collection will be found one of these ancient alliterative poems ;—a style of composition for which, for a length of time, the Northern Poets were particularly renowned ; for, although the use of alliteration was not entirely peculiar to them, it was, at least, one distinguishing feature of their compositions. Thus* Chaucer *makes ' his Persone ' to say*

> ——"I am a Sotherne man
> I can not geste, Rom, Ram, Ruf, by my letter,
> And, God wote, rime hold I but litel better."

George Gascoigne, *an English poet of the age of Queen Elizabeth, has the following reference to this curious pas-*

*sage :—" In making a delectable poem," he says, "it is not enough to roll in pleasant woordes, nor yet to thunder in* Rym, Ram, Ruff *by letter, (quoth my maister Chaucer,) nor yet to abounde in apte vocables, or epithets, unlesse the invention have in it also* aliquid salis."

*Of the Pystill of Susan, there are various ancient manuscripts.*[1]

*The copy which has been followed, is contained in the very large collection, or* ingens volumen, *as it is properly enough styled, in the Bodleian Library, called, from its donor, the* Vernon Manuscript, *and was probably compiled about the end of the XIVth century. In a volume of old metrical romances in the Cotton Library, written about the middle of the XVth century, is another copy which has afforded some various readings, but which wants the first eight stanzas of the poem. A third copy forms part of a volume once in Mr Heber's possession, which had successively belonged to Sir Henry Spelman, Dr Taylor, (the Editor of Demosthenes,) and Richard Gough, Esq. : it is described by* Dr Whitaker, *the learned Editor of Piers Plouhman's Vision, as a manuscript, which, 'from the handwriting, might probably be assigned to the reign of Richard the Second.'*

*He thus mentions* Hucheon's *Poem :—*

*"One specimen of alliteration, combined at once with rhyme and a very complicated stanza has never been published, and of which it is not to be wondered at that it has had no imitators. The story is that of* Susanna, *and from the style and orthography it appears to be nearly as ancient as Piers Plouhman, with one of the copies of which, now before the Editor, it is bound up, as it has evidently been transcribed by the same hand."—Preface to the Vision, &c., p.* xvii.

---

[1] It was, indeed, printed by Ritson, about the year 1803, as the commencement of a projected volume of 'Select Scotish Poems ;' similar in size to his excellent Collection of Scotish Songs. This volume, the Editor learnt, was to have been published by Mr Constable, but, owing to the death of Ritson, it was never completed, and a few copies only, it is believed, of the two sheets that were actually printed off, have been preserved.

VI.

# 'The Pistill of Susan.'

I.

THER was in Babiloine a bern, in that borw riche,
   That was a Ieugh ientil, and Ioachin he hiht;
He was so lele in his lawe, ther lived non him liche,
Of alle riche that renke arayes he was riht:
His innes, and his orchardes were with a dep dich,   5
Halles and herbergages, heigh uppon heiht;
To seche thoru that cite ther nas non sich,
Of erbes, and of erberi, so auenauntliche i-diht
      That day.
   Withinne the sercle of sees,      10
   Of erberi and alees,
   Of alle maner of trees,
      Sothely to say.

II.

He had a wif hight Susan, was sotil and sage,
Heo was Elches doughter, eldest and eyre,    15
Lovelich and lilie-whit, on of that lynage,
Of alle fason of foode frelich and feire:
Thei lerned hire lettrure of that langage,
The maundement of Moises, thei marked to that deire,
To the mount of Synai that went in message,    20
That the Trinite bi-tok of tables apeire
      To rede;
   Thus thei lerne hire the lawe,
   Cleer clergye to knawe,
   To God stod hire gret awe,    25
      That wlonkest in weede.

### III.

He hedde an orchard newe, that neighed wel nere,
Ther Iewes with Ioachin priveliche gon playe;
For he real and riche of rentes ever there,
Honest, and auenaunt, and honorablest aye.          30
I-wis, ther haunted til her hous, hende, ʒe mai here,
Two domes of that lawe, that dredde were that day,
Preostes and presidens preised als peere,
Of whom vr soverein lord sawes gan say,
    And tolde,          35
 How heor wikkednes comes
 Of the wrongwys domes
 That they haue gyue to gomes,
    This iuges of olde.

### IV.

Thus this dredful demers on daies thider drewe;          40
Al for gentrise and joye of that Iuwesse,
To go in his gardeyn, that gayliche grewe,
To fonge floures and fruit, thought thei no fresse;
And whon they seigh Susan, semelich of hewe,
Thei weor so set uppon hire, might thei not sese;          45
Thei wolde  enchaunte  that  child:  hou  schold  heo
  eschewe?
And thus this cherles unchaste in chaumbre hir chese,
    With chere,
 With two maidenes al on,
 Semelyche Suson,          50
 On dayes in the merion,
    Of murthes wol here.

### V.

Whon theos perlous prestes perceyved hire play,
Tho thoughte the wrecches to bewile that worly in
  wone,
Heore wittes wel waiwordes thei wrethen awai,          55

And turned fro his teching, that teeld is in trone.
For siht of here souerayn, sothli to say,
Heore hor heuedes fro heuene thei hid apon one,
Thei caught for heor couetyse the cursyng of Kai,
For rightwys jugement recordet thei none,          60
          They two.
    Euery day bi day
    In the pomeri thei play,
    Whiles thei mihte Susan assay,
          To worchen hire wo.          65


### VI.

In the seson of somere, with Sibell and Jone,
Heo grethed hire til hire gardin, that growed so grene,
Ther lyndes and lorers were lent vpon lone,
The sauyne and sypres, selcouth to sene,
The palme, and the poplere, the pirie, the plone,          70
The iuniper ientel, jonyng bi-twene,
The rose ragged on rys, richest on rone,
I-theuwed with the thorn trinaunt to sene,
          So tiht;
    Ther weore popeiayes prest,          75
    Nihtyngales uppon nest,
    Blithest briddes o the best,
          In blossoms so briht.


### VII.

The briddes in blossoms thei beeren wel loude
On olyues, and amylliers, and al kynde of trees,          80
The popeiayes perken and pruynen for proude,
On peren and pyn-appel thei ioyken in pees;
On croppes of canel keneliche thei croude,
On grapes the goldfinch thei gladen and glees;
Thus schene briddes in schawe schewen heore schroude,
On figges and fygers thei fongen heore sees,          86
          In fay;

Ther weore growyng so grene
The date, with the damesene,
Turtils troned on trene,                              90
      By sixti, I saygh.


### VIII.

The fyge and the filbert were fode med so fayre,
The chirie and the chestein, that chosen is of hewe,
Apples and almaundes that honest are of ayre,
Grapes and garnettes gayliche thei grewe,            95
The costardes comeliche in cuththes thei cayre,
The britouns, the blaunderers, [the] braunches, the
    bewe,
Fele floures and fruit, frelich of flayre,
With wardons winlich and walshe notes newe,
      They wald                          100
  Ouer heor hedes gon hyng,
  The wince and the wederlyng,
  Spyces speden to spryng,
      In erbers enhaled.


### IX.

The chyue, and the chollet, the chibolle, the cheue, 105
The chouwet, the cheuerol, that schaggen on niht,
The parsel, the passenep, poretes to preue,
The pyon, the peere, wel proudliche i-piht ;
The lilye, the louache, launsyng with leue,
The sauge, the sorsecle, so semeliche to siht ;      110
Columbyne and charuwe clottes thei creve,
With ruwe and rubarbe, ragget ariht,
      No lees ;
  Daysye, and ditoyne,
  Ysope, and aueroyne,                              115
  Peletre, and plaentoyne,
      Proudest in pres.

### X.

Als this schaply thing ʒede in hire ʒerde,
That was hir hosbondes and hire, that holden with
    hende;
Now folk be faren from us, thar us not be ferde    120
Aftur myn oynement, warliche ʒe wende.
Espieth now specialy, the ʒates ben sperde
For we wol wassche us I-wis bi this welle strende.
For-thi the wyf werp of hir wedes vnwerde,
Vnder a lorere ful lowe that ladi gan lende,    125
        So sone:
    By a wynliche well,
    Susan caste of hir kelle,
    Bote feole ferlys hire bi-felle,
        Bi midday or none.    130

### XI.

Now were this domes-men derf drawen in derne,
Whiles thei seo that ladi was laft al hire one,
For to heilse that hende thei highed ful ʒerne,
With wordes thei worshipe that worliche in wone:
"Wolt thou, ladi, for loue, on vre lay lerne,    135
And vnder this lorere ben vr lemmone?
Ʒe ne tharf wonde for no wight vr willes to werne,
For alle gomes that scholde greue of gardin ar gone
        In feere.
    Ʒif thou this neodes deny,    140
    We schal telle trewely
    We toke the with avoutri;
        Vnder this lorere."

### XII.

Then Susan was serwful, and seide in hire thought,
"I am with serwe bi-set on eueriche syde,    145
Ʒif I assent to this sin, that this segges haue sought,

I be bretenet and brent in baret to byde:
And, ʒif I nikke hem with nai, hit helpeth me nought:
Such toret and teone taketh me this tyde.
Are I that worthlich wrech, that all this world wrought,
Betere is wemles wende of this world wyde."      151
With this
Tho cast heo a careful cri,
This loueliche ladi,
Hir seruauns hedde selli,      155
No wonder, I-wis.


XIII.

Whon kene men of hir court comen til hir cri,
Heo hedde cast of hir calle and hire keuer-cheue,
In at a prive posterne thei passen in hi,
And findes this prestes wel prest her poyntes to preue;
Tho seid the loselle aloude to the ladi,      161
"Thou hast gon with a gome, thi God to greue,
And ligge with thi lemon in avoutri,
Bi the lord and the lawe that we onne leeue."
They swere,      165
Alle hire seruauns, thei shont,
And stelen awey in a stont;
Of hire weore thei neuer wont
Such wordes to here.


XIV.

Hir kinrede, hir cosyns and al that hire knewe,      170
Wrong handes, I-wis, and wepten wel sare,
Sykeden for Susan, so semeliche of hewe,
Al onwyse of that wyf, wondred thei were.
Thei dede hire in a dungon, ther neuer day dewe,
While domes-men were dempt this dede to clare;      175
Marred in manicles, that made wer newe;
Meteles, whiles the morwen to middai and mare,
In drede.

Ther com hir fader, so fre,
With al his affinite ;                                    180
The prestes sauns pite,
   And ful of falshede.


### XV.

Tho seide the iustises on bench, to Ioachim the Iewe,
That was of Iacobes kynde, gentil of dedes,
Let senden after Susan, so semelych of hewe,          185
That thou hast weddet to wif, wlonkest in wedes ;
Heo was in trouthe, as we trowe, tristi and trewe ;
Hir herte holliche on him that the heuene hedes.
Thus thei brought hir to the barre, hir bales to brewe,
Nouther dom ne deth that day heo ne dredes,          190
   Als thare ;
 Hir hed was ȝolow as wyre
 Of gold fyned with fyre,
 Hire scholdres schaply and schire,
   That bureliche was bare.                195


### XVI.

Nou is Susan in sale, sengeliche arayed,
In a selken schert, with scholdres wel schene.
Tho ros vp with rancour the renkes reneyed,
This comelich accused, with wordes wel kene ;
Homliche on her heved heor hondes thei leyed :      200
And heo wepte for wo, no wonder, I wene.
We schul presenten this pleint, hou thou euer be paied,
And sei sadliche the soth, right as we haue sene,
   O sake.
 Thus with cauteles waynt,                        205
 Preostes presented this playnt.
 Ȝit schal trouthe hem ataynt,
   I dar vndertake.

M

### XVII.

" Thorw-out the pomeri we passed us to play,
Of preiere and of penaunce was vre purpose,          210
Heo com with two maidens, al richeli that day,
In riche robes arayed, red as the rose ;
Wylyliche heo wyled hir wenches away,
And comaunded hem kenely the ȝates to close ;
Heo ȝode to a ȝong mon, in a valay,          215
The semblaunt of Susan wolde non suppose,
   For soth :
  Be this cause that we say,
  Heo wyled hir wenches away,
  This word we witnesse for ay,          220
    With tonge and with toth.


### XVIII.

Whon we that semblaunt seigh, we siked wel sare,
For sert of hir souereyn, and·for hir owne sake,
Vr copes weore cumberous, and cundelet vs care,
But ȝit we trinet a trot, that traytur take ;          225
He was borlich and bigge, bold as a bare ;
More mighti mon then we his maistris to make :
To the ȝate ȝaply thei ȝeoden wel ȝare,
And he lift vp the lach, and leop ouer the lake,
   That ȝouthe.          230
  Heo ne schunte for no schame,
  But bouwed aftur for blame,
  Heo nolde cuythe us his name,
   For craft that we couthe."


### XIX.

Now heo is dampned on deis, with deol thaugh hir deue,
And hir domes-men vnduwe do hir be withdrawen. 236
Loueliche heo louted, and lacched hir leue,
At kynred and cosyn, that heo had ever i-knawen,

Heo asked merci with mony, in this mischeue:
" I am sakeles of syn," heo seide in hir sawen,    240
" Grete God of his grace ʒor gultus forʒive,
That doth me derfliche be ded and don out of dawen, .
      With dere.
   Wolde God that I miht
   Speke with Ioachim a niht,    245
   And sithen to deth me bediht;
      I charge hit not a pere."


XX.

Heo fel doun flat in the flore, hir feere whom heo fand,
Carped to him kyndeli, as heo ful wel couthe:
I wis I wrathyed the neuere, at my witand,    250
Neither in word, ne in werk, in elde, ne in ʒouthe.
Heo keuered vpon hir kneos, and cussed his hand:
For I am dampned, I ne dar disparage thi mouth.
Was neuer more serwful segge, bi se, nor bi sande,
Ne neuer a soriore siht, bi north, ne bi south,    255
      Tho thare.
   Thei toke the feteres of hire feete,
   And euere he cussed that swete:
   In other world schul we mete.—
      Seide he no mare.    260


XXI.

Then Susan, the serwfol, seide uppon hight,
Heef hir hondes on high, bi-held heo to heuene:
" Thou maker of middelert, that most art of miht,
Bothe the sonne and the see, thou sette vppon seuene;
Alle my werkes thou wost, the wrong, and the riht, 265
Hit is nedful nou thy names to nempne.
Seththe I am deolfolich dampned, and to deth diht,
Lord, herteliche tak hede, and herkne my steuene,
      So fre!

Seththe thou maight not be sene,                    270
With no fleschliche eyene,
Thou wost wel that I am clene,
    Haue merci now on me!"


### XXII.

Nou thei dresse hire to deth withouten eny drede,
And lede forth that ladi, louesum of lere;          275
Grete God, of his grace, of gultes vngnede,
Help with the Holi Gost, and herde hir preyere.
He directed this dome, and this delful dede
To Danyel, the prophete, of dedes so dere,
Such ȝiftes god him ȝaf in his ȝouthehede,         280
Ȝit failed hit a fourteniht, ful of the ȝere,
    Nouht sayne.
  Tho criede that freoly fode,
  " Whi spille ȝe innocens blode?"
  And alle thei stoteyd and stode,                285
    This ferlys to frayne.


### XXIII.

" What signefyes, gode sone, these sawes that thou
    seeth."
Thus these maisterful men mouthes can mele,
Thei be fendes all the frape, I sei hit in feith,
And in folk of Israel be foles wel fele.             290
" Vmbiloke ȝou, lordes, such lawes ben leith,
Methinketh ȝor dedes vnduwe such domes to dele,
Aȝein to the ȝildhalle, the gomes vngreith,
I schal, be proces apert, disproue this apele,
    For nede.                              295
  Lat twinne hem in two,
  For now wakneth heor wo,
  Thei schal graunte, ar thei go,
    Al heore falshede."

### XXIV.

Thei diseuered hem sone, and sette hem sere,    300
And sodeynly askede, thei brought into the sale,
Bifore this ȝonge prophete this preost gom apere,
And he him apeched sone, with chekes wel pale :
" Thou hast I-be presedent, the peple to steere,
Thou dotest nou on thin olde tos, in the dismale ;   305
Now schal thi conscience be knowen that euer was
       vnclere,
Thou hast in Babiloygne on benche brewed much bale,
         Wel bolde :
    Now schal ȝor synnes be seene,
    Of fals domes bideene,    310
    For theose in Babiloyne han bene
        Jugget of olde.

### XXV.

Thou seidest thou seghe Susanne sinned in thi siht,
Tel nou me trewly, vnder what tre ? "—
" Mon, bi the muche God, that most is of miht,   315
Vnder a cyne, sothli, myseluen I hir se."—
" Now thou lyest in thin hed, bi heuen vppon hiht,
An angel with a naked swerd the neighes wel nei,
He hath brandist his brond, brennynde so bright,
To marke thi middel at a mase in more then in thre,
        No lese :    321
    Thou brak Godes comaundement,
    To sle such an innocent,
    With eny fals juggement,
        Vnduweliche on dese."    325

### XXVI.

Now is this domes-mon withdrawen withouten eni
    drede,
And put into prison aȝeyn into place,
Thei broughten the tother forth whom the barn bede,

To-fore the folk and the faunt, freli of face :
" Cum forth, thou corsed caytif, thou Canaan," he sede,
" Bi cause of thi couetise, thou art in this case,      331
Thou hast disceyuet thi self, with thi oune dede,
Of thi wit for a wyf biwiled thou wase,
    In wede.
  Thou sey nou, so mote thou the,      335
  Vnder what kynde of tre
  Semeli Susan thou se
    Do that derne dede.


XXVII.

Thou gome of gret elde, thin hed is grei hored,
Tel hit me treweli, ar thou thi lif tyne."      340
Tho that rothly cherl ruydely rored,
And seid bifore the prophet, thei pleied bi a prine.—
" Now thou liest loude, so helpe me vr lorde ;
For fulthe of thi falshed thou schalt ha euel pine,
Thou and thi cursed cumpere, ȝe mon not acorde ;  345
Ȝe schul be drawen to the deth, this dai ar we dine,
    So rathe.
  An angel is neih honde,
  Takes the domes of ȝor honde,
  With a brennynge bronde,      350
    To byte ȝou bathe."


XXVIII.

Then the folk of Israel felle vpon knees,
And lowed that loueli lord, that hir the lyf lent ;
All the gomes, that hire God wolde gladen and glees,
This prophete so pertli proues his entent,      355
Thei trompe bifore this traitours, and traylen hem on
  trees,
Thorw-out the cite, by comuyn assent ;
Hose leeueth on that lord, thar him not lees,
That thus his seruant saued that schold ha be schent,
    In sete.      360

This ferlys bifel
In the days of Danyel,
The Pistel witnesseth wel
      Of that Profete.

  Ihesu Crist with mylde steuene
  Graunt vs alle the blisse of heuene.

         Amen.

ANE BALLET OF THE NINE
NOBLES

## VII.

# ANE BALLET OF THE NINE NOBLES.

---

*ON the margin of the ancient MS. copy of* Fordun's Scotichronicon, *that once belonged to the celebrated historian,*
Hector Boece, *is written the following translation of some
barbarous Latin verses, added by* Bower *about the year*
1440, *and occurring in most copies of the same Chronicle,*[1]
*which may be termed the Counsel of* Robert the Bruce, *as
to the proper mode of defending Scotland :—*

> ON fut suld be all Scottis weir,
> Be hyll and mosse, thaim selff to "steir."[2]
> Llat wod for wallis be bow and speir,
> That innymeis do thaim na deir.
> In streit placis gar keip all stoir ;
> And byrne the plane land thaim befor :
> Thane sall thai pass away in haist,
> Quhen that thai find na thing bot waist.
> With wyllis and waykene of the nycht,
> And mekill noyis maid on hycht :
> Thane sall thai turne with gret affrai,
> As thai war chassit with suerd away.
> This is the consall and intent
> Off gud KING ROBERTIS Testament.

*The following ballad, however, may serve to show the
esteem in which the memory of* Robert the Bruce *was long*

---

[1] Lib. xii. cap. x.          [2] In the MS. "weir."

*held by the people of Scotland. After enumerating the exploits of the Nine Worthies, our valiant Monarch is brought forward, leaving the reader to draw his own conclusion as to who " was doughtiest in deeds."  It occurs at the end of the large and splendid copy of* Fordun's *Chronicle, in the* University Library of Edinburgh, *and is written in the same hand with the rest of the Manuscript.  Another copy occurs at the end of a little MS. volume in the same library, containing an Abbreviation of the* Scotichronicon, *written in the year* 1521, " *Editum per Johannem Law, Canonicum Sanctiandreæ."*

*The Nine Worthies mentioned in this ancient ballad often make a conspicuous figure in old English poems.  Thus* John Gower, *in his 'Balade to King Henry the Fourth,' says :—*

> See Alexander, Hector and Iulius,
> See Machabeus, Dauid and Iosue,
> See Charlemaine, Godfray, and Arthus,
> Fulfilled of warre, and of mortalite,
> Ther fame abitte, but all is vanite,
> For death, which hath the warres vnder fote,
> Hath made an end, of which there is no bote.
> —Chaucer's Works, Speght's Edit., 1597, Fol. 332.

*The reader will remember the amusing Pageant of the Nine Worthies, introduced by* Shakspeare *in Love's Labour's Lost, where the king says :—*

" Here is like to be a good presence of worthies : He [Don Adriano de Armado] presents Hector of Troy ; the swain, Pompey the Great ; the parish curate, Alexander ; Armado's page, Hercules ; the pedant, Judas Machabeus.
> And if these four worthies in their first show thrive,
> These four will change habits, and present the other five." [1]

*Schir Frollo, mentioned in line* 41, *is a personage introduced to exemplify the prowess of Arthur, and according to the Chronicles was a Roman knight, governor of Gaul.  His name and that of " Lucyus the Emperour of Rome " are alluded to in the 'Legend of King Arthur,' printed in* Percy's *Reliques, vol. iii. p.* 79.  *He is also thus referred to in the Ancient Chronicles of Scotland—" Becaus that*

---

[1] Act v. ii.

the aire of Britane was maryit with a Scottis man, quhen the kynryk vakit and Arthur was xv. ʒeris ald, thay maid him king be the deuilry of Merlyn. . . . And sekirly thare is mekle thing said of this Arthure quhilk is nocht suth, and bot fenzeit; as thay say that he slew Ffrelle King of Ffrance, and als Lucius the Procurator of Rome; ffor in his dayes thar was nanè sik, as all storyes of Ffrance beris witnes; and sik mony othir besynes are maid of him as Maister Walter Mapes fenzeit in his buke of ane callit Lanslot the Lake," &c.

The ninth in order, Godefroy Earl of Bologne, at times gave place to Sir Guy of Warwick in the enumeration of these Worthies; and indeed it appears that one of them might be changed at pleasure. Strutt, in his 'Sports and Pastimes of the People of England' (Int., p. xli), states that in preparing the pageants for a royal procession, orders were given "to set up the frames, and to space out the rooms that the Nine Worthies may be so instauled, as best to please the eye. The Worthies are thus named in an heraldic MS. in the Harleian Library—Duke Iossua; Hector of Troy; Kyng Dauid; Emperour Alexander; Iudas Machabyes; Emperour Iulyus Cesar; Kyng Arthur; Emperour Charlemagne; and Syr Guy of Warwycke; but the place of the latter was frequently, and I believe originally, supplied by Godefroy Earl of Bologne. It appears, however, that any of them might be changed at pleasure: Henry VIII. was made a 'Worthy' to please his daughter Mary."

It is interesting, in conclusion, to remark that Sir David Lyndsay, in his Register of Arms, 1542, has emblazoned the armorial bearings of the Nine Worthies. In his manuscript volume preserved in the Advocates' Library, they are thus described :—" Heir followis the Armys off the nyne maist nobill; off the quhilkis thair wes thre Iowis, as Dauid, Iosue, and Iudas Machabeus :—Thre gentilis, as Iulius Cesar, Alexander Conquerour, and Hector off Troy :—Thre crissynhed men, as Charlis the Magne Empriour and King of France, Arthur King off the greit Britannie, and Godefroie Duk off Bollonie, conquerour off Ierusalem."

# ' De nouem nobilibus.'

Hᴇᴄᴛᴏᴜʀ of Troy throu hard feichthyngis,
    In half thrid ʒeris slew xix kyngis ;
And ammirallis a hunder and mare,
Wyth small folk at vnrackynnit war ;
He slew ·sa fell, at wes ferly,          5
Qwham Achileʒ slew tresnabili.

    Alexander als nobil a kyng,
In xij ʒeris wan throw hard feichtyng
Al landis vnder the formament !
Egwhethir adai in till parlement,       10
He said, he had but variance,
Our litill in till his gouernance.

    Iulius Cesar wan hailily
The ilis of Grece, and all Surry ;
Affrik, Arab, Bretan wan he,         15
And discumfit his mawche Pompe :
Throw hard batell, and stalward stour,
He was the first was emperour.

    The gentill Iew Schir Iosue,
Anek xxx kyngis throw weir wan he ;    20
And conquirit the landis also,
The flum Iordan pertit in two

Throw Goddis grace, and strang power;
Men suld hym loff on gret maner.


    Dauid slew mychtthy Golias,        25
And Philistens at felon was;
He wes so wycht, et weill feichtand,
That he wes neuer sene recriand;
Thairfor men call him, loud and still,
A trew prophet, of hardy will.        30


    Michty Iudas Machabeus
In bathell slew Antiochus,
Appolonius and Nichanore,
At in his dais wald neuer schor
No multitud be adred of men,        35
Thoff he war ane eganis ten.


    Arthur wan Dace, Spanʒe, and France,
And hand for hand slew tua giantis,
Lucius the publik procuratour
Of Rome, wyth milleonis in stalwar stour;    40
And in till Pariss Schir Frollo,
In lystis slew wythoutin mo.


    Charleʒ of France slew Aygoland,
And wan Spanʒe fra hethoun land;
He slew the sowden of Pavi,        45
And wan the Saxonis halily;
And quhar God deid for our safte,
He put haly the Cristante.


    Godefrey Bolʒone slew Solimant,
Befor Antioche, and Corborant,        50
Quham he throu ful strak had ourtane,
Throu cops and harmez his glave is gane;
Sere hethownis he slew throu hard feychttyng,
And of Ierusalem a ʒeir was kyng.

Robert the Brois throu hard feich[t]yng,          55
With few, venkust the mychthy kyng
Off Ingland, Edward, twyse in fycht,
At occupit his realme but rycht;
At sumtyme wes set so hard,
At hat nocht sax till hym toward.          60


Ʒe gude men that thir balletis redis,
Deme quha dochtyast was in dedis.

THE DUIK OF ORLYANCE IN
DEFENCE OF THE SCOTS

N

## VIII.

## THE DUIK OF ORLYANCE IN DEFENCE OF THE SCOTS.

---

*THE following lines, transcribed from the* Maitland Col-*lections of Scotish Poetry, deposited in the* Pepysian Li-brary, Cambridge, *are merely an extract, with some occa-sional variations, from* Androw of Wyntown's *Chronicle,—a work, the publication of which was fortunately under-taken, and executed with an unrivalled degree of care and elegance, by the unwearied assiduity of its learned Editor, the late* David Macpherson.

*These lines, however, may be allowed to stand in opposi-tion to some of the many ancient rhymes which the English are known to have scattered abroad against the Scots. The jealous and hostile spirit which, for so many ages, existed betwixt the inhabitants of the two Kingdoms, has long happily ceased, and, we trust, for ever. Nevertheless, it is curious and interesting to observe the various manifestations of this long-cherished, and deep-seated animosity;—whether we may read in our Annals of strife and bloodshed in the field of battle ;—of border forays and predatory excursions ; or, discover it in the more harmless, but not less vehement and sarcastic effusions in which they mutually seem to have indulged.*

*The question put by the illustrious* Duke of Orleans *is
sufficiently simple and dispassionate, and leads to a natural
and satisfactory conclusion, when he asked, how it came that
the English, with all their boasting, never were able to van-
quish* " the puir folk of Scotland "—

> —— —— "whose gaddering into weiris
> Micht nocht exceid five hundreth speiris—"

*but allowed themselves to be harassed night and day, by
those whom they pretended to hold in despite; nor could
enforce that homage and obedience which, at times, they
presumed to say, we owed to the Crown of England.*

VIII.

# '𝔇efence of the 𝔖cots.'

ANE thowsand ȝeir thre hundreth nyntye and ane
   Fra Jesus Chryst had manheid tane
The bischop of Sanct Androis se,
Maister Waltir Traill callit was he,—
Be counsale and be ordinance          5
Of Scottismen, he passit in France:
Ffor, in to Scotland men hard tell,
At the duik Johne of Longcastell,
Be ane ordinat delyuerance
Off Inglismen, he passit in France.——    10
And quhatsoeuir thay tretit had,
Our bischop thair tuell monethis baid.
And thair sayrlie the Inglismen
The Scottismen diffamit than:—
Thai said, thair gaddering in to weiris,    15
Micht nocht exceid fyve hundreth speiris:
The king of France, thai said, forthy,
Suld lat of Scottis men bot lichtlye.
Thir wourdis war said in the presence
Of the duchtie Duik of Orlyance,    20
Quhilk had ane speciale effectioun
Till Scottismen and thair natioun;
And than in haist he maid ansueyr,
As it was said on this maneyr:—
Ȝe wein to lak, bot ȝe commend    25
That natioun, as ȝe mak it kend:
Was neuer realme, nor regioun,
Wourth mair commendatioun,

Than ar the few folk of Scotland,
As that ȝe gar ws vnderstand.     30
Ȝe say, thair gaddering in to weiris,
May nocht exceid fyve hundreth speiris;
And ȝe ar ane michtie natioun,
Excelland in presumptioun,
Ffor all landis lyand ȝow by     35
Ȝe suppress with ȝour senȝory;
Owthir ȝe win thame to ȝour croun,
Or haldis thame in subjectioun;
Bot the few folk of Scotland,
Quhilk by dry marchis ar lyand     40
Neir on to ȝow, thai hald thair awin,
As it is maid vntill ws knawin;
And will cum with thair poweir,
Playn ȝe, or ȝour land, of weir,
And day and nycht will ly thairin,     45
And in ȝour sicht ȝour landis ' bryne; '
Ȝour cattale, and ȝour gudis, thay ta;
And spairis nathing ȝour self to sla;
Thus suffer thay on na kin wyss,
Ȝow of sic micht to do suppryss;     50
Bot euir thay quyt ȝow lill for lall,
Or that ȝe skaill the market all:
That natioun may ȝe nocht defame,
Bot gif ȝe smyt ȝour awin with schame!
The king of France thairfor think me,     55
Suld hald thame in to mair daintie,
That so few folk, of so lytill micht,
Aganis ȝow can manteine thair fecht,
Vpon the dry merchis lyand,
As it is gart ws vnderstand.—     60
   Quhen this was said the Inglismen,
War schamit of thair wourdis than,
And held thame still, and spak no mair,
In till dispyt as thai did ayr.

ffinita responsio Illustrissimi ducis Orlianensis
in honorem et defensionem Scotorum.

# THE BLUDY SERK

IX.

# THE BLUDY SERK.

*THE author of this admired ballad, which owes its pre-
servation to Bannatyne's Manuscript, was our fine moral
poet* Robert Henryson, *who flourished in the latter part of
the Fifteenth Century.  His poems are now very generally
known by the edition of his works printed in* 1865, *and, in
particular, his* Robene and Makyne *is allowed to be the
earliest and one of the finest pastorals in our language.
This ballad is probably derived from one of the* Tales *in the*
Gesta Romanorum, *of which the following summary is
given by* Warton *in his* History of English Poetry.[1]—
"A knight offers to recover a lady's inheritance which had
been seized by a tyrant, on condition that if he is slain, she
shall always keep his bloody armour hanging in her chamber.
He regains her property, although he dies in the attempt;
and as often as she was afterwards sued for in marriage,
before she gave an answer, she returned to her chamber, and
contemplating with tears her deliverer's bloody armour, reso-
lutely rejected every solicitation."  The poem of* Henryson
*differs in several particulars, but principally in his descrip-
tion of the tyrant as a "fowll gyane."*

*In the Bannatyne MS., where this poem is preserved, it
is included amongst various 'Fabillis' there contained.*

[1] Vol. i. Diss. iii. p. ccii.

Henryson *was one of the first of the British poets to employ Fables as a distinct class of popular literature. His collection was proposed to be published from a MS. preserved in the British Museum, and was on the eve of being sent to press, when our ancient literature lost one of its most zealous and active supporters, in the late* Sir Alexander Boswell.

*This manuscript, written in the year* 1571, *the Editor conceives may have been a transcript from a printed copy, as the* Fables *certainly were printed more than once about that period. In the Sale Catalogue of the curious library of* Sir Andrew Balfour, M.D., *which was dispersed by auction at Edinburgh in* 1695, *an edition printed there in* 1570 *occurs ; but no copy of so early a date is at present known. Some curious elucidations of these* Fables *might have been received from an English version by* Richard Smith, *which appeared at London in* 1577, *under the title of* "The Fabulous Tales of Esope the Phrygian, compiled moste eloquently in Scottishe Metre by Master Robert Henrison, and now lately Englished." *The translator, who is likewise the printer of the volume, speaks of these fables as* "*verie eloquent and full of great invention,*" *and, referring to one of the printed copies, exposed, as the custom was, for sale, he says,*—

> " Late passing thorowe Paules Church yarde,   Aside I cast mine eye
> And ere I wist, to me appearde,   Sir Esope by and by
> Apparelled both braue and fine,   After the Scottish guise," &c.[1]

---

[1] This curious volume, however, which was at one time in the Library of Sion College, is stated in the notes to Henryson's Works, ed. Laing, p. 267, to have fallen aside.

# '𝕿𝖍𝖊 𝖇𝖑𝖚𝖉𝖞 𝕾𝖊𝖗𝖐.'

THIS hindir ʒeir I hard be tald,
  Thair was a worthy King ;
Dukis, Erlis, and Barronis bald,
  He had at his bidding.
The Lord was anceane and ald,         5
  And sexty ʒeiris cowth ring ;
He had a dochter fair to fald,
  A lusty lady ʒing.

Off all fairheid scho bur the flour,
  And eik hir faderis air ;         10
Off lusty laitis and he honour,
  Meik, bot and debonair.
Scho wynnit in a bigly bour,
  On fold wes none so fair,
Princis luvit hir paramour,         15
  In cuntreis our allquhair.

Thair dwelt alyt besyde the king
  A fowll gyane of ane ;
Stollin he hes the lady ʒing,
  Away with hir is gane ;        20
And kest hir in his dungering,
  Quhair licht scho micht se nane :
Hungir and cauld, and grit thristing,
  Scho fand in to hir waine.

He wes the laithliest on to luk                    25
  That on the grund mycht gang :
His nailis wes lyk ane hellis cruk,
  Thairwith fyve quarteris lang.
Thair wes nane that he ourtuk,
  In rycht or ȝit in wrang,                         30
Bot all in schondir he thame schuke ;
  The gyane wes so strang.

He held the lady day and nycht,
  Within his deip dungeoun ;
He wald nocht gif of hir a sicht                    35
  For gold nor ȝit ransoun.
Bot gife the king mycht get a knycht,
  To fecht with his persoun,
To fecht with him, both day and nycht,
  Quhill ane wer dungin doun.                       40

The king gart seik baith fer and neir,
  Beth be se and land,
Off ony knycht gife he micht heir,
  Wald fecht with that gyand.
A worthy prince, that had no peir,                  45
  Hes tane the deid on hand,
For the luve of the lady cleir ;
  And held full trew cunnand.

That prince come prowdly to the toun,
  Of that gyane to heir ;                           50
And fawcht with him, his awin persoun,
  And tuke him presoneir ;
And kest him in his awin dungeoun,
  Allane, withouttin feir,
With hungir, cauld, and confusioun,                 55
  As full weill worthy weir.

Syne brak the bour, had hame the bricht,
  Vnto hir fadir deir :

Sa evill wondit was the knycht,
  That he behuvit to de.
Vnlusum was his likame dicht;
  His sark was all bludy;
In all the warld was thair a wicht
  So peteouss for to se!                          60

The lady murnyt, and maid grit mone,    65
  With all hir mekle micht:
" I luvit nevir lufe, bot one,
  That dulfully now is dicht!
God sen my lyfe wer fra me tone,
  Or I had sene ȝone sicht;                       70
Or ellis in begging evir to gone,
  Furth with ȝone curtass knycht."

He said, " Fair lady now mone I
  De, trestly ȝe me trow:
Tak ȝe my sark that is bludy,              75
  And hing it forrow ȝow;
First think on it, and syne on me,
  Quhen men cumis ȝow to wow."
The lady said, " Be Mary fre,
  Thairto I mak a wow."                           80

Quhen that scho lukit to the serk,
  Scho thocht on the persoun:
And prayit for him with all hir harte,
  That lowsd hir of bandoun:
Quhair scho was wont to sit full merk      85
  In that deip dungeoun:
And evir quhill scho wes in quert,
  That wass hir a lessoun.

L. 61. 'his likame' is, *his body* (from the Isl. lykame, *corpus*), which
Sibbald, supposing it an error of the transcriber, chose to alter to 'lynkome,'
*linen*, and then bring forward this as an additional presumption that Henryson *was* the author of ' Christ's Kirk on the Greene,' because, forsooth, the
word *lynkome* occurs in it !

Sa weill the lady luvit the knycht,
  That no man wald scho tak:       90
Sa suld we do our God of micht
  That did all for ws mak;
Quhilk fullely to deid wes dicht,
  For sinfull manis saik:
Sa suld we do, both day and nycht,     95
  With prayaris to him mak.

## 𝔐oralitas.

This King is lyk the Trinitie
  Baith in hevin and heir:
The Manis saule to the Lady:
  The Gyane to Lucefeir:       100
The Knycht to Chryst, that deit on tre,
  And coft our synnis deir:
The pit to hell, with panis fell;
  The syn to the woweir.

The Lady was wowd, but scho said nay,   105
  With men that wald hir wed;
Sa suld we wryth all syn away,
  That in our breist is bred.
I pray to Jesu Chryst verrey
  For ws his blud that bled,     110
To be our help on domysday,
  Quhair lawis ar straitly led.

The saule is Godis dochtir deir,
  And eik his handewerk,
That was betrasit with Lucifeir,     115
  Quha sittis in hell, full merk.
Borrowit with Chrystis angell cleir,
  Hend men! will ӡe nocht herk?
For his lufe that bocht ws deir,
  Think on the Bludy Serk!     120

ffinis q; m̄r. R. Henryci.

# SIR JOHN ROWLL'S CURSING

X.

# SIR JOHN ROWLL'S CURSING.

Dunbar, *in his Lament for the Death of the* Makkaris, *bewails the fate of two contemporary poets named* Rowll, *with whom he seems to have been familiar. He says—*

Death hes tane Rowll of Abirdene
And gentill Rowll of Corstorphyn ;
Two bettir fallowis did no man sie ;
    *Timor mortis conturbat me !* [1]

*But so little is known concerning these two ecclesiastics, as to leave it uncertain which of them should be considered author of the following singular invective :—which, indeed, is the solitary memorial that remains of the talents of either one or other of two men, who received from their illustrious friend this testimony to the excellence of their natural dispositions.*

*Sir David Lyndsay also names Rowll with other Scotish Poets, of whom he says—*

" Thocht thay be deid, thair libellis bene levand,
  Quhilkis, to reherse, makith reidaris to rejose." [2]

Rowll's *poem has been preserved both in* George Ban-

---

[1] Bann. *MS.* fol. 104.         [2] Lyndsay's Works, vol. i. p. 285.

natyne's *and* Sir Richard Maitland's *collections of old* Scotish *poetry.* Lord Hailes *says, " Whether it was written by him, or only in his name, I know not. The following passage in it (he adds) determines the aera at which he lived :—*

> ——'and now of Rome that beiris the rod,
> Vndir the hevin to lowse and bind,
> Paip Alexander.'

*The Pontiff here meant must have been the virtuous* Alexander VI., *who was* Divine Vice-gerent *from* 1492 *to* 1503." [1] *And* Dunbar's *poem, which commemorates their death, was printed in the year* 1508.

Pinkerton *mentions the following poem with great contempt, styling it a stupid and despicable production, and quoting the last lines—*

> " This *tragedy* is callit, but dreid,
> Rowlis cursing, quha will it reid,"

*says the author " might have put a point of interrogation at the close." [2] The name of* Tragedy, *in the language of those times, was applied to any descriptive poem, nor was it appropriated to dramatic compositions in England before the reign of* Henry VIII., *although no regular tragedy was produced earlier than* January 1561, *when* Ferrex and Porrex *was first represented.*

Sir John Rowll's *Cursing may be considered as a religious satire, being, as* Lord Hailes *justly observed, " an invective against those who defraud the clergy of their dues, and has no resemblance to any sort of dramatic composition." [3]* Dr Leyden [4] *thought that in acrimony it was little inferior to* Sterne's *chapter of curses : and the author's invocation of all the devils to revenge the stealing of his geese, he considered as forming a curious contrast to Sir John of Grantam's curse for the Miller's eels that were stolen, recorded in* Harsnet's *Detection of Egregious Impostures :—*

[1] Bannatyne Poems, 1770, p. 272.
[2] Maitland Poems, 1786, p. 451.
[3] Bannatyne Poems, 1770, p. 270.
[4] Glossary to the Complaynt of Scotland, 1801, p. 329.

O

> " All you that have stolen the Miller's eelis,
>     *Laudate Dominum de cœlis :*
> And all that have consented thereto,
>     *Benedicamus Domino.*"

*After the author has excommunicated—*

> " Baith the halderis and conceilaris
>     Ressettaris and the preve steilaris,"

*and bade them* " hy to the pot of hell," *the lines—*

> " In hellis hoill quhair nevir is licht,
>   Nor nevir is day, bot evir nicht,
>   Quhair nevir is joy evin and morrow,
>   Bot endles pane, dule and sorrow ;
>   Quhair nevir is petie nor concord,
>   Nor amitie, bot discord,
>   Malice, rancour and invy, &c."

*are very striking, and remind us of the impressive descrip-*
*tion by a greater poet, of—*

> " A dungeon horrible on all sides round,
>   As one great furnace flam'd ; yet from those flames
>   No light ; but rather darkness visible
>   Serv'd only to discover sights of woe,
>   Regions of sorrow, doleful shades, where peace
>   And rest can never dwell ; hope never comes,
>   That comes to all ; but torture without end
>   Still urges, and a fiery deluge, fed
>   With ever-burning sulphur unconsumed."
>                                             —MILTON.

X.

## Heir followis
## the cursing of S<sup>r</sup> Johne Rowlis
## Upoun the steilaris of his fowlis.

DEVYNE power of michtis maist,
    Of Fadir, Sone, and Haly Ghaist,
Jesu Chryst and his appostillis,
Petir, Paule and his discipillis,
And all the power vndir God,           5
And now of Rome that beiris the rod
Vndir the hevin to lowse and bind,
Paip Alexander, that we do fynd
With that power that Petir gaif,
Godis braid malesone mote thay haif,    10
And all the blude about thair hairt.
Blak be thair hour, blak be thair pairt,
For fyve fat geiss of Schir Johine Rowlis,
With caponis, henis and vthir fowlis,
Baith the halderis and conceilaris,    15
Ressettaris, and the preve steilaris,
And he that saulis saifis and dammis
Beteich the devill thair guttis and gammis,
Thair toung, thair teith, thair handis, thair feit,
And all thair body haill compleit,    20
That brak his зaird and stall his frutt,
And raif his erbis vp be the rute,

His quheit, his aitis, his peiss, his beir,
In stowk or stak, to do him deir;
In barne, in houss, in kill or mill,                    25
Except it had bene his awin will;
His wow, his lamb, his cheis, his stirk,
Or ony teyndis of haly kirk;
And all that lattis vnkend or knawin
The vicar to dispone his awin                           30
Kirkland hay, or gerss to awaill,
Be thair support, red or counsall;
Now cursit and wareit be thair werd,
Quhill thay be levand on this erd,
Hungir, sturt and tribulatioun,                         35
And nevir to be without vexatioun,
Of vengance, sorrow, sturt and cair,
Graceless, thriftles and threid bair;
All tymes in thair legasie,
Fyre, sword, watter and woddie;                         40
Or ane of thir infirmeteis
Off warldly scherp aduerseteis,
Pouertie, pestilence or poplecy,
Dum, deif or edroposy,
Maigram, madness or missilry,                           45
Appostrum or the perlocy,
Ffluxis, hyvis or huttit ill,
Hoist, heidwark or fawin ill,
Kald, kanker, feistir or feveris,
Brukis, bylis, blobbis and bleistiris,                  50
Emeroidese, or the sair halss,
The pokkis, the spaving in the halss
The panefull gravell and the gutt,
The gulsoch that they nevir be but,
Seattica and arrattica,                                 55
The cruke, the cramp, the collica,
The worme, the wareit wedonympha,
Rimbursin, rippillis or bellythra,
The choikis that haldis the chaftis fra chowing,
Golkgaliter at the hairt growing,                       60

The stane wring, stane and stane blind,
The berne bed, and morbehind
The strangelour, and grit glengloir,
The harchatt in the lippis befoir,
The mowlis, and in thair sleip the mair,          65
The kanker and the kattair;
[And never to be but schot of blude,
Or Elf-schot, thus to conclude,
And mony utter malleteis,
Bayth for his hennes and his geis,]              70
Mott fall vpoun thair kankart corss,
With all the evil that evir had horss,
Fische, fowll, beist or man,
In erd sen first the warld began,
Till thay remember or thay de,                   75
Repentand thair iniquitie,
And draw thair inclinatioun
Fra stowth to contemplatioun,
Fra feyndis fell subiectioun
To haly kirkis correctioun.                      80
Sua thay mak plane confessioun
Thair gud will and contritioun,
Confessand thame to thair curatt,
That in thair hairtis is evill indurat.
Na vthir preist hes power, nor freir;            85
And thay that daly will perseveir,
Nocht dreidand God in work nor word,
Nor ȝit of haly kirk the suord,
Bot in thair cursit and sinfull wayis
Levand and dryvand our thair dayis,              90
Nor ask God mercy nor repent,
Than, this salbe thair sacrament;
Fra God, our Lady and all thair hallowis,
To the feynd thair saulis, thair craig the gallowis
I gif, and Cerberus thair banis sall knaw,       95
For thair dispyt of the kirkis law,
Gog and Magog, and grym Garog,
The devill of hell, the theif Harog,

Sym Skynnar and Schir Garnega,
Julius appostata,                                                100
Prince Pluto and quene Cokatrice,
Devetinus the devill that maid the dyce,
Cokadame and Semiramis,
Fyremouth and Tutivillus,
And Browny als, that can play kow                               105
Behind the claith, with mony mow.
All thir about the beir salbe
Singand ane dolorus dergie;
And vthiris devillis thair salbe sene,
Als thik as mot in sonis beme;                                  110
Thair sall thay kary in thair clukis,
Sum libberlais, and sum hell crukis,
Sum with kamis, and sum with kardis,
Sum with quhippis of leddrin tardis,
Sum with clubbis and mellis of leid,                            115
Sum with brandrathis birnand reid,
Sum with rumpillis lyk a skait,
And geiss and caponis rostit hait,
That sal be laschit on thair lippis,
Cum thay within the devillis grippis,                           120
With skulʒeoun clowttis, and dressing knyvis,
Platt for plat on thair gyngyvis;
Sayis richt thus " Of Rowlis geiss
Thame chaftis thame chowit every peiss;
For thow art he, and thow art scho                              125
That Rowlis blak robene put in bro;
And thow art scho that stall the hen,
And put her in the pot thair ben.
Lo! this is he that with his hairt
Wald nevir gif the vicar his pairt,                             130
Bot ay abowt for to dissaif
The haly kirk that it sowld haif."
Than ruffy Tasker with his flaill
Sall beit thame all fra top to taill;
And ruffy Ragmen with his taggis                               135
Sall ryfe thair sinfull saule in raggis;

And quhen the devillis hes thame tirvit,
All thair saulis sal be transformit,
Sum in bichis, and sum in beiris,
Sum in mvlis, and sum in meiris,                    140
Aganis the statour that thay wer in,
For vengence of thair deidly sin,
To ryd and tak possessioun
Throw all hell vp and doun,
And with grit din and deray                         145
Compeir sall Sathan but delay,
Sayand richt thus with sentence he,
" Vpoun the day that thow sall de,
I devill of deillis, I ȝow condame
For geis, for ȝowis, for woll, for lame.            150
Thairfoir hy ȝow to the pott of hell,
With Sathan our Abirone to dwell ;
As feyndis spreitis perpetualy
For to remane in mesary.
Deip Acheron ȝour saulis invaid                     155
As blak, as ruch as ony taid ;
Snaykis, serpentis and edderis
Mott stuf ȝour bellyis and ȝour bledderis,
In hellis hoill quhair nevir is licht,
Nor nevir is day, bot evir nicht,                   160
Quhair nevir is joy evin and morrow,
Bot endles pane, dule and sorrow ;
Quhair nevir is petie nor concord,
Nor amitie, bot discord,
Malice, rancour and invy,                           165
With magry and malancoly ;
[Quhair thair is hunger, cald and thrist,
Dirknes, mirknes, rouk and mist,
And cair, but consolatioun,
With eternall damnatioun."]                         170
Than fra the sentence be on thame said,
Grit Baliall sall gif a braid,
And bakwart leip vpon a beir,
Sum on ane mvle, sum on a meir,

    Sum on wolffis, and sum on wichis,                    175
    Sum on brod sowis sum on bichis.
    [Sum on dragounis, and sum on devillis,
    And sum on gillattis just up creilis,]
    Than is thair nocht bot sadill and brydill,
    Thir outtit meiris hes lang gane ydill;               180
    Bot sic ane clawing with thair clukis,
    And sic ane reirding with thair rukis,
    Rampand with ane hiddowis beir,
    Cryand "All is ouris that is heir."
    [Gif thai be weirun of grit pane                      185
    All thair saulis sall be slane
    Quhair with the feynd thai salbe furrit
    Becaus the kirk thai have incurrit.]
    The memberis of tha wickit men
    That staw the guse, the cok, the hen,                 190
    Thay salbe revin be the throttis,
    For cutting of tha fowlis croppis;
    [Salbe bordourit and buttonit als,
    In sign that thai war mansworne and fals;]
    Syne led in towis and in lang tedderis,              195
    And daly etin with taidis and edderis,
    That all the court of hevin may knaw
    Thay war the thevis that Rowlis geiss staw.
    For quhy! grit God our hiest juge,
    He gaif decreit but refuge,                            200
    That all pykaris of pultre
    Gais nocht to hevin, bot thay sall fle
    To hell without redemptioun,
    Quhair is no remissioun.
    The forme of thir vgly devillis,                      205
    Thay hafe lang tailis on thair heilis,
    And rumpillis·hingand on thair tailis,
    Dragoun heidis, and warwolf nalis,
    With glowrane eyne as glitterand glass,
    With bowgillis and hornis maid of brass,              210
    And dyverss facis repleit with yre,
    Spowtand vennum and sparkis of fyre;

And sum with teith and tegir tungis,
Attour thair chin with bludy fangis
Spottit and sprinklit vp and doun,                215
Reid attry lyk a scorpioun,
And sum ar smeith and sum are ruch,
And sum ar lyk ane serpentis sluch,
With prik mule eiris sum ar lyk,
Thair neifs ar lyk ane midding tyk,              220
With gaippand mowth richt ʒaip to swelly
The mair the less devill in his belly.
Of thair fowle fegouris na man can tell,
Thocht thay wer sevin ʒeiris in hell,
To leir to paynt, portour or blasoun,            225
Thair forme and thayr feyndly fassoun,
Thair vgsum horribiliteis.
Nor ʒit na that schaipis with scheiris,
Thocht infineit he be of ʒeiris,
Maist principaly to schaip thair graith          230
In hell, for steiling heir of claith,
Can conterfit nor mak it meit,
Ane gabart for a deill compleit;
And ʒit in hell ar mony ane
That said thai war als trew as stane.            235
Gif thair be ony in this houss
That beiris the nedill, gorrit the lowss,
I thame beseik thay be nocht wraith
Suppois they clyit haif parte of claith;
Bot seik the causs, and leif the deid,           240
And blame the scheiris that raif the skreid;
And quha that steilis, and on stowth levis,
Cursit mot thay be amang thir thevis.
Now to the effect ga will I,
And speik of feyndis phantesy,                    245
In court nocht with the quene of fary
But heltaris, heidtailis, sonkis or sadillis,
But butis or spurris, crukis or ladillis,
With full berdis blasand in the wind,
And hett speitis in thair taill behind.          250

Than Inflar Tasy with his jaggis,
And Belly Bassy with his baggis,
At hellis ʒettis sall mak sic reirding,
On thir steillaris of geiss sall ding,
That it beis hard in middil erd                255
The grit flappis with sic faird;
Thunder blastis and fyre sall blaw,
That na devill may ane vthir knaw
For reik, stynk, and bryntstane birnand,
Devillis ʒelpand, gaipand and girnand;        260
Than sall bla Baliall gif ane brattill,
And all the thevis in hell sall startill.
Lyk to ane gaid of yrne or steill
That doun war sinkand in ane weell,
Sa sall thay ga to endles pane,               265
And nevir to cum hame agane.
  Now Jesu, for thy passioun,
That deit for our redemptioun,
Of mankynd haif mercy sone.
Latt never this sentence fall thame vpone,    270
Bot grant thame grace ay till forbeir
Resset or stowth of vthir menis geir;
And als agane the geir restoir
Till Rowle, as I hafe said befoir;
And to repent thay may in tyme,               275
Pray we to God.   Thus endis the ryme.
This tragedy is callit, but dreid,
ROWLIS CURSING, quha will it reid.            278

*Finis quod* ROWLL.


ffinis.

TAYIS BANK

XI.

# TAYIS BANK.

—————

*TWYSBANK, one of the popular airs mentioned in* Colkelbie's Sow, *has been conjectured*[1] *to be the appropriate
tune of the following beautiful song, a conjecture, however,
proceeding entirely on the resemblance of the name to that of
the* River Tay, *which occurs in the poem; but still it may
not be inappropriately designated by the title we have given it.
We owe its preservation to the care of* George Bannatyne,
*in whose MS. collection it is inserted at fol. 229. Although
an affected quaintness has somewhat disfigured it by a re-
dundance of alliteration, yet as a descriptive poem, it is
possessed of considerable merit; and as few, if any, of the*
Scotish *songs now extant, are of equal antiquity, it is remarkable that* 'Tayis bank' *should have escaped the notice
of* Ritson, *and other collectors of our Lyric poetry. Not
many years since, however, a copy of it appeared in the*
British Bibliographer,[2] *to which work it was transmitted
by the late* Henry Weber, *whose services in publishing,
with great fidelity and care, several of the early Metrical
Romances in our vernacular tongue, have not been duly
appreciated.*

*From the context of this poem, says* Mr Weber, *" it ap-*

[1] *Leyden,* Complaynt of Scotland, Introd. p. 283.
[2] Vol. iv. p. 186.

pears to have been composed on a lady of the noble family of Perth, *named* Margaret; *and it may be conjectured with almost more than probability, that the subject of the. poem was* Margaret, *eldest daughter* of Sir John Drummond, *lord of that ilk, and Stobhall, who is stated to have been contracted to* King James IV. *and had a daughter by him, afterwards married to* Alexander, Earl of Huntley." *Should this supposition respecting the lady be deemed well founded, the reader may feel some interest in the. description contained in the quotation that is annexed. The poem itself may unquestionably be attributed to the reign of our gallant Monarch* James IV.

XI.

# 'Tayis bank.'

QUHEN Tayis bank wes blumyt brycht,
  With blosomes blyth and bred,
Be that riuer ran I doun rycht,
  Vndir the ryss I red;
The merle melit with all hir mycht,       5
  And mirth in mornying maid,
Throw solace, sound, and semely sicht,
  Alswith a sang I said.

Vndir that bank, quhair bliss had bene,
  I bownit me to abyde;       10
Ane holene, hevinly hewit grene,
  Rycht heyndly did me hyd.
The sone schyne our the schawis schene,
  Full semely me besyd;
In bed of blumes bricht besene,       15
  A sleip cowth me ourslyd.

About all blomet wes my bour
  With blosummes broun and blew,
Ourfret with mony fair fresch flour,
  Helsum of hevinly hew;       20
With schakeris of the schene dew schour,
  Schynnyng my courtenis schew,
Arrayit with a rich vardour
  Of natouris werkis new.

Rasing the birdis fra thair rest,      25
  The reid sone raiss with rawis;
The lark sang lowd, quhill lycht mycht lest,
  A lay of luvis lawis;
The nythingall woik of hir nest,
  Singing, 'The day vpdawis;'      30
The mirthfull maveiss merriest
  Schill schowttit throw the schawis.

All flouris grew that firth within,
  That man cowth haif in mynd,
And in that flud all fische with fyn,      35
  That creat wer be kynd:
Vndir the rise the ra dyd ryn
  Our ron, our rute, our rynd,
The dvn deir dansit with a dyn,
  And herdis of hairt and hynd.      40

Wod winter, with his wallowand wynd,
  But weir, away wes went:
Brasit about with wyld wodbynd
  Wer bewis on the bent:
Allone vnder the lusty lynd,      45
  I saw ane lusum lent,
That fairly war so fare to fynd
  Vndir the firmament.

Scho wes the lustiest on lyve,
  Allone lent on a land,      50
And farest figour, be sic fyve,
  That evir in firth I fand.
Hir cumly cullour to discryve
  I dar nocht tak on hand;
Moir womanly borne of a wyfe      55
  Wes neuer, I dar warrand.

To creatur that wes in cair,
  Or cauld of crewelty,

A blicht blenk of hir vesage bair
  Of baill his bute mycht be;        60
Hir hyd, hir hew, hir hevinly hair
  Mycht havy hairtis vphie;
So angelik vnder the air
  Neuir wicht I saw with E.

The blosummes that wer blycht and brycht  65
  By hir wer blacht and blew;
Scho gladit all the foull of flicht,
  That in the forrest flew;
Scho mycht haif confort king or knycht
  That ever in cuntre I knew,        70
As waill, and well of wardly wicht
  In womanly vertew.

Hir cullour cleir, hir countinance,
  Hir cumly cristall ene,
Hir portratour of most plesance       75
  All pictour did prevene.
Off every vertew to avance,
  Quhen ladeis prasit bene,
Rychttest in my remembrance
  That rose is rutit grene.        80

This myld, meik, mansuet Mergrit,
  This perle polist most quhyt,
Dame Natouris deir dochter discreit,
  The dyamant of delyt;
Neuer formit wes to found on feit    85
  Ane figour more perfyte,
Nor non on mold that did hir meit,
  Mycht mend hir wirth a myte.

This myrthfull maid to meit I ment,
  And merkit furth on mold;      90
Bot sone within a wane scho went,
  Most hevinly to behold;

The bricht sone with his bemys blent
  Vpoun the bertis bold,
Farest vnder the firmament        95
  That formit wes on fold.

As parradyce that place but peir
  Wes plesant to my sicht;
Of forrest, and of fresch reveir,
  Of firth, and fowll of flicht,       100
Of birdis, bath on bonk and breir,
  With blumes brekand bricht,
As hevin in to this erd doun heir,
  Hertis to hald on hicht.

So went this womanly away      105
  Amang thir woddis wyd,
And I to heir thir birdis gay
  Did in a bonk abyd;
Quhair ron and ryss raiss in aray,
  Endlang the reuer syd:      110
This hapnit me in a tyme in May
  In till a morning tyd.

The reuer throw the ryse cowth rowt
  And roseris raiss on raw;
The schene birdis full schill cowth schowt  115
  Into that semly schaw:
Joy wes within and joy without,
  Vnder that wlonkest waw,
Quhair Tay ran down with stremis stout
  Full strecht vnder Stobschaw.     120

ffinis.

---

" Margaret Drummond, eldest daughter of John Lord
Drummond, was a Lady of rare perfections and singular

P

beautie.　With her, the young King James the 4th was [so] deeply enamoured, that without acquainting his Nobles or Council, he was affianced to her in order to have made her his Queen.　But so soon as his intentions were discovered, all possible obstructions were made both by the Nobility, who designed an allyance with a daughter of England, as a mean to procure Peace betwixt the Nations, and by the Clergie, who declared against the lawfulness of the marriage, because they were within the degrees of consanguinity forbidden by the Canon Law.　Nevertheless, the King, under promise, gott her with child, which proved a daughter, [in the year 1497,] and was called Lady Margaret Stewart ; but he was so much touched in conscience for the engagement he had made to the young Lady, that, notwithstanding the weakness of the Royal family, he rejected all propositions of marriage, so long as she lived : for he was crowned in the year 1488, at the age of sixteen, and did not marry untill the year 1502, when he was near thirty, and about a year after her death, which was effected not without suspition of poison, for the common tradition goes, that a potion was provided in a breakfast to dispatch her for liberating the King from his promise, that he might match with England ; but so it happened that she called two of her sisters, then with her, Lady Flemyng and a younger [sister] Sybilla, a maid, whereby it fell out all the three were destroyed with the force of the poyson.　They ly buried in a curious vault, covered with 3 fair blue marble stones joined closs together, about the middle of the quyre of the Cathedrall church of Dumblane : for about this time the buriall place for the family of Drummond at Innerpaffray was not yet built.　The Monument which contains the ashes of these three lady's stands intire to this day, and confirms the credit of this sad story."— HISTORY OF THE FAMILY OF DRUMMOND. [by William, Viscount of Strathallan,] 1681. MS. folio 188. DRUMM. CASTLE.

# WELCUM TO MAY

XII.

# WELCUM TO MAY.

*THE finest poetical descriptions of external nature, not unusually are found referable to the month of May*—'fair May,' (*in the words of the gentle* Spenser [1])—

—"the fairest maid on ground,"

*who comes*

"Deck'd all with dainties of her Season's pride
And throwing flowers out of her lap around."

*The present poem, which has something of a lyrical character, is a pleasing specimen, to shew how attentive our ancient poetical writers were in celebrating the praises*

"Of lusty May, that mudder is of flouris."

*It is given from* Bannatyne's *manuscript,*[2] *which likewise contains the earliest copy of the well-known song* 'O lusty Maye, of Flora Quene,' *mentioned in the* Complaynt of Scotland, *and supposed to have been written by* Alexander Scott.

*It is rather singular that in the following poem no allusions should be found to the games and pastimes peculiar*

—"to the mery moneth of May
Whan loue lads masken in fresh aray."

*This circumstance might warrant us in fixing the date of*

---

[1] Faerie Quene, B. vii. 34.　　　　[2] MS. fol. 229 b.

*its composition between the year* 1555, *when all such re-creations were forbidden by an Act of Parliament,*[1] *(which enjoined, that* 'gif ony wemen or vthers about simmer treis singand makis perturbatioun to the Quenis liegis in the passage throw burrowis and vtheris landwart townis the wemen perturbatouris for skafrie of money or vtherwise salbe takin handellit and put vpone the Cukstulis of euerie burgh or towne,')—*and the year* 1568, *when the manuscript, from which the poem is given, was compiled.*

[1] Acts of Parl. vol. ii. p. 500.

XII.

# '𝔚elcum to 𝔐ay.'

BE glaid all ȝe that luvaris bene,
For now hes May depaynt with grene
The hillis, valis and the medis;
And flouris lustely vpspreidis.
Awalk out of ȝour sluggairdy,     5
To heir the birdis melody;
Quhois suggourit nottis loud and cleir
Is now ane parradice to heir.
Go walk vpoun sum rever fair;
Go tak the fresch and holsum air;     10
Go luke vpoun the flurist fell;
Go feill the herbis plesand smell;
Quhilk will ȝour comfort gar incres,
And all avoyd ȝour havines.
The new cled purpour hevin espy,     15
Behald the lark now in the sky,
With besy wyng scho clymis on hicht,
For grit joy of the dayis licht.
Behald the verdour fresch of hew,
Powdderit with grene, quhyt, and blew,     20
Quhairwith dame Flora, in this May,
Dois richely all the feild array;
And how Aurora, with visage pale,
Inbalmes with hir cristal hale
The grene and tendir pylis ȝing,     25
Of every gress that dois vpspryng;

And with hir beriall droppis bricht
Makis the gresys gleme of licht.
Luk on the saufir firmament,
And on the annammellit orient; 30
Luke or Phebus put vp his heid,
As he dois raiss his baneris reid;
He dois the eist so bricht attyre,
That all semis birnyng in a fyre;
Quhilk confort dois to every thing, 35
Man, bird, beist, and flurissing.
Quhairfoir, luvaris, be glaid and lycht,
For schort is ȝour havy nycht,
And lenthit is ȝour myrry day,
Thairfoir ȝe velcum new this May: 40
And, birdis, do ȝour haill plesance
With mirry song and obseruance,
This May to velcum at ȝour mycht,
At fresch Phebus vprysing bricht:
And all ye flouris that dois spreid, 45
Lay furth ȝour levis vpoun breid,
And welcum May with benyng cheir,
The quene of euery moneth cleir.
And euery man thank in his mynd
The God of natur and of kynd, 50
Quhilk ordanit all for our behufe,
The erd vndir, the air abufe,
Bird, beist, flour, tyme, day and nycht,
The planeitis for to gif ws licht.


ffinis.

THE

# TALE OF COLKELBIE SOW

XIII.

# THE TALE OF COLKELBIE SOW.

*THE following Tale, which is of considerable antiquity, is now printed for the first time, from* BANNATYNE'S MANUSCRIPT, *preserved in the Library of the Faculty of Advocates. It is contained in the* Fifth *part or division of this valuable Collection, commencing—"Heir followis the "fyift pairt of this buik, contenying the ffabillis of Esop, "with diuerss vthir fabillis and poeticall workis maid and "compyld be diuers lernit men,* 1568." *On the back of this Title is the following Address:*

"TO THE REDAR.

My freindis thir storeis subsequent,  
Albeid bot fabillis thay present,  
3it devyne doctowris of jugement  
 Sayis thair ar hid, but dowt,  
Grave materis wyiss and sapient  
Vnder the workis of poyetis gent,  
Thairfoir be war that thow consent  
 To blame thir heir set owt."

*From internal evidence, the date of* Cowkelbie Sow, *or* Colkelbie, *although posterior to* Chaucer,[1] *evidently appears, from the Prohemium, to have been written during the æra of Minstrelsy. With little hesitation, therefore, it may be assigned to some time previous to the middle of the Fif-*

[1] The first wes the samyn Chantecleir to luke,  
Of quhome Chaucer treitis in to his buke.  
   *—Vide* stanza 99, part iii.

*teenth Century—since it seems, at least, to have been very popular considerably anterior to the age of Dowglas and Dunbar, both of whom flourished in the reign of James IV.*

*Gawin Dowglas thus enumerates Colkelbie, among other heroes of romance, represented in the Mirror of Venus—*

> " I saw Raf Coilȝear with his thrawin brow,
>    Craibit Johne the Reif, and *Auld Cowkewyis Sow.*" [1]

*In " Ane interlude of the laying of a Gaist," a burlesque poem contained in Bannatyne's manuscript, and printed for the first time in the Minstrelsy of the Scottish Border, it is also noticed—*

> " To reid quha will this gentill geist
>    ȝe herd it nocht at *Cokilbys feist.*" [2]

*Dunbar, in his ' General Satire,' alludes to the poem in the following passage—*

> " Sic knavis and crakkaris to play at cartis and dyce,
>    Sic halland schekkaris, whilk at *Cowkelbyis gryce*
>    Are haldyn of pryce, when lymmaris dois convene." [3]

*He also refers to this strange and whimsical rhapsody (the moral of which, however, is expressed in no obscure terms) in his poem called ' A Remonstrance to the King,' ll. 61-68 :—*

> " And thocht this nobill cunning sort,
>    Quhom of befoir I did report
>    Rewardit be, it war bot ressoun
>    Thairat suld no man mak enchessoun ;
>    Bot quhen the vthir fulis nyce,
>    That feistit at Colkelbeis gryce
>    Ar all rewardit, and nocht I,
>    Than on this fals warld I cry, Fy ! "

*The humour of this very singular composition, which is professedly satirical, is certainly coarse, and the versification exceedingly irregular. But the poem, although refer- ring in its allusions (as Dr Leyden has observed) to local and temporary circumstances, which are not obvious at this distance of time, throws much light on the manners and*

---

[1] Palice of Honour, part iii. St. 48.     [2] Bann. MS. fol. 114 b.
[3] Ll. 56-58.

*rustic festivities of the Scottish peasantry during a very early period. From the minuteness of its description, it is also highly illustrative of the music, dances, and musical instruments in common use in Scotland in the Fifteenth Century. And what adds in no small degree to its interest, is the consideration, that the names of the greater proportion of the airs, dances, and songs, enumerated in Colkelbie's Sow, are otherwise unknown.*

*No other copy of the poem than that from which the present transcript was made, is known to exist. In the Asloan Manuscript, formerly possessed by Sir Alexander Boswell of Auchinleck, Baronet, alluded to elsewhere in the present Collection, there appears to have been a copy; but most unfortunately it has shared the same fate with* Ralf Coilȝear, *and some others of the curious tales and romances which that MS. once contained.*

*Of the Author of this Popular Tale, there is no trace whatever in the manuscript; and neither Dr Leyden, who, in his learned introduction to the Complaynt of Scotland, has given various extracts from it, nor any other writer who notices its existence, seems to have known his name. The Arms at the end of the* Prohemium, *of which an accurate* facsimile *has been made, seem to be those of George Bannatyne the transcriber, as they very closely correspond with the Arms of the family of Bannatyne.*

*The orthography of the manuscript has been strictly followed; and no liberties have been taken, with the exception of a few of the contracted words, the preservation of which could have answered no good purpose, and would no doubt have been embarrassing to those unaccustomed to the perusal of ancient manuscripts.*

R. P.

Edinburgh, *November* 1821.

*[To the above notes by Robert Pitcairn, it may be added that the scene of the first part of the poem appears to be laid in Ayrshire, as the lands of Colkelbie are described in the* Retours *as lying in the parish of Stewarton in that county.*

*The following is an outline of the tale :—A 'merry' man*

*named Colkelbie, who possibly took his name from the lands, sold a sow for the sum of three pence, and the disposal of the separate pennies forms the subject of the three parts into which the poem is divided.*

*The first penny fell into a lake, and was found by a woman, who purchased with it a little pig wherewith to make a feast. While the guests, however, are assembling, the pig makes its escape, and afterwards becomes a mighty boar.*

*The second part of the poem contains a tale of chivalry, and in it the scene is transferred to the neighbourhood of Paris, such disregard of geographical accuracy not being unusual with the versifiers of the period. When walking one day by a river, Colkelbie meets a young and beautiful damsel leading an old man, who tells her story :—A foreign couple once lived with him who both died suddenly, leaving their young daughter Adria unprovided for. He adopts her, and in his blindness she leads him about. Colkelbie induces the old man to resign Adria to him on his providing a substitute. He also bestows on him the second penny. Under the care of Colkelbie's wife Bellamerous, Adria grew up to be a handsome woman, and Colkelbie's son Flannislie, a strong man and skilful archer, marries her. The king of France, happening to visit at their house, is struck with the stalwart appearance of Flannislie. He then makes him a squire of his bodyguard, and gives him a grant of land. This became the earldom of Flanders or Flandria, the name being derived from the first syllable of Flannislie, and the latter part of the name Adria.*

*In part three the scene apparently is again shifted to Scotland. Colkelbie with the third penny purchases twentyfour eggs, which he offers as a baptismal gift to the son of his neighbour Blerblowan. The child's mother rejects the gift as too trifling. Colkelbie, however, hands the eggs over to one of his domestics, who from them raises such a stock of poultry, that in fifteen years a thousand pounds were accumulated, which he presents to his godson, and thus lays the foundation of an immense fortune.]*

## XIII.

# Heir begynnis Colkelbie Sow.

### [Prohemium.]

QUHEN riallest, most redowttit and he
  Magnificat crownit kingis in maieste,
   Princis, duces and marquis curious,
Erlis, barronis and knychttis chevelrous,
And gentillmen of he genolegye,     5
As scutiferris and squieris full courtlye,
Ar assemblit and sett in a ryell se,
With namit folkis of he nobilite,
Thair talk that tyme in table honorable,
Befoir lordingis and ladeis amiable,    10
Is oft singing and sawis of solace,
Quhair melody is the mirthfull maistrace,
Ermy deidis in auld dayis done afoir,
Croniculis, gestis, storeis and mich moir,
Manestralis amang mvsicianis merely,   15
To haif hairtis in hevinly armony,
So semis it weill that suthly so war ay.
Quhat is the warld without plesance or play,
Bot passionale? Than lat ws mak sum sport
And recreatioun the cumpany to confort.   20
Wold my lordis do se quho wold begin it?
Quho sall furthschaw or quho sall first fall in it?
Quho with discreit correctioun of ʒow
Bot I, quho hath begune this mater now.

For begynnyng without end quhat availis,                25
Bot lyk a tre flureist quhair the fruct falis,
To quhich all man of quhat estait he be
With recent mynd suld evir haif his E,
Nocht to begin flureist and syne decress,
The langir lyfe the gud loss than to cess?          30
Quhat salbe said bot at his ending he
Frome on fair ymp fell doun a widderit tre;
The lyfe is gone, the loss lesting is lost,
The begynnyng thay say was bot a wost.
Quhairfoir ӡe men most honorable at all,            35
Quhich eternall wald haif memoriall,
Gyd ӡow so that first ӡour God plesit be,
And obtene name and wirchep quhen ӡe de;
And quho will nocht eftir his gudly powere
Considering his estait go profess him a mertere, 40
Or sustene lak, so may he lyknit be
A fair flureiss fadit in a falty tre;
All be my self is this symylitude,
Suld I begin to sport and nocht conclude,
Than wold ӡe all belyve say, " Lo him ӡondir,   45
That set to bourd and left it in a blondir."
Quhairfoir I will say of my fantesy
Sum solasing to glaid this cumpany;
Bot, for Godis luve and his appostill Petir,
Pardoun the fulich face of this mad metir.          50
Sen the sentence to feill is fantastike
Lat the lettir and langage be such like;
Sen all the world changis so mony facis
I trest I will cast caissis vpon caisis.
And so lat se quhat cais ӡe think most nyce.      55
Wisdome vmquhile holdis the nycest wys,
So that it be sport in discretioun,
Without odius crewale comparisoun.
Perticular malice and all such thing removit,
The wyss nycest the wisest quhile is provit,       60
For quhich, knawing myne vnsufficience
To be comprysit perticiane with prudence,
I propone, nocht as wiss presumpteouss,

Bot rathir sport myne awin spereit to reioss,
And my lordis to heir that will deden ;     65
Now I begin with Titill est, Amen.

EXPLICIT PROHEMIUM

ET SEQUITUR PRIMA PARS.

[𝔉itt 𝔉irst.]

H EIR I gife ȝow caiss,
     Vmquhile a merry man wais
Callit Cokkelbe :
He had a simple blak sow,
And he sald hir, bot how,     5
For penneis thre, as eftir ȝe may see ;

L. 6. "As eftir ȝe may see," are added in the manuscript, perhaps by
the same hand, but evidently written with different ink,

And verrely as I hard
Thus the mony he ward;
THE FIRST PENNY of the thre
For a girle gaif he;                                        10
The secund fell in a furde;
The thrid he hid in a hurde.
Now quhilk penny of the thre
Wes best bestowit, say ȝe?
The lost penny wes vplesit,                                 15
The girle for the tyme plesit;
Bot the penny that wes hid,
I hold leist gude did;
For in old prouerbe we sing,
Cumis littill gud of gaddering,                             20
Quhair wrechit awerice birnis,
Hyding hurdis in to hirnis,
And knawis nevir quhome till,
Latting wirschep to go will.
Gret laubor is to get geir,                                 25
And to conserue it is feir,
And moir angir is to leiss
Thir thre peruerst propirteiss,
I find in skarss keping,
And auaritious wynnyng,                                     30
Quhair mesur is nocht maistress,
Bot gaddering for gredeness.
The hid penny, thinkis me,
Wes werst bestowit of the thre,
For it waiss fro the vse of man;                            35
Lat warldis gudis go than,
With messur and merines.
Ȝit thair is moir of this cais,
The penny lost in the lak
Wes fundin and vptak,                                       40
And he that fand it did by
With the samyn penny

L. 10. "Maid" on the margin, and the word "girle" put within
brackets.

Q

A littill pig for his prow
Off Kolkelbeis sow.
A harlot wynnit neir by,                                45
And scho wald mak a mangery,
And had no substance at all,
Bot this pur pig stall,
To furniss a gret feist,
Withouttin stufe, bot this beist.                       50
And ʒit scho callit to hir cheir
On apostita freir,
A peruerst perdonair
And practand palmair,
A wich and a wobstare,                                  55
A milygant and a mychare,
A fond fule, a fariar,
A cairtar, a cariar,
A libbar and a lyar,
And riddill revar,                                      60
A Tuttivillus, a tutlar,
And a fanʒeit flatterar,
A forfarn falconar,
A malgratious millare,
A berward, a brawlar,                                   65
And ane aip ledar,
With a cursit custumar,
A tratlar, a tinklar,
And mony vthir in that hour
Off all evill ordour.                                   70
First with a fulisch flour,
An ald monk, a lechour,
A drunkin drechour,
A dowble toungit counsalour,
A trumpour, a trvcour,                                  75
A hangman, a hasardour,
A tyrant, a tormentour,
A truphane, a tratlour,
A faynit nigramansour,

L. 43. "Gryce" on the margin, written in the same hand.

A japer, a juglour,                                          80
A lase that lufis bot for lour,
And a man merrour,
An evill wyffis mirrour,
In all thair semblance sour
With a noyefull nychtbour,                                   85
A lunatik, a sismatyk,
An heretyk, a purspyk,
A lumbard, a lolard,
Ane vsurar, a bard,
Ane ypocreit in haly kirk,                                   90
A burn grenge in the dirk,
A schipman on se and sand,
That takis lyfe and gud on hand,
And knawis nowthir courss nor tyd,
Bot presumpteouss in pryd,                                   95
Practing no thing expert,
In cunnyng, cumpass, nor kert,
A skeg, a scornar, a skald,
A balestrod and a bald,
An vnthrifty dapill man,                                     100
A rebald, a ruffian,
A murderer of leil men,
A revischer of wemen;
And two lerit men thame by,
Schir Ockir and Schir Symony,                               105
Ʒit mony in a grit rout
For lak of rowme stud about.
Now wald I wit at this feste
Quho fure best of this beste;
I hald the folk best fure,                                   110
That stud fer without the dure
Fro this cursit cumpany,
And mensles mangery.
Ʒit of this caiss thair is moir,
The puir pig gaif a rore,                                    115
Him to kill quhen thay pynit;
So soir the silly pig quhrynit,
Quhill all the swyn thairabout

Ruschit furth in a rout.
I keip nocht now to commoun                    120
All beistes for to blassoun
Of thair diuerss naturis,
Complexionis and cullouris,
Quhom the law levis ete,
Or quho suld be no manis meit;                 125
Nor of the foulis of the are,
How sum with closs feit thay fare,
And sum diuidit the nalis;
Nor of the fische with thair scalis.
All this I set asyd now,                       130
Haif at Cokilbeis sow;
For to say the verite,
Luvand beistis swyne be,
Contrair houndis nature;
For brawle doggis at the dure                  135
All settis on the sory hound,
That lyis euir at the grund,
And he that cryis most and roris
Ourthrawin, schent and most soiris,
All the remanent him ruggis,                   140
Sum be leggis, sum be luggis,
Thay are luving to men,
Bot nocht to thame self than,
For wo is him that hes royne;
Bot nocht so of the swyne,                      145
And on of thame be ourthrawin,
That his cry may be knawin,
All the remanent that heiris
Cumis in thair best maneiris,
To reskew as thay may;                          150
So did thay this day.
That sowis sonis hard I nevir
Win so grit wirschep for euir,
For Stiftapill all the store
Ruschit out with a rore.                        155
This pig, quhen they hard him,
Thay come golfand full grim;

Mony long tuthit bore
And mony galt come befoir,
And mony grit gunnald,                    160
Gruntillot and gamald,
Wrotok and Writhneb,
Hogy evir in the eb,
With the halkit hoglyn,
Suelly Suattis Swankyn,                   165
Baymell bred in the bog,
Hog hoppit our hog;
Mage of the Milhill,
Grom Gym of the Gill,
The suddill sow and the sord,             170
Reid Kit that oft rord,
Patypull of the Pappourtis;
And Knvtknot of the Kuppourtis,
The gray, the gorot and the grym;
Hurlhekill hoblit with him,               175
Sigill Wrigill our sow,
Gret bore Tusky the grow;
Mony galt, mony gilt,
Come let the pig to be spilt.
Rowch rumple out ran,                     180
Weill mo than I tell can,
With sick a din and a dirdy,
A garray and a hirdy girdy,
The fulis all afferd wer,
And the harlot hurt thare                 185
With bair Tuskyis tuth.
And for to say the verry suth,
In that fellon affray
The littill pig gat away,
And ilk bore and ilk beist                190
Defoulit the fulis of the feist;
Sum mokit, mengeit and merrit;
Thus wer thay fro the meit skerrit.
Is nocht this a nyce caiss?
Bot ʒit a fer werss it waiss;             195
A new noyment and nois

With a rumour vprois,
That of that caiss to degest,
It mycht be callit a tempest,
For all the suynis awnaris                          200
Said, seilis how the fulis fairis,
And seis so curst a cumpany,
Herand thair awin swyne cry,
With thir myligantis machit,
Afferd the fulis had thame kachit,                  205
As to steill thame away,
Than dyn raiss and dirray,
Stok hornis blew stout,
Mony on ischit out,
Gilby on his gray meir,                             210
And Fergy on his sow fair
Hoge Hygin by the hand hint;
And Symy that was sone brint,
With his lad Loury,
And his gossep Gloury;                              215
Fergy in frunt past,
And Fynny followit him fast;
Thurlgill thrang till a club
So ferss, he flaw in a dub,
Quhill Downy him abak drewgh;                       220
Than Rany of the Reidhewch
With Gregry the bowman,
For lufe of his leman
Licht lap at a lyn;
He felȝeit and he fell in,                          225
And Hoge was sa haisty,
That he sualterit him by,
Quhill Thoby cariour him tuk
To land with a scheip cruk.
Schipirdis schowit to schore,                       230
And Fergy Flitsy ȝeid befoir,
Chiftane of that cheif chak,
A ter stowp on his bak,
With his lad Luddroun,
And his hound Hunddroun;                            235

Mony schiphird with him is,
Fro brokis, brois and brymmis,
Off two ram crukit hornis
Thair baner on a birk born is,
With Barmyberd thair banerman,      240
And his cousing Cachran.
Thair menstrall Diky Doyt
Fur befoir with a floyt ;
Than dansit Doby Drymouth
*The sone schene in the Sowth,*      245
And as thay lukit on a lee
Thay saw an vthir menȝe.
Than all thay fled full afferd,
And the maister schipherd,
Fergy Flitsy, befoir      250
Thocht wes litill on his store,
His feit maid sic dynnyng,
He lakkit breth for rynning.
"How," quod Hobby, "herk me,
We neid nocht to fordir fle,      255
Ȝone folk our awin freindis ar,
I knaw be thair banar."
Than wer thay nevir half so fane,
And glaidly turnit all agane,
And knew be thair array,      260
That all nolt hirdis wer thay
That ischit out to the cry,
And thair banar borne by,
Of Crumhorne the cowis taill,
Festnitt on a lang flaill.      265
Besyd thair capitane, I trow,
Callit wes Colyne Cuckow,
And Davy Doyte of the dale
Was thair mad menstrale,
He blew on a pype he,      270
Maid of a borit bourtre ;
Waytstath him by
Dansit ane dandy.
The thrid fallowschip he saw,

That thay windir weill knaw,                      275
The swynehirdis in a rowt,
And Sueirbum with his snowt
Wes captane of thame thair,
And borne wes his banair,
Vpoun a schule for to schaw,                      280
A flekkit sowis skyn faw,
With terletheris tyit hy.
Quho bur it bot Botgy,
And Clarus the long clype
Playit on a bag pype.                             285
Haggysheid and Helly,
Ballybrass and Belly
Dansit, and his sone samyn.
Than all assemblit with a gamyn,
And all the menstralis attonis                    290
Blew up and playit for the nonis ;
Schiphird, nolt hirdis,
And swynhirdis outgirdis,
For to dance merily.
A maistir swynhird Swanky,                        295
And his cousing Copyn Cull,
Fowll of bellis fulfull,
Led the dance and began
Play us *Joly lemmane*,
Sum trottit *Tras and Trenass*,                   300
Sum balterit *The Bass*,
Sum *Perdowy*, sum *Trolly lolly*,
Sum *Cok craw thow quhill day*,
*Twysbank and Terway*,
Sum *Lincolme*, sum *Lindsay*,                    305
Sum *Joly lemman, dawis it nocht day*,
Sum *Be зon wodsyd* singis,
Sum *Late, laite on evinnyngis*,
Sum *Joly Martene with a mok*,
Sum *Lulalow, lute cok*,                          310
Sum bekkit, sum bingit,
Sum crakkit, sum cringit,
Sum movit *Most mak revell*,

Sum *Symon sonis of Quhynfell,*
Sum *Maister Peir de Conʒate,*                    315
And vthir sum in consate
At leser drest to dance.
Sum *Ourfute,* sum *Orliance,*
Sum *Rusty bully with a bek,*
And *Every note in vtheris nek,*                  320
Sum vsit the dansis to deme
Of Cipres and Boheme,
Sum the faitis full ʒarne
Off Portingall and Naverne,
Sum countirfutit the gyss of Spane,              325
Sum Italy, sum Almane,
Sum noisit Napillis anone,
And vthir sum of Arragone,
Sum *The Cane of Tartary,*
Sum *The Soldane of Surry,*                       330
All his dansis defynd,
Sum *Pretir Johine of grit Ynd,*
Sum as the Ethiopis vsit,
Sum futit and sum refusit,
Sum had dansis mony ma,                           335
With all the dansis of Asia;
Sum of Affrickis age,
And principale of Cartage.
Thair pressit in *Pery Pull,*
Full of bellis fulfull,                           340
Maister Myngeis *The Mangeis,*
Maister Tyngeis *La tangeis,*
Maister Totis *La toutis,*
And *Rousty rottis the routis,*
Maister Nykkis *La nakkis*                        345
And Sir Jakkis *La jakk[is],*
The *Haryhurlere husty,*
And *Calby the curst custy.*
Mony laddis, mony lownis,
Knowf, knois, kynnis, culrownis,                 350
Curris, kenseis and knavis
Inthrang and dansit in thravis;

With thame Towis the mowis,
And Hary with the reid howis.
Than all arrayit in a ring                    355
Dansit *My deir derling*,
And all assentit in a sop
To *The vse of Ewrop;*
That for so much thay beleuit,
That expert and weill preuit                  360
Thay war in the Est warld,
As is heir breuly ourharld.
Thay conclud the vse plane
Of ylandis in occiane,
And of the fermeland of France,               365
And how the Empriour dois dance
*Suesis in Suauia* syne,
And als the *Reuir of Ryne*,
Off *Bretane the brod Ile*,
Off *Yrland* and *Argyle*,                     370
*Burgone* and *Breband*,
*Hanyngo* and *Holland*,
*Flanderis, Freisland,* and eik
*Brandeburcht* and *Broinsweik*,
*Dittmer* and *Baywer*,                        375
*Pruce, Poill* and *Pomer*,
*Lubwick land* and *Lunaburcht*,
*Malestrand* and *Makilburcht*,
*The steidis sevin and sevinty*,
And all boindis thame by,                      380
The *Rerall* and *Rusland*,
*Sclauia* and *Gotland*,
*Denmark* and *Norroway*.
All thair dansis and play
Thay movit in thair mad muting,               385
And all thay falit in futing,
For merrit wes thair menstralis,
Thair instrumentis in tonis felis,
And all thair plat pure pansis
Coud nocht the fete of ony dansis             390
Bot such thing as affeiris

To hirdis and their maneiris;
For thay hard speik of men gud,
And small thairof vndirstud,
Bot hurlit furth vpoun heid,  395
A Copyne Cull coud thame lede.
And so thay wend thay weill dansit,
And did bot practit and pransit,
And quhen thay had all done,
It was a tratlyng out of tone.  400
Than thay began for to chyd,
Quhill Quhorlorehusty cryd,
Ceiss this brangling and bere,
Remembir quhy ȝe come here,
That ilk knave and ilk cust  405
Comprysit Horlorehust,
For a witte man commendit,
And thus thair dansing thay endit.
And so concluding thay past
To thair maisteris als fast,  410
The silly pig to reskew,
All the samyn ar thay met trew;
Be than wes machit on mold
Als mony as thay wold;
Lord God, so lowd as thay cryd,  415
Full oft the fulis thay defyd,
And on thame semblit attonis,
Bot thair wes breking of bonis;
Hold how he wes heir
Thay chace with a fresch cheir,  420
Fyll on the foirsaid sottis,
And ourthrew all the ydiottis,
Both of the swyne and the men.
Be this ȝe may weill ken
That foly is no sapience,  425
For multitud in negligence
He seldin palme of victory,
Bot God and gud wit gy;
And all' this grit brawling,
Babling and vthir thing,  430

Wes for a pig as ȝe hard sayn,
Ȝit he eskapit vnslane.
Now juge as ȝe list by,
For this is bot a fantesy,
And littill poynt of poetry,                    435
Bot sport to mak ws mirry ;
And ȝit this is a strange caiss,
Bot eftirward this pig waiss
Growin to a grit boir.
Lo, such is this warldis glore,                 440
Now law, now he,
Nothing stable we se
In this warld of variance,
Ȝit fell a caiss and new chance.
This pig, quhen he a boir wes,                  445
Off micht he grew maikles,
As to fecht for awant
With antelop or oliphant,
Tiger, pard or pantere,
Bull, wolf or wyld bere,                        450
With the awfull vnicorne,
Nor ony beist that wes borne ;
For he faucht wichtly with Wad,
And with Melliager mad,
With anterouss Hercules                         455
He did a battell in pres,
And huntit was in the plane
Befoir the goddes Dyane,
Bot he eskapit harmeles,
And killit hundis in the chase.                 460
The rich king of Sydon
And his knychtis ilk on,
For thir bere afferd wer,
For vmquhile he wonit thair,
And gaif a battell curious                      465
To Eglamoir of Artherus.
The vgly worme nevir so weill preuit
Quhill this bald bore leuit,
Nor ȝit as I vndirstand

The dragone in the Holy Land.    470
Is nocht this a nyce cais,
That first this pig so pure waiss,
And in so mony dengeris,
He eskapit with weris?
ȝe may consaue be this twich,    475
That oft of littill cumis mich,
To contempt a small fo,
Quhill he haith grace to ryd or go
At liberty and fredome,
I hold it no wisdome,    480
Or for loif of pennyis
To suffer honour perreis.
And thus is the cais endit
Of the penny that wes spendit,
That grew to so grit priss;    485
Scarss spending skathis gentriss.
Thus haif I tald ȝow a caiss
To sett ȝow in solaiss,
For our exceding study
May causs quhyle malancoly;    490
Thairfoir to mak ws mirryar
Thus did my fantesy fair,
And this hirdy girdy I,
And dirdy, cry ȝow mercy.

ffinis.

## [Fitt Secound.]

OFF thir mokking meteris and mad matere,
ʒour he reuerence, humly eft I requyre
All ʒe hereris pardoun with pacience
My noyous noyiss nycetie and negligence ;
And to satisfie my foirsaid symple dyte,              5
In recompance of it now will I wryte
Of the SECUND PENNY, ffor the girle cost,
How it did thryve that onis was thrall half lost.
A ʒeir eftir, walking in his disport
By a rever, Cokelby saw resort                        10
Ane auld blind man with a pretty maid,
Nocht twelf ʒeir old[1] I hold of age scho haid ;
Bot suth to say scho was nocht lyk to be
A wordly wicht, so windir fair wes sche ;
So weill nurtourit as scho had nurischeit bene        15
In closter or court, dochter to kyng or quene.
Innocentlie scho salust on hir kne
This carlage man, this foirsaid Colkelbe ;
ʒit for to tell the werray treuth of it,
He was ane man boith of substance and wit,            20
And said, " Dochter, haue Goddis blyssing and myne."
The auld man askit *le pour amour deuine*
*Cherite*, and he said, " Father, cum to my houss."
He had him home and gaif him fair almouss,
And intentlie inquireit quhair he had                 25
Gottin that fair innocent gudelie maid,
And gif scho war his dochter or kyn to say.
He said, " Suithlie scho is nother *parfay ;*
Bot one palmar, ane honest man was he,
One aliane come frome beʒond the se,                  30

---

[1] MS. hold.

With his awin wyf, a blyssit createur,
Lougeit with me, suppoiss that I be peur,
And throuch the will of God, so as it was,
Thay war weseit with suddane soir seikness,
And deceissit thairin boith in ane hour;     35
This little maid, this tender createur,
Was thair dochter, and beluiffit with me,
That leiddis me now sence myself may nocht se."
Colkelbe said, " I beleif it is so,
Bot quhat cuntre that ewer thai folk come fro,     40
It semis thai war of kynreid full potent,
Be the dochteris feris this innocent.
Bot, guid father, gif that ȝe wald aggree
To lat the maid remane heir still with me
For hir honour, and elss so wald I reid ȝow,     45
Bot ȝe sall haif ane boy of myne to leid ȝow."
The blynd man said, "Thre soneis at home I haue,
And war I thair no moir gyding I crawe,
Bot for the maide hath bene a quhill with me,
And ȝe hir haue I suld the better be."     50
Cokkelby said, " I had thre pennyis round,
The first wes lost onys in a lak and found,
And with it coft a pig sum callis a gryss,
Quhich increscit to he wirschip and pryss,
So mervellous mony men of him reidis;     55
He wes the caus of feill ferlifull deidis,
As his legend beris witness, luke quho so list;
The secound penny I haif heir in my fist,
On lyis in hurd; this is the caiss of thame;
Thre silly pennyis suthly I hald the same.     60
The said secound penny I sall gife the
For this ȝoung maid, gif that thow will and sche,
With my favouris in tyme to cum also:"
Thay agreit, and thus I lat thame go.
This Colkelby nvreist hir in his houss,     65
Quich grew so fair and verry verteouss,
So gentill in all his gestis and appliable,

L. 56. The words "the caus" are repeated by mistake in the manuscript.

And sobir in seruice and amiable,
That all that hir saw thay luvit hir as thair lyfe,
And specialy this Colkelbeis wyfe,                          70
A worschepfull woman in to hir houss,
Thay callit hir to name Bellamorouss.
Betuix hir and hir husband Colkelby
Thay had a sone callit Flannislie;
Galland he wes and gud in all his feir,                     75
And of all vtheris odly the best archeir
In ony land, rycht wirschepfull and wyse,
Big of bonis, a strong man of dewyse.
And, as his fader and moder did oft espy,
He coppeit this ʒong wench attentely                        80
In his consait with sad degestioun,
Hir most plesand perfyt pure persoun,
Hir fresche figour formyt, of forme and face,
Gevin to all gud, fulfillit of Godis grace,
That all bonty and bewty that mycht be                      85
Worthy compryssis thairof anewch had sche.
He lovit so weill thair was non vthir,
Bot with consent of freindis, fadir and moder,
He weddit hir to wyfe, wit ʒe for ay.
This amiable innocent Adria                                 90
Wes callit to name, and this in France fell
Into the first orising of it to tell,
Or it prevelit planeist and popelus,
Quhair now Pareiss citie is situat thus.
This Colkelby wonit thair, quhair the caiss                 95
Of the pig, fulis, and all that foirsaid was,
Till on a tyme that he France the king
Roid to vesy the boundis thair as regne;
And in the place thair as Cokkelby dwelt,
A man of stoir with such thing he delt,                     100
For than non could haif craft cornis to win;
That king of mycht lugit in to his In,
And on the morne a grit schoting thay did cry,
Quhair Flanislie our all wan victory.
The king saw him so big a man and strang,                   105
And gudly als, to tary ʒow nocht lang,

For his body a squyer he him maid;
And in his weiris so weill he him behaid,
He was maid knycht in court to continew;
And than he send for his fair lady trew,  110
Dame Adria, quhome the king did commend
In his chalmer vpoun the quene to attend;
Best belouit and most perfyte wes sche,
For hi[r] gestis and bewtie and bontie,
Our all the laif the ladeis that thair ware.  115
And Flannislie so weill in weiris him bare,
That the king eftir maid him erle ryall,
And a cornar of a cuntre seuerall,
Nocht than invent inhabit as it lay,
Gaif him be seile heretable for ay,  120
Quhich he plenyssit with peple and polesy,
And namit it eftir him and his lady,
This is to say Flannislie and Adria,
His hole erldome callit Flandria,
Flan fra the first sillab of Flannislie,  125
And Dria drevin fra Adria the fre,
The quhich famouss erldome of Flanderis ay
Haldis of Frankland and Duchpeir to this day.
Off the secound penny thus come grit grace
With correctioun, and this I call a cace;  130
I reid nocht this in story autentyfe,
I did it leir at ane full auld wyfe,
My gritgraundame, men callit hir Gurgunnald;
Scho knew the lyfe of mony faderis ald,
Notable gestis of peax and weiris in storye,  135
Fresche in hir mynd and recent of memorye,
Nochtwithstanding scho was weill sett in eild;
Hir aige I hald of sevin scoir of winteris heild,
And saw sumdeill; bot for to say the suth,
Into hir heid I trest was nocht a tuth,  140
Thairfoir grwew most gredely eit sche,
And laking teith famvlit hir faculte,
That few folk mycht consaue hir mvmling mowth,

L. 141. The word "grwew" in the manuscript seems unintelligible. Perhaps it is an error of the transcriber for "grwell."

Bot I that was expert thairin of ʒowth.
Than wald I say scho had grit grace of God ;          145
" Quhy so," quod scho, " my son ? " and maid a nod.
" Madame," quod I, " for thair be mony wyffis
Throw haboundance of spech that nevir tryffis,
And I wald chenge, mycht it be at my reid,
For a gud toung all the teith in thair heid ;          150
As ʒe ar now, so suld thay nocht be nemit
Skaldis, baldis, and thairthrow schent and schamit."
Than angrit scho and said, "Sanct Johne to borrow!
Thow lichit boy, thow menis mekle sorrow,
And sall do moir gife thow in lyfe may byd."          155
" Madame," quod I, " that tak I on ʒour syd."
Than wald scho preiss bett me in angry wyss,
Bot weill was me, scho mycht nocht ryn nor ryss,
And I wald vp and wisk away full wyld ;
Than wald scho flattir, " Cum in agane my chyld,    160
And thow sall haif, lo, standing in the skelf,
Quheit breid and reme, conservit for my self."
Than sett scho me to leir littill at the scule,
Nowdir lyk to be a wysman nor a fule,
And oft with pyne scho maid me to report             165
Of hir tailis ; and to conclud in schort,
Scho said, " My sone be this said taill thou sall
Lerne fyve wittis, and the first of thame all
Is to concidder of fulis the foly ;
Set in nummer thay ryss and multeply,                170
Thay may nevir moir fruct in felicity,
Thair ignorance requyris nocht it so be ;
Experience and testimoniall
Off the saidis fulis, my sone, consaif thow sall,
That a pure pig in thair possessioun                 175
Thay had, and tuk for ferme conclusioun
To kill the samyn, and mak of it a feist ;
And syne thay war ourthrawin, most and leist,
For sory swyne for thair golfing affraid,
Till that the pig brak fra thame in a braid,         180
And syne knavis ourcome thame with a crye ;
Thairfoir, my sone, fra sic fulich foly,

And fallowschip, keip the, for the *first* wit.
The *secund* is, my sone, will thow lerne it,
Presome nevir bot povert may prewaill,                185
Be it rychtwiss, aganis men of grit availl,
That ar nocht wyiss, bot wranguss in thair deidis,
In cais thai mak the quhiles vexit at nedis;
Witnes this pig, sone, be experience,
That was fangit in the fulis offence,                190
To be killit, and recouerit agane
To so grit grace, as is foirsaid certaine.
Thairfoir, my sone, leif nocht thy gud quarrell
For apperance of dangeris and parrell,
For be thow just God sall thy juge be                195
In all perrellis, and weill deliuer the;
And the danger passit, thow art alss sure
As evir thow was, and stranger in nature,
To aventure agane in richtowsnace.
Bot quho so will cowardly hyd his face                200
In defens of his just actioun,
Quhen he trestis him for such fowll affectioun
Most in surty suppressit sone sal he be,
Quhair the richtouss frome all feir sall go fre.
Lychtly nevir thy gud querrell for feir                205
Off all perellis, dowt, domage or dangeir,
Suld it so be, nevir suld mertirdome
Fortefie fath, nor win the sege of Rome;
Quho that surest dois keip him sonest dois slyd,
Bot gud quarrell and grace God be thy gyd.                210
The *thrid* wit is, my sone, gif thow will ken,
Quhair evir thow seis grit wit in virtewiss men,
Thocht thay be pure, auld or ȝong specialy,
Contempne thame nocht sone, and lo the quhy,
This maid, this girle, this pure Adria, wes                215
ȝoung, faderles leuit, and eik modèrles,
In strenge lond, and ȝit the Holy Gost
Vpliftit hir for wit to wirschep most;
And in lykwayiss hir lord Erle Flannysle.
Quho wold haif thame opprest for thair pouirte!  220
Remembir now in such hicht as thay are,

Quhat may thay do to thair party contrare,
Thay may weill quyt and ouirthraw thame at all;
Dispyss nevir wyiss vertewis in purall.
The *ferd* wit is, lat nevir thy penny be,　　225
Nor warldis gud, my sone, mastir of the;
For littill thing weill spendit may incres
To he honour, wirschep and gritt riches,
As did thir tuo pennyis spendit weill
Vpoun the pig and the pure damesell.　　230
I neid no moir of thame to multeply,
Thow knawis befoir how thay did fructefy,
Thairfoir hald nocht pennyis our pretiouss,
Bot suffer thame pass prospering commodiouss.
Forsuth a tyme a penny thow may spend,　　235
That may awaill the to thy lyvis end.
Thairfoir, my sone, gife thow thinkis to indure,
Spend with mesure for luk, wit and mesure.
The *fyift* wit is, my sone, set nevir thy harte
To mak an hurd, suffering honour by starte,　　240
For littill watt thow how sone that thow may slid
Frome it slely, or it fra the to glid;
And at the leist in the hurd quhill it lyis,
It servis nowdir the warld nor multeplyis,
And gif thow deis it is vnknawin to men;　　245
In avarice quhat cheir is with the then?
For quich this man, this worthy Colkelby,
That in his dayis gat nevir bot pennyis thre,
Saw two thryve weill, and the thrid did nocht,
Incontinent that penny out he brocht,　　250
And awowit to God in solempnit word,
That he suld nevir study to mak ane hord.
Rycht so, my sone, I chairge the to dude,
Spend with wirchep and spair nocht Godis gud;
How littill wat thow ane vdir tyme quho may　　255
Bruk thy wyfe and baggis eftir thy day."
Thus Gurgunnald, my grit grandame, me kend;
Haif I myssaid in ocht I sall amend.

EXPLICIT

SECUNDA PARS.

## [Fitt Third.]

A ND with pardoun now of ȝour he lordschippis,
    And correctioun of ȝour reuerend maisterschippis,
Heir wald I tell of THE THRID HID PENNY,
As I haif told ȝow two did fructefy.
This Cokelby concidering weill the cais,     5
That of wrechit awarice grew nevir grace,
Having in hairt the hole experience,
How that the two pennyis raiss in ascenss,
Thocht he wald preve the thrid penny quhyle hid,
Quhilk for the tyme no fruct nor proffeit did,     10
To suffer it spreid in warld and fructefy,
And gif sum folk wald say that I go by,
How suld a penny fruct contrair nature,
Sen gold, siluer, mettell, and alkyn vre
Fynit be folkis, vanisis and nocht incressis,     15
Sum wold allege my lewit langage a less is,
Bot, or I waid moir in this wildirnas,
Off such weir I will declair the cass.
Quhill that the vre is in the awin nature,
And nocht fynit nor forgit be manis cure,     20
So long the forss of the four elementis,
And most the erth mynisteris it nvtrimentis
To incressing as herbis, stone or tre,
Frome thair orising stok cuttit quhill thay be,
And frome thair ferm first rutit grund dewydit,     25
Thay may nocht than be natur so abscidit,
Do fructifie and flureiss as afoir,
Lyk as a man heidit he may no moir,
Bot that the saule throw grace of God only,
In spirituall joyis only dois fructefy.     30
So the mettell, abscidit be the man,
Nocht fructefeis of nature, bot quhat than?

Manly resoun, and wit of Godis gift
Fyndis menis the money to vplift,
And multeply in moir memor and mycht,                    35
Than evir it did in erd quhill it plycht.
For quhy, so long as it lay on the ground,
It was vnfynit as fruct nevirmoir found,
And quhan it was vptak be manis wit,
Throw out the warld alway welcome wes it,                40
And set in cas and menissit alyte,
Vsit and handlit be men, ʒit quhair a myte
Failis thairof manis wit bringis agane
A thowsand pundis fynit out of vris plane ;
The examplis that quhoso hath a vertew,                  45
Vss it wysly oft syiss ten frome it grew.
And in schort my long legend quho so lestis,
The euwangell the trewth thairof attestis,
Goddis awin word, quhich tuk frome on fule man
A pure penny having no moir as than,                     50
And gaif the wyss that had ten pennyis tald ;
Bot quhy was that ? for the fule man no wald
Dispone wysly his penny, bot abuss it,
Hyd it, and he that had ten weill tham vsit,
Thairfoir God tuk frome the vnverteouss men             55
A penny, and gaif to the gud having ten ;
Rycht so he that has science and it abusis,
Nocht following fast the fruct, bot it refusis,
God will it geif to him that hes far moir.
I cast me nocht alday to gloiss in gloir,                60
Or to langar legendis that ar prolixt,
Thairfoir I turne vnto my first text,
As to declair the thrid penny, quhyle hid,
Eftir out brocht, and gydit grace it did,
As followis heir, quho lykis to adwert,                  65
Throw consaitis of Colkelby expert ;
Lyk to sede sawin in erd mortificat
Fflouris money fructis viuificat,
Lyk martiris killit, off quhome the mirreitis rysis,
Sanctis in hevin quhome sinfull man supprysis ;         70
And herkynnis how, besyd this Colkelby,

Thair duelt a man was rich of stoir and fie,
Quhair Bodyvincant castell standis now in plane,
His big nychtbour men callit him Blerblowane;
A wirthy wyfe had he weddit, and sche     75
Was callit Susane, on quhome a sone gat he,
And Colkelby was gossep to the same,
And he callit him Cokalb to his rycht name.
Colkelby with the said thrid penny bocht
xxiiij hen eggis, and with thame socht     80
To his gud sone, for godfadirly reward,
Him to remembir, as schawit is eftirward.
Susan angrit heirat, as oft woman is,
Quhile passionat that all consaitis kennis,
Tuk in disdane this gift, this symple thing,     85
And said, "Gossap, beir hame ʒour pure offring;
Mene ʒe to mok my sone and me, no moir
I will heirof, fure it away thairfoir."
He said, "I sall keip thame to my gud sone;"
And had thame home to his place quhair he wone,     90
And chairgeit sone his henwyfe to do hir cure,
And mak thame fruct: than to set thame scho fure;
Hir best brod hen callit lady Pekle-pes,
And ʒoung Cokrell, hir lord and lemman wes,
Scho maid brud on thir eggis, that in schort space     95
Twenty-four chikkynis of thame scho hes,
Twelf maill and twell famell be croniculis cleir;
And quhat thay war with thair names we sall heir.
The first wes the samyn Chantecleir to luke,
Of quhome Chaucer treitis in to his buke,     100
And his lady Partlot, sister and wyfe,
Quhilk wes no lyse in detis of that lyfe;
For quhy, folkis levit be naturall lawis than.
The tuther bruthir was clipit Cok Cademan,
He tuk to wyfe his fair trew sister Toppok;     105
Cok Crawdoun was the thrid, and his wyfe Coppok;
And to compt just the fourt, Cok Lyk ouris,
And littill Hen-pen his pretty paramouris.
The fyift lord was Lyricok in hall,
And Kekilcrouss thay did his lady call.     110

Reid Kittilcok that sat on reid caill stok,
And Feklefaw farest of all the flok
Was the sext, and Cokrusty the sevin,
Dame Strange his wyfe, quhilk had a stout stevin;
Cokky the aucht, his lady clepit Lerok;                  115
Cok Nolus the nynt spowsit his sister Erok;
Cok Coby the tent and Sprutok his speciall;
Cok Obenar the levint, his maik thay call
Dame Juliane; the twelf wes Cok Jawbert,
And lady Wagtaill his joy and all his hairt.            120
So stout a stoir come of thir brethir twelf
And thair sisteris, I can nocht say my self
The fyiftie pairte, thay wer so fructeouss,
And at schriftis evin sum wes so battalouss,
That he wald win to his maistir in feild               125
Fourty florans with bill and spuris beild.
Sum of this stoir this Cokkelby did sell,
Sum auld, sum ȝung, sum eggis in the schell,
And coft thairwith vthir ware, and so it turnit,
This penny, that xv ȝeir it nocht soiornit,            130
He mvlteplyit moir than a thowsand pound.
Than his gud sone he callit to him a stound,
Befoir his fader, moder and freindis all,
And said, Cakkalb, my sone, ressaif thow sall
All thir gudis, for justly thay ar thyne,              135
Off thy chyld gift, storit throw grace devyne,
Fro xxiiij hen eggis quiche I the gaif,
Set, thi moder, sone, wald thame nocht ressaif.
Than as ȝe hard he tald all the caiss;
This Cokelb grew eftir to so grit richess              140
Throw this penny, he grew the michtiest man
In ony realme.   Quhat did the penny than?
First hid in hurde, to vertew nocht applyit,
And syne outbrocht that so fer fructefyit.
Thairfoir, my sone, study nevir in thy day            145
With auarice warldis gud in hurd till ley,
Nor be thow nocht disparit of Godis grace.
The thrid penny this was, and the last caice,
As my beledame, old Gurgunnald, told me,

I allege non vthir auctorite. 150
In this sentence maid on revill raill,
Quhich semys most to be a wyfis taill,
With correctioun quhite now I thus conclud.
God that ws bocht with his awin blissit blud,
Both ȝow and me to consarue he deden, 155
Throw meik mirreitis of his only sone.   Amen.


EXPLICIT

TERTIA PARS ET VLTIMA.

# KING BERDOK

XIV.

# KING BERDOK.

---

*THIS singular fragment, preserved in George Banna-
tyne's well-known Manuscript 'Ballat Buik,'*[1] *has been
overlooked by the different editors of early Scotish poetry,
except by* Leyden, *who alludes to it in his interesting and
learned introduction to the* Complaynt of Scotland,[2] *as
follows:* "*In a ludicrous poem in the* Bannatyne Manuscript on King Berdok of Babylon who wooed the golk
'sevin ȝeir' of Maryland, and was pursued and besieged
by the King of Fary assisted by*

> ——'the kingis of Pechtis and Porlingaill,
> The king of Naippillis and Navern alhaill'—

*it is said—*

> 'Weill cowd he play in clarschocht and on lute.'"

*This was the harp known in the Highlands of Scotland.
It is enumerated as one of the instruments with which the
Irish or rather Erse bard in* Holland's Houlate *was
acquainted.*

> "The Chenachy, the Clarshach,
> The Beneschene, the Ballach,
> The Crekrye, the Corach,
> Scho kens thame ilk ane."

*Although it may now be impossible to ascertain the indi-
vidual work, the nature of this fairy tale plainly intimates
that it was intended as a burlesque of some 'geste' or
romantic story, which may have been popular at the time
of its composition.*

[1] Fol. 142 b.  [2] P. 152.

## XIV.

# '𝕶ing 𝕭erdok.'

SYM of Lyntoun, be the ramis horn,
   Quhen Phebus rang in sing of Capricorn,
And the mone wes past the gussis cro,
Thair fell in France ane jeperdie forlo,
Be the grit kin[g] of Babilon, Berdok,      5
That dwelt in symmer in till ane bowkaill stok ;
And into winter, quhen the frostis ar fell,
He dwelt for cauld in till a cokkil schell :
Kingis vsit nocht to weir clayis in tha dayis,
Bot ʒeid naikit, as myne auctor sayis ;     10
Weill cowd he play in clarschocht and on lute,
And bend ane aiprim bow, and nipschot schute ;
He wes ane stalwart man of hairt and hand ;
He wowit the golk sevin ʒeir, of Maryland,
Mayiola, and scho wes bot ʒeiris thre,     15
Ane bony bird, and had bot ane e ;
Neuirtheless king Berdok luvit hir weill,
For hir foirfute wes langar than hir heill.
The king Berdok he fure our se and land,
To reveiss Mayok the golk of Maryland,     20
And nane with him bot ane bow and ane bowtt ;
Syne hapnit him to cum amang the nowtt,

L. 5 MS. reads 'kin.'

And as this Berdok about him cowd espy;
He saw Mayok milkand hir mvderis ky,
And in ane creill vpoun his bak hir kest;　　　25
Quhen he come hame it wes ane howlat nest,
Full of skait birdis, and than this Berdok grett,
And ran agane Meyok for to gett.
The king of Fary hir fadir than blew out,
And socht Berdok all the land abowt,　　　30
And Berdok fled in till a killogy;
Thair wes no grace bot gett him or ellis die;
Thair wes the kingis of Pechtis and Portingaill,
The king of Naippillis and Navern alhaill,
With bowis and brandis with segis thay vmbeset him,
Sum bad tak, sum slay, sum bad byd quhill thay get
　　　him;　　　36
Thay stellit gunis to the killogy laith,
And proppit gunis with bulettis of raw daich:
Than Jupiter prayit to god Saturn,
In liknes of ane tod he wald him turn;　　　40
Bot sone the graciouss god Mercurius
Turnit Berdok in till ane braikane buss;
And quhen thay saw the buss waig to and fra,
Thay trowd it wes ane gaist, and thay to ga:
Thir fell kingis thus Berdok wald haif slane,　　　45
All this for lufe, luveris sufferis pane,
Boece said, of poyettis that wes flour,
Thocht lufe be sweit, oft syiss it is full sour.


EXPLICIT.

# THE GYRE-CARLING

XV.

# THE GYRE-CARLING.

GYRE-CARLING *is the name of the Hecate, or Mother
Witch, of the Scotish peasantry, who is sometimes identified
with the queen of the Fairies.  Carling*, Dr Leyden *explains
as being the feminine of carl, and as used " to denote an old
hag or witch; hence compounded with the* Isl. *gier;* R.
*gier;* Al. *geyr; the Gyre-Carling, the Queen of Faries,
the Great Hag, Hecate, or Mother Witch of the peasants,
concerning whom many popular stories were formerly cur-
rent, and rude burlesque verses are still repeated."* [1]  *Frequent allusions in our early writers occur respecting these
superstitions.*  Sir David Lyndsay, '*who feinzeit many
fabillis' for the amusement of his royal pupil*, James V.,
*reminds him how, in his tender years, he was accustomed
with*

> —" mony plesand storye,
> Of the Reid Etin, and the Gyir Carlyng.
> Confortand the, quhen that I saw the sorye." [2]

—*And* Montgomery, *with great minuteness, in the* Flyting,
*describes the array of* Nicnevin (*another of her popular ap-
pellations,*)—*and  her 'elrich' company in their processsion
on All-hallow-evin.* [3]

[1] Glossary to Complaynt of Scotland, 8vo, 1801, p. 318.  See also Dr
Jamieson's Dict, *sub v.*; and Mr Chalmers's Glossary in his edition of
Lyndsay.

[2] Lyndsay's Works, ed. Laing, vol. i. p. 3.

[3] Montgomery's Poetical Works, edit. 8vo, 1821, p. 113.

*After the Editor transcribed the following burlesque frag-
ment from* Bannatyne's *manuscript,[1] he found that it had
been introduced into the Minstrelsy of the Scottish Border,[2]
in the interesting and valuable dissertation " on the Fairies
of Popular Superstition."* Leyden *had previously remarked
the peculiarity of its commencing in the same manner as
' The Warris of the Jowis,' an alliterative poem preserved
in the British Museum,[3] which is cited by* Warton.[4]

[1] Fol. 136, b.
[2] Vol. ii. p. 174, edit. 1803, where Scott remarks, " The Gyre-Carling
is termed the Queen of Jowis (Jovis or perhaps Jews), and is with great
consistency married to Mohammad."
[3] MSS. Cotton, Calig. A. II. 109.
[4] Warton's Hist. of Poetry, vol. i. p. 311.

XV.

# [𝕿𝖍𝖊 𝕲𝖞𝖗𝖊=𝕮𝖆𝖗𝖑𝖎𝖓𝖌.]

I N Tiberius tyme, the trew Imperiour,
   Quhen Tinto hillis fra skraiping of toun henis was
     keipit,
Thair dwelt ane grit Gyre-Carling in awld Betokis
     bour,
That levit vpoun christiane menis flesche, and rewth
     heidis vnleipit;
Thair wynnit ane her by, on the west syd, callit
     Blasour,                              5
For luve of hir lawchane lippis, he walit and he weipit;
He gadderit ane menȝie of modwartis to warp doun
     the tour:
The carling with ane yrne club, quhen that Blasour
     sleipit,
   Behind the heill scho hatt him sic ane blaw,
     Quhill Blasour bled ane quart           10
     Of milk pottage inwart,
     The carling luche, and lut fart
North Berwik Law.

The king of Fary than come, with elffis mony ane,
And sett ane sege, and ane salt, with grit pensallis of
     pryd;                              15
And all the doggis fra Dumbar, wes thair to Dumblane,
With all the tykis of Tervey, come to thame that tyd;

Thay gnew doun with thair gomes mony grit stane,
The Carling schup hir in ane sow, and is hir gaitis
     gane,
Gruntlyng our the Greik sie, and durst na langer byd, 20
    For bruklyng of bargane, and breking of browis :
       The Carling now for dispyte
       Is mareit with Mahomyte,
       And will the doggis interdyte,
    For scho is quene of Jowis.                    25

Sensyne the cokkis of Crawmound crew nevir a day,
For dule of that devillisch deme wes with Mahoun
     mareit,
And the hennis of Hadingtoun sensyne wald nocht lay,
For this wyld wilroun wich thame widlit sa and wareit :
And the same North Berwick Law, as I heir wyvis
     say,                                        30
This Carling, with a fals cast wald away carreit :
For to luk on quha sa lykis, na langer scho tareit.
    All this langour for luve befoirtymes fell,
       Lang or Betok wes born,
       Scho bred of ane accorne ;                  35
       The laif of the story to morne
    To ʒow I sall tell.


EXPLICIT.

THE

# TALIS OF THE FYUE BESTIS

# XVI.

# THE TALIS OF THE FYUE BESTIS.

---

*[THESE tales, which have not hitherto been printed, are contained in the* Asloan *manuscript, preserved at Auchinleck, Ayrshire, already referred to. The MS. in which they are preserved is a large folio volume, written on paper, and contains miscellaneous pieces in prose and verse, collected and transcribed about the year* 1515, *by* John Asloan *or* Sloan, *who seems to have been a writer or notary at Edinburgh.[1]*

*The tales are related by the Horse, the Hart, the Unicorn, the Bear, and the Wolf, before the Lion as King; and these five beasts are his counsellors. The first tale, that of the Horse, is imperfect; enough, however, remains to show its nature. A foolish person induces a wise friend to leave the strait and correct path and go with him in 'the plesand way of dissait.' They are seized by robbers, who are at last captured, and all are condemned to death. The moral of the tale is to keep the way of penance, and avoid the temptations of the 'foul flesche.'*

[1] In 1494 John Sloan appeared as procurator for several persons of the name of Herries, who were summoned at the instance of Lord Herries of Terregles (Robertson's Index). He was probably a native of Kirkcudbright, as in 1531 a charter was granted to John Asloane, and Jonet Maxwell his spouse, of the lands of Garreauch (Great Seal Register, by Paul and Thomson, A.D. 1531. No. 1003). His name occurs as a witness to various deeds, in which he is designated a notary public (*Ib.* Nos. 567, 804).

*The second tale, that of the Hart, is also imperfect, a large corner of the leaf of the MS. which contains it being torn away. Its subject is worthy* Sir William Wallace, *and his heroic defence of Scotland against 'the Sutheren,' and 'Saxon blude.'*

*The third tale, that of the Unicorn, fortunately is complete, and the scene of it is laid in Kent.* Gundulfus *the young son of a bondman or farmer, when in the farmyard throws a stone at a cock and breaks its leg. The bird is nursed by the other fowls, recovers, and becomes the chief cock of the farm :—*

> ——" quhill he clapit durst thar na cok craw,
> Quhen he had clapit, than crav thai all on raw."

Gundulfus *goes to Oxford, and in due time is ready to take holy orders. The day before he expects to be appointed to a benefice, he visits his home, and is induced to stay over the night. He and his friends carouse freely, in the expectation that he will be aroused in time to make an early start by the crowing of the cock, which is considered as good as a clock. The bird, whose leg he had broken, however, overhears the conversation, and refuses to crow till long after daybreak. When he at length began, and was followed by the others,* Gundulfus *awakes, and finding he is late, mounts a horse and rides at full speed through the village. At last the horse falls and leaves him in the mud. He returns home, and has the mortification to find the vacant church filled up and all his hopes of preferment at an end. The moral is, that rulers should not injure the poor, as the time may come when they may fall into the hands of the oppressed.*

*The story of* Gundulfus *forms part of the well-known Latin poem called* Speculum Stultorum, *written about the year* 1190 *by Nigellus Wireker, precentor in the Church of Canterbury. In that poem the tale is called '*Narratio Arnoldi de filio presbyteri et pullo gallinæ.'[1]

*The fourth tale, that of the Bear, relates how* Alexander, King of Macedon, *was induced to withdraw from the*

---

[1] 'The Anglo-Latin Satirical Poets of the Twelfth Century.' Edited by Thomas Wright, M.A., vol. i. p. 54.

*siege of the city of "Lapsat in Araby" which he was about to attack and destroy.*

*The fifth and last tale, that of the Wolf, narrates how that wily animal counsels the Lion to live on venison for a year, and allow the sheep to increase during that time. While complaining that the latter were scarce, he has an 'allya' or confederate who is scouring the country and destroying them. The Lion, however, exiles the Wolf and all beasts of prey from his Court, and the four counsellors who remain represent the four virtues 'that in a kyng suld ryng'—viz., prudence, justice, magnanimity, and continence.*

*With regard to the authorship of these tales, we may observe that they were compiled by a Scottish versifier, who may have borrowed the subjects of them from various sources. The second, however, must be an original composition, as it certainly would not be that of an English author.]*

## XVI.

# The Talis of the Ffyue Bestis.

## [The Horsis Tale.]

*     *     *     *     *     *     *<br>*     *     *     *     *     *     *

" And in this faireway persaif I wele a thing,  
To no gud rest this nycht it sall us bring;  
This plesant way the way is of dissait,  
And in this firth ar thevis in our gait."  
Bot neuertheles for ony argument,       5  
This plesand streit this werray fule furth went;  
Richtso this wys man did, and left the tother,  
Ffor werray effectioun of his carnale brother.  
So has this waye tham to the brigantis brocht,  
Takin thai war, and with thaim went and wrocht.       10  
So come the kingis justice of the land,  
And tuke thaim all, and to law gart thaim stand.  
So quhen thire theifis all ware iustifyed,  
Than euerilk brother for himself replyed.  
This wysman said, " Of all this gret trespas       15  
Hereof the quilk that I accusit was,  
This werray fule, my brother, had the wyte,  
That tuke the way of plesance and delyte,  
And left the way that suld ws bring to rest,  
And brocht ws baith vnto the thefis nest,       20  
And with him furth the samyn way I ȝud  
Bot for affectioun naturale of his blud,

So, sen this fule was causar of this scaith,
Richtso suld he be pvnist for ws baith,
That with no ressoun rewlit wald he be."                25
" Nay," said this fule, " the falt was nocht in me
Bot all in ȝow, that God has gevin to wit
To rewle ws baith and nocht disponit it ;
Ffor quha wald trow a wysman wald assent,
And I a fule, so sone to myne entent,                30
Bot ȝour affectioun, se I weile be this,
Has blyndit ws, and gart ws baith go myss.
Thus in this mater all the falt ȝe haf."
And so furthwith this juge the sentens gaf,
And sen this wysman left his awne entent,                35
And to this fulis deid gaf his assent,
And left the wit that God gaf him of grace,
Ffor the affectioun naturale that he has,
And for this fule he wald nocht rewlit be,
Be this sentence he jugit baith to de.                40
And in rememberance euer of thare deidis,
Gart thaim sit dovne, and straik of baith thar heidis.

*Moralitas fabule.*

In more effect of this mater I mene,
Thir brethir two in euery man thai bene.                45
The wantone flesche it is the foly brothir,
The sely saull forsuth it is the tothir,
So quhen the saull affermes the delyt
Off the foule flesche, lust and appetit,
Alsone with dedly synnis ar thai wrocht,                50
Takin and slane, and to confusioun brocht.
Fforbere this way of lust that ȝe se heire,
And take the way of bushis, thorne and brere.
That is the way of pennance and of grace,
To bring our saulis to that joyfull place                55
Of paradys, and of perfectioun richt,
Now Ihesus bring ws to that blysfull sicht.

———

So quhen this riall hors his tale had endit,
This ryall hart richt gentilly it commendit.

His statly hed with tyndis set on hicht,                60
Of polist gold and siluer birnist bricht,
Before this king he laid his tyndis law,
And in this wys his tale began to schaw :—


## The Hart[is Tale.]

I hald in bretta   .   .   .   .   .   .
That euer was   .   .   .   .   .   .            65
William Wallace worth .   .   .   .
Saif reuerence of the   .   .   .   .
He tuke fro no man t   .   .   .   .
He wan all Scotland in .   .   .   .
Tharfor in hevin is his   .   .   .   .            70
And that I trow be richt   .   .   .

The samyn day the sutheren   .   .
Had wroch thair will apon .   .   .
As thai had done befor in d   .   .
With sanct Edmond and sanct   .            75
Ane haly heremed quhare he   .   .
As in autentik writ we reid
The staitis of this warld but dreid
Desyrit to se throcht Goddis grace.

Sa come ane angell fra the hicht,                80
And schew him baith of hevin and hell,
The joye amang thire angellis bricht,
The fyre amang thire fendis fell.
Of purgatory, thus hard I tell,
And of thaim all he had a sicht,                85
That deit as that day and nycht,
And quhare thair saulis thaim schupe to duell.

And so he saw in colour sabill,
Of saulis dovne to hell declyne,
Ane multitud innomerable,                90

Perpetually for to suffer pyne,
To purgatory he saw pas syne.
.   .   .   .   .   .   .   .   . e,
.   .   .   .   .   .   . tin fable,
.   .   .   .   .   .   .   . fra hyne.          95

.   .   . thre,
.   .   . ais in,
.   .   . degre,
.   . dedly syn,
.   . thai begyn,          100
.   . may se,
. ace fulfillit be,
. of hevin thai wyn.

.   .   .   .   .   . re to hevin up ran,
.   .   .   .   . . lyf of religioun,          105
.   .   .   .   . it was the tothir man,
.   .   .   . aly mes and confessioun,
.   .   . .rid a lord for his regioun,
In his defence deit as than
Wallace, with his woundis wan,          110
That day tholit deid at Londoun toun.

Thar was na force mycht gar him fald,
Na ȝit reward of warldly gud,
Bot Scotland ay defend he wald,
Ffra subiectioun of Saxonis blud.          115
Thus for his realme stedfast he stud,
And to his deid was bocht and sauld,
Tharfor in hevin his saull I hald,
Or he was cald, thus I conclud.

Now be this tale. I wald ȝe wnderstud,          120
Movand awort to haf ane querell gud,
Quhat corage in a mannis hart it bringis,
The fame of it how lovably it ryngis;
And quhat of grace the sely saull encressis,
Throw just batale quhoso tharin decessis,          125

Bot neuertheles quhat euer the pepill deme,
The gud of pece, thar can no man expreme.

On fut than gat this gentill vnicorne,
This gentill best this king he came beforne.
So fair a best, so sweit vnto my sicht                130
Was neuer sene with only erdly wicht.
The only tynd that on his hed he baire,
A kyngis ransoun it was worth and maire :
To luke on him it did me sic delyte,
And on this wys he tald his tale perfyte.             135

## The Vnicornis Tale.

Before this tyme in Kentschire it befell,
A bonde thare was, his name I can nocht tell,
Gundulfus was his sonis name I ges,
Of tender age of nyne ȝeris ald he wes,
And wele he vsit for to rys at mornys                 140
To kepe the grange and his faderis cornis
Ffra cokis, crawis, and vther foulis wyld.
So on a day this litill prety child
Seand thir birdis lukand our the wall
Toward the grangis, Gundulfus gois withall,          145
And with the casting of a litill stone,
Of ane littil bird the theis bone
Brokin he has in sounder at a cast,
And sone the fowlis flokit about him fast.
Quhat will ȝe mare, he was bot slane or schent,      150
Sore for him wepit all the hennis of Kent.
Wp was he takin, and in a garding led,
Amang thir herbes thai haf maid him a bed,
And quhat throu comfort and throu medecyne,
Within the space of days viii or nyne,               155

This bird was mendit hale and sound,
Of all the panys of his bludy wound.
And Gundulfus, with his frendis assent,
To Oxinfurd to study is he went.
Sone efter this this bird wax a cok,                     160
The gudliest and farest of the flok,
Clerast of voce and wysest in his entent,
The cruellest of all the cokis of Kent ;
And he had Coping to be his wyf,
And he had chosyn hir for term of lyf,                   165
And scho agane till him hire treuth plicht,
To luf him best of ony erdly wicht.
And so at evyne apon his perke he gat,
On his richt hand dame Copok nixt him sat ;
And quhill he clapit durst thar na cok craw,            170
Quhen he had clapit than crav thai all on raw.
So wele he had the houssis obseruance,
That of the flok he baire the gouernans.
Thus was he cheif cok of the bondis place,
And baire the rewle threttene zeris space.              175
And all this tyme he had this child in thocht
That brak his leg quhen he trespassit nocht.
[Creverat et multum jam jam Gundulfus in altum,
    Jamque suo patri substituendus erat.] [1]
He was na master in diuinite
Bot he wald preche in to that science hie.
Weile couth he cast the bukis of decres,                180
Bot tharin nothing had he of his greis.
Prentis in court he had bene for a zere ;
He was a richt gud syngare in the quere.
He couth wele reid and sumpart write and dyte,
And in his grammere was he wele perfyte.                185
He was na gret bachillare in sophistry,
With part of pratik of nygramansy,
Of phesik he baire ane vrinale,

---

[1] There is no break in the MS. here, but two lines seem wanting to
complete the sense.   Those inserted are from the Latin original, which
makes Gundulfus the son of a presbyter, not of a farmer.

To se thire folk gif thai war seike or hale.
And in his clething was he wele besene,                    190
Ffor govne and hude was all of Lyncome grene.
Gret was the joy that in the place was than,
To se the meting of that noble man.
In come his frendis till him fast anone,
And notwithstanding that the day was gone,                195
"Ffader," he said, "I can nocht byde this nycht,
To Rochister I mon thir wayis richt,
To morne is the day of my promocioun,
Of haly ordour to resaif the crovne,
And tharin standis myne awansing hale,                    200
Vnto ane benefice perpetuale,
And falʒe this, the kirk gais to ane nothir."
Than spak our dame that was the childis modir,
"Son, for my blissing this nycht with ws abyde,
And all at eis to morne son sall ʒe ryd,                  205
Oure houss cok sall the houris of the nycht
Alswele devyde as ony orloge richt,
And at the first cok walkinn sall ʒe be,
And at ʒour hors sone be the houre of thre.
ʒe haue bot nyne myle of the farest way,                  210
At Rochister ʒe sall be sone be day,
And haf ʒour tonsour be the houre of nyne."
And so he baid, and drank with thaim the wyne.
Quhen thai war full of mychti ale and wyne,
Thai gat to rest and slepis as ony swyne.                 215
The nycht ʒeid oure, the freindis thocht nocht lang,
Ffor all thare trast was on the cokis sang.
And all this sawe the cok apon the balk,
And quhen he hard the matir of thair talk,
And on the breking of his theis bone,                     220
This cok had mynd, Gundulfus he had none.
Sone come the tyme that he suld say his voce,
The houre ʒeid oure, the cok he held him clos:
With that dame Coppok putis on hir maike,
Said, "Slepe ʒe schir! get wp for Cristis saik,          225
ʒour houre is gone, quhy syng ʒe nocht, for schame!
Wait ʒe nocht weile ʒone clerk suld ryde fra hame.

And all thare trast apon ʒour sang thai lay,
Schir! syng ʒe nocht, ʒone clerk sall slepe quhill day.
And so in vane is all thing that thai wirk,          230
It war gret pete he suld tyne his kirk,
And of the tynsall ʒe sall haf the blame."
Syng wald he nocht, bot schrewitly said, "Madame,
Wysest ʒe are quhen that ʒe hald ʒow still,
And ʒit ʒe wyffis evir speike ʒe will,          235
Dame, intromet ʒow in ʒour wyfis deid,
Lytill ʒe wist quhen that my leg couth bleid,
And ʒone is he that brak my leg in sounder,
Gif I suld crawe, madame, it ware gret wounder,
Ffor thocht my leg be werray haile outwart,          240
Quhen I him se, it bledis at my hart."
As thai ware talkand this fer thaim amang,
Lang efter that the cok tuke wp a sang,
And all the birdis with ane woce thai cry,
Get wp! get wp! we se the dayis sky.          245
And wp he gat and saw that it was day.
Said kirk and worshipe fastly war away.
On hors he gat, fast throw the tovne he raid,
And all the doggis intill his tale he had;
Quhill at ane stone he styntit with sic fors,          250
That to the erd ʒeid baith the man and horss.
This hors gat wp and ran oure to the hill,
And in the myre this worthy clerk lay still.
And still he lay quhill it was tyme of none,
The kirk disponit, and all the seruice done.          255
Than wp he gat, and hame agane is went,
Ane hevy man forsuth in his entent.
His garment grene that was of colour gud
Was sa mismaide in the myre and mvde;
And quhat for schame he was so pale of hewe,          260
Quhen he come hame, thar was no man him knewe.
So quhen this clerk with schame come hame agane,
Than was this cok quyt of his legis pane,
And said, " Madame Coppok mak gud cheire,
Now wepis he that leuch this hender ʒeire,          265
Quhen with ane stone my thees bone he brak,

Bot for I lukit till his faderis stak,
And quhen I bled he said the feild was his,
Now, God I loif this day has send ws this."

    Now be this tale ȝe sall wele wnderstand,     270
Gif ȝe be lord and rewlare of this land,
Ȝe schape ȝow nocht for till oppres the pure ;
Ffor and ȝe do, forsuth I ȝow assure
The tyme may cum that ȝour awentour standis
Perawenture into sic mennis handis.     275
Quha schapis him the pure for to oppres,
At Goddis hand the mater has to addres.
Quhill that ȝe haf space tharfor ȝe suld amend,
Byde nocht the straik of vengeans at ȝour end,
Ffor till amend als oft as ȝe do mys,     280
And we beseke Jhesu of his bliss.

                        Amen.

    It was ane blyth sicht of this baire,
  Of reid gold was the birs he baire.
Of reid gold schynand was his haire,
His scheldis war richt sad and sure,     285
His tuskis scharp that he with schure,
Of stele thai ware, baith stark and sture.
This was the taile that he tald thare,
I coppyit it with all my cure.


## The Baris Taile.

    Gret Alexander King of Massedovn,     290
  The quhilk of the nyne nobillis was one,
Of his conquest the tyme nere by the end,
To the cite of Lapsat in Araby he send ;
And of the folk desyrit sic a thing,
To knaw him for thar souerane lord and king,     295

T

And to be subiect to his hie empyre,
And tak example at the tovne of Tyre,
That was so strang and for rebellioun
Was wtterly distroyit and cassyn dovn.
To this desyre and quhat thai wald haf done,          300
Thire worthy folk ware awysit sone,
And in thire termes answer haue thai send,
That quhill we leif we will this tovne defend,
In sic fredome as our antecessouris
Has left till ws, and till this tovne of owris.       305
Erare we cheis with worschipe for to de,
Than for to leif in subiectioun to be ;
And in this querell maid thaim ilkone bovne,
With ane assent to defend this tovne.
This riall prince he was amouit so,                   310
Quhen he this herd he micht no forder go.
Bot to this tovne this king agane is gone,
And with ane of the riallest of one
Of kyngis and princis and worthy men of weir,
And with the cost nane vther man mycht beir.          315
And in entent to cast the cite dovn,
And put ȝone pepill to confusioun,
But hope of grace for trety and debait,
Into remembering of his hie estait.
Into this tovne thar was a noble man,                 320
Ane worthy clerke, the best of ane was than,
And had bene master to this riall kyng,
In his scoling quhen at this prince was ȝing.
And our all thing this tovne he lufit best,
And of this prince he trastit grace of rest.          325
So or this ost was cummyn to this tovne,
This clerk on kneis befor this king fell dovne.
This king was ware, and weile this clerk he saw,
Said, " Master, ces, ȝour erand weile I knawe,
Desyre na thing at me this daye, for quhy,            330
Quhat evire ȝe ask that thing I will deny,
And in the contrare wirk at all my micht."
Than spak this clerk, and set this word on hicht :—
" A kingis word in more effect suld be,

Than ony of laware degre. 335
Excellent hie and mychti prince, but peire,
Now of this grace that ȝe haf grantit heire,
I thank ȝour hienes, and I ask no more,
Bot hald the purpos that ȝe are cummyn fore,
To sla ȝone folk, and to distroye ȝone tovne, 340
To do no grace to cast ȝone wallis dovne.
Now may ȝe cheis to lat ȝour wordis stand,
And tyne the cost, or tak this tovne on hand,
And brek ȝour word befor this riall rowte."
The king was wo, and to remuf that dowt 345
To counsall ȝeid, and quhen he was degest
To tyne this cost, erare he thocht it best
Than for to breke the wordis that he spak,
And left this towne and wald nocht tak the lak.
So throw the wit of his philosophouris, 350
And the gret worschipe of his conquerouris,
In rest and pece with fredome ȝit thai ryng,
And boith ar deid, this gret clerk and this king.
  Nowe be this taile it may richt wele be sene
  Ane kyngis word in till effect suld bene 355
More precious in worschipe of his crowne,
Than gud or gold or ony wallit tovne.
Richt sad of langage suld he be ane kyng,
And weile avysit or he said the thing,
That suld him greif or muf in his entent, 360
Erare speike nocht, than speike and syne repent.
Or gif a kyng has said or done amys,
In that to iustice oucht grevand is,
It is more worschipe till his hie estait
For to revoke, than to be obstinat. 365
And to forbeire sic lust and sic delyte,
And tak tharfor euerlestand lyf perfyte,
Vnto the quhilk the lord of lyf, but end,
Quhen we depart, mot all our sawlis send.

## The Wolfis Tale.

This wretchit wolf neir by this lyoun lay,                     370
His habit was, me thocht, of cottoun gray,
And so weile fauorit was his face on far,
The laif semed fere farere than thai ware.
Thinkand to put this counsall fra that king,
And his allya to the court inbring,                           375
He umbethocht him gretly of his wylis,
And to thire staitis gaif he weile thair stylis.
Said, "Souerane lord, I can nocht fabillis fene,
Bot for the commoun proffet I complene,
In all this land thare is no schepe to get,                   380
Within ten myle a mutone to ȝour meit,
Bot schepe and nolt distroyit are and deid;
And for the quhilk, schir, this is the remeid,
To lat tham stand still that thai may store
And multiply, as thai ware of before.                         385
Of wenysoun and wyld meit mak gud cheire,
And of gret bestis feid ȝow for a ȝeire.
Schir, tak gud heid, and wnderstand me wele."
Than said the king, " Be ȝour complaint I feile,
That for I haf na mutoun to my mete,                          390
My cosingis of my counsall I suld ete.
Na, neuer more, thocht in defalt I de,
Than quha wald byde and of my counsall be,
Bot with my counsall will I seike remeid,
Fynd how my schepe and how my nolt ar deid."                  395
So quhill this wolf was in this court, thai fand
That his allya forrayd all the land,
And so this lyoun sentence gaf he plane,
No beist of reif suld in his court remane,
Nor of inwy nor ȝit of covatis.                               400
So was this wolf, with all thare hale awys,
Exild the court and fled with all his micht.
So sodanely this court went out of sicht,
That all was gone in twynkling of ane E,
And so gois all the warldis rialte.                           405

Now be this wolf schortly, be myne awys,
Is wnderstand the syn of covatis,
And be thire foure of counsall to the king,
The wertuis foure that in a king suld ryng,
Prudence, justice, and magnanimite,                    410
And continence that is content to be.
The wertewe no tyme suthly lestis
In no persone that covatis in restis.
Quha may be prudent with that desyre,
Or ȝit content had he the hale empyre.                 415
Curage throw covatis is set at nocht,
And be that mayne is justice sauld and bocht.
Now mak this wyce exild for to be,
Tak lawe, and luf, and leif in cherite,
And think quhat suld this warldis fals wanglore,       420
And for the joye that lestis euermore,
Beseike we him, that bocht ws with his blud,
Eternale God the ground of euery gud.

Amen.

HEIRE ENDIS THE TALIS OF THE FYUE BESTES,
PER M. JO. ASLOAN.

# THE MANER OF THE CRYING
## OF ANE PLAYE

XVII.

# THE MANER OF THE CRYING
# OF ANE PLAYE.

[IN *the following curious Interlude, the personification of*
Wealth *is represented as announcing a dramatic performance, to be given at the Cross of* Edinburgh, *which city is
described as a place where there is* 'plesans, disport and
play.' *To make the intimation as attractive as possible, the
person representing* Wealth *describes himself as descended
from* Hercules *and the race of giants. He informs his
audience that his grandfather is the Ossianic hero* Fyn
M'Kowle *or* Fingal, *whose wife was a giantess, and that
his father is the great* Gow Macmorne, *a man also of extraordinary size.*

*In the* Bannatyne Manuscript *where the poem occurs, the
following title is given to it :* "Ane littill interlud of the
Droichis part of the play,'—*and at the end there are the
words* "Ffinis off the droichis part of the play," Droich
*being a person of small size, or a dwarf. It seems, possibly,
to have been intended that the description of the extravagant
proportions of the persons mentioned in the poem should be
recited by the dwarf, to make the contrast more amusing.*

*The other characters in the comedy are* Weilfare, Wantoness, and Play, *who*

—" with all sportis and merynes,<br>
ȝour hartis hald euer on hicht."]

*It is difficult to say whether this poem actually formed part of any drama, as assuredly no composition of the same period now exists that can be dignified with the title.*

*The earliest drama that belongs exclusively to our country is* The Satire of the thrie Estaits, *which it is certain was not written before the year* 1535; *and therefore, to connect this interlude with that most singular production, or assign them both to the same author, as has repeatedly been done, is very erroneous. The present poem evidently belongs to the reign of* James IV. *and not of his successor; and instead of being the work of* Sir David Lyndsay, *it seems to bear sufficient evidence of the more masterly hand of his predecessor* Dunbar.

*The volume that has furnished the present copy, (written by* John Asloan, *apparently in or before the year* 1515,) *is preserved at* Auchinleck, *and has been already described. Besides presenting the text in a more genuine state, it contains several stanzas of a local nature and of no inconsiderable interest, that do not occur in* Bannatyne's *later manuscript, from which it has hitherto been printed.*

XVII.

# '𝕳eir followis the maner of the crying of ane Playe.'

HARRY, harry, hobillschowe!
    Se quha is cummyn nowe,
Bot I wait nevir howe,
      With the quhorle wynd?
A Soldane owt of Seriand land,        5
A gyand strang for to stand,
That with the strenth of my hand
      Beres may bynd.

Ȝit I trowe that I wary,
I am the nakit, blynd Hary,        10
That lang has.bene in the fary,
      Ffarleis to fynd;
And ȝit gif this be nocht I,
I wait I am the spreit of Gy,
Or ellis go by the sky,        15
      Licht as the lynd.

The God of most magnificence,
Conserf this fair presens,
And saif this amyable audiens,
      Grete of renovne;        20

L. 5. Bann. MS. reads 'A sargeand out of Sowdoun land.'

Prowest, ballies, officeris,
And honerable induellaris,
Marchandis, and familiaris,
    Of all this fair towne.

Quha is cummyn heir, bot I,      25
A bauld bustuoss bellamy,
At ȝour corss to mak a cry,
    With a hie sowne?
Quhilk generit am of gyandis kynd,
Ffra strang Hercules be strynd,      30
Off all the occident of Ynd,
    My eldaris bair the crovne.

My fore grantschir, hecht Fyn McKowle,
That dang the devill, and gart him ȝowle,
The skyis ranyd quhen he wald scowle,      35
    And trublit all the air:
He gat my grantschir Gog Magog;
Ay quhen he dansit, the warld wald schog;
Ffive thousand ellis ȝeid in his frog,
    Of Hieland pladdis of hair.      40

Ȝit he was bot of tendir ȝouth;
Bot eftir he grewe mekle at fouth,
Ellevyne ell wydemet was his mouth,
    His teith was ten myle sqwair.
He wald apon his tais stand,      45
And tak the sternis dovne with his hand,
And set tham in a gold garland
    Aboue his wyfis hair.

He had a wyf was lang of clift;
Hir hed was hiear than the lift;
The hevyne rerdit quhen scho wald rift;      50
    The lass was no thing sklender:

L. 43. 'Ellevyne mylle' in Bann. MS.

Scho spittit Loch-Lomond with hir lippis ;
Thunder and fyreflaucht flewe fra hir hippis ;
Quhen scho was crabit, the son tholit clips ;      55
    The fende durst nocht offend hir.

Ffor cald scho tuke the fever cartane ;
Ffor all the claith of Fraunce and Bertane,
Wald nocht be till hir leg a gartane,
    Thocht scho was ging and tender ;      60
Apon a nycht heir in the North,
Scho tuke the grawell, and stalit Cragorth,
Scho pischit the mekle watter of Forth ;
    Sic tyde ran efter hender.

A thing writtin of hir I fynd,                      65
In Irland quhen scho blewe behynd,
At Noroway costis scho rasit the wynd,
    And gret schippis drownit thar.
Scho fischit all the Spange seis,
With hir sark lape befor hir theis ;                70
Sevyne dayis saling betuix hir kneis,
    Was estymit and mair.

The hyngand brayis on athir syde,
Scho poltit with hir lymmis wyde.
Lassis mycht leir at hir to stryd,                  75
    Wald ga to lufis lair.
Scho merkit syne to land with myrth ;
And pischit fyf quhalis in the Firth,
That cropyn war in hir count for girth,
    Welterand amang the wair.      80

My fader, mekle Gow Makmorne,
Out of that wyfis wame was schorne ;
Ffor litilness scho was forlorne,
    Sic a kempe to beir :

L. 62. Cragorth, supposed to be Craigforth, near Stirling,—"a bold
bosky crag of similar formation to Stirling Hill and Abbey Craig " (*see*
Nimmo's History of Stirlingshire, 3d edit., p. 291).
    L. 71. 'Thre dayis sailing,' Bann. MS.   L. 79. Bann. MS. reads 'geig.'

Or he of eld was ȝeris thre,  85
He wald stepe our the occeane se;
The mone sprang neuer aboue his kne;
  The hevyn had of him feir.


Ane thousand ȝer is past fra mynd,
Sen I was generit of his kynd,  90
Ffull far amang the desertis of Ynde,
  Amang lyoun and beir:
Baith the King Arthour and Gawane,
And mony bald berne in Brettane,
Ar deid, and in the weris slane,  95
  Sen I couth weild a speir.


I haue bene forthwart euer in feild,
And now so lang I haf borne scheld,
That I am all crynd in for eld
  This litill, as ȝe may se.  100
I haue bene bannist wnder the lynd
Ffull lang, that no man couth me fynd,
And now with this last southin wynd,
  I am cummyn heir parde.


My name is WELTH, thairfor be blyth,  105
I am come heir comfort ȝow to kyth;
Supposs that wretchis wryng and wryth,
  All darth I sall gar de;
Ffor sekerly, the treuth to tell,
I come amang ȝow heir to duell,  110
Ffra sound of Sanct Gelis bell,
  Nevir think I to fle.


Sophea and the Soldane strang,
With weris that has lestit lang,
Ffurth of thar boundis maid me to gang,  115
  And turn to Turky tyte.

The King of Frauncis gret army,
Has brocht in darth in Lombardy;
And in ane cuntre he and I
    May nocht baith stand perfyte.        120

In Denmark, Swetherik, and Noroway,
Na in the Steidis I dar nocht ga;
Amang thaim is bot tak and sla,
    Cut thropillis, and mak quyte.
Irland for evir I haue refusit,        125
All wichtis suld hald me excusit,
Ffor neuer in land quhar Erische was vsit,
    To duell had I delyte.

Quharfor in Scotland come I heir,
With ȝow to byde and perseveir,        130
In Edinburgh, quhar is meriast cheir,
    Plesans, disport and play;
Quhilk is the lampe, and A per se
Of this regioun, in all degre,
Of welefair, and of honeste,        135
    Renovne, and riche aray.

Sen I am Welth, cummyn to this wane,
Ȝe noble merchandis euerilkane,
Address ȝow furth with bow and flane,
    In lusty grene lufraye,        140
And follow furth on Robyn Hude,
With hartis coragiouss and gud,
And thocht that wretchis wald ga wod,
    Of worschipe hald the way.

Ffor I, and my thre feres aye,        145
WEILFAIR, WANTONESS, and PLAY,
Sall byde with ȝow, in all affray,
    And cair put clene to flicht:
And we sall dredless ws address,
To banniss derth, and all distress;        150
And with all sportis and meryness,
    Ȝour hartis hald euer on hicht.

[Sen] I am of mekle quantite,
Of gyand kynd, as ȝe may se,
Quhar sall be gottin a wyf to me                    155
    Sicklyke of breid and hicht ?
I dreid that thair be nocht a [bryde]
In all this towne may me abyd,
Quha wait gif ony heir besyde,
    Micht suffer me all nycht.                    160

With ȝow sen I mon leid my lyf,
Gar serss baith Louthiane and Fyf,
And vale to me a mekle wyf,
    A gret vngraciouss gan ;
Sen scho is gane, the Gret FORLORE               165
[Of BABYLON, that I full yore
Espousit, quhan we tochir store
    Fra gud sanct Dawy wan.]

Adew ! fairweill ; for now I go,
Bot I will nocht lang byd ȝow fro ;               170
Chryst ȝow conserve fra every wo,
    Baith madin, wyf, and man.
God bliss thame, and the haly rude,
Givis me a drink, sa it be gude ;
And quha trowis best that I do lude,              175
    Skynk first to me the kan.


**FFINIS OFF THE DROICHIS PART OF THE PLAY.**


'Sen' in l. 153, and 'bryde' in l. 157, are supplied from Bann. MS.;
the Asloan MS. for 'bryde' reads 'maide.'

Ll. 166-168. This Interlude in Asloane's MS. is incomplete ; the leaf
which had the conclusion being lost. As Bannatyne's MS. from which the
subsequent stanza is given does not contain the former, these three lines
were kindly supplied by Robert Jamieson, Esq., editor of 'Popular Songs
and Ballads.'

L. 168. 'He was a sair Sanct to the Crown,' as James the First very
feelingly observed to the Abbot of Dumferling, who was extolling David's
munificence to the Church, which had been so disastrous to his successors. —
MS. Note, R. Jamieson.

# LAYING OF LORD FERGUS'S GAIST

# XVIII.

# THE LAYING OF LORD FERGUS'S GAIST.

## ANE INTERLUDE.

---

*THIS amusing* Interlude, *preserved by* Bannatyne *in his 'Ballet Buik,'* [1] *has already been printed in the 'Minstrelsy of the Scottish Border,'* [2]*—where it is said to be "in the same strain with the verses concerning the* Gyre Carling. *As the mention of* Bettokis Bowr *occurs in both pieces, and as the scene of both is laid in* East Lothian, *they are perhaps composed by the same author."* Sir Walter Scott, *with his usual discrimination, at the same time observes, " The humour of these fragments seems to have been directed against the superstitions of Rome, but it is now become very obscure. Nevertheless the verses are worthy of preservation, for the sake of the ancient language and allusions."*

Calderwood, *in his highly valuable History of the* Church of Scotland, *mentions* James Wedderburn *as one of those who, before the Reformation, being persecuted on account of their religious opinions, fled from Scotland;—*

[1] MS. fol. 114.  [2] Vol. I. p. clx.

*and says, that "he had a good gift of poesie, and made diverse Comedies and Tragedies in the Scotish tongue, quhairin he nipped the abuses and superstitions of the time." The historian adds, that "he counterfeited also the conjuring of ane gaist, quich was indeed practised be* Frier Lang, *beside Kinghorn, quich* Frier Lang *had been Confessor to the King:—But after the conjuring the King was constrained for shame to remove him." A curious allusion to this story occurs in* 'Ane Epistill direct from the halie hermeit of Alareit, to his brethren the Gray Freirs,' *which was written by* Alexander, Earle of Glencairn :

> ——Bot ordourlie to dress this thing
> A gaist I purpois to gar gang
> By counsaill of Frier Walter Lang — —
> That practick he provit anis befoir
> Betuix Kyrkaldie and Kinghorne,
> Bot Lymmaris maid therat sik skorne
> And to his fame mad sik digressioun,
> Sensyne he hard not the Kingis confessioun,
> Thoicht at that time he come no speid.[1]

*From the allusion by* Calderwood, *it has been conjectured that* Wedderburn *was the author of the following burlesque poem.*

[1] Knox's History, edit. 1732, p. 25.

# 'Ane Interlude
# of the Laying of a Gaist.'

L ISTIS lordis, I sall ȝow tell
    Off ane verry grit mervell,
Off Lord Ferguss gaist,
How mekle Schir Andro it chest
Vnto Beittokis bour,          5
The silly sawle to succour:
And he hes writtin vnto me,
Auld storeiss for to se,
Gif it appinis him to meit,
How he sall coniure the spreit:      10
And I haif red mony quarss,
Bath the Donet, and Dominusque parss,
Ryme maid, and als reiddin,
Baith Inglis and Latene:
And ane story haif I to reid      15
Passis Bonitatem in the creid—
To coniure the littill gaist ȝe mon haif
Off tod tailis ten thraif,
And kast the grit haly watter
With pater noster, patter patter;      20
And ȝe man sitt in ane compass,
And cry, Harbert tuthless,
Drug thow, and thiss draw,
And sitt thair quhill cok craw.

The compass mon hallowit be                     25
With Aspergis me Domine;
The haly writt schawis als
Thair man be hung abowt ȝour hals,
Pricket in ane woll poik,
Off neiss powder ane grit loik.                 30
Thir thingis mon ȝe beir,
Brynt in ane doggis eir,
Ane pluche, ane paiddill, and ane palme corss,
Thre tuskis of ane awld deid horss,
And of ane ȝallow wob the warp,                 35
The boddome of ane awld herp,
The heid of ane cuttit reill,
The band of ane awld quheill,
The taill of ane ȝeild sow,
And ane bait of blew wow,                       40
Ane botene, and ane brechame,
And ane quhorle maid of lame,
To luke owt at the litill boir,
And cry, Chrystis cross! ȝow befoir:
And quhen ȝe se the littill gaist,              45
Cumand to ȝow in all haist,
Cry lowd, Chryste eleisone!
And speir quhat law it leivis on?
And gif it sayis on Godis ley,
Than to the littill gaist ȝe say,               50
With braid benedicitie;
Littill gaist, I coniure the,
With lierie and larie,
Bayth fra God, and Sanct Marie,
First with ane fisschis mowth,                  55
And syne with ane fowlis towth,
With ten pertane tais,
And nyne knokis of windil strais,
With thre heidis of curle doddy;
And bid the gaist turn in a boddy.              60
Than eftir this coniuratioun,
The littill gaist will fall in soun,
And thaireftir doun ly,

Cryand mercy petously;
Than with ȝour left heill it sane,                    65
And it will nevir cum agane,
Als mekle as ane mige amaist. — — —
He had ane littill rod leg,
And it wes cant as ony cleg,
It wes wynd in ane wyndinscheit,                    70
Bayth the handis and the feit:
Suppois this gaist wes littill
Ȝit it stall Godis quhittill;
It stall fra peteouss Abrahame,
Ane quhorle and ane quhum quhame;                    75
It stall fra the carle of the mone
Ane pair of awld yrn schone;
It ran to Pencaitlane,
And wirreit ane awld chaplane.
This littill gaist did na mair ill,                    80
Bot clok lyk a corne myll;
And it wald play and hop,
Abowt the heid ane stre strop;
And it wald sing and it wald dance,
Ourefute, and Orliance.                    85
Quha coniurit the littill gaist, sa ȝe?
Nane bot the littil Spenȝie fle,
That with hir wit and ingyne,
Gart the gaist leif agane;
And syne mareid the gaist the fle,                    90
And cround him kyng of Kandelie;
And they gat thame betwene,
Orpheus king and Elpha quene,
To reid quha will this gentill geist,
Ȝe hard it nocht at Cokilbys feist.                    95


EXPLICIT.

Line 68. .Apparently one or more lines are here omitted.

# SYMMIE AND HIS BRUDER

XIX.

# SYMMIE AND HIS BRUTHER.

*IN a satirical poem*[1] *included in the present collection, the*
'swyngeour coife,' *(a character in which the lewd and
inordinate lives of the secular clergy is drawn from existing
manners,) at times, is spoken of, as,*

> " Peipand peurly with peteouss granis,
> Like fenȝeit Symmie and his bruder."

*These persons are no doubt the heroes of the following poem,
which, as Lord Hailes has observed, seems to intimate that
they were what is termed in the Canons of the Scotish Church,
A.D.* 1242 *and* 1296, quæstionarii, *or persons sent out by
the Church upon a begging mission.   Kennedy, in order to
throw ridicule upon* Dunbar, *represents him as one of these*
quæstionarii, *or begging friars, and says to him, with*
'cloutit cloke, skryp, burdoun, and clam-schellis,'

> " Fra Etrike Forest furthward to Dumfrese,
> Thow beggit with a pardoun in all kirkis,
> Collapis, cruddis, mele, grotis, grisis, and geis,
> And ondir nicht quhyle stall thow staggis and stirkis."[2]

*The poem itself is certainly obscure, and perhaps not quite
entire, but possesses a considerable share of humour in its*

---

[1] ' Ane Descriptioun of Peder Coffeis.'          [2] Flyting, ll. 425-428.

*descriptions, even although it falls very far short of* Peblis
to the Play, *or* Christis Kirk on the Grene, *of one or
other of which it may be considered as an imitation. The
stanza in which it is written, however, was popular during
the 15th and 16th centuries; and, amidst the contrariety
of opinions that have been expressed respecting the age of
these compositions, it might be difficult to assign the present
poem, with any degree of certainty, to a particular age. It
has hitherto been inedited, except the first seven stanzas,
which appeared in* Sibbald's *Chronicle of Scotish Poetry.*[1]

[1] Vol. i. p. 360.

## XIX.

# Followis Sym and his Bruder.

THAIR is no story that I of heir,
   Of Johine nor Robene Hude,
Nor ȝit of Wallace wicht but weir,
That me thinkis half so gude,
As of thir Palmaris twa but peir,       5
To heir how thay conclude ;
In to begging, I trow, fyve ȝeir
In Sanct Androis thay stude
               Togidder,
      Bayth Sym and his bruder.     10

Thocht thay war wicht, I warrand ȝow,
Thay had no will to wirk ;
Thay maid them burdownis nocht to bow,
Twa bewis of the birk,
Weill stobbit with steill, I trow,     15
To stik in to the mirk ;
Bot sen thair bairdis grew on thair mow,
Thay saw nevir the kirk
               Within, ·
      Nowthir Sym nor his bruder.    20

Syne schupe thame vp to lowp our leiss,
Twa tabartis of the tartane ;
Thay comptit nocht quhat thair clowtis weis,
Wes sewit thairon incertane :

Syne clampit vp sanct Peteris keiss,							25
Bot of ane auld reid gartane :
Sanct James schellis on the tothir syd sleuis,
As pretty as ony pertane
          Ta,
      On Sym and his bruder.							30

Thus quhen thai had reddit thair ragis,
To Rome they war inspyrit ;
Tuk vp thair jaipis and all thair jaggis,
Fure furth as thay war hyrit ;
And ay the eldest bure the baggis,							35
Quhen that the ȝungest tyrit ;
Tuk counsall at Kinkellis craggis,
Come hame as thay war hyrit
          Agane,
      Baith Sym and his bruther.						40

Than held thay houss, as men me tellis,
And spendit of thair feis ;
Quhen meit wes went, thay flew our fellis
Als bissy as ony beis ;
Syne clengit Sanct Jameis schellis,							45
And pecis of palme treis,
To se quha best the pardone spellis.
I schrew thame that ay leiss
          But lauchter,
      Quod Sym to his bruder.						50

Quhen thay wer welthfull in thair wynning,
Thay puft thame vp in pryd ;
Bot quhair that Symy levit in synnyng,
His bruder wald haif ane bryd ;
Hir wedoheid fra the begynning							55
Wes neir ane moneth tyd ;
Gif scho wes spedy ay in spynning,
Tak witness of thame besyd
          Ilk ane,
      Baith Sym and his bruder.						60

The carlis thay thikkit fast in cludis,
Agane the man wes mareit,
With breid and beif, and vthir budis,
Sym to the kirk thay kareit;
Bot or thay twynd him and his dudis,                    65
The tyme of none wes tareit:
Wa worth this wedding, for be thir widis,
The meit is all miskareit
    To day!
   Quod Sym and his bruder.                  70

Our all the houss, be lyne and levall,
The ladis come to luk him;
To tak a justing of that javell,
The bryd wount nocht to bruk him;
Thay maneist him with mony nevell,                      75
Than Symme rais and schuk him,
I cleme to clergy, quod the cavell,
How dar thow cum to luk him
    Ʒondir,
   Quod Sym and his bruder.                  80

With that the carle begowth to crak,
Glowrit vp and gaif a glufe;
His beird it wes als lang and blak,
That it hang our his moif;
He wes als lang vpoun the bak,                          85
As evir wes Angus Dufe;
He sayis, "This justing I vndirtak,
My coit is of gud stuffe,
    Call to,"
   Quod Sym and his bruder.                  90

He hoppit sa mycht na man hald him,
Said "Blame me bot I bind him;
I sall ourtak him, and that I tald him,
In ʒone feild gife I fynd him,"
On his gray meir fast furth thay cald him,              95
The flokis flew furth behind him,

Thay daschit him doun, the dirt ourhaild him,
Than start thay to and tied him
    Tycht,
   Baith Sym and his bruder.    100

Than brak he lowss, the horss that bair him
Ran startling to Stratyrum,
And he gat vp, and Symme swair him,
ʒe meit nocht bot ʒe myr him;
Off that fowll courss for to declair him   105
The cairlis come to requyr him,
Than all the laddis tryd with a lairrum
To flud him and to flyr him
    Bayth,
   Quod Syme and his bruder.    110

This was no bourdene to brown hill,
That gatt betwene the browis,
And had no thing ado thairtill,
As mony vder trowis;
Bot come furth on his awin gud will,    115
To Squyar Johine of Mowis,
He gatt ane sit vp in the schill,
And that the laddis allowis
    Ilk ane,
   To Sym and his bruder.    120

Yob Symmer was the stirrepman,
Was nolt hird of the toun,
He said " I will just as I can,
Sen he is strickin doun."
He gatt twa plaitis of ane awld pan,    125
Ane breist plait maid him boun,
The first rynk raif his mowth a span,
And thair he fell in swoune
    Almaist,
   Bayth Sym and his bruder.    130

Doun fra the leggis quhen he wes laist,
He maid a peteouss panting,
He swownit and he swelt almaist,
For gaping and for ganting ;
Abyd, quod the leich, I se a waist,                135
His wrangtwch is in wanting,
God saif him, and the Haly Gaist,
And keip the man fra manting
    Mekle,
   Quod Sym and his bruder.                140

His mowth wes schent, and sa forschorne,
Held nowdir wind nor watter ;
Fair weill all blast of blawing horne,
He mycht nocht do bot blatter :
He endis the story with harme forlorne,                145
The nolt begowth till skatter,
The ky ran startling to the corne,
Wa worth the tyme thow gat hir
    Now !
   Quod Symme till his bruder.                150

EXPLICIT.

# ANE BALLAT OF ALLANE-A'-MAUT

XX.

# ANE BALLAT OF ALLANE-A'-MAUT.

*THIS ballad, transcribed from* Bannatyne's *Manuscript,* 1568, *is doubtless the most ancient which we now have of a numerous class of compositions, that still preserve no ordinary share of popularity among the peasantry both of Scotland and England, respecting this celebrated personage,* Allane-a'-Maut, *or, as he is more frequently styled,* Sir John Barleycorn. *It has never been printed, except by* Mr Jamieson, *in his valuable collection of* Popular Ballads and Songs,[1] *where it is accompanied with five or six other curious pieces of a similar kind, taken from tradition, or English copies of a more recent period. Among the later productions of the same class, the Editor cannot help alluding to a wild and romantic story, by his friend* Mr Allan Cunningham, *lately published in his two volumes of* Traditional Tales.[2]

*A curious mistake has arisen from the jocular signature affixed to the poem in the Manuscript, as, instead of reading* 'quoth Allane Matsonis suddartis,'[3] *or soldiers, the name of* Allan Watson *has found a place in the different lists and lives of the early Scotish Poets as its author. In the same manner has the name of* John Blyth *been registered among the Scotish Poets, as author of a* 'Ballat of Gude*

---

[1] Edin. 1806, vol. ii. pp. 231-260.  [2] Lond. 1822, 12mo, vol. i.
[3] The signature is not affixed to the copy in Mr Jamieson's collection.

*Fallowis.'—Surely it requires very little discernment to ascertain that such names were assumed for 'the nones,' and suggested by the nature of the verses. The only Poet, to whom the following ballad can with any degree of likelihood be attributed, is* Dunbar, *among whose works will be found a few pieces of a like kind, and who, perhaps, assumed no feigned character when he so designated himself.*

x

# 'Quhy sowld nocht Allane honorit be?'

QUHEN he wes ȝung, and cled in grene,
    Haifand his air abowt his ene,
    Baith men and wemen did him mene,
Quhen he grew on ȝon hillis he ;—
Quhy sowld nocht Allane honorit be ?       5

His foster faider fure of the toun,
To vissy Allane he maid him boun ;
He saw him lyane, allace ! in swoun,
For falt of help, and lyk to de ;—
Quhy sowld nocht Allane honorit be ?      10

Thay saw his heid begin to ryfe ;
Syne for ane nvreiss thay send belyfe,
Quha brocht with hir fyfty and fyve
Of men of war full prevely ;—
Quhy sowld nocht Allane honorit be ?      15

Thay ruschit furth lyk hellis rukis,
And every ane of thame had hukis ;
They cawcht him schortly in thair clukis,
Syne band him in ane creddill of tre ;—
Quhy sowld nocht Allane honorit be ?      20

Thay brocht him invart in the land,
Syne every freynd maid him his band,
Quhill they micht owdir gang or stand,
Nevir ane fute fra him to fle ;—
Quhy sowld nocht Allane honorit be ?          25

The grittest cowart in this land,
Ffra he with Allane entir in band,
Thocht he may nowdir gang nor stand,
Ʒit fowrty sall nocht gar him fle ;—
Quhy sowld nocht Allane honorit be ?          30

Schir Allanis hewmond is ane cop,
With ane sege feddir in his top :
Fra hand till hand so dois he hop,
Quhill sum may nowdir speik nor se ;—
Quhy sowld nocht Allane honorit be ?          35

In Ʒule, quhen ilk man singis his carrell
Gude Allane lyis in to ane barrell
Quhen he is thair, he dowtis no parrell
To cum on him be land or se,—
Quhy sowld nocht Allane honorit be ?          40

Ʒit wes thair nevir sa gay a gallane,
Fra he meit with our maistir Schir Allane,
Bot gif he hald him by the hallane,
Bakwart on the flure fallis he ;—
Quhy sowld nocht Allane honorit be ?          45

My maistir Allane grew so stark,
Quhill he maid mony cunning clerk,
Vpoun thair faiss he settis his mark,
A blud reid noiss besyd thair E ;—
Quhy sowld nocht Allane honorit be ?          50

My maistir Allane I may sair curss,
He levis no mony in my purss,
At his command I mon deburss
Moir nor the twa pairt of my fe ;—
Quhy sowld nocht Allane honorit be ?        55

And last, of Allane to conclude ;
He is bening, courtass and gude,
And servis ws of our daly fude,
And that with liberalitie ;—
Quhy sowld nocht Allane honorit be ?        60


FINIS  QUOD  ALLANE  MATSONIS  SUDDARTIS.

# ANE DESCRIPTIOUN OF PEDER COFFEIS

## XXI.

# ANE DESCRIPTIOUN OF PEDER COFFEIS.

*THIS satirical Poem was originally published by* Lord Hailes, *among his selections from the MS. 'Ballat Buik' of* George Bannatyne.[1] *"What the author meant by* Coffeis," *says* Lord Hailes, *(and we cannot use better words than his own to describe the poem,) "he explains in l.* 3, *where he speaks of 'Pedder* Knavis.' Coffe, *in the modern Scottish language means* rustic. *The sense here is peddling merchants. The seven sorts are:* 1. *An higgler and forestaller;* 2. *A lewd parish priest;* 3. *A merchant who traffics in company upon too small a stock;* 4. *Though obscurely expressed, is a low-born fellow, who intrudes himself into the magistracy of a royal burgh;* 5. *A fraudulent bankrupt;* 6. *A miser;* 7. *A dignified churchman: the character of each is drawn from the living manners of that age."*

*The Notes[2] subjoined by* Lord Hailes, *in explanation of this satirical description, and which* Sibbald,[3] *with a few slight alterations, adopted without acknowledgment, are too valuable to be withheld. They are therefore annexed without either mixture or alteration.*

[1] 12mo; Edinburgh, 1770, p. 170.　　　　　[2] Id. p. 298.
[3] Chronicle of Scottish Poetry, vol. i. p. 368.

*There is one thing, however, that in this place ought
to be remarked, since the Poem has hitherto been published
as an anonymous composition. In the same manner that
other pieces are attributed to their respective authors, the
signature* "quod Linsdsay" *appears in the manuscript. Although the name be written in a different-coloured ink, the
hand is apparently of the same age with that of the poem
to which it is affixed. Nor does internal evidence in any
degree invalidate the propriety of its being so attributed.
This circumstance having been unnoticed, was perhaps the
cause why it did not find a place in the elaborate edition
by* Mr George Chalmers, *of the poetical works of* Lyon
King at Arms.

XXI.

# Ane descriptioun of Peder Coffeis having na regaird till honestie in thair vocatioun.

I T is my purpoiss to discryve
   This holy perfyte genolagie
Of pedder knavis superlatyve,
Pretendand to awtoretie,
That wait of nocht bot beggartie.     5
Ʒe burges sonis, prevene thir lownis,
That wald distroy nobilitie,
And baneiss it all borrow townis.


Thay ar declarit in SEVIN PAIRTIS;
1. Ane scroppit cofe, quhen he begynnis,     10
   Sornand all and sindry airtis,
For to by hennis reid-wod he rynnis;
He lokis thame vp in to his innis
Vnto ane derth, and sellis thair eggis,
Regraitandly on thame he wynnis,     15
And secondly his meit he beggis.


2. Ane swyngeour coife, amangis the wyvis,
   In landwart dwellis with subteill menis,
Exponand thame auld sanctis lyvis,

And sanis thame with deid mennis banis;　　20
Lyk Rome-rakaris, with awsterne granis,
Speikand curlyk ilk ane till vder;
Peipand peurly with peteouss granis,
Lyk fenȝeit *Symmye* and his bruder.

3. Thir cur coffeis that sailis oure sone,　　25
　And thretty-sum abowt ane pak,
　With bair blew bonattis and hobbeld schone,
　And beir bonnokkis with thame thay tak;
　Thay schamed schrewis, God gif thame lak,
　At none quhen merchantis makis gud cheir,　　30
　Steilis doun, and lyis behind ane pak,
　Drinkand bot dreggis and barmy beir.

4. Knaifatica coff misknawis him sell,
　Quhen he gettis on a furrit goun;
　Grit Lucifer, maistir of hell,　　35
　Is nocht sa helie as that loun;
　As he cumis brankand throw the toun,
　With his keis clynkand on his arme,
　That calf, clovin futtit, fleid custroun,
　Will mary nane bot a burgess bairne.　　40

5. Ane dyvour coffe, that wirry hen,
　Distroyis the honor of our natioun,
　Takis gudis to frist fra fremmit men,
　And brekis his obligatioun;
　Quhilk dois the marchandis defamatioun;　　45
　Thay ar reprevit for that regratour,
　Thairfoir we gif our declaratioun,
　To hang and draw that common tratour.

6. Ane curloreouss coffe, that hege-skraper,
　He sittis at hame quhen that thay baik,　　50
　That pedder brybour, that scheip keipar,
　He tellis thame ilk ane caik by caik;
　Syne lokkis thame vp, and takis a faik,

Betuix his dowblett and his jackett,
And eitis thame in the buith, that smaik ;　　55
God, that he mort into ane rakkett.

7. Ane cathedrall coffe, he is ovir riche,
And hes na hap his gude to spend,
Bot levis lyk ane wareit wretche,
And trestis nevir till tak ane end ;　　60
With falsheid evir dois him defend,
Proceding still in averice,
And leivis his saule na gude commend,
Bot walkis ane wilsome wey, I wiss.

I ȝow exhort, all that is heir,　　65
That reidis this bill, ȝe wald it schaw
Vnto the provest, and him requeir
That he will geif thir Coffis the law,
And baneiss thame the Burgess raw,
And to the Scho streit ȝe thame ken ;　　70
Syne cutt thair luggis, that ȝe may knaw
Thir peddir knavis be burges men.

ffinis quod Linsdsay.

# NOTES ON THE PRECEDING POEM,

## BY LORD HAILES, 1770.

St. 2. 1. 11. "*Sornand* all and sindry *airts.*" This *scroppit* or *contemptible* dealer is represented as going about in every quarter *sornand ;* a contraction from *sojournand.* Hence *sorners,* or *sojourners,* which so often occurs in our more ancient statutes. He is here described as solicitous in

purchasing fowls, profiting by the sale of their eggs, forestalling the
market, and drawing advantage from a dearth. These are topics of
popular discontent, which the legislature has sometimes sanctified by inex-
tricable statutes.

My reason for imagining that *scroppit* means contemptible, is founded
on the following passage in Knox, p. 93. "Thair was presentit to the
Quein Regent a calfe having two heidis; whairat she *scorppit*, and said, it
was bot a common thing."

St. 3. A rascally wencher among the married women, resides in the
country, versant in the arts of subtilty; he interprets to them the legends
of the saints, and sanctifies them with dead men's bones or relics. Such
persons seem to have raked the streets of Rome for every superstitious
foolery. Sometimes they growl like dogs, in the offices of religion; sometimes they pitifully whine like the hypocritical *Symmye and his brother*.

The first part of this description alludes to the lewd and inordinate lives
of the secular clergy.—The description of their employment in the country
resembles that which the younger Vossius profanely gave of a friend of his:
"Est sacrificulus in pago quodam, et decipit rusticos."—In Lord Hynd-
ford's MS. [the 'Ballat Buik' of Geo. Bannatyne], there is a poem relative
to *Symmye and his bruder*; it is obscure; but seems to import, that they
were what is termed *quæstionarii* in the ancient Scottish canons, c. 48.
—that is, persons sent out by the church upon a begging mission.

St. 4. l. 25. "Thir cur coffeis that sailis oure sone,<br>
And thretty-sum about ane pak."

These lines are unintelligible without the aid of the statute-book. By
Act 24. parl. 4. James V. it is provided, "That na merchand saill, *without he have ane halfe last of gudes of his awin*, or else in governance, as
factour, to uthir merchandes." And by Act 25. "That na schip be
frauchted out of the realme, with ony staple gudes, fra the feast of Simon's
day and Judes, [28. Oct.] unto the feast of the purification of our lady,
called Candlemas." The reader will now perceive what it was to sail too
early, and wherein they offended, who, to the number of thirty, were joint
adventurers in one pack of goods.

St. 5. l. 33. "*Knaifatica* coff misknawis himself." The word *knaifatica*
has been invented to describe a pedlar of mean servile original. Every one
knows, that *knave* formerly meant a servant. It is probable that this
stanza was aimed at some living character, remarkable for the insolence of
office.[1]

———L. 38. "With his keis clynkand on his arme." The keys of a
city are considered as the symbols of trust and power, and therefore they
may have been borne by Magistrates. It is an ancient custom for the
chief magistrate of a city to deliver the keys to the Sovereign, upon his
first entry.

St. 6. l. 41. "Ane dyvour coffe." This stanza describes, in very em-
phatical terms, the offence of one who, while unable or unwilling to pay,
deals upon credit with foreign merchants.

St. 7. l. 55. "And eitis thame in the buith, that *smaik*." The word

---

[1] Those who most frequently held the office of Provost of Edinburgh, during the latter
part of this reign [Queen Mary's], were Lord Seaton, Douglas of Kilspindie, and Symon
Prestoun of Prestoun.—SIBBALD.

*smaik* means a pitiful ignominious fellow.   It occurs in a curious poem by the Earl of Glencairn, preserved in Knox, p. 25.

> "They *smaikis* dois set their haill intent,
> To reid the Inglische New Testament."

The churl here described, after having carefully numbered his cakes, conveys one of them under his cloaths, and eats it in his booth or shop.

> St. 9. l. 70. "And to the *scho-streit* ye thame ken,
> Syne cut thair luggis," &c.

Shoes are still sold at Edinburgh in the upper part of the *Grassmarket*, which is [formerly was] also the place of execution.   It is probable that lesser punishments, such as that of cutting off the ears of delinquents, were anciently inflicted in the same place.   It has been suggested to the editor, that by *Scho-streit*, a street in Perth, still termed the *Shoe-gate*, is understood.   But there seems no reason for supposing that this poem was composed at Perth, or that the *Shoe-gate* in Perth was a place of punishment.

THE

# THE
# WYF OF AUCHTERMUCHTY

# XXII.

## THE WYF OE AUCHTERMUCHTY.

*THE* ' Wyf of Auchtermuchty ' *has long continued to be a favourite among all classes of the people of* Scotland :—*and few poems of the same nature have oftener been printed, though seldom, it must be added, with a due regard to accuracy. Having been preserved by tradition, as well as by writing, there is no cause for surprise at finding the different copies vary considerably from each other. Of these, the one contained in* Bannatyne's *Manuscript ' Ballat Buik' is the most ancient.* Lord Hailes *indeed was inclined to think that it "had been transcribed at some later period than* 1568, *when most of the MS. was written." But there is no reason for entertaining such an opinion, since it occurs in the middle of the volume, and, as appears from the original series of paging, could not possibly have been inserted at a later period than the rest of the collection. From this copy the text is carefully given, and the most important variations of other editions are pointed out at the foot of the page. The only one, however, which requires particular notice is written in a hand not much later than the year* 1600, *and is distinguished as MS. A. This copy is now preserved in the* Advocates' Library. *It was discovered among some old law-papers which had belonged to the family of* Skene of Halyards, *in Fife.*

*For genuine humour, and as a faithful picture of rustic manners, 'The Wyf of Auchtermuchty' has seldom or never been equalled.* Ritson, *who intended to republish it in a projected volume of 'Select Scotish Poems,' says, in a manuscript note, "The subject of this poem seems to be borrowed from the first part of a story in the 'Silva Sermonum jucundissimorum,' Basil.* 1568, 8vo, *p.* 116; *though certainly from a more ancient authority. It has been very popular (he adds), and given rise to several imitations." The story referred to is quoted at full length in the* Appendix, *(the volume from which it is taken being of rare occurrence,) so that the reader may be enabled to draw his own conclusion respecting its originality. There is indeed a striking similarity in many of the incidents; but the poem has too much of a natural character and propriety, to make us think of depriving the old* Scotish *author of the merit of its invention.*

Allan Ramsay, *who, so far as we learn, was its earliest publisher, has, as* Lord Hailes *observed, altered six lines, and added no fewer than twenty. "It must be admitted* (Lord Hailes *adds) that his alterations and additions are in the style of the original. They prove him to have been a better poet than a publisher of other men's works." After such an encomium by one every way so well qualified to estimate their merit, it would have been improper to have withheld these additions.*

*Respecting the author of this poem, it may be observed that in* Bannatyne's *Manuscript,*[1] 'quod Mofat' *is subjoined, in a different, if not in a more modern hand. Accordingly it has been attributed to a* Sir John Moffat, *('one of the Pope's knights,') the only* Scotish *poet of the name,—who is conjectured to have lived in the earlier part of the* 16th *century. All we know concerning him is, that he was author of the fine moral poem, beginning*

"Bruthir be wyiss I reid ȝow now ;"

*that has been printed in* Lord Hailes's *collection. The*

---

[1] Fol. 120. b.

' Wyf of Auchtermuchty ' *may therefore be supposed to have been written about the year* 1520. *Should the solitary evidence, just referred to, respecting its author, be relied on, there is but too much cause to justify our regret in not possessing more considerable remains of a poet, whose claims to original genius, it is presumed, will not be disputed.*[1]

[1] I find there was a Sir John Moffat, a chaplain of the morn (morning) service, in the parish kirk of Dunfermline, 21st January 1493-94. And probably the same person, 12th February 1578-79, called Master of the Grammar School, was the proprietor of landis (houses) in the north part of the Tolbooth. — *Court-book of the Regality of Dunfermline.*

## XXII.

# The Wyf of Awchtirmwchty.

IN Awchtirmwchty thair dwelt ane man,
    Ane husband, as I hard it tawld,
Quha weill cowld tippill owt a can,
And nathir luvit hungir nor cawld.
Quhill anis it fell vpoun a day,        5
He ȝokkit his plwch vpoun the plane ;
Gif it be trew, as I hard say,
The day was fowll for wind and rane.

He lowsit the pluche at the landis end,
And draif his oxin hame at evin ;        10
Quhen he come in he lukit bend,
And saw the wyf baith dry and clene,
And sittand at ane fyre, beikand bawld,
With ane fat sowp, as I hard say :
The man being verry weit and cawld,        15
Betwene thay twa it was na play.


L. 1. thair wind an honest man.        L. 2. a rach husband.
L. 3. Sa weill can tipple vpon a good can.    L. 4. this man.
L. 8. It came on a foull day.
Ll. 9-16. *This stanza in MS. A. has only four lines.*
        He loosed the pleuch hame as he came,
          He saw the goodwife sitting baith fair and clene,
        Sitting before a good beikman bald,
          A good fat sowp his handis betuene.


Y

Quoth he, " Quhair is my horssis corne?
My ox hes naithir hay nor stray;
Dame, ʒe mon to the pluch to morne,
I salbe hussy, gif I may."                                    20
" Husband," quoth scho, " content am I
To tak the pluche my day abowt,
Sa ʒe will rowll baith kavis and ky,
And all the houss baith in and owt.


Bot sen that ʒe will husyskep ken,                           25
First ʒe sall sift, and syne sall kned ;
And ay as ʒe gang but and ben,
Luk that the bairnis dryt not the bed.
Ʒeis lay ane soft wisp to the kill,
We haif ane deir ferme on our heid ;                         30
And ay as ʒe gang furth and in,
Keip weill the gaislingis fra the gled."


The wyf was vp richt late at evin,
I pray God gif hir evill to fair,
Scho kyrnd the kyrne, and skwmd it clene,                    35
And left the gudeman bot the bledoch bair ;
Than in the mornyng vp scho gatt,
And on hir hairt laid hir disjwne,
Scho put als mekle in hir lap,
As micht haif serd them baith at nwne.                       40


L. 18. My cattell.          L. 19. Ye shall go to the pluch the morne.
L. 20. Ise gyde the hous als well as I may.
L. 21. Goodman.                          L. 22. To gang to the pleuch.
L. 24. Gyde my hous well.
L. 25. A gude husband if ye will be.
L. 28. Misvse not the bed.
Ll. 29-32.  And a good husband as ye wold be,
                  Some spottis in the house ye man outspy ;
               We have a deare ken [q. kane] to the ladie,
                  See that the calfes swk not the ky.
Ll. 37-40.  *These lines in MS. A. read thus:—*
               The goodwife gat up soone in the morning,
                  Vpon hir heart laid a fine disjune,
               Sho preind mair to Jock in hir lap
                  Nor wold have serued three honest men at noone.

Sayis Jok, " Will thow be maister of wark,
And thow sall had, and I sall kall;
Ise promiss the ane gud new sark,
Athir of round claith or of small.
Scho lowsit oxin aucht or nyne,                        45
And hynt ane gad-staff in hir hand;
And the gudman raiss eftir syne,
And saw the wyf had done command.


And cawd the gaislingis fwrth to feid,
Thair was bot sevensum of thame all;                   50
And by thair cumis the gredy gled,
And likkit vp five, left him bot twa :
Than owt he ran in all his mane,
How sone he hard the gaislingis cry;
Bot than or he come in agane,                          55
The calfis brak lowss and sowkit the ky.


The calvis and ky being met in the lone,
The man ran with ane rung to red;
Than by thair cumis ane ill-willy cow,
And brodit his buttok quhill that it bled.             60
Than hame he ran to an rok of tow,
And he satt doun to say the spynning;
I trow he lowtit our neir the low,
Quoth he, this wark hes ill begyning.


Than to the kyrn that he did stoure,                   65
And jwmlit at it quhill he swatt :

L. 41. &c. *This address to Jock, the servant, is not in MS. A.; nor indeed are several other lines.*
    L. 53. The good man ran forth in a great anger.
    L. 54. Soon ever as he.
    L. 55. Ere he came in what thought ye of yt.
    Ll. 61-64. He gat the rock soone in his bosome,
            He thought well to have begun his spinning;
        But alace ! he leand our neir the low;
            Alace ! (quo he) this work hes a hard beginning.

Quhen he had jwmlit a full lang houre,
The sorow crap of butter he gatt.
Albeit na butter he cowld gett,
Ȝit he wes cummerit with the kyrne,          70
And syne he het the milk our hett,
And sorrow a spark of it wald ȝyrne.

Than ben thair come ane gredy sow,
I trow he cund hir littil thank;
And in scho schot hir mekle mow,             75
And ay scho winkit and scho drank.
He cleikit vp ane crukit club,               ·
And thocht to hitt the sow ane rowt,
The twa gaislingis the gled had left,
That straik dang baith thair harnis out.     80

He gat his foot vpon the spyre,
To haue gotten the flesch doune to the pat,
He fell backward into the fyre,
And brack his head on the keming stock :
Ȝit he gat the mekle pat vpon the fyre,      85
And gat twa cannes and ran to the spout,
Er he came it, quhat thought ȝe of that ?
The fyre brunt aw the pat arss out.

Than he beur kendling to the kill,
Bot scho start all vp in ane low,            90
Quhat evir he hard, quhat evir he saw,
That day he had na will to mow.
Than he ȝeid to tak vp the bairnis,
Thocht to haif fund thame fair and clene ;
The first that he gat in his armis           95
Was all bedirtin to the ene.

Ll. 67, 68. And wold he haue jumblit while the dumsday,
            Sorrow a bit butter that ever he gat.
L. 73. And in there came.                L. 75. Hir ill fard mow.
L. 79. The glaidis had chaped.          L. 80. He chanced to ding.
Ll. 81-88. *This stanza, which does not occur in MS. Bann. nor in the
ordinary printed copies, is given from MS. A.*

The first that he gat in his armis,
It was all dirt vp to the eine;
"The Diuill cut of thair handis," quoth he,
"That fild ȝow all sa fow this strene."          100
He trailit the fowll scheitis doun the gait,
Thocht to haif wescht thame on ane stane;
The burne wes rissin grit of spait,
Away fra him the scheitis hes tane.


Than vp he gat on ane know heid,              105
On hir to cry, on hir to schowt,
Scho hard him, and scho hard him not,
Bot stowtly steird the stottis abowt.
Scho draif the day vnto the nicht,
Scho lowisit the plwch and syne come hame;   110
Scho fand all wrang that sowld bene richt,
I trow the man thocht richt grit schame.


Quoth he, " My office I forsaik,
For all the dayis of my lyf,
For I wald put ane howss to wraik,           115
Had I bene twenty dayis gudwyf."
Quoth scho, " Weill mot ȝe bruke ȝour place,
For trewlie I will nevir excep it;"
Quoth he, " Feind fall the lyaris face,
Bot ȝit ȝe may be blyth to get it."          120


Than vp scho gat ane mekle rung,
And the gudman maid to the doir;
Quoth he, " Deme, I sall hald my tung,
For and we fecht I'll get the woir."

L. 106. 'cray,' *MS. Bann.*
L. 106. Vpon the goodwife he cryed mony good shout.
L. 113. Dame I'le ge ouer my hussies skep.
L. 114. Forsooth of my life.          L. 122. dur, *MS. Bann.*
L. 121-124 *are not in MS. A.*

Quoth he, " Quhen I forsuk my plwche,          125
I trow I bot forsuk my seill,
And I will to my plwch agane,
Ffor I and this howss will nevir do weill."


FINIS QUOD MOFAT.


L. 128. Goodwife your houss and I will nere doe well. MS. A.

------

## ADDITIONAL VERSES AND EMENDATIONS,
### BY ALLAN RAMSAY, 1724.


L. 7, 8. But schort the storm wald let him stay,
         Sair blew the day with wind and rain.
L. 12. He blinkit ben.
L. 13. Set beikand by a fire full bauld.
L. 14. Suppand fat sowp.
L. 15. Being weary.
L. 18. My owsen has nae.
L. 20. *After this line are added,—*
         This seid-time it proves cauld and bad,
            And ʒe sit warm, nae troubles se;
         The morn ʒe sall gae with the lad,
            And syne ʒeil ken what drinkers drie.
L. 21. Gudeman, quod scho.
L. 24. *After this line are added,—*
         And now sen ʒe haif made the Law,
            Than gyde all richt and do not break;

They sicker raid that neir did faw,
   Therefore let naithing be neglect.

L. 49. He draif the gaislingis.
L. 59. Than by come an ill-willy roan.
L. 61. Syne up he tuk an rok of tow.
L. 63. He loutit doun.
L. 65. *Before this line the following stanza is inserted :—*

The leam up throw the lum did flow,
   The sute tuke fyre it flyed him than,
Sum lumps did fall and burn his pow;
   I wat he was a dirty man:
Ȝit he gat water in a pan,
   Quherwith he slokend out the fyre:
To soup the House he syne began;
   To had all richt was his desyre.

L. 77 He tuke the kirnstaff be the shank.
L. 79. The two left gaislings gat a clank.
L. 97-100. *These lines* Ramsay *has altered thus :—*

The first it smelt sae sappylie,
   To touch the lave he did not grein:
The Deil cut aff thair hands, quoth he,
   That cramd ȝour kytes sae strute ȝestrein.

'A BALLET SHEWING HOW A DUMB
WYFF WAS MAID TO SPEIK'

# XXIII.

## 'A BALLET SHEWING HOW A DUMB WYFF WAS MAID TO SPEIK.'

---

*THE folio* Maitland *MS. in the* Pepysian *Library, contains a fragment of the following humorous tale;*[1] *and a less imperfect copy occurs in one of* Bishop More's *MSS. in the* University Library, Cambridge. *The stanzas in the latter MS. having been awkwardly transposed by the writer, both copies are made use of in order that this ballad might be given in its most perfect state.* [*There are, however, some deficiencies which have been ingeniously supplied by* Charles Kirkpatrick Sharpe, Esq.]

*The incident on which this story is founded might be traced back through a long series of writers of various nations, both in prose and verse. The original of the present tale may perhaps be found in one of the numerous French* fabliaux, *which doubtless were well known at an early period in* Scotland, *owing to the great intercourse which subsisted between the two nations.*

*Part of a vulgar Scotish ballad of a similar kind, which never seems to have been printed, is still remembered. The husband takes his wife to a Surgeon* 'to cure her of the dumb, dumb, dumb,' *who, by cutting the strings of her tongue, brings her faculties of speech to* 'a pretty tolerable

Ll. 5.-84.

consistency : '—*or rather, enables her* ' to rattle with her tongue, tongue, tongue,' *at such a rate, that the poor man is fain to apply a second time for assistance, and beg of the doctor to make her dumb again. Instead of pointing out some remedy, or even answering him as we might suppose him to do, like* Sganarelle, *in the admirable Comedy of* Le Medecin malgré lui, *on a similar application,*—

" That's impossible, sir : all that I can do to serve you, is, I can make you deaf, if you please,"—

*he is so malicious as to say, like the Devil in the following tale, that though it is an easy matter to make a woman speak, it is beyond the skill of all the Doctors in the land afterwards to silence her.*

XXIII.

# '𝕿𝖍𝖊 𝕯𝖚𝖒𝖇 𝖂𝖞𝖋𝖋.'

[THAIR dwelt a larde in Fyffe
    (Sic menne ar countit madde)
Quha weddit ane gude-wyffe
Ritche, dumb, and wondirous sadde;]¹
Quhan wthair wyfes war glaid          5
To mak thair husbandis blyth,
Scho sat, and nothing said;
And comfort nane could kyth.
    Than, to be brief,
    He tuik sic grief,          10
That deiplie he did sweir,
    That he forthoucht,
    That he had brocht,
Ane dum wyff hame for geir.


And so wpone ane day,          15
He went alone to pance;
So met he in his way
Ane greit grim man be chance:

---

¹ The beginning of this poem has been lost, but only four lines in the first stanza appear to be wanting; they have been supplied by C. K. Sharpe, Esq.

Quhilk fast at him did fraine
Quhy he sa sadlie went ?                          20
Quhat angwisch, greiff, or paine,
Perturbit his intent
  He bad him schaw
  And lat him knaw,
Of all his grief the ground—                      25
  He sould remeid,
  Haif he na dreid,
Gif remeid micht be found.


Than he declairis cleir
The mater all and sum ;                            30
How he had tane for geir
Ane woman deif and dum.
For hir riches and rentes
He wedit hir to his wyfe ;
Bot now he sair repentes,                          35
And irkis sair of his lyfe.
  His eirdlie joy
  Is turnit to noy ;
He wist him self war deid.
  Quod he agane,                         40
  " Tak na disdane,
And I sall find remeid.


Gif thow will counsall keip,
And trow weil quhat I say,
This nicht in hir first sleip,                     45
Vndir hir towng thow lay
Off quaiken espein leif,
The quhilk betaiknis wind ;
And scho sall haif releif
Of speikeine thow sall find ;                      50
  Quhat kind of taill,
  Foroutin faill,

That thow of hir reqwyreis,
   Scho sall speik out,
   Haif thow na dout,        55
And mair than thow desyreis."

Than was he glaid of this,
And thoucht him self weill chewin:
And hame he cam with blis;
Thocht lang quhill it was ewin.     60
Quhill scho was fallin on sleip
Ay warlie watchit he;
And than he tuik guid keip,
And laid in leifes thrie;
   Thinkand his cuir        65
   To wirk most suir,
He lay walkand quhill day;
   Quhill scho awoik
   Guid tent he tuik,
To heir quhat scho suld say.     70

Na rest than could he tak,
Bot tumbillis heir and thair:
The first word that scho spak,
Scho said, " Ewill mot ȝe fair !
That wald nocht lat me rest,     75
And I sa seik this nicht!—"
—For joy he hir imbraist,
His hart was hie on hicht.
   Than furth scho schew,
   All that scho knew,       80
Quhen that scho could nocht speik.
   Fra scho began,
   Scho spairit nocht than,
And [lyit na lyk] ane seik.—

[To daill wyth sic ane spreit     85
The carle hee was nocht faine—

L. 84 in MS. almost illegible; the words in brackets were supplied by
J. Pinkerton.
   Ll. 85-98 supplied by C. K. Sharpe, Esq.

Bot ance hee chancit to meet
The grit grim man again.
" Allace, sweit schir," hee said,
" Ʒow thocht to doe mee joy,                    90
Ʒit now the play is playd,
I thole bot deip annoy:
    The leiffis applyed
    War scantlie tryed,
Till scho began to trattil                      95
    Wi sic ane soun,
    That auld Mahoun
Himselfe wald flee the battil!]

And quhan I did hir pray
In licence for to sitt,                         100
That is the neirest way
To putt hir by hir witt:
God knawis the drerie lyff
I had sen scho was dum;
Off ane gud quyet wyff                          105
Is now ane feind becum;
    Hir speiche but sessoun,
    But ryme or ressoun,
Now deiffis vp all the hous;
    Allace! this day,                   110
    That, I may say,
That euer scho spak sa crous."

" Blame thyselff," quod he,
" That gaif hir superflew;
Thow laid in leifis thrie,                      115
Quhair ane mycht bene enew;
Had thow don as I bad,
Or now thow sould haue seine,
[Thy wyff in myrthe y-clad,]
Weill temperet toung betwene;                   120

L. 106. '-begun' *MS.*
L. 119 omitted in *MS.*, supplied by C. K. Sharpe, Esq.

Bot quha may latt hir
Ane wyfe to clatter,
Syne no man can conuert hir;
The mimest wyff
That euer tuik lyff,                                   125
Will warie sum wordis, and start hir."


Quod he, "Tak quhat I haiff,
And leif hir as ȝe fand hir."—
"Allace!" quod he, "ȝe raiff,
I dar nocht cum neir hand hir;                          130
I am devill but doutt,
Ffirst langage learnit hir till,
I dar nocht be so stoutt,
To bid hir hald hir still;
Fra scho delyte                                        135
To fecht, and flytt,
I dar nocht with hir mell;
Scho will speik out,
Haue ȝe na doutt,
Off all the deuillis in hell.                          140


The leist deuill that is in hell
Can gif ane wyff hir toung;
The gritest, I ȝow tell,
Cannot do mak hir dum.
Ffra scho begin to clatter,                            145
Scho will claver quhair scho pleis,
We deuillis can na wayis latt hir;
'Gude' man tak ȝow the waneis!
Thocht nighbouris aboutt
Wis hir toung outt,                                    150
It dois thame nocht availl,
I say for me
Scho will chyde 'till' scho die,
Scho is best with littill daill."

L. 121. 'latter' *MS.*        L. 148. waneis or uneis, annoyance.
L. 153. 'will' *MS.*

Quod he, " Than tell me plane,  155
Quhat counsall best ȝe call ? "—
Quod he, " Gang hame agane,
Ffor it is ill over all :
Latt thy wyff speik hir fill,
Sen scho thairto was borne ;  160
Ffor wyffis will haue thair will
Thocht ȝe and I had sworne.
 Quhat euer hir happin,
 Hir toung is hir wapin,
To speik than quha may latt hir,  165
 Quha may ganestand,
 Or contramand
Ane crabit wyff to clatter ? "

Thus thai depairtit plane :
The feind flew ouir ane hill ;  170
The guidman hame agane,
And with his wyff baid still :
Quod he, now I perseaue
Thair is na leid in land
That has, as I wald haiff,  175
His wyff at his command.
 Ffra thine furth ay,
 He leit hir say,
And neuer was offendit,
 Bot at hir wourdis  180
 Maid quyet bourdis,
Quhill death thair dayis endit.


ffinis hujus.

THE

# WOWING OF JOK AND JYNNY

## XXIV.

# THE WOWING OF JOK AND JYNNY.

*THE* Wowing of Jok and Jynny *is the most ancient, and not the least humorous of many similar songs and ballads which still retain their popularity in this country.* Lord Hailes *observed—and his words are quite applicable at the present time, that ' this well-known poem, by frequent publication, has been much corrupted. Every publisher took the liberty of adding or altering just as his fancy led him. It is now given faithfully from the manuscript,[1] and exhibits a ludicrous picture of the* curta supellex *of the Scottish Commons in the sixteenth century.'* [2]

*Even since the time that* Lord Hailes *presented the text in a genuine state, the interpolated copies have been generally adopted, by its different editors. But the original poem has too much merit, and possesses too close a resemblance to the nature of the present collection, to justify its exclusion, merely because it has been already published.*

*We possess no information with respect to the author, unless it be worth observing that the signature quod* Clerk, *attached to his poem in the manuscript, has, at an early period, been intentionally obliterated. The name, apparently,*

[1] Bann. MS. fol. 137.
[2] Ancient Scottish Poems. Edin. 1770, p. 340.

*is written in the same hand (not that of the transcriber) which attributes* The Brash of Wowing, *and two other poems in the same collection, to a writer of this name,— supposed to have been* Maister Johne Clerk, *the poet mentioned by* Dunbar *as having been taken by Death*

' Fra balat making and trigide.'[1]

*The explanations by* Lord Hailes, *which will be found in the* Appendix, *may be useful to some readers.*

[1] Lament for the deth of the Makars.   Edin. 1508.

# 'The Wowing of Jok and Jynny.'

ROBEYNS Jok come to wow our Jynny,
  On our feist-evin quhen we wer fow;
Scho brankit fast, and maid hir bony,
And said, " Jok, come ʒe for to wow?"
Scho birneist hir baith breist and brow,     5
And maid hir cleir as ony clok;
Than spak hir deme, and said, "I trow,
ʒe come to wow our Jynny, Jok."

Jok said, "Forsuth I ʒern full fane,
To luk my heid, and sit doun by ʒow."     10
Than spak hir modir, and said agane,
" My bairne hes tocher-gud annwch to ge ʒow."
"Te he," quod Jynny, "keik, keik, I se ʒow;
Muder, ʒone man makis ʒow a mok."
" I schro the, lyar! full leis me ʒow,     15
I come to wow your Jynny," quoth Jok.

" My berne," scho sayis, "hes of hir awin,
Ane guss, ane gryce, ane cok, ane hen,
Ane calf, ane hog, ane fute-braid sawin,
Ane kirn, ane pin, that ʒe weill ken,     20

L. 12. 'annwch' is inserted after 'tocher-gud,' but has been scored
through in the MS. by the transcriber.

Ane pig, ane pot, ane raip thair ben,
Ane fork, ane flaik, ane reill, ane rok,
Dischis and dublaris nyne or ten:
Come ȝe to wow our Jynny, Jok?

Ane blanket, and ane wecht also,               25
Ane schule, ane scheit, and ane lang flail,
Ane ark, ane almry, and laidillis two,
Ane milk-syth, with ane swyne-taill,
Ane rowsty quhittill to scheir the kaill,
Ane quheill, ane mell the beir to knok,        30
Ane coig, ane caird wantand ane naill:
Come ȝe to wow our Jynny, Jok?

Ane furme, ane furlet, ane pott, ane pek,
Ane tub, ane barrow, with ane quheilband,
Ane turf, ane troch, and ane meil-sek,         35
Ane spurtill braid, and ane elwand."
Jok tuk Jynny be the hand,
And cryd ane feist, and slew ane cok,
And maid a brydell vp alland;
"Now haif I gottin ȝour Jynny," quoth Jok.     40

"Now, deme, I haif ȝour bairne mareit;
Suppoiss ȝe mak it nevir sa twche,
I lat ȝow wit schoss nocht miskareit,
It·is weill kend I haif annwch:
Ane crukit gloyd fell our ane huch,            45
Ane spaid, ane speit, ane spur, ane sok,
Withouttin oxin I haif a pluche;
To gang to gidder, Jynny and Jok.

I haif ane helter, ahd eik ane hek,
Ane coird, ane creill, and als ane cradill,    50
Fyve fidder of raggis to stuff ane jak,
Ane auld pannell of ane laid sadill,

L. 26. originally 'four lang flailis.'

Ane pepper-polk maid of a padill,
Ane spounge, ane spindill wantand ane nok,
Twa lusty lippis to lik ane laiddill;                    55
To gang to gidder, Jynny and Jok.

Ane brechame, and twa brochis fyne,
Weill buklit with a brydill renʒe,
Ane sark maid of the Lynkome twyne,
Ane gay grene cloke that will nocht stenʒe;             60
And ʒit for mister I will nocht fenʒe,
Fyive hundreth fleis now in a flok.
Call ʒe nocht that ane joly menʒe,
To go to giddir, Jynny and Jok?

Ane trene truncheour, ane ramehorne spone,             65
Twa buttis of barkit blasnit ledder,
All graith that ganis to hobbill schone,
Ane thrawcruk to twyne ane tedder,
Ane brydill, ane girth, and ane swyne bledder,
Ane maskene-fat, ane fetterit lok,                      70
Ane scheip weill keipit fra ill wedder;
To gang to giddir, Jynny and Jok.

Tak thair for my parte of the feist;
It is weill knawin I am weill bodin;
Ʒe may nocht say my parte is leist."                    75
The wyfe said, "Speid, the kaill ar soddin,
And als the laverok is fust and loddin;
Quhen ʒe haif done tak hame the brok."
The rost wes twche, sa wer thay bodin;
Syne gaid to giddir bayth Jynny and Jok.               80


EXPLICIT.

# THE

# FERMORAR AND HIS DOCHTER

FERMORAR AND HIS DOCHTER

## XXV.

# THE FERMORAR AND HIS DOCHTER.

*THIS lively and spirited dialogue between a Farmer and his Daughter, on the subject of her marriage, is apparently of English composition, although the Editor found it written on the fly-leaf of an ancient copy of* Wyntoun's Chronicle, *which appears to have formerly belonged to the Abbey of* Cambuskenneth, *now preserved in the Library at Wemyss Castle,* Fife. *The date of the manuscript itself is about the latter part or middle of the* 15th *century ; that of the poem is not much later than the reign of James V.*

*In a foolish and vulgar English song of the last century, not worth preserving, entitled* The Maid's resolution to marry a Rake, *we find reasons nearly similar to those expressed in the following dialogue, for choosing a Gentleman, instead of a Ploughman or Farmer, as her husband.*

> My Mother would have me to marry a Clown
> That hedges and ditches all week for a crown ;
> But to marry a Rake is all my delight ;
> If he rambles all day he will please me at night.
>
> The name of a Clown I highly disdain,
> My Father and Mother they love the same :
> A Clown is a Clown both at home and abroad,
> When a Rake he is comely, and sweet in his bed.

> A Ploughman I own is good in his kind,
> But I'm resolved to alter my mind ;
> For a Rake dress'd in scarlet and trimm'd with gold
> Is handsome and pleasant, and lovely to behold.

*The sixth stanza of this poem is defective of three lines; but possibly we have no great cause to regret the loss which it has sustained.*

*Among the ballets entered in the Stationers' Register to John Wallye and Mrs Toye, was one " Betwene a Ryche Farmer and his Daughter "*—Herbert's Ames, vol. i. p. 588.

# 'The Fermorar and his Dochter.'

A S I did walk onys be ane medo side,
    In ane symmer sessoun, quhen men wynnis thair
        hay,
I hard ane riche fermorar with his dochter chide,
Tuiching hir meriage, and thus he did say;
"Here duellis Symkin my nychtbour, ourthort ʒone
        way,                       5
    He hes thre welthy childering, choiss the one of
        thoiss;—
    Thow sall haue one of thame, with myche of my
        poiss."

"Ffader," quoth the dochter, "that goith aganis my
        hart,
Sen I haue bene ʒour drevill this xx ʒeris and more,
Now wald ʒe gar me go at pleuch and cart,      10
And leif my liff in sklavary, as I haue done to fore;
Tak it for ane ansuer, I will do so no more:
    ʒe can nocht compell me to mary one of thois,
    For I will haue ane gentill man, with plesand cloiss."

"Dochter," quoth the fader, "quhy dois thou thaim
        refuss,                  15
Sen thai be gudlie ʒemen that be in all this land?—
In all this cuntrie, I think, thou can not choiss,

More nymlar fallowis of fute, nor of hand;
More panefullar, more thrifty, I lat the vnderstand:
  Thou can nocht do better than mary one of thoiss;
  No! thou sall mary one of thame, in spite of thi
     noiss." 21

" Ffader," quoth the dochter, " I put ȝow out of dout,
I rak nocht of thare manheid, nor thair thriftynes
    at all;
I am nocht disposit to mary Hob Klout,
To leif like my mothir, in messerie and thrall, 25
Servand the swyne, and the oxin in thare stall,
  With ane pare of clamper kynnis clowtit to my hoiss;
  No! I will haue ane gentill man, in spyte of ȝour
    noiss.

" Gif I gett ane gentill man, I can nocht lychtly myss
Of doctouris of phesik, and necessary fude; 30
Gif I say bot onys, ' Gude husband gett me this,'
I can nocht lychtly laik it, and it will do me gude;
Sic qualiteis hes ane gentill man that is cum of gentill
    blude:
  How mony of this cuntre, dois laik one of thoiss?
  No! I will haue ane gentill man, in spite of ȝour
    noiss. 35

[1]

" Ane gentill man is lusty, luvand, and faithfull of fay,
He is worthy to be luvit, he is plesand and gay:—
  Fader, content ȝou, in spite of ȝour noiss,
  And euir I maryt be, I will haue one of thoiss.

" Giff I get ane gentill man, his sycht will do me
    gude, 40
He will hals me, and brais me, and lufe me out of
    mesour;

_______________
[1] Three lines of this verse are wanting in the MS.

So sall I haue my silkan gowne, with my Franche hude,
I sall haue aboundance, and infinite tressour,
And I salbe accumpanyit with ladeis of plesour,
   And I sall haue my chois of veluot, to my fine
     hoiss,                           45
   So will I haue ane gentill man, in spite of ʒour noiss.


"Ane gentill man is lusty, and will lay on the laid,
With ane swerde, and ane dagar glitterand by his side,
Quhen Symkin standis quhisling, with ane quhip and
     ane gaid,
Prikand and ʒarkand one ald ox hide,         50
With one pare of stro buskynis, he gois to ride,
   Moist like one spittell man :—suld I haue one of
     thoiss !
   No ! I will haue ane gentill man, in despite of ʒour
     noiss."

# ANE BALLET OF MATRYMONIE

## XXVI.

## ANE BALLET OF MATRYMONIE.

--------

*THIS humorous poem may serve as a counterpart to ‘The Wife lapped in Morels skin,’ and some other well-known pieces of* English *poetry, which were coeval with it. The original is preserved in a very curious volume* [1] *of miscellaneous poetry among the* Cotton Manuscripts *in the* British Museum, *described as having once been the property of* Sir Henry Savile.*

*It was first printed in a posthumous collection of* Joseph Ritson,[2] *whose antiquarian pursuits were not, with the prejudices entertained for a length of time by his countrymen, bounded by ‘the cold river of Tweid.’ In* Ritson's *volume this poem is entitled* The Honey Moon, *which has here been altered, as there seems to be no authority to show that the period, usually regarded as at least the positive term of matrimonial happiness (but during which the following ludicrous adventure is stated to have occurred), had, so early as the latter part of the 16th century, received such an appropriate denomination.*

[1] MSS. Cotton, Vesp. A. 25.
[2] The Caledonian Muse. London, printed 1785, and first published 1821. 8vo, p. 172.

See app. p 400 for the ballet.

# 𝔅allet.

B Y West of late as I dyd walke,  
   In the pryme tyme of the day,  
Yt was my chaunce to here the talke  
Of two yonge folkis in 'fay';  
They had not bene marred at the kyrke       5  
Thre dayes then fully past,  
The good man bad his wyffe to worke,  
Nay soft, quod she, no hast,  
               For now  
     I wyll, quod she,                10  
     Not worke for the,  
     I make to God a vowe.

And yf thow wylt not worke, quod he,  
Thou drab! I shall the dryve.  
I would to God, thow knave, quod she,     15  
Thow durst that matter 'pryve.'  
The godman for to beate his wyffe  
In hande a pase he went,—  
He caught two blowes vpon his head  
For every one he lent,                    20  
              In dede;  
     He never 'blan'  
     Beating her than—  
     Tyll both hys eares dyd blede.

V. 4. say.       V. 16. preve.       V. 22. blande.

He was so stowte and sterne that stoure,          25
And fearsse with her in fyght,
That even vpon the stony flowre
She knokt his head full ryght.
The good wyffe was wonderous wake in hande,
Fearefull and nothing bold,                       30
But he had never a fott to stande
When she of hym caught hold
                          By the crage;
          And with her fyst,
          His mouth she kyst,                      35
          As fast as yt myght wagge.


Now then, she cryed lowd, alacke!
I do you well to wytt;—                        .
But he lay downe vpon his backe,
And she stode on her fett;                         40
Bending her selffe to hym a pace,
She cryed him mersy then
And pylled the barke even of hys face
With her commaundements ten;
                          And oft                  45
          She dyd hym dosse
          Abowt the nosse,
          Tyll 'al' his face was softe.


Now when the neybowres hard the noyse,
So longe betwen them twayne,                       50
They wyst yt was no wanton toyes,
And fast thether they ranne;
But when they came, in vayne yt was,
The dores was sparred rounde,
The good wyffe cryed owt alas!                     55
But he lay on the grounde,

V. 41. pacce.          V. 48. at hys facce.

Well beate ;

Lying alonge
He sayd among
That better he would her heate.     60

Hys neybowres they were sore afrayde
That he would kyll hys wyffe,
Then hym full instantly they prayde,
To stynt and leave hys stryffe,
And not hys wrath vpon her ' wreache,'     65
They dyd hym all exorte ;
Nay, nay, quod he, I shall her teache
How she shall be so shorte

With me ;—

Yet on his face     70
She layd apace,
And cryed him styll merse.

Whiche thing to here the neyboures all
Dyd pytty her so sore,
That to the good man they dyd call,     75
And sayd, for shame, no more :
He bad them then go pyke them home,
And there go medle them now ;
I am, quod he, not suche a one,
To leave fighting for yowe,     80

I trow :

Yet for all this,
They sayd, I wys,
Smale neybourehede he dyd showe.

Some prayed hym, in avoyding cryme,     85
That he hys hande would hold ;
Let her, quod he, another tyme,
Not be with me so bolde ;
For suredly, and owght I were
To bede her taunt or cheke,—     90

V. 65. wyrke, *MS.*

But he could scante the same declare,
She held so fast hys neke,
     In a bande;
  " Alas," quod she,
  " Wyll ye kyll me?      95
  Swete husbaund, hold youre hande."

His neyboures then were sore afrayed,
That he would her devoure,
The dorres then being fast sparred
They threw them in the flowre;    100
The good wyffe lepte away apace,
When shame had put to flyght,
And he, well blowen abowt the face,
Began to stand vpright,
     Nere made;     105
 . No wyght of skill,
  I think, judge wyll
  But he thereoff was glade.

Allthoughe his bake were somewhat dust
After a folyshe guysse,     110
Yet was the man hym selffe so lust,
That scarcly he could rysse.
The good wyffe dyd her chamber take,
Shewing her selff in drede;
To neyboures the goodman myrth dyd make, 115
To them that sawe that dede,
     All and some;
  To whom he sware,
  That he had thare,
  Slane her had they not come.   120

' Wish ' all yong marryed wyves I wyll
No such masters to ' pryve,'
But even obey your husbandes styll,
Lesse they to worke yowe dryve;

  V. 121. with, *MS.*    V. 122. preve, *MS.*

And seeing that yt ys not the best     125
To leve in debate and stryffe,
God send all 'then' that quiet rest
May be with man and wyffe,
                To the end :
      ' Lat' vs all pray     130
      Both night and day,
      That God such grace may sende.


FINIS.


V. 127. them, *MS.*                 V. 130. grant, *MS.*

THE PROMINE TO KING JAMES
THE SEXT

XXVII.

# THE PROMINE TO KING JAMES THE SEXT.

*AT the time when the Editor was engaged in collecting the poetical works of the author of* The Cherrie and the Slae, *which (accompanied with* "Biographical Notices," *from a more learned pen) have recently appeared, he was not aware of the existence of* this Promine *otherwise than from the notice given of its title by our typographical historians;* [1] *and from observing, that in the sale of Mr West's highly curious and valuable Library, in the year 1773, a copy of it was sold in a lot of* "Fragments of old English and Scottish verse." *After many fruitless inquiries, it appeared that this identical copy was in the possession of* Francis Douce, Esq., *who, with great politeness, allowed a transcript to be made for the present publication.* [2]

*The author of this poem was* Sir Patrick Hume of Polwart, *the antagonist of* Montgomery, *in the well-known* Flytings, *which they are said to have carried on 'in friendly emulation.'* Among "The names of the xxv. gentlemen pensioneris appointit to attend on the Kingis Majestie at all tymes of his ryding and passing to the feildis." xvij. of Maij. 1580. *we find our author mentioned as* 'The young Laird of Polwart.' *We are told that he was in great favour with King James VI. who appointed him Master of his Household, 1591; one of the gentlemen of his bed-chamber; and Warden of the Marches. This last office was suppressed upon the Union of the Crowns in 1603. He died 15th* June 1609. [3] *His brother,* Alexander Hume, Minister of Logie, *is known as the author of some beautiful descriptive poems contained in a volume which nearly rivals the present tract in rarity.*

[1] Ames, p. 585. Herbert, p. 1501.
[2] [It is now preserved in the Bodleian Library.]
[3] Crawford's Peerage, p. 313.

# The Promine,

## Contening the maner,

place, and time, of the maist Illuster King James
the Sext his first passing to the feildis: directit
to his hienes: Be P. H. familiar ser=
uitour to his Maiestie.

❧ Imprentit at Edin=
burgh be Johne Ros, for Henrie Charteris. 1580.
Cum Priuilegio Regali.

O REUEREND Rois, and maist redowtit Roy,
    O peirles Prince, and Perll superlatiue;
Our hope, our helth, our help, and warldlie Joy,
Comfort to Scotland Indefinitiue:
Cleir lamp of licht aboue all that dois liue;                5
Patrone of prudence, precious and perfite;
Gem of Ingine, to quhome God lykis to giue
Gracis far ma nor I can think or write.


¶Thocht ouir all quhair thy famous louing springis
In reputatioun, and greit reuerence;                       10
Thocht thy renoun out throch al Europe ringis
As flowand fountane full of sapience,
To offer this ʒit to thine Excellence,
For feir of fault, I wald haue bene effrayit,
Gif I had not be sure experience                           15
Thy gracious gudenes prouin and assayit.


¶For this respect, maist cunning courtes King,
As I desire, and wischis eirnestlie
To pleis and serue ʒour grace in euerie thing,
Swa I beseik ʒour mightie Maiestie                         20
For to accept this mater, maid be me
To glaid ʒour grace, conforme to Intentioun
Of Clerkis commending, mirth with honestie,
As Comedeis, and sic vther Inuentioun.

¶ Schir reid thairfoir, and mak me to reiois;    25
I hecht ȝour hienes, helping Goddis grace,
That I sall pen sum Poetrie, or prois,
Mair profitabill, gif I get time and space:
And sen ȝour wit all verteweis dois Imbrace,
Schortlie I sweir, bot gif ȝour grace allow it,    30
That I sall curs my cairfull catiue cace,
Sine quite this quair, and neuer sall awow it.

¶ To tak this peice in proper patronage,
Ȝour Prencelie prudence will me not deny;
Than gif thay speir, the Author to alledge    35
Quha wrait the veirs, I sall say it was I,
And sall not sussie men geuin to Inuy,
Bot quhen thay lak, or lauchis at my letter,
Bauldlie sall say in geuing the defy
Vpon the subiect, se quha can do better.    40

¶ FINIS.

*¶ Ȝour Graces humbill seruand to command,*
*I P. H. with faithfull hart and hand.*


¶ **The Promine.**

*¶ On the xij. day at fiue houris before none*
*1500 seuentie nyne in Iune.*

GOLDIN Titan with burning bemis bricht,
  Be kindlie cours, and reuolutioun,
Appeirandlie, to the Astrologues sicht,
Was in the first degre of Cancer wone;
Or neir hand by, in his Ecliptyk rone,    5
Against the force quhilk daylie had him rent,
Be the first Mobillis, weltering violent.

¶Sa in his Solstice glemand gloriouslie,
Throw nature of his proper motioun,
That Pompous Planeit, placit properlie,                    10
In that North Signe, of richt ascensioun
Quhair Juppiter hes exaltatioun,
Did with his bemis on bankis, and brayis beit,
The frutes to foster, with his hailsum heit.

And flowand Phæbe, Lady of the seyis,                      15
Not retrograd, reuoluing in hir ring,
Beheld the west with fixit face and eyis
In Joyfull June, quhen the xij. day did spring
Befoir the furthcome of that cumlie King:
Quhilk as the Sone out of the cloudes gray,               20
Fra Snawdoun Castell, did discend that day.

¶With manlike maneris, maikles to behald,
With Princelie port, and visage glorious,
With gentill gesture, wordis wise and cald,
In taikning of the maist victorious,                      25
Richt gaylie garnist with giftis gracious,
Quhais heuinlie hauingis stonischit the Air,
As efterward, I purpois to declair.

¶At his first furthcome on the Gowane hillis,
To write how euerie circumstance befell,                  30
Quhat beir began of Hagbutis, bowis, and Billis,
Quhat din of daggis, with clink of mony bell
At Falcounis fair, war tedious to tell:
For to be schort, I schaw not how the steidis
On bridillis bait, quhil famie mouthis bleidis.           35

¶Ʒit wald my Muse Inspire me with the spreit
Of Poetrie, and pairt of Eloquence
To schaw the maner, I esteme it meit,
How euerie thing maid haill obedience,
Vnto his Royale hie Magnificence,                         40
Reiosit swa, with suddand semelie sicht
Of that leidsterne, and luifsum lamp of licht.

¶His Princelie presence superexcellent,
As lemand Lanterne maist delectabill,
Did euerie leuing creature content,                          45
And to thingis senceles semit amiabill;
Quhais Celsitude was sa acceptabill,
That in thair kind Ilk thing did obseruance,
His heich honour and worschip to auance.   ·


¶I mene not onlie thingis Inferiall                          50
That subiect ar vnto corruptioun;
Bot also celeste, and Superiall,
Quhais substance is but alteratioun;
As fair Phebus, or vtherwayis the Sone,
Quhilk is composit of na Element,                            55
That day brak vp in his bricht birneist Tent.

                                              ·

¶And schew his radious visage rubicound,
Quhilk all the day lay hid vnto the howr
That his grace Ischit furth vpon the ground;
Thairefter did on eirth his presence powr,   ·              60
Excluding than all signes of the schowr,
Sa glaid he was to se his gudlie grace,
And farleit fast the phisnome of his face.


¶Sine in the praises of that Prince preclair,
Spred furth his Purpour springis aureat                      65
Into sic sort to purifie the Air,
Quhill all the skyis skaillit violat;
The Hemispheir become Illuminat
Vpon the eirth, be heuinlie Influence,
Distelland dewis on vapouris sweit as sence.                 70


¶The ground ouirgiltand all with goldin glemis,
Quhill throw his michtie operatiounis,
Furth of fresche fludes, bet with buriall bemis,
Rais sappie subtil exhalatiounis,
Quhais potent pithie Inspiratiounis                          75

Makis treis, frutes, and flouris for to spreid,
Nicelie enamaling mony mirthfull meid.

¶ Than fair dame Flora glaiding gardings gay,
Syilit with schaddow of the blumand bewis,
Hir minglit Mantill meiklie did display ;  80
Richt curiouslie, ouircleithand all the clewis,
With flouris of ane hundreth heuinlie hewis,
Quhair besilie the bummand honie Beis,
Tuik nurischement on natures tapestreis.

¶ Thair micht be sene the dewie perllis round, 85
Reuest the Rosis, and the Lilleis quhite ;
Into dulce humouris herbis did abound
Bathing the bony Daseis of delite
With ane sweit liquour on the leiffis lite,
Comforting all the fragrant freklit fiouris  90
That spreidis in Maij, throw hailsum balmis schouris.

¶ Obedientlie begouth than to vnfald
The beiraris bricht, thair flouris to his eis,
Quhen thay his potent presence did behald,
Sa tender twistis trimling on the treis,  95
His prudent hie precellence for to pleis.
Thair Cristall croppis me thocht thay did Incline
In signe of homagè to that Prince diuine.

¶ Into the Park did properlie appeir,
Richt trimlie trottand into trowpis and twais, 100
The wilde quhite cullourit Ky, and falow deir,
With brawland bowkis, bendand ouir the brais,
The flingand Fownis, followand dune dais ;
Sa curage causit beistis mak besines
His Maiestie muifand to merines.  105

¶ Bot to behald it was ane perfite Joy,
And as ane eirdlie plesand Paradice :
To heir and se, thair at the Kingis conuoy,
The Merle and Maweis, changeing notes nice ;

The Kiddis skippand, with Rais throw the rice,      110
Quhair birdis blyithlie on the branches sang,
With sic ane reird, quhill all the Rokkis rang.

¶Swa schortlie throw sic heuinlie harmoneis,
Become richt coy, heiring the fowlis sing,
Baith Eolus, and Neptune God of seis,      115
Behalding fast the cumming of that King;
Quhilk was sa welcum vnto euerie thing.
Quhat misteris mair, the Goldspinkis was sa glaid,
Culd thai haif spokin, doutles thai had said:

¶Welcum maist maikles Mirrour, and A per se,   120
With euerie princelie prerogatiue possest;
Welcum worschip, vertew, and honestie;
Welcum in warld, the wise, and worthiest;
Welcum blist birth, as bountifull and best;
Welcum but peir, the maist Imperiall King,      125
That is, or was, or in the warld sall ring.

¶Thow Salomon fecund in sapience,
Ane Job in Justice, Jonit with pietie,
Perfitelie pleneist with all abstinence,
Discreitlie mixt with Magnanimitie,      130
Meik, mercifull, kind but Inconstancie,
To all gude men luifing and liberall:
In the thair wantis na wit Heroicall.

¶Thy liuelie licht, o leidar Laureat!
All Christiane men may cleirlie knaw and se,      135
Dois glance as gyde, lyifis to Illuminat,
Instructing Kingis, and thair Nobilitie,
Be gude exampill, for to follow the,
As worthiest, but feinʒe to confes
Nixt vnder God the haill eirth to posses.      140

¶Thow onlie may be callit verteous,
In quhome na vertew is deficient:
Indewit with the giftis plenteous

Of bodie, mind, and fortoun, to the lent;
Thairfoir ȝe Knichtis, and Clerkis, with ane consent,
And pynit pure men, from all panis relaxt          146
Salute ȝour Souerane, sweit King James the saxt.

¶ For vicious folk, with filthie faultis defylit,
Into his Court sall haue na praise nor place.
And gredie godles men sall be begylit,              150
Gif thay presume for to obtene his grace.
All fenȝeit flatteraris sall ay fle his face;
And as the snaw meltis from the Sone away,
Sa from his sicht the wickit sall decay.

¶ Quhairfoir now Scotland sing with ane accord   155
Baith greit and small, of Ilk stait and degre,
Perpetuall praise, and thankis to the Lord,
That hes ȝow geuin sa gude ane King as he,
Ȝow to mantene in eis and Equitie.
Wald God his dayis, for euer micht Indure,         160
Swa of all seill, but sorrow war ȝe sure.

¶ God grant his grace the Euerlasting gloir,
Lang life, gude helth, praise and prosperitie:
Baith worschip, welth, and weilfair euermoir,
And of his fois the vailȝeand victorie,             165
With heuinlie, eirthlie, full felicitie:
And that in him (God) be ay glorifeit,
Luifit, honourd, feird, and euer sanctifeit.


¶ FINIS.

## ¶ L'Enboy.

*¶ Thir wordis few the Authour dois reheirs*
*Into this maner, speikand to his veirs.*

M Y bony bill, of barbour language breuit,
   Gif thow be euill, thow will be wors repreuit,
Be witles, vaine, enuyous, Ignorantis,
Quhilk to speik euill, and do na gude thame hantis.
For sum will say thy febill Eloquence     5
Is euill cullourit, but Intelligence.
Sum will say this, sum vtheris will say that,
And pairt will speik in deid, and wait not quhat.
Syne sum seditious craftie knaifis Inding,
Will say, perhaps, thow dois bot fleiche the King.   10
Thus, gif thow heir fals knaifis calumniat the,
I pray the, baith to say, and sweir thay le.
Schaw to sic fuillis, quhair euer that thow fairis,
Thy mening gude, and honester than thairis.
Gif, for all this, thay ceis not to maling,    15
Than say thow art ressauit of the King
Vnto quhais serene Celsitude I send the:
Thay ar ouir pert: syne gif thay vilipend the:
Ʒit of ane thing greitly thow may reiois
In Burgh or land, quhair euer that thow gois,   20
All men of knawledge, and Clerkis will commend the,
And honest folkis will euer mair defend the.

¶ Fin de l'enuoy.

# FINIS.

# The Appendix

# THE APPENDIX.

---

## Ralf Coilȝear.

THE woodcut of the two heads on the title-page occurs also
in the edition of Sir David Lyndsay's poems, 'Imprentit
at Edinburgh be Johne Scot at the expensis of Henrie Charteris,'
1571, 4to; and likewise in an edition of Barbour's 'Bruce,' 4to,
probably printed about the same time; but the title-page of
the only copy known has been unfortunately lost. [The
woodcut at p. 40 was omitted in Edition of 1822.]

---

## Awntyrs of Arthure.

THE Editor has been favoured by his friend, Dr ROBERT
ANDERSON, whose attachment and valuable contributions to
our National Literature are well known, with a sight of some
remarks on this ancient romance, by the late ALEXANDER
THOMSON, Esq., the ingenious author of Whist, Paradise of
Taste, and other poems. They occur among the Collections
which he had made for a History of Scotish Poetry. Mr
Thomson appears to have been engaged several years in the
formation of such a work, after the plan and example of
Warton's valuable and amusing, but unfinished and ill-digested

History of the Poetry of England. Although he has not accomplished much, he nevertheless seems to have examined with diligence the earlier remains of Scotish Poetry which were then accessible to him; having done little more than sketch out the plan of so desirable a work, and filled up occasional portions of it, with careful analysis and critical examination. The following extract will evince the discrimination which he was capable of showing, and the value that might have been attached to his labours had he proceeded farther in completing such an important undertaking :—

"The most glaring imperfection of this Romance [Gawan and Galoran of Galloway] is undoubtedly its deficiency in unity of action, the two parts being entirely unconnected. In this respect it is inferior to the former, although the appearance and behaviour of the ghost displays more of fancy and of poetry than anything to be found in the Gawan and Gologras. It is, however, to be wished that this marvellous incident had constituted the latter half of the Poem, as the entrance of *Galoran*, at the banquet of Arthur, would have opened the piece in a striking manner; and the whole of that story must have been more interesting, had it preceded and not followed the supernatural adventures.—The same error, in point of arrangement, I have often regretted, in the *Romance of the Forest*, where the woes and wanderings of the two lovers, although sufficiently interesting in themselves, are read almost with a perfect indifference after the terrific scenes at the castle.

"Although the characters are not marked with that strength of pencil which distinguished those of Gawan and Gologras, that defect is perhaps compensated by the introduction of two female personages; and the circumstance of a wedding making part of the catastrophe, gives it more the air of a modern performance."

---

The Lincoln Manuscript, which has furnished the text of this ancient romance, is a thick volume of more than 300 leaves, in folio, consisting of a variety of old English poems and romances, written in the earlier part of the fifteenth century. It appears to have been compiled between the years 1420 and 1430, or perhaps later, by ROBERT DE THORNTON of East Newton, Yorkshire, who held some situation in the Cathedral, and was afterwards translated to the Archdeaconry of Bedford. He died in May 1450, and lies buried in the Cathedral of Lincoln. To the Reverend Mr GRAY OF LINCOLN, the Editor owes his best thanks for the kind and friendly manner in which he facilitated his object, during the time required in making some transcripts from the curious volume alluded to—the most important contents of which are as follows :—

The Lyf of gret Alexander, conquerour of all the worlde (in prose), imperfect at beginning.

Morte Arthur (in English verse).

The Romaunce of Octavyane.

The Romaunce off S<sup>r</sup> Ysambrace.

The Romaunce off Dyocleoydois the Empo<sup>r</sup>, and the Erle Berade of Tholous, etc.

The storye of saynte Christofre.

Sir Degrenante (q. Sir Degoré).

Sir Eglamour of Arteas.

Lyarde (an absurd story of an old horse).

Thomas off Ersyldoune (printed in the present collection).

The Awntyrs of Arthure at the Terne Wathelyn (printed in the present collection).

The Romance of S<sup>r</sup> Perciuell of Gales, cousin to Kynge Arthur.—Also various Prayers, Homilies, etc. with the Miracles of S<sup>t.</sup> Edmond, Archbishop of Canterburye.

## Orfeo and Heurodis.

SINCE this poem was printed, the Editor has had an opportunity of examining the copy referred to as being preserved in Ashmole's Collection, at Oxford.  It approaches as close as was anticipated to the present text, except that it contains the prologue, which, as supplying the deficiency in the Auchinleck MS. is here inserted.

### King Orfeo.

Mery tyme is in Aperelle
That mekyll schewys of manys wylle,
In feldys and medowys flowrys spryng,
In grovys and wodes foules syng,
Than wex ȝong men jolyffe,
And than prevyth man and wyffe.
The Brytans as the boke seys
Off diuerse thinges they made ther leys,
Som they made of harpynges,
And som of other diuerse thinges,
Som of werre and som of wo,
Som of myrthe and joy also,
Som of trechery and som off gyle,
Som of happys that felle som whyle,
And som be of rybawdry,
And many ther ben of fary,
Off all the venturrys men here ore se
Most off luffe for soth thai be
That in the leys ben iwrought,
Ffyrst fond and forth brought ;
Off aventours that fell som deys
The Bretonys therof made ther leys,
Off kinges that before vs were,
When thai myȝt ony wondres here

They lete them wryte as it wer do,
And ther among is sir Orfewo.
He was forsothe a nobill kyng
That most luffyd gle and herpyng :
Wele sekyr was euery gode herper
To haue off mekyll honour.
Hymselue he lernyd for to herpe,
And leyd thereon hys wytte so scherpe ;
He lernyd so wele, with outen les
So gode herper neuer non was,
In all this werld was no man bore
That had kyng Orfeo ben before
And he mycht hys herpe here
Bot he wold wene that it were
A blyssedfull note of peradis,
Suche melody therin is.
The kyng jorneyd in Tracyence,
That is a cyte off grete defence,
And with hym hys quen off price,
That was callyd dame Meroudys ;
A feyrer lady than sche was one
Was neuer made off flesch ne bone ;
Sche was fulle off lufe and godnes,
Ne may no man telle hyr feyrnes.
Yt befell in the begyning of Mey,
When ffoules syng on euery sprey,
And blossom spryng on euery bouȝhe,
Ouer all wexyth mery inowhe,
Than the quen, &c.

In the same Manuscript are several curious Pieces of old
English verse. One of these is a fragment, entitled THE
KYNG AND THE HERMYT, consisting of about 522 lines.
Although possessed of considerable humour, it seems to have
remained unnoticed, except in the pages of the British Bibli-
ographer, a work replete with curious and interesting matter

of antiquarian lore, in which it is printed (vol. iv. p. 81—95) from a transcript communicated by Professor Conybeare of Oxford. This story is now more especially worthy of notice, from the conviction which the present writer has of its having suggested one of the happiest scenes, of a humorous description, that occurs in the works of our great Novelist. It would be unnecessary to give anything like an analysis of it in this place, as the poem itself can so easily be referred to, but there is certainly a striking similarity in some parts,— as in the King's losing his way in Sherwood forest; his prayer to Saint Julyan, the patron of pilgrims and wayfaring men 'for harborow'; his meeting with the hermit, from whom he seeks a night's shelter, and the reception he meets with; his supper of bread, cheese, and '*thyn drynke*,' before the hermit is induced to bring forth 'whyte bred' and venyson, with 'a pott of galons foure'; the bows and broad arrows about the friar's bed; and the tenour of their conversation,— all which seem to have somewhat more than a casual resemblance to the truly graphic and delightful scene of Richard and Friar Tuck, in the splendid story of Ivanhoe. The adventures of the Hermit at Court, where, like Ralf Coilȝear (without being aware of his quality), he engaged to return the King's visit, might have been interesting, but this part of the story is lost: that the fragment, however, has been excelled, in the scene alluded to, it need hardly be said. We find nothing, for instance, that will bear a comparison with the conclusion of the adventure—when Locksley, in the morning, knocks at the cell, and addressing the jolly Friar of Copman-hurst, says to him, "'Art thou mad? to give admittance to a knight thou didst not know? Hast thou forgot our articles?'

"'Not know him,' replied the friar boldly; 'I know him as well as the beggar knows his dish.'

"'And what is his name, then?' demanded Locksley.

"'His name,' said the hermit,—'his name—is Sir Anthony of Scrablestone; as if I would drink with a man, and did not know his name.'"

Another poem, contained in the same Manuscript, may also be here shortly noticed, as the Editor can find no allusion to it in particular. It is an ancient *bowrde*, of 255 lines, which might be entitled THE COKWOLD'S DAUNCE, and it might serve as a companion, or counterpart, to the well-known poem of the *Boy and the Mantle*, published by Bishop Percy, in the 'Reliques of Ancient Poetry.' The trial of the *Horne* is there alluded to in the following lines :—

> " The litle boy had a horne,
>     Of red gold that ronge :
>     He said, there was noe cuckolde
>     Shall drinke of my horne ;
>     But he shold itt sheede
>     Either behind or beforne.
>     Some shedd on their shoulder,
>     And some on their knee ;
>     He that cold nott hitt his mouthe,
>     Put it in his eye ;
>     And he that was a cuckold
>     Every man might him see."
>         —Percy's Reliques, vol iii. p. 10.

From this 'bowrde—that ys full gode and trew,' we learn that King Arthur, who loved and honoured cokwolds both day and night, had a 'bugill horne,' out of which he was accustomed to drink, 'for myche craft he couthe thereby,'— it having the peculiar property assigned to it in the above extract ; for

> " Iff any cokwold drynke of itt
>     Spyll he schuld withouten lett."

This, we are told, afforded much amusement to the King, who entertained a number of cokwolds at Court, where a table was set apart for them 'and none other,' at which they sat, dressed in scarlet kirtells, with garlands of willow on their heads, and were fed with the best meat from the King's own

table.   It so happened that the Duke of Gloster came to
Court, where he was received with mirth, honour, and great
solace; and on a day, when set at meat with the King, he
looked about in surprise, and inquired what these men had
done who wore these willow-garlands.   The King satisfies his
curiosity on this point,—and,

> ——" after the Erlys word,
> Send to the cokwold's bord,
>     To make them mery among
> All maner of mynstralsy,
> To glad the cokwoldes, by and by,
>     With harpe, fydell, and song "—

and likewise bids them 'take no greffe,' but prepare themselves for their Daunce.   The King asks, in the meanwhile,
for his drinking-horn, and informing the Duke of its pro-
perties, who asked by what skill he might know a cokwold,
says to him,

> " Syr Erle, take and begyn."

To this the Duke, with commendable politeness, answers,

> ——" Nay ! be seynt Austyn,
>     That wer to me vilony ;
> Not for all a reme to wyn,
> Befor ʒou I schuld begyn,
> Ffor honour off my curtassy."

Accordingly, the King takes the horn to drink as he had often
done, for, as this poem goes on to say,

> ——" he wend to haue dronk of the best,
> Bot sone he spylled on hys brest,
>     Within a lytell whyle ;
> The cokwoldis lokyd iche on other,
> And thocht the King was thair owne brother,
>     And glad thei wer of that :

> He hath vs scornyd many a tyme,
> And now he is a cokwold fyne,
>   To were a cokwoldis hate."

Finding himself to be thus unexpectedly qualified to 'daunce in the cokwold's rowte,' and that he could not better himself, he, with all possible good nature, says to his

> —"lordynges, sykerly,
> We be all off a freyry,
>   I am ȝour awne brother"—

and thinking it best 'to make mery, and take no care,' offers to join in the dance, at which

> " Euery cokwold seyd to other
> King Arthour is owr awne brother"—

and, as might on such occasions have been expected,

> —" the cokwoldes wer full blythe
> And thankyd God a C. syth,
>   Fforsoth, withouten doute."

The poem then concludes with the following lines :—

> " Kyng Arthour left [lived ?] at Skarlyon,
> With hys cokwoldis euerychon,
>   And made both gam and gle ;—
> A knyght ther was, with outen les,
> That serued at the Kyngis des,
>   Sir Corneus hyght he ;
> He made this gest in hys game,
> And named it after hys awne name,
>   In herpying, or other gle ;
> And after nobull Kyng Arthour,
> Lyued and dyghed with honour,
>   As mony hath done sene,
> Both cokwoldis, and other mo :
> God gyff vs grace, that we may go
>   To Heuyn.  Amen.  Amen."

## Thomas of Ersyldoune.

THE reader will no doubt be glad to receive the following illustrations of the prophetical parts of this poem, coming, as they do, from one who is so well qualified to elucidate both the historical and literary remains of our country. SIR WALTER SCOTT (in a letter to the Editor) says,—" I am much delighted, and considerably puzzled, with *Thomas the Rhymer.* It seems to me made up of different patches, which have been added from time to time in the true spirit of English prophecy,— for you may remember Comines says, 'Le Chancelier d'Angleterre, commença par une prophetie *dont les Anglois ne sont jamais despourveus.*' Pinky Cleugh is in one place distinctly mentioned by name; in another, Black Agnes of Dunbar is spoken of as alive, and her captivity is prophetical. There must have been a lapse of more than two centuries betwixt the composition of these two different passages. As well as I can, without books, I will endeavour to guess at the different historical events which are obscurely or more directly alluded to :—

"Fytt 2d, line 21. 'The Baylliolfe—Comyns—Barlays (rather Barclays)—as well the Fresells (Frasers),' were all distinguished during the wars of David II.'s minority, or shortly before, as probably were the Russells.

"Line 44. The fight at Eldone Hill here alluded to, may, perhaps, be that in which Oswin, a pretender to the throne of Northumberland, was defeated and slain by Ethelwold, about the middle of the eighth century. The field of battle is still called Corpse-cleugh, or some such name, and distinguished by barrows, and other marks of ancient contest: bones, and remnants of armour are even yet turned up by the plough.

"Line 52. The battle of Falkirk is obviously that in which Wallace was defeated by Edward I.

"Line 71. Bannockburn is mentioned by name. The allusion to the defeat of the English chivalry by stratagem is worth remarking; it shows the country of the pseudo-prophet, who is naturally disposed to apologise for the defeat of the English at that memorable occurrence.

"Line 97. Dupplin Moor is distinctly mentioned; and the subsequent capture of Perth, line 102.

"The battle of Durham, and the captivity of David II. is alluded to from line 120 to line 140, and the three last stanzas of the Second Fytt seem to me a variation of the same passage; or it may relate to the previous battle of Halidon, where the Regent, Archibald Douglass, may be the 'full doughty that was slain.'

"All these personages and events hitherto noticed relate as distinctly as can well be expected to the middle of the fourteenth century, when, in the beginning of Fytt Third, we light all at once upon 'Spynkarde Cleugh,' being clearly our unlucky battle of Pinkie. I cannot help thinking this stanza much more modern than the rest of the poem.

"The battle at Pentland hill, Fytt 3, l. 20, appears to be a wild guess at future events. In former times the prediction might have been deemed oracular; but now, few will be disposed to allow that it hath any reference to the battle of Pentland, in Charles II.'s time, any more than the press of banners between Seton and the sea refers to the battle of Prestonpans. But Thomas, or more properly his imitator, has made a chance hit in both cases. In the latter, especially, a staunch Jacobite would say the rout of the dragoons was foretold, line 53.— Only they did not stay for the *hewing*, mentioned line 57.

"The story of the Cross of Stone is a favourite presage in Nixon's prophecy, and I know not how many besides.

"Line 132. The rivulet, near to Flodden field, is called Sandyford, or something like it. Flodden is therefore probably alluded to in this and the following stanza.

"Line 156. Here the story returns to the Fourteenth Century, and to Black Agnes of Dunbar, which makes it probable that this part of the poem must have been written when she was in the height of renown.

"It is singular that Thomas should be represented as speaking of himself as one in disgrace with Agnes of Dunbar, though her bounden vassal. Unquestionably it is highly probable that Thomas of Ercildoune held his lands of the Earl of Dunbar, as he resided in the very village which took the name of Earlstown, from its dependence on these great Earls. An antiquary is tempted to guess that the obscure hint, here thrown out, may possibly allude to some dispute between Thomas and his supe:ior, which, making a part of the remembered history of the former, was introduced by the English imitator, who writes prophecies in his name."

After all, it may in general be admitted that the whole of the prophecies attributed to

'Thomas the true, that never spak false,'

in the corrupted and modernised state in which those bearing his name now appear, are little better than spurious. If he attempted any such predictions, which cannot reasonably be doubted, after the uniform tradition of more than five centuries, and the concurring testimony of so many ancient writers to his prophetical character, they were not, it is highly probable, committed to writing in his own time, but being circulated and handed down by tradition only, every person, no doubt, considered it lawful to alter or accommodate them to his own views. At least we find occasionally the same prophecy, either by accident or design, bearing the most opposite construction. But if there be one exception, it is that which follows, given exactly as it occurs in a very ancient manuscript, in the Harleian Collection (No. 2253, fol. 127), supposed to be of the time of Edward I., and which, as it approaches so near the period in which he flourished, may be considered as exhibiting a genuine specimen of the language of the author. This *Response* assuredly bears reference to the Wars in Scotland during the time of Edward I. A contrary opinion, however, has long been held (see Border Minstrelsy, vol. iii. p.

282-5—Sir Tristrem, p. xvi); and Sir Walter Scott still thinks that "the Battle of Dupplin is distinctly referred to in line 16, and that line 11 alludes to the dreadful famine in the reign of David II. The only line of the prophecy still remembered and quoted, is that of a hare kindling on the hearthstone, a prophecy which Thomas is said by tradition to have uttered concerning the desolation of his own house."

> The hare sall kittle (litter) on my hearth stane,
> And there will never be a laird Learmont again.

Every circumstance, however, warrants us in referring the following lines to some time before the end of the thirteenth century; and their application to the wars of Edward I., just previous to the commencement of a long series of war and desolation (about which time Thomas appears to have died) is certainly more appropriate, than conceiving him to overlook these in a foresight of what should take place more than half a century after his death. The erroneous supposition of this response having been addressed to Black Agnes, the heroic Countess of March, seems first to have given rise to the conjecture, which has thrown discredit on the idea of its being uttered by the Poet of Ersyldoune. In his time, the title of that powerful family had. not been changed from Dunbar to March.

> "*La Countesse de Donbar demanda a Thomas*
> *de Essedoune, q'nt la guere descoce pren-*
> *dreit fyn/ e yl la repoundy et dyt.*[1]

When man as mad a kyng of a capped man/
When mon is leuere other mones thyng then is owen/
When Londyon ys forest an forest/ ys felde/
When hares kendles o the herston/
When wyt and wille werres togedere

[1] This title is evidently added by the English transcriber,—otherwise it would have been *la guerre d'Angleterre.*

When mon makes stables of kyrkes and steles castles wyth
    styes
When Rokesbourh nys no burgh ant market is at Fforwyleye
When the alde is gan ant the newe that dou notht
When Bambourne ys donged with dede men
When men ledes men in ropes to buyen and to sellen/
When a quarter of whaty whete is chaunged for a colt of ten
    marks/
When prude prikes and pees is leyd in prisoun,
When a Scot ne may hym hude ase hare in forme/
    that the Englyssh ne shal hym fynde/
When rycht ant wronge ascenteth to gedere/
When laddes weddeth louedis
When Scottes flen so faste that for faute of ship hy drouneth
    hemselve/
    Whenne shal this be/
    Nouther in thine tyme ne in myne,
    Ah comen and gone
    Withinne twenty wynter ant on/[n]

The prophecies attributed to Thomas the Rhymer, in the common collection of 'The Whole Prophecies of Scotland, England, France, Ireland,' &c. have not the slightest marks of authenticity. They are, besides, too darkly veiled in allegory, or shadowed forth in obscure allusions, to interest any one.—But the persons or events prefigured must·have, at one time, been more intelligible than now, else it would be difficult to account for their extensive popularity; unless, on the idea which the common people may have entertained of their actually bearing reference to future national occurrences; as it is said, 'though thir sayis be selcouth, they shall be sooth found.' Without, therefore, being possessed either of historical value, or poetic merit, they are now to be regarded merely as literary curiosities.

## The Pistill of Susan.

THE Editor has it not in his power to give the various readings which occur in the text of this poem between the different manuscripts; but, in order to show in what these might have consisted, the first stanza of the one manuscript, as selected and printed by Dr Whitaker, in his very elegant and elaborate publication, is here inserted (p. xvii).

Ther was in Babyloyn a biern in that burgh riche
    That was a Jewe Jentil and Joachym he highte
He was so lele in his law. ther was non hym liche
    Of al richesses that rewke. arayed was right
His ynnes and his orchardes. wer with a depe diche
    Hallis and herbgages. hye upon hight
To seek thurgh that cite. ther was non siche
    Of arbres and herbes. so avenntly dight
              That day
       Within the cercle of the sees
       Of arborye and aloes
       Of all mannè of trees
              Sothely to say.

And the last stanza of the Cotton MS. may be added for the same intent. By comparing these readings with the adopted text, it will be perceived how far the ancient copies often vary from each other, even when the sense of the passage and the words themselves are in substance the same.

Then the folk of Israell fellen vpon knees
    And lowely thanked our lord/ that her the lyf lent
All gomes that her god wolde/ glades and glees
    That thys prophete so pertly preued hys entente
They trumpped before the traytores/ and trayled hem on trees
    Thorow out the cyte/ be comune assente

He that loueth that lorde/ thar hym not drede no lees  
　That thus his seruant con saue/ that shuld haue be schent  
　　　　　　So swete.  
　　　Thys ferly befell  
　　　In the dayes of Danyell  
　　　The wytnesse wyll well tell  
　　　　　　Of the same prophete.

---

## [Sr Johne Rowlis Cursing.

As stated in the Introductory Notice, this poem is preserved
both in the Bannatyne and Maitland MSS., and it is somewhat curious that while both texts have evidently been copied
from the same source, the Maitland MS. has sixteen lines more
than the Bannatyne. These additional lines are supplied in
the present edition, and are distinguished by being put within
brackets. The present Editor is indebted to R. HUTCHISON,
Esq. of Carlowrie, for the use of a copy of the Maitland
version, which Dr Laing, in 1834, printed among the poems
of the contemporaries of Dunbar, which he afterwards can-
celled, and of which only one or two copies now exist.]

---

## Colkelbie's Sow.

FOR completing the transcript of COLKELBIE, and carefully
collating it with the Manuscript, the Editor may take this
opportunity of acknowledging, that he is indebted to his
friend ROBERT PITCAIRN, Esq., whose zeal and knowledge
in antiquarian pursuits have lately been shown in his curious
publication of QUEEN MARY'S FUNERALS.

# [The Talis of the Fyue Bestis.

THE 'gentill Vnicorn' is thus described in an heraldic MS. of the period of Sir David Lyndsay, preserved in the Advocates' Library: "The Vnicorne is ane strenthy beist, the quhilk is lyk ane hors of body, bot scho hes feit of ane eliphant, and taile of ane hart, and hir voice is marvalouslie fleand; and aboue, in the middis of hir heid, ane mervalous horne, scheynand and thrawand ewin to the eird; the quhilk is sa stark and scharp, that it peirsis with it all that it overtakis, and na man may byde it; for na ingyne may be in the warld, and may not be tane leifand, bot gif the huntaris send ane gratious Virgine quhair the Vnicorne repairis; for it is hir nature to byde and repos in the Virginis skirt, and takis all the feirtnes fra hir; and on this maner huntaris sleyis thame, and signifyis he that first bure thame in armes wes stark in mony maneris, and his voice fleis, and is fleand to· his innemeys, and that he had wit in his intent and in his heid attour all vtheris to cum to his intent, and all his rest wes in deidis of virginitie."—MS. dated 1586, marked 31. 3. 20.

The tale which the Unicorn relates being taken from the *Brunellus*, or *Speculum Stultorum*, of Nigellus Wireker, a short account of that well-known Latin poem, written as a satire on the monastic orders, may here be given: Its hero is an ass named Brunellus or Burnellus, who is very much discontented with his position. He believes that the tail he possesses is too short for him, and he is anxious to obtain one of longer dimensions. He consults Galen, who expostulates with him on the folly of his desire, stating that in this respect he is as well provided as other people; in fact, that Louis the King of France and his highest priests have no greater share of tail. As he is still anxious, Galen gives him a prescription to make his tail grow longer. To prepare this, it is necessary first to obtain the necessary ingredients, which can only be done at Salernum, the great medical school of the period.

Brunellus accordingly goes to Salernum, where, first of all, he is cheated by a London merchant. On his return journey he encountered a variety of misfortunes. Near Lyons, a Benedictine monk named Fromundus, set his four great mastiffs upon him, and they bit off more than half of his tail. A still more serious loss then occurred,—his baggage containing the precious ingredients for lengthening that appendage was lost. Brunellus being quite crestfallen, proceeds to Paris to study at the celebrated schools, that he might, at least, return a scholar. He meets with another traveller, called Arnoldus, going to Paris with the same view. In the course of their journey, Arnoldus relates to him the story of Gundulfus, to warn him against provoking those weaker than himself.

In the Latin original, Gundulfus is described as the son of a priest named Longius, who had retired to the country, and the scene is laid in Apulia. The boy, instead of throwing a stone at the cock, as in the Scottish version, carries a small stick with which he breaks the fowl's leg.

The Latin poem of Wireker is written in elegiac verse, and consists of 3800 lines. It was extremely popular in its time, and is familiarly quoted by Chaucer[1] :—

> " I haue wel red in Dan Burnel the asse
> Among his vers, how that there was a cok,
> That for a preestes sone yaue him a knok
> Upon his leg, while he was yonge and nice,
> He made him for to lese his benefice."
>
>         —*Canterbury Tales*, v. 15, 318.

---

[1] Brunellus is also referred to in the 'Palice of Honour' of Gawin Douglas :—

> " With mony vther clerk of greit auaill
>    Thair was Brunell, Claudius and Bocchas."
>
>        —Works by Small, vol. i. p. 36.]

# The Wyfe of Auchtermwchty.

The story from which RITSON supposes that this admirable comic poem may have been borrowed, is contained in the following quotation from the *Silva Sermonum Jucundissimorum*, 1568 :—

CONUENIUNT UIR ET UXOR, UT QUISQUE EORUM EXERCERET OFFICIUM ALTERIUS, QUO POSSET ALTER EORUM IN POSTERUM EXERCERE UTRUMQUE.

RVSTICVS quidam non potuit conuenire cum sua coniuge, sed semper improbabant sibi mutuo officia sua. Vno dierum Laurentius, (sic enim uocabatur ille, & illa Adelheidis) cogitabat penes se, quid agendum esset, quo possent tot inimicitiae, rixae ac tumultus sedari inter eos : dicit uxori, in posterum se oportere agere partes suas, ipse uero uxoris acturus est. Oportere eam arare, triturare, serere, ac similia opera uirilia facere : ipse domi uellet exercere quæ muliebria sunt : utpote curare prolem, nutrire ac prouidere gallinis, anseribus, anatibus, porcis, pullo equino, coquere & uerrere pauimentum, &c. per quod quisque posset alterius munus ac officium scire. Arrisit consilium mulieri, quae alioqui cupientes sunt freni ac dominij. Accessit stabulum, parat equos ac aratrum, adit campum, iubet marito (qui iam uxor erat) mittat sibi prandium in campum, curet prolem, & uideat ne excidat ex cunis, aut inuertantur cunae, ac coquat diligenter. Curabo omnia diligenter, ait uir, simulque satagit in domo, cantillat argute, ut uideatur mulier in domo esse ; satagendo inuertit magnam ollam lactis, quo butyrum debuit contudisse & coxisse pultem pro puero. Hæc erant primordia eius œconomiae, quibus tantum horruit, meminitque eius quod dixerat dominus : curam gereret pueri ac cunarum, ne inuertantur, quare capit magnum ac latum lapidem, superponit puero atque ita sistit cunas. Subit etiam Laurentio se debere coquere, iam instabat tempus prandij, quare capit duodenam ouorum, diffringit ea in sartagine cum butyro, ad coquendum aut frixendum : abit interim in penum, ad promendum uinum, & ibidem meminit ouorum, recurrit cito superius, detinens spinam epistomij in manu. Quum uenit in coquinam, decidit coctura in ignem, cui assidet felis ac deuorat oua. Meminit & prolis, uisit num dormiat, & amoto lapide, reperit eam mortuam. Bone Deus quam tristatur, ac cogitat quid incœptet ? concutit ac constringit manus : quod faciendo, excidit ex eius manibus spina epistomij, quam oblitus erat in manu : quare currit actutum in penum, & reperit uinum penitus effluxum esse. Volens rapide amouere poculum, in quo prompserat uinum, collidens illud uasi, excidit ex manibus eius, atque ita uniuersum uinum perditum est. Quis bono hoc Laurentio magis perplexus ? uoluit subinde apud se : Tu uis esse hera, & effudisti lac, non potes iam contundere butyrum, proles extincta est, oua ac butyrum arserunt, ac comesta sunt à felibus, uinum natat in penu, poculum uini effusum est. Quid fiet cum redierit uir famelicus & sitibundus, uideritq ; hanc bellam œconomiam ? Ex quo ego me interposui rebus domesticis, & illa uirilibus, ob hoc baculo mea latera contunderet, & me oneraret ictibus, mihi æquum fieret, ita uolui, cur non mansi uir ? In-

terim cogitat bonus Laurentius quomodo agat. Venit illi in mentem equulus
oblitus in stabulo, capit seculam, & exit. Veniens secundum uiuarium, uidet
lupum in margine, lætatur, projicit seculam post lupum, putans se nacturum
eundem, natando aufugit ille, & falcula manet in limo. Exuit se Laurentius,
& intrat aquam, quærit seculam, uerrens diu in limo : interim uenit quidam qui
furatus est eius uestes. Post diutinam quæsitionem in uanum, erigit se, & quæ-
rens indusium in ripa, uidet uniuersas uestes ablatas. Exit aquis nudus, &
digitis uellit tot herbas, ut fasciculum collegerit : simul uellens pugillum graminis,
quo contegat ea, quæ natura tegenda suadet. Deinde currit celeriter domum,
retro per hortum, (ne quis eum posset ita animaduertere nudum) ad stabulum, uolens equulo dare gramen seu herbas. Ille ualde esuriens inuadit herbas ac gramina,
simul & quod natura tegendum suadet, & amordet omnia simul. Quis posset
esse in maiori anxietate, quam hic pauper Laurentius? Nesciuit introitum nec
exitum, nec quò posset confugere, nisi in furno, ubi se retro locat, expectans
misericordiam. Interim uenit uxor, uel tunc temporis arator ex agro, putans
coniugem bene obijsse sua munia. Videns autem quid actum esset de puero, in
penu, coquina ac lacte, attonita erat, & uocat circumquaque, Lentzo, Lentzo.
Is absconditus in furno nolebat primo respondere, timebat enim sibi. Post
paululum uocat iterum, Lentzo. Respondet ille in furno : Heho. Vocat iterum
arator; Vbi es? Respondet Laurentius : Hic in furno. Quid agis ibi, procede.
Nequaquam here, ait alter, malè exercui rem domesticam. Quid actum est,
ait illa? Prolem ego necaui, uolens sistere cunas. Eia bone Laurenti, nil refert (inquit illa) nos satagemus alias proles progignere, exi saltem ex furno,
nihil fiet tibi. Sed plus feci, bone here. Quid fecisti praeterea? Laurentius
dixit ; Vinum siui effluere ex uase in penu, & poculum uini effudi etiam. Nil
nocet, mi Laurenti, (inquit illa) exi, bibemus aquam. Sed plura feci, ô here.
Quid sit, rogat illa? Dispersi butyrum & oua, & feles comederunt illa. Non
adeò magnum est hoc damnum, prodi, satiabimur pane ac caseo. Plus adhuc
perpetraui. Quid est illud rogat illa? Volebam praebere equulo nostro gramen, & seculam amisi in limo uiuarij : interim quod quaero eam, ablatae sunt
mihi uestes. Nil refert nec hoc, gramen demetemus cultro, & uestes alias
curabimus resarciri widersdorfij, prodi saltem. Sed aliud adhuc perpetraui
quod omnium est maximum & pessimum. Quærit illa : Quidnam est hoc
mali? Volui ait inijcere gramen nostro equulo, ille importunus ac famelicus,
ex quo eram nudus uolens rapere gramen, quo supellectilem meam conabar
tegere, abmordit unà cum gramine meum compositorem discordiarum, uentre
tenus, Hæc est causa cur non audeo prodire. Audiens hoc Adelheidis, capit ilico
furcam furnariam, ac ait ; Videbatur mihi aliud in hoc negocio quàm oua, lac,
uinum, uestes & proles. Vis tu curare rem domesticam, & destruere omnia,
perdere ac deuastare : quin & sinis auferri tibi (quod omnium maximum est) nos-
trum compositorem discordiarum? Siste, pro tua hac œconomia te remunerabo.
Contrudit eum furca furnaria ita, ut necessariò confregerit furnum supernè, & effu-
geret nudus in domum : & ita nudus ac sanguinolentus, exiliuit per fenestram.
Illa insequitur furca illa furnaria, clamat ille, imprecatur illa. Vicina audiens
hunc tumultum, miratur, prospicit, uidet uicinum suum Laurentium currentem,
uxorem insequentem, ac malè se habentem. Mota autem uicinali misericordia,
dixit : Eia commater Adelheidis, quid ita conmota es erga compatrem Laurentium? qui semper bonus ac probus extitit, desine parumper ab ira hac, & da ei

saltem indusium. Ego dedero illi fel potius (ait illa) omnia deuastauit in domo, prolem oppressit magno lapide. Omnia condonanda forent, sed unum & præcipuum designauit, quod celandum est; à nostro equulo in stabulo, siuit amorderi praecipuam supellectilem nostram, uentre tenus. Cactera condonanda forent, sed hoc unum nullo modo potest expiari nec condonari. Audiens hoc uicina, quòd deprædatus esset eo, quod praecipuè expetitur, fit & ipsa infesta suo compatri, ac concitat caniculum quem habuit complosis manibus in eum, dicens : Hurss, hurss, cape eum, ad nibil enim utilis est. Miser hic Laurentius penitus abdicatur, nullus restat ei locus ulterius, sed aufugit nudus quaqua uersum. Vicina autem dixit: Age commater Adelheidis, compone mentem tuam, habeo ego seruum bonum, fortem ac uigilem, qui erit in rem tuam ; scio enim ualere : nam ego sum usa eo his sex aut septem annis. Hoc pacto perdidit Laurentius optimum suum pugionem, & cogebatur deleri omnino ex libro uiuentium. Suadeo ergo uiris obire sua munia, & mulieribus similiter sua : sic poterit neuter improperare alteri. Ita fiet, ut uiro maneat sua uigil ales salua ac uegeta, & uxor reddetur pacatior, nec cogatur diffringere furnum, & tandem aufugere nudus & mutilatus.

---

## The Wowing of Jok and Jynny.

LORD HAILES, in his notes to this poem, says : " Instead of encumbering the glossary with a minute detail of the wretched goods and chattels of the bride and bridegroom, I subjoin a list of whatever might be dubious or unintelligible to an English reader.

"*Almry,* cupboard. *Ark,* large chest for keeping corn or meal. *Blasnit-ledder,* probably basnit, tanned-leather. *Brechame,* the collar of a work-horse. *Brochis,* clasps. *Brydill-renye,* the rein of a bridle. *Coig,* a pail or trough. *Creill,* basket. *Dublaris,* probably dishes with covers. *Ell-wand,* an ell measure or rod. *Fetterit-lok,* fetter-lock. *Fidder,* 128 C. weight. *Flaik,* hurdle. *Furme,* form or bench. *Furlet,* a measure containing one fourth of a boll. *Fute-braid sawing,* corn sufficient to sow a foot-breadth. *Graith,* girth. *Gryce,* pig. *Guss,* goose. *Heck,* rack. *Hobbil schone,* clouted shoes. *Hog,* a sheep of two years old. *Jak,* that piece of warlike dress called a *doublet of fors,* or defence. *Kaill,* coleworts. *Kirn,* churne. *Laid-saddill,* load-saddle.  *Maskene fatt*, vessel to boil malt in for brewing. *Milk-syth*, milk-strainer.  *Nek*, button of a spindle.  *Pek*, a measure containing one sixteenth of a boll.  *Polk*, poke, bag.  *Quhittill*, knife.  *Raip*, rope.  *Rok*, distaff.  *Sark*, shirt.  *Schule*, shovel.  *Spounge* probably *spung*, purse. *Spurtill, spattula*, flat iron for turning cakes.  *Thraw-cruk*, a crooked stick for twisting hay or straw ropes.  *Trene*, spout.  *Truncheour*, trencher, platter.  I do not know the signification of *padell*."  [Sibbald explains *Padell*, " a small leathern bag or wallet for containing a pedlar's wares."]

Stanza 1, l. 1.  "*Robeyns Jok ;*" *i.e.*, Jok the son of Robin, or Robin's son.  Proper surnames came late into Scotland.

— l. 3.  "*Scho brankit fast, and maid hir bony.*"  She tript away hastily, and dressed herself out to the best advantage.

— l. 6.  "*Cleir as ony clok.*"  Clear as a *clok*, or beetle ; a proverbial expression, alluding to the bright polish on the body of that insect.

St. 2, ll. 1, 2.

> "*I ȝern full fane,*
> "*To luk my heid, and sit doun by ȝou.*"

This is obscure : I understand it to mean, "I earnestly long to sit down at your side, after having first searched my head, that there be no animals about me."  A refinement in rustic courtship !

St. 2, l. 7.  "*I schro the lyar, full leis me ȝow.*"  The young lady having told her mother that she suspected the sincerity of her wooer, he tenderly answers, "Curse you for liar, I love you heartily."

St. 3, l. 3.  "*Ane fute-braid sawing.*"  Corn sufficient to sow a foot-breadth, or a foot-breadth of ground on which one may sow.  Here the author, straining to make a ludicrous description of braggart poverty, has transgressed the bounds of probability.  The idea, however, has pleased ; for in a more modern Scottish ballad the following lines occur :—

> "I ha a wie lairdschip down in the Merse,
> *The nynetenth pairt of a gusse's gerse,*
> And I wo' na cum every day to wow."

St. 7, l. 3. "*Fyve fidder of raggis to stuff ane jak.*" A quantity of rags, wherewith to quilt any coat of mail. By 87th statute, parliament 6, James V., it was provided, "That all *yeamen* have *jackes of plate.*"

St. 7, l. 6. "*Ane spounge.*" This probably means a *spung*, or purse, which closes with a spring. A.S. *bung* or *pung*. In Scotland the word *spung* is still used for a *fob*. Skinner gives an example of what he calls *lingua mystica erronum*, or Gypsy cant. "To nip a bung:" this is from A.S. niipen. digitis vellicare, and *bung* or *pung*, marsupium. It would be curious to inquire whether the cant of Gypsies be anything more than corrupted Anglo-Saxon or corrupted French, just as these outcasts from civil society are of Anglo-Saxon or French original.

St. 8, l. 3. "*Ane sark maid of the Linkome twyne.*" A shirt made of the *Lincoln* twine ; a sort of cloth so called. Thus in *Chrystis Kirk of the grene,* st. 2, l. 5 : "'Thair kirtillis wer of *Lincome* light."

St. 10, l. 1. "*Tak thair for my parte of the feist.*" Such are my effects, sufficient to set off against yours ; or, in the vulgar phrase, to pay my share of the reckoning.

St. 10, l. 5. "*And als the laverok is fust and loddin ;*" i.e., the lark is roasted and swollen. It seems to be a cant proverbial expression for dinner is ready.

— l. 6. "*When ʒe haif done, tak hame the brok.*" After you have dined, you may carry the remnants home.

THE END.